Praise for Orchids and Stone

Daphne is both physically tough and emotionally vulnerable, a heroine readers will love and root for in this fast-paced, gripping read.

—Laura Moriarty

Gritty and powerful.

—Jo-Ann Mapson

A mesmerizing debut that is part mystery, part modern love story, and thoroughly gripping. *Orchids and Stone* stars a bright, uniquely independent woman who is strong enough to define her own future and tender enough to rediscover both love and forgiveness. Lisa Preston's deftly layered narrative crescendos to a nail-biting climax that surprises and satisfies.

—Carol Cassella

Daphne is a strong central character, complex and fundamentally stunted by tragedy in her life. With lyrical writing and nuanced characterization, *Orchids and Stone* will have you rooting for Daphne's redemption amid pulse-pounding car chases. It's a book that has something for every reader!

—Kate Moretti

ORCHIDS
AND STONE

ORCHIDS
AND STONE

LISA PRESTON

THOMAS & MERCER

No part of this book may be reproduced, or stored in a retrieval system, or transmitted in any form or by any means, electronic, mechanical, photocopying, recording, or otherwise, without express written permission of the publisher.

Published by Thomas & Mercer, Seattle

www.apub.com

Amazon, the Amazon logo, and Thomas & Mercer are trademarks of Amazon.com, Inc., or its affiliates.

ISBN-13: 9781503952324
ISBN-10: 1503952320

Cover design by Mumtaz Mustafa

Printed in the United States of America

In memory of C

CHAPTER 1

Daphne didn't quit college to become a roofer. When the first day of spring break became the night her father killed himself in a hotel room, she drove his car the two-plus hours back to the university the next morning. Gathering her clothes, photos, and a shoebox of desk items, she abandoned her textbooks and extra school supplies in the quad atrium, free to any takers.

College was supposed to be more than an escape from her half-empty bedroom and stymied parents, but she left Western Washington University thinking she'd always been a poser there, never a good fit with dorm life. Finishing part of a semester more than her dead big sister counted, like all half measures, for nothing.

No solace waited at home. For the first time since she was eleven, her father wouldn't be there in the evening, burning. No restive three-word chant or even his less common complaint, "Nobody makes an effort," would burst from him after the hours whiled away and he slumped up the stairs.

Quiet and comfort were not the same thing. In the wake of her impulse to drop out of school, she dreaded surreal days and evenings to be passed at home. Her trembling mother offered no answers.

Haunted since childhood about the thing she never found and things she never said, Daphne drove slower as the miles brought her near home and she took an earlier exit into Seattle. Wondering what her mother knew and should have known, Daphne told herself she was a rotten daughter for not returning home without delay. She idled the car in the far lane, honked at by drivers with deadlines.

A roadside placard in front of bulldozed black dirt announced: Openings, Training Available, Ask about our Women-In-Construction Program. Daphne parked her father's sedan among the pickup trucks and SUVs. Beyond the sign, construction bustled on numerous six-plex apartments; some building exteriors appeared finished and others bore open-framed walls. Concrete slabs ghosted the footprint of apartments to come. New building skeletons took hammer blows as men raised sheets of siding to the exteriors.

Men in hard hats, leather work gloves, flannel shirts, and brown Carhartts or heavy blue jeans moved with burly purpose. Suspenders burdened their shoulders with the weight of enormous tool belts.

These men drove beeping forklifts packing stacks of lumber. They spread blueprints on truck hoods, shot nails with powered guns, and pointed at other men, tools, pallets, and buildings. They gave and received orders in shouts.

"You lost?" The man in front of her wore boots, jeans, and a sneer.

"You . . . you h-have jobs open." She winced at her childish stammer, awash in the feeling of being half-adult. She'd told her best friend, Thea, about this sensation, upon Thea's graduation the previous spring. But Thea, with one year on Daphne and all about getting a job with her new journalism degree in order to move permanently out of her parents' house, pretended not to understand how matriculation to adulthood loomed as a daunting milestone for Daphne.

"I mean, the sign says . . ." Daphne ended with a wave at the driveway placard.

The construction worker in front of her snorted. "Yeah, you'll last an hour." His next comment came with a giant wad of spit while he muttered to the ground about her—her balls? Then he pointed toward a white trailer. "Check in at that Atco."

What's an Atco? Daphne wanted to ask. At the trailer, she accepted a form to fill out, checking the NONE block next to the words: Experience Level?

You'll last an hour.

The words hung over her. Outside, a guy named Bob handed her a hammer after a guy named Dick welcomed her and said to listen to the foreman, who would let her know after a full day tomorrow if she was hired.

Foreman, Daphne puzzled as they handed her a scrap board, a handful of nails, and told her to drive them. "Seriously?"

Bob nodded. Dick went back into the Atco. *Is Bob the foreman? You'll last an hour.*

Daphne caught her tongue between her teeth and drove the first nail, keyed with self-consciousness. She couldn't remember hammering anything before but pretended competence with a starting tap before pounding the nail home with mean, targeted blows.

"Good eye, but you don't want to chew up the wood too much," Bob said.

She drove more nails, stopping when the heads nestled the plank.

"Okay, I need you to load a roof."

"Load a roof," Daphne repeated, not understanding but happy for any comment not taunting her about how long she'd last.

"Yep. Can you carry these up?" He pointed to a pallet laden with packages of shingles, thumbed open a pocket knife, and sliced the plastic binders securing the packages.

Daphne pulled one long bundle of shingles from the top. It weighed perhaps thirty-five or forty pounds. Healthy college girls could lift forty pounds, but they usually didn't. They didn't heft sharp-edged packages of shingles onto one shoulder and climb a ladder. They didn't repeat the chore a dozen times in an hour. They didn't labor hours on end.

You'll last an hour.

She lasted, shaking, bringing bundles up the ladder with her jaw set. Thin, screaming muscles engaged over and over.

Ignoring the physical pain, there was an upside. Climbing a ladder at a construction site felt fun and naughty. Aloft, after the challenge of walking the bare, slanted roof to the peak, she saw a particular way to stack shingle bundles.

Daphne worked with vicious determination, surviving each minute, proving the first man wrong. Extreme work beat driving a few more miles to her sister-less, father-less childhood home.

Bob honked a truck horn mid-afternoon and all the men stopped working for fifteen minutes, gathering at his truck's tailgate to take water from a yellow cooler. Daphne kept working in a dreamy daze, hauling shingles up the ladder, stacking them near the apartment's ridge. She toiled through lunchtime and the afternoon break as well.

At five thirty, when everyone below stopped working, her body and brain were so woozy she considered skipping dinner and going straight to bed. Maybe she'd sleep in the car at the construction site. It was real, this work. Guts and grit.

The naysayer who'd sent her to the Atco cast a sidelong look, booting the empty pallet. "Most of us carry two bundles of roofing at once."

"Not all day, most of us," a man walking past with a coil of nails said.

"Most companies use power loaders," snapped another guy, unbuckling his tool belt.

"More than enough," Bob said, and they all shut up. He turned to Daphne, "Can you be here at six? Load another roof?"

The other men laughed and hooted about the power loader not being available to carry shingles onto the roof mechanically. Grunt work had to be done by hand this time and no one wanted the short straw. Bob raised a palm, the jeers stopped, and he asked again. "Six a.m.?"

Daphne nodded.

"Don't forget your lunch."

That night, she cleaned her plate and was in bed by seven thirty. Her mother hugged her, but they didn't talk. If her mother cried that night for her long-dead daughter or her looming first week as a widow, Daphne didn't hear the weeping.

Daphne didn't imagine echoes of her father's old mantra about Suzanne—*someone saw something*—when she went upstairs. She didn't think about how hollow the house felt, how he would never come home. She didn't think of questions and answers and comfort never to be given or received.

The last she heard were faint sounds of her mother going outside to smoke then plunking on the living room sofa. She didn't look across her bedroom at Suzanne's empty bed or at the window beyond and think about promises lost or aching years gone by. She slept the unmoving sleep of the spent and knew no more.

The alarm clock went off at five thirty but not because her big sister had snuck out and might need a safety net.

Daphne's body was so sore, she held her breath. The motion of allowing her chest to expand lanced her ribs. Opening her hands to wiggle her fingers hurt all the way up her arms. Her shoulders felt too battered for contemplation.

Bad as the pain was, she found she could make her body move. This discovery was so amazing, she tested the possibilities. She pulled on jeans and an old shirt over her underwear, limped downstairs to wolf three times as much cereal as she'd ever eaten in one sitting, and made a peanut butter and jelly sandwich. Leaving her mother a note about being out all day, she shoved away thoughts of notes her father and sister left, then drove her father's car back to the construction site.

This time, no one sneered about how she'd last an hour. One man bid her good morning, waving a handful of flat cardboard packages and a weird tool.

"Staple hammer," he said. "I'm Hal. We're working together. After we lay paper, I'll show you how we start shingles, get things square. Has to be perfect from the start."

Perfect sounded like a lofty goal, but the world of construction appeared to be an alternate universe, where new things were possible. She could force her screaming body to bend.

"Perfect." Daphne realized the foreman never intended to make her carry shingles today. He just wanted to see if she'd show up expecting to haul deadweight up a ladder.

"Got a scribble stick?"

"What?"

"Do you own a pencil?"

"Oh." Daphne turned for the sedan amongst the pickups. Her father's car was still packed with her college things. She rummaged for a pencil plus her little sharpener, then followed Hal to another section of the building project. This six-plex had a plywood-sheeted roof but was not yet tar papered.

"First we have to load it," Hal said.

Daphne saw rolls of tar paper on a pallet by a ladder and allowed herself a satisfied smirk at the coming labor. When her scrawny muscles protested, she closed the part of her mind that listened to complaints of pain and worked.

Hal nodded. "It's the legs."

"It's the legs." And she pressed on, hefting tar paper, scaling the ladder.

It seemed no time until Hal called for her to stop, said they had enough rolls of paper loaded and they needed to lay it out.

Laying out tar paper on a roof turned out to be kind of cool. She liked kicking the roll after one end was attached, liked watching it unwind itself across the roof. She liked the repetition, smacking the staple hammer fast and hard along the length of the straightened paper. Before a horn honk announced the morning break, her first roof was papered. The building was huge, but they'd covered it with tar paper hauled up from a pallet down below. Hal said they were ready to roof.

She didn't like holding what Hal called "the dumb end" of the tape measure and she asked enough questions about what he was doing with his fancy metal triangle and T-square that he promised she could start the other side of the roof if they got that far.

I'll get that far, she promised, rolling her battered shoulders with satisfaction, studying the marks he made on their fresh tar paper, and noting the precise way he cut and fit two shingles in halves and thirds to get the process started.

"This is the reveal." Hal indicated the space where the shingles would overlap, marked the tar paper with his pencil at both ends of the roof and had her hold a chalk line, let her snap it. They lined yards of roof, readying to work.

His pencil was an outsized, rectangular-shaped instrument that would never work in a pencil sharpener. When he broke the point, she was glad she'd grabbed her little hand-twist pencil sharpener when raiding the car for supplies. But Hal just used his razor knife, the same one he'd cut shingles with, and whittled a point back onto his pencil.

She set shingles when and where he directed and didn't wince when firing the nail gun. Construction was beautiful and reassuring. Something hard had to be done right and repeated ad nauseam.

They stayed on the roof for their break. Hal ate a sandwich and she surveyed the site like an eagle after its first flight. The next time the horn honked and Hal reached for his lunch box, he hesitated. "Didn't you bring a lunch?"

"Oh, right." Daphne went back to the car for her sandwich, happy to guzzle cups of water from Bob's huge yellow cooler, happy to take her PB&J sandwich up the ladder to what now seemed like *her* roof.

She'd built something.

Below them, framers and plumbers and electricians and floorers scuttled like ants for their lunches. Daphne sat on the peak of her half-shingled roof and swallowed her sandwich.

"That's not enough to eat," Hal said. "You'll need at least four sandwiches a day. Eat one on the morning break, two for lunch, and one on the afternoon break." He downed another meaty grinder.

When she got to start the shingles on the other side and her pencil rolled off the roof, Hal loaned her his flat-sided carpenter's pencil and they plowed on.

The roof ridge was hard, much harder than she'd figured, with careful fitting of hand-cut shingles, but at the end of the day, she and Hal had roofed a building.

"You're hired," Bob called out while she was coming down the ladder for the last time.

Men sipping water at the cooler tipped their cups to her.

"You'll be on a framing crew next week."

"M'kay." She stepped off the ladder.

Bob proffered a humongous hammer with a toothed head and claws that looked like they could rip concrete. "You're gonna need tools."

Hal and the other men laughed. One introduced himself, said he ran the framing crew. She thought she might miss the rooftops but nodded, making a mental note about things she'd buy, a staple hammer, a roofing hammer, a framing hammer. A T-square, a metal triangle. A lot of rectangular pencils and a knife to keep them sharp. A tool belt with suspenders.

"Bob let a guy go yesterday," Hal said, getting into his truck as she headed to her dad's car. "He doesn't keep people with a bad attitude or people who don't work their butts off."

Daphne wondered if Bob fired the guy who said she'd last an hour. She hadn't seen him today. How long had he lasted?

At her father's graveside service, Daphne swayed between confusion and anger. A black wrought iron fence separated them from the consecrated ground where people who died without mortal sins on their souls were buried.

Reginald Mayfield's coffin was plain. Suzanne's coffin had been more ornate, the centerpiece in a well-attended church service that twisted into a spectacle and struck then-eleven-year-old Daphne to her core. The boy Suzanne loved had pushed forward, caressing the coffin's carved wooden edges, weeping in a singsong voice about touching her perfect body and Jesus being broken. The congregants' collective gasps as that funeral morphed into something darker—as men in suits came forward and pulled the boy from the altar and police were summoned to quell the disturbance—all left young Daphne bewildered and helpless next to her parents' anguish.

Her mother wept alone now, promising flowers every year. Daphne made no promises. She felt the threads between her and her mother fray. The family had survived ten years since Suzanne's death, survived the murder case being suspended. Why had her father found a limit to the pain he could endure? Why hadn't her mother known his sorrow had driven him so deep? Or had she known?

The next week, with her new tools, Daphne learned rudimentary framing. She accepted a new rectangular carpenter's pencil from Bob and learned where to mark the bottom and top plates. She crowned boards, pulling them lengthwise to see where the lumber was bowed. Phrases like "sixteen inch centers" rolled off her tongue while sweat rolled off her face. She ate four fat sandwiches a day, in addition to a huge breakfast and a heaping dinner. Following time on the framing crew, a different guy took her on. He said he ran the drywalling crew.

She was pleased to discover that drywallers also had to load a house before they could work, carrying in the drywall to be hung on the interior. The special thing about loading drywall was: the loaders ran.

Instead of walking through the house with one person on each end of a sheet or multiple panels, these workers jogged the material through the building. The physical labor of carrying dozens of heavy, hard-edged slabs of man-made rock wasn't difficult enough. They improved the exertion factor by adding speed to the equation.

Because of the running, loading drywall was as hard as carrying tar paper or shingles up a ladder. When she asked why drywallers ran while loading, everyone said they ran to save time. But roofers didn't run bundles up ladders to roofs.

She learned to hang drywall then, gasping for breath, dripping with sweat, turning hard-bodied.

The following week, Bob had her join the siding crew. Siders didn't run siding from the truck to the framed buildings' exteriors.

She could see subcontractors working in the more finished six-plexes and noticed floor men didn't run rolls of carpeting and linoleum inside. She'd seen electricians and the furnace guys wire and duct the buildings. They didn't run. No, drywallers just made things hard, creating wonderful, cleansing work.

One day Bob asked what job she liked best, and she understood they'd had her try all a laborer could do at the construction site. The journeymen plumbers and electricians were above them. The subcontracted carpet layers and painters were below them. Bob and his crews had seen her work and she'd made the grade.

"Roofing," Daphne said. "I like being up there."

He nodded and assigned her to the roofing crew, his pencil hesitating when she added, "But I like loading drywall, too. Happy to help whenever they need someone."

Learning roofing meant mastering how to use bond breaker between layers, how to hot mop, how to puncture screws through sheet metal, what to conceal and what to reveal as she fit hip roofs, parapets, butterflies, gambrels, gables, façades, and mansards. She got roof legs, feeling secure on the rake of a steep slope, even on bare rafters or trusses, harnessing only when the foreman demanded they rope up.

Her body morphed, dropping sizes in jeans while needing larger shirts. And she had no idea why people bought expensive memberships to gyms when paying work—it paid so handsomely she banked half her checks and started a retirement fund—provided incredible muscles.

When Thea called, having found a job and an apartment and needing a roommate, Daphne left her mother, left the house of memories she'd silenced through days of toil. She cleaned out her half of the bedroom closet and liberated the big box of her sister's private papers from the top shelf.

Thea howled when Daphne related what she did all day. Her mother adopted an enormous gray cat from the animal shelter but took months to stop staring at Daphne and asking, "What about finishing your last semester of college? What about graduating and getting a good job?"

"I've got a good job."

Daphne joined the roofers' union but never went to meetings or voted. She paid her dues, roofed, and jumped in with the drywallers when they loaded. She got a lot of strange looks.

No one understood Daphne's choice.

She'd done it without thinking. But in the succeeding decade—living now with her boyfriend of four years and (sometimes) his kids—owning a pickup truck, her hands calloused and her body built, Daphne understood her choice.

For her sister.

For her father.

For not knowing, Daphne had sentenced herself to a life of hard labor.

CHAPTER 2

Trapped in Vic's front seat as he backed out of the driveway, Daphne suffered glares from his kids and pretended not to know. For a Wednesday, she'd have ranked this a decent afternoon, but it fell before the darkest weekend of the year. Everything was relative. While Jed and Josie argued about who would have gotten to sit up front if she weren't beside their father and Vic burned about returning the kids to his ex early, Daphne debated calling her mother or waiting for the dreaded annual request to keep their unspoken double vigil.

Everybody had a grievance, felt pain, found something hard in a world of rare possibility. She couldn't fix things for anyone. Saturday's ten-year anniversary of her father's death called up more sorrow and confusion and unanswered questions than she wished to bear again.

She rolled her shoulders, relishing the ache of sore muscles. Yesterday, she'd re-shingled a small garage on her own. Roofing—putting the lids on, as the guys at work called it—remained where she made peace and money, where she found pleasure out of pain. Instead of a sad visit with her mother Tuesday afternoon, she'd earned a thousand dollars.

"I forgot my history book," Josie said, her knees pushing into Daphne's backrest.

"Hmm?" Vic twisted, alternating his gaze between the road and his daughter. He had just shifted to drive and the car lurched forward.

Then a robin startled from the neighbor's yew, bounced off the Honda's plastic grille and flopped twice in the street before falling still. The dead bird's body stayed in the traffic lane, feathers fluffed as though awaiting a final execution from the next car. Daphne sat wordless, sure she was the only one who noticed the death.

At the front door, with the book retrieved and the kids headed down the brick steps, Daphne cast a long look at Grazie, their decrepit Springer-Golden mix panting on the kitchen floor. Turning her back on her boyfriend's dog felt like punishment and Daphne trailed the family of three back to the car.

There, she asked Vic, "Mind if I stay?"

She knew he'd like her to come along, but he gave a sympathetic smile and glanced back at the house. "You begging off?"

"Yes."

"No, I don't mind." He kissed her, held the car door open for his son and daughter, then backed over the dead bird as he brought the sedan onto the street.

Daphne knew Vic thought she wanted to ponder the Grazie Decision. She was willing to let him believe this because his assumption made her appear like a better person than someone who wanted to think about the perils of being thirty-one while being with a man whose kids were torn. And she warned herself that expecting the worst weekend of the year to hit her in the face in a few days placed her in a dangerous position to make a life decision.

Forever, that's how long the battle would go on. She thought of Vic's habit of thinking problems through by articulating the best- and worst-case scenarios, and she felt no better about her prospects, or the dog's.

Grazie thumped her tail and slumped back to the floor when Daphne jiggled the leash on its hook by the refrigerator. The dog passed on many walk offers these days, and watching her gait fail when she did agree to an outing was painful. Daphne smoothed Grazie's fur and went solo, crossing the street to let the Peace Park swallow her.

Being so close to the park was the best thing about Vic's house. Daphne cut across the outer path and greenbelt, walking the distance to the center fountain, the one that caught any available sun.

Climbing the fountain steps would offer glimpses of green and white ferries churning the Sound, but Daphne didn't want to catch the city's sights. She wanted to pretend she wasn't in a city, wasn't suspended in sorrow, wasn't in a worthwhile relationship with a nice man whose divorce from a wicked ex stood to negatively impact Daphne forever.

The park's center was a good place to pretend. No one else was visible save an elderly woman hurrying across the far path.

If that woman hadn't ducked behind the near end of a long rosebush, a dose of tranquility might have come easier. The number of street crazies in Seattle seemed to go up every year. Daphne doubled over on the bench, folding her arms against her legs. The stretch to her back tugged as a painful reminder of the masochistic pleasure she took in overwork.

"They're trying to take me. Goodness sakes." The old lady's cry was faint, and Daphne shut her eyes to force the stranger's craziness away, reconsidering the craziness of her world.

Vic's kids. Their venomous mother's self-appointed mission of tormenting Daphne and twisting the kids had no end. And Jed and Josie? They treated Daphne at turns with hostility and their uncommon, heartbreaking, vulnerable goodness. This would be something Daphne lived with at home every Wednesday afternoon and every other weekend, plus any of the kids' activities Vic and Daphne attended beyond Vic's allotted times with his children.

"Help. Help me, please! They're trying to kidnap me. They're trying to steal all my money." The cries came straight for Daphne.

She looked up, elbows on her knees. The elderly woman's hair, thin and bluish-white, stuck out sideways in stiff curls, the top flat. She wore a tan raincoat over a lavender polyester pantsuit, blue loafers, and white bobby socks.

The woman rushed forward to clutch Daphne's arm. "Please help me."

Daphne rose from the bench, casting about as the old lady jostled her. "Um . . ." She studied the bony hand on her arm, the liver spots and blue veins.

"They're trying to rob me. Please, don't let them."

"There's no one else here."

"They want to steal all my money."

"Ma'am, I don't . . ."

"Don't let them take me," the older woman begged.

"Them?" With no *them* present, Daphne felt walls build in her mind, the coming decision to separate from other people's lives.

A black-haired woman in dark clothes appeared beyond dormant rosebushes.

Daphne pressed her lips tight. "Do you live around here?"

The old lady's hair flapped as she nodded and pointed beyond the distant woman.

"I live right there." She indicated the dense bank of trees on the east side of the park. "They want to steal my house, too."

Daphne closed her eyes for a split second of solitude, begging with her silence, *Can't you see I want to be alone?*

The lady peered without flinching. "Do you live nearby?"

"On the other side." Daphne pointed at thick trees, thinking of Vic's blue saltbox house on Westpark.

"They're trying to steal my house." The old woman cried. "They're trying to rob me."

The other woman, in a luxurious black wool coat that would weigh a ton when the rain came, shot a hand up and started hustling toward them but not fast enough to save Daphne from more demented beseeching.

"My name is Minerva Watts. I'm Mrs. John Watts, but my husband's passed. It's been fourteen years. What's your name, dear?"

"Um, Daphne."

"Mother!" The woman in black charged, her coat opening like a cape.

"I'm not her mother. I don't know her, Daphne. They're robbing me."

Daphne wished someone else were there, wished she were anywhere else. The skies were going to open up and it would blow. Wind on wet skin. The thought made her shiver and zip her lined, fleece jacket.

Shouldn't the elderly woman have more than a thin raincoat? The skin on the backs of her hands, translucent as onion paper, begged for protection. And she was skinny, Old Lady Skinny. The kind who couldn't be hugged too hard, lest they break. *Would it be all right*, Daphne wondered, *to give the little old lady a quick hug before they went their separate ways?*

The old lady started to say something to Daphne but was drowned under the louder voice of the younger woman. "Mother, stop this."

The old lady pulled her raincoat tight, huddling her shoulders as though protecting an invisible purse. "I don't know her. I'm not her mother. She's robbing me. Please, Daphne, you have to help me."

"It's so hard when she's like this," the woman in black wool whispered to Daphne in a strained voice, then touched one finger to her temple. "Are your parents . . . healthy?"

Daphne felt her face tighten. Strangers should not accost each other, exchange names, or inquire about one another's families. That's how it is, especially in big cities. A stranger should not inquire about her parents, making her think about her father's death, which made her think of her beautiful, wild sister who would have been forty on Sunday. The woman in black shouldn't be making a demeaning gesture about her crazy, old mother. And Daphne shouldn't be bothered by an Alzheimer's patient wandering in the Peace Park. She shouldn't be in their world at all, and they shouldn't be in hers.

"I'm not her mother," the old woman snapped at Daphne. "She's trying to steal all my money. Please help me."

The Northwest's bipolar weather, offering holes of sunshine minutes earlier, darkened and allowed a few drops of rain. The old woman grabbed at Daphne's arm. The younger woman blocked the effort and began marching the old lady away with forced cheer in her voice. "It's time to go now. You have to come with me."

Daphne sank back to the bench. She couldn't force Jed and Josie to be more pleasant, to not make snide remarks when Vic wasn't close enough to hear. To appreciate a dinner Daphne prepared. To enjoy a movie Daphne picked out. To say thank you when Daphne remembered where Josie left her history book.

The old woman shouted over her shoulder to Daphne. "Please help me! Really, I don't know her."

What if the old lady were telling the truth? If Daphne had her phone, she could call someone. But who? Who should she call over a sad, crazy-sounding old lady pushing her day further off-kilter? Was this a 911-type call? She'd left her phone charging by the stove, right where Josie had left her schoolbook with the history assignment that was due tomorrow. And if Josie hadn't forgotten the book, Daphne and Vic might now be through dropping the kids off at Vic's ex, might have weathered it well. Might be laughing and kissing their way home or pulling up at some corner bakery, ready to share a cappuccino. They might talk. Or they might put off the talking they sorely needed to do.

One robin would be alive.

Daphne looked back across the park toward the house, thinking of Grazie and the Old Dog Decision. Voices carried from beyond the curve on the path to Eastpark.

"Come on, Mother."

"Someone, help me!"

Daphne wished for a graceful exit. *Come on, Mother.* She'd be saying the same words by the end of the week. She took a few half-hearted steps after them but looked over her shoulder toward the direction she wanted to go. At home, she could take a hot shower alone. Or maybe Vic would be back. He'd said he didn't mind her not going. He'd be in a good mood. She could see them having a good rest-of-the-day, alone together.

Perhaps five minutes ago, she'd come into the park for peace. No more than ten minutes. A quarter of an hour ago, she'd been in the car with Vic and the kids. The difference a bit of time makes, it floored Daphne. How things change. Her father had said a few minutes was all it took. A bit of effort and everything could change, if only people would make the effort.

"Look, wait a minute," she called, but not loud enough to make a difference. She half-walked, half-jogged for the last place she'd seen the two women, then continued down the path.

"I'm being kidnapped! They're going to rob me!" The cries came from the edge of the park. Daphne ran until she could see them again.

They were almost to Eastpark Avenue. A silver boat of a car waited there, a big, late-year American model. The vehicle purred. A stocky man waited in the driver's seat. Words passed between them, but Daphne couldn't make them out.

Two teenage boys in Seahawks coats loitered at the curb, not far from the car. The old lady called out to them, making a high-pitched plea Daphne couldn't hear but could imagine.

"Almost there," came the high, tense voice of the younger woman.

The old lady begged the boys, on the verge of tears. "Help me, please."

"Mother, stop it. Just cooperate." The woman in black kept the old lady moving to the car. The teens paid them no attention. Daphne ran headlong toward the two women as they reached the car.

"I'm not your mother. Leave me alone." The old lady's wail was pitiful.

"Look," Daphne called, "is everything okay here?"

The driver, a man in jeans and a black leather jacket, swung from the driver's seat, ran around, and opened the car's right rear door. The old lady balked at the gaping doorway, but the other woman overcame her feeble resistance and both women disappeared into the backseat. The man shut the door, ran around to the driver's seat, and lurched the transmission as Daphne reached one hand up in a silent request for them to wait, her other palm slipping off the car's trunk as they pulled away.

If only the old lady hadn't turned to stare at Daphne through the back window. If only Daphne hadn't been there to absorb the wistful gaze, as sad as any that old Grazie gave when she sighed and kept her head on the floor instead of rising for her dinner or a walk.

"Do you have a phone?" Daphne asked the kids.

One glared and the other looked away, unfocused eyes keeping him apart from civility. Daphne decided they were the sort of scowlers people crossed the street to avoid. The sort who breathed up more of the city's wet air than they deserved. They wore ear buds, the wires mingling with stringy hair before disappearing into their long dark coats.

It was penance, Daphne decided. All of this.

For a nonreligious person, she was a big believer in penance. Working through time and debts owed, not quitting—this was an idea that crystallized for her in youngest adulthood.

She should have gone with Vic to take his kids back to their mother.

He said he didn't mind, so he got points for that. She thought she'd get points because she had been in the car to go with them at first. She just didn't see it all the way through, didn't finish doing the uncomfortable part.

If I'd stayed with him, kept a smile on my face in front of the kids, in front of Cassandra, I wouldn't be here.

"Do you mind?" Daphne snapped her rhetorical question as she pushed by the boys to cut across the park. She hoped Vic was home, a loving, supportive face waiting. She hoped he was out, so silence could serve as peace.

And leaving the greenbelt to cross Westpark Avenue, she saw the robin's body, flattened into the pavement save a few wing feathers bristling in the wind.

CHAPTER 3

"So, they just drove away . . ." Vic said, pulling food purchases from green canvas totes with the same aplomb he'd displayed throughout her breathless rush into the house and description of her encounter in the Peace Park.

Daphne nodded, her mind pinging with the contrast of mental and physical stress while watching his methodical putting away of the groceries.

Soup was on sale, she saw. And bread was two-for-one. Almost everything Vic bought wore an orange discount sticker.

"Right," she said, wiping sweat from her hairline. "I didn't know what to do."

"You didn't do anything."

"Right."

Vic grabbed a can of kidney beans before it rolled off the kitchen counter. "So this old woman . . ." Daphne gave him a sharp look and he amended, "This older lady, you think she's really in trouble?"

"No. Right? I mean, it had to be . . . nothing." She shouldn't get after Vic for referring to an old lady as an old woman.

The woman had said her name, hadn't she? Daphne squinted but couldn't recall.

Vic squeezed her hand and she smiled, studying his face. Calm and amiable, wavy hair and glasses, sweet smile. The kind of guy a girl fell in like with right away and fell in love with as she got to know him.

Damp and getting chilled now, Daphne pulled on a fleece sweater, wishing for the millionth time that Vic didn't keep the house so cold. "She's not in trouble, right?"

He looked at her. "I wasn't there, Daph, but I'm sure you're right. She's fine. You did fine. I'd have done the same thing."

"You'd have done nothing?"

"Well . . ." He stacked two cans in a cabinet. "Maybe."

Irritation percolated. She grabbed his arm, saw her fingers on his denim shirt, then imagined her hand thin-skinned, blue-veined, and covered in age spots. Facing her dim reflection in the microwave, she half-expected to see her hair white, short, and flapping, not dark and grown-out, loose from its usual ponytail. And her skin, while showing the effects of spending days on rooftops in all weather, was of a woman in her thirties, much firmer than a thin old lady's.

Daphne turned from the microwave, unwilling to allow the lady's image to haunt her. "Maybe what? What would you have done?"

Vic's gaze landed on the fridge calendar. "Depends. Whatever you think's best."

Daphne studied the calendar. The next day showed a soccer game for Jed and a volleyball game for Josie. Friday listed Vic on day shift and Saturday bore the note: G-Pop!

Shouldn't the old lady in the park have been in as safe a situation as Vic's dad? Many of the residents at Green Springs babbled nonsense. Others were mentally sharp but needed close monitoring for medical or safety reasons. G-Pop forgot things he should know, but he still did crossword puzzles and enjoyed the care facility's activities. Daphne sighed. "I just didn't know what to do. I didn't want to overreact. It's so far-fetched that there was a real problem, but . . ."

"But you'd feel better if you told someone." He kissed her mouth then caressed her face as he put a large sack of no-brand frosted corn-flakes on top of the fridge.

"I doubt it," Daphne said. "I just told you and I don't feel any better."

"Thanks for that." His smile flickered and he reached for the tele-phone. "Oh, we missed messages."

Daphne looked at the phone and took in the double-blink of the little red light indicating two missed messages. Her mom? Thea? Prob-ably the calls were for Vic, but she leaned forward when he hit the play button. At times like this, she was glad Vic hadn't updated electronics when he'd moved into his father's home.

The machine's mechanical voice announced "Message one." Then her mom's voice sighed and asked Daphne to call. Daphne hit the delete button. Resistance born ten years back, in the wake of their second fam-ily disaster, left Daphne forever torn in dealing with her mother.

She refused to meet Vic's look, knowing he didn't understand.

The machine announced message two and Vic's ex's shrill voice made Daphne wince, made Vic hold his breath.

Cassandra's voice scolded. "Vic, I'd appreciate it if you'd pick up Jed's bike at the repair shop tomorrow. He's your kid, too. Don't leave me to do everything while you're over there partying with no responsibilities."

Delete it. Hit delete the second you hear how bitchy she's being, Daphne wanted to say.

He hit the delete button then got a dial tone.

"Who are you calling?" she asked.

"The police."

"What? Seriously?"

"Sure. This thing in the park, it's their job."

23

"But I don't even know if there was a real problem."

"You don't have to."

"And they're gone now. There's no problem *now* anyway."

"You can still report it," Vic said, then turned his attention to a voice in his ear. "Yes, this is regarding something my girlfriend saw in the park. Possibly suspicious. Suspicious, let's say. We'd like to talk to an officer."

Daphne yanked the fridge door open, pulled out a leftover casserole, and set it down hard on the ceramic counter, wincing as she clinked the glass dish. She scooped two lumps of casserole onto a plate while he talked to the dispatcher.

"I could have done that," Daphne said when he hung up. She set their single heaping plate in the microwave and punched a button. "I should have done that. Is that just a weather service thing, making a call?" He'd often said that for all his evaluating and predicting climate patterns, at the end of the shift, meteorologists merely made a few phone calls and sent e-mails to tell people what the weather might be. He didn't control the storms, the fronts, the wind.

"Doesn't matter," he said, folding tote bags and tucking them into the space between the fridge and cupboards. "Coffee? Wine? Anything?"

They settled on cider, making a fuss of warming it on the stove, adding a cinnamon stick and cloves. She didn't want alcohol before talking to the police and didn't want caffeine, lest she couldn't sleep when alone tonight.

"Just us on a Wednesday evening," Daphne said, as they shared the plate of noodles and veggies under cheese. Wednesday nights without kids didn't happen, according to the custody schedule.

"You know Jed and Josie are here this weekend?" Vic said.

"Yeah, I know. We'll stay home."

The previous weekend, Vic's ex wanted the kids, though it was Vic's turn. He'd agreed rather than fight, but the swap meant they'd have the kids this weekend. Daphne had scheduled Thursday afternoon and all of Friday off for this week, in hope of escaping her mother's annual tears. A long weekend getaway with Vic wasn't going to happen now.

"Daph, I have an all-day training thing Friday. We wouldn't have been able to run off Thursday afternoon anyway. And I'd have never guessed you'd want to be out of town this, of all weekends."

"When I asked for the time off last month, I didn't know you'd be on day shift this Friday," she said. They'd had this conversation two other times. She was glad he didn't say again: *And what about your mother?* "But I still get to sigh over not going away for the weekend, don't I?"

"Sure. Sigh away. You get to wish for whatever you want. Me, too. I wish for you to be happy." He pulled his chair closer to Daphne's and slid his arm around her. "Are you up for watching Josie play tomorrow? It's a home game."

Getting out of his hug, Daphne wondered if Cassandra would be at Jed's soccer game or Josie's volleyball match. Vic alternated between the kids' events, scrupulously fair, and this time was Jed's turn for Vic to attend.

—ɯ—

When a police officer knocked on their door, Daphne hesitated, cloaked in the memory of police coming to her parents' home on spring break her senior year of college. That morning, Daphne was barely awake, going for orange juice. When the knock came, her mother had dropped a coffee cup—her father's coffee cup—then crunched over the broken bits of ceramic to open the unlocked door. The Mayfields were door-lockers, and Daphne had assumed her father was upstairs, on his way down to see what had broken and who was at the door. Though she'd missed the first hints that her mother had already known something was wrong, she absorbed her mother's dreading demeanor as the door was opened and they listened to news that her father had been found in a motel room and he had left a note. It became the day she learned why a family man would go to a hotel room in the city where he lived, a reason less common than dirt and more painful than infidelity.

The officer at Vic's door was of average build but looked stocky under his uniform and gear. He held a notebook but wrote nothing down while Daphne gave a halting account of being accosted in the park. When she was unable to give a detailed description of the two women, the man, or the big silver car on Eastpark Avenue, when she couldn't recall the name the old lady gave, Daphne felt the urge to point out how much like any other cop he appeared.

"Nothing distinctive?" he asked.

The one distinctive thing about this cop in their living room was he wore black leather gloves while holding his pen and notebook. Who wrote while wearing gloves?

"The guy was wearing a black leather jacket," she blurted.

The police officer promised to be on the lookout and to do extra patrol around the park.

"Nothing will happen," Daphne said, her voice glum. "I haven't helped anybody."

"Look, miss," he said, tucking his notebook into a hip pocket, "I understand you saw something upsetting, but it probably wasn't a crime. And you've done more than most people would have."

His tone offered encouragement, forgiveness. Daphne wanted none. She knew her size deceived. Strangers couldn't see her muscles. The large shirt tucked into her small jeans fit. Were she decisive, a fighter, she could have bested the woman in black and maybe the man. But she hadn't even been the one to call for the police officer who now thanked her and left.

She wasn't a fighter. She teared up at sappy commercials. At Grazie's agedness and the mean-spirited barbs of Vic's ex. The Hawai'ian version of *"Somewhere Over the Rainbow"* choked her up. She wanted to cry now over the coming ten-year anniversary of her dad's death. Over her dead sister's nonbirthday this Sunday. And Christmas was the worst, a season of sorrow ever since she was an eleven-year-old kid.

The act of calling the police and reporting the suspicious incident evaporated into a feeling of having done nothing. Daphne pulled a scrunchie ponytail holder out of her pocket, toying with the red elastic fabric. In another mood, she'd have unbuckled Vic's belt, lowered his zipper, and slid her scrunchie onto him. He'd have laughed and played back. But tonight they sat at opposite ends of the green leather sofa, feet stretched toward each other, her hand on Vic's knee, him rubbing her feet. When he clicked the TV on, a number of movie advertisements flashed by: thrillers, dramas, and comedies. Daphne jumped to her feet and headed for the kitchen. Vic clicked the TV off and followed her, looking baffled when he saw Daphne grab a coat and the dog's leash.

"Vic, you know how in movies, bad guys kidnap an ordinary person and make the family withdraw all their money?"

"Like that old Michael Douglas movie we saw part of last year?"

"That wasn't Michael Douglas; it was Kurt Russell. You always confuse them. I don't know how you do it."

He shrugged.

"They don't even look alike," she said, wishing she'd persisted today when it might have mattered. "There was another movie like that. With that British guy."

"Hopkins?" Vic gave a mild smile. "He became American. But I think I did see the movie you're talking about now. I remember a gratuitous butt shot of inconsequential characters. Young women. Nice butts."

"You're a good man in many ways, but I'm finding you lacking tonight."

"Again?"

"Yes. What if people did that to old ladies?"

"What people?"

"The people who do it to ordinary families."

"Do what to them, Daph?"

She bounced on her toes, agitation growing with her theory. "Like that couple on the road trip in the movie. They had car trouble and she gets kidnapped. The bad guys make the husband liquidate all the assets he can in one day in order to get her back."

Vic shook his head, blank-eyed.

She pressed on. "Why wouldn't bad people do that to old people? Just . . . overbear them, make them sign everything over super fast?"

"Bad people who kidnap an average Joe and tell the Joe's family to hand over everything they can right away?"

"Yes," she said, pleased he'd come around.

"I suppose they could, but you know, those are just movies."

"But . . . it's possible." She squirmed, tucking her shirt in, zipping up. "The old lady said they were taking her house, her car, all her money. She said they were kidnapping her."

"Honey, she's fine. That woman you saw in the park, she's probably as fine as she can be. She's with her daughter and her son or son-in-law."

"You said you would have done more."

He put his palms up. "I said maybe. And I didn't say what."

When she entreated the dog to rise, Vic hung the leash back on the hook and spooned his body against hers in a full body hug, pressing her against the fridge. "Look, Daph, I know lightning has struck twice for you—"

"That's not it," she protested. "I'm going to the park. Now. I'm going to where she was when I first saw her, and where I last saw her. She was in trouble, Vic."

"This was not lightning. I don't think so, Daph."

"You don't?"

"No. This was some strangers having a bad day, that's all. It's difficult with older people, sometimes. They can be trying."

"They just need time," Daphne said, thinking of Vic's father and how she'd learned to deal with how he forgot who she was, how he could take forever to answer a question. "They need patience. When it seems like they're . . . trying, as you call it, old people just need time."

"And young people?"

She soured at his prompt, looking away. He could leave her efforts with his kids out of this.

Vic smoothed her hair and said, "Daph, you saw people you don't know having a bad moment. You know, in your heart of hearts—"

"My heart of hearts." Her hands made fists over her breasts.

Vic placed his hands over hers, resting his chin on her head and softening his voice. "You know this happens all the time, all over the world. People have little crises. Strangers see glimpses and keep their noses out of other people's business."

"Some of those strangers help."

"Daph."

"Some of them do. And others should. Just like . . ." But she couldn't finish.

She didn't have to. Vic knew what happened when she was in college. He even knew what happened when she was a kid.

"This was not lightning again. Not again."

"What if it was? Imagine, like you always say, what's the worst-case, the best-case scenario?"

"Please stop this."

"Worst-case is she was in real trouble and—"

"That is very unlikely. Let's leave the drama to Josie in this family. She's quite good at it."

Daphne would have none of his attempt at levity. "And no one, not even me, would help her."

"Can we be done with this, please?" Vic asked. "Can we both just take it as an opportunity, a reminder? We'll be more thoughtful. Nothing in the past can be changed. Whatever happened in the park— and probably nothing bad happened—it's over. There's nothing to be accomplished now, no good purpose served in agonizing."

"But . . ."

"Daphne, the best-case is some little old lady has family taking care of her when she goes off in la-la land. You're with me on that?"

"I am. I get it. That's the best-case."

"So, okay," he said.

"But, Vic, what's the worst-case?" When he wouldn't answer, she hesitated then whispered. "The worst-case is some little old lady needed help—begged me for help—and I didn't help her. I did nothing."

No matter how many times Vic told her she was being a nut, that they would freeze, that it was dangerous at night, Daphne brushed away his protests.

"We'll bring Grazie," she said, reaching again for the dog's leash.

The fluffy tan tail thumped on the kitchen linoleum at the leash's advertisement of a late-night walk. Still, she stayed lying down. The old hips ached and she sometimes needed a physical boost to get to her feet.

"That'll be a big help," Vic said. "She'll scare off all the thugs. Look at her."

"If people would just *do* something . . ." She wiped her eyes. "Vic, I have to *do* something. Grazie, come *on*, get up."

Grazie chortled, lifting one front paw.

"Look, she wants to go. Don't be a killjoy." Daphne clapped her hands against her thighs, beseeching the dog. "Come on, girl. Come on!"

Grazie roused herself. After the leash snapped onto her collar, she was first out the door, crossing the street, making for the greenbelt.

CHAPTER 4

In the heart of the Peace Park, Vic brought up the elephant: What should they do for the old dog with failing hips? "Surgery or not?"

The Grazie Decision, as they called it, wasn't coming to them with grace, but they'd agreed it was not a choice to be abdicated through procrastination. They'd spent enough time considering and needed to decide whether or not to put the dog, the kids, and themselves through the hip replacement procedure. If they decided against it, they had to admit to drawing a line in the sand, making a proclamation against extending Grazie's life a year or two, saying she wasn't worth the expense and inconvenience. In his more reluctant moods on the subject, Vic talked about not being a bleeding heart.

"She's looking great tonight." Daphne said it hoping Vic would become enthusiastic and carry them forward with a burst of determination she didn't feel but ached for.

"It's over five thousand dollars."

"I know," she said. "And weeks of recovery."

"The stairs would be out of the question for six weeks. She'd hate not being upstairs with us at bedtime."

"But we could always sleep in the living room for a month and a half," Daphne finished for him. She knew the next line in the debate, too. "But the whole thing may not help all that much."

This was the finish they both understood.

Vic nodded. "Plus, she's old."

"Right." Daphne scuffed a toe along the path. "But the decision's yours."

This was the kind of decision-making abdication Daphne could warm to. Grazie predated her, had been Vic's Divorce Dog, the middle-aged sweetheart he'd pulled from the pound when his wife told him to move out and he'd moved in with his father.

Grazie had given him an enticement for the kids when their mother had them embittered, got him through putting his dad into assisted living, gave him a way to date Daphne, who'd been so wary in the beginning she wouldn't see him at his place or hers nor anywhere that demanded they get in a car together.

Her parents had forced such caution onto Daphne from the age of eleven.

Never get picked up by a guy. Never get in a car with one. Never meet one somewhere he's arranged. At the rare school-related party, never drink anything other than tap water she'd poured herself or a soda she'd opened herself, and never leave that benign drink unattended.

You're never safe, her dad had warned when he and her mom had taken her up to Bellingham for college. She'd winced for him, knowing he felt a father's job was to keep his daughters safe, knowing he felt he'd failed Suzanne.

Daphne inhaled, realized it sounded like a gasp, and cleared her throat. "Seriously, you should decide," she told Vic, using both hands to massage Grazie's hips, wishing they could know if the dog would choose to have surgery were she given the choice.

Big into choices, Daphne recoiled at imposing her selection—whichever it might be—on a being as sweet and soulful as Grazie, good old Grazie, who wagged her tail in pleasure as she snuffled in the border grass and made quick, watery eye contact before inspecting a fir cone on the path. Grazie. Their Grazie.

The grass was already dewy with nightfall. It would soak their shoes if they strayed from the park's curving asphalt path, but Daphne meant to stray, to retrace her path from earlier in the day. With the leash in one hand and Vic holding her other hand, she led them across the grass, up the slope toward the bench near the fountain. She stiffened in the cool night, her memory and muscles sharpening as she thought of the old woman's odd behavior.

Had she been hiding? The memory offered more clarity than the moment had. Now Daphne could believe the old lady was hiding from the woman in black. Daphne understood her own isolation, lost in her thoughts at the time, not tuning in right away and being naturally standoffish with strangers. But the woman had been trying to hide when she had ducked into the bushes.

"It's our decision," Vic said. "We are an *us*, a couple."

Such words should have melted Daphne, but nothing would thaw her tonight, not this weekend, and she shook her head. "She's your dog."

"Come on. Grazie thinks she's yours now."

It was true. Four years ago, Grazie had chosen Daphne to be the person she loved best. Maybe a dog rescued from the pound could form fiercer attachments than other animals. Maybe she recognized a kindred searcher. Maybe she and Grazie just found each other at the right time in their lives, at Vic's father's house. It had been a home of changes. Long before Daphne moved in, Vic's dad moved out to the assisted living facility. Every other weekend the kids stayed over. In between those visits was the Wednesday night visitation—or vigil, as Daphne thought of the experience.

The kids were jealous, she decided, of Grazie's affection for her. The dog's easy love chafed them just as they bristled over Vic loving Daphne.

Looking at Vic's profile in the low light under cloud-cloaked stars, she saw the essence of the man beside her. A good man, a guy who hadn't gotten the cards he'd hoped for, a guy who'd been nothing but good to her. A guy with complications he made the best of, including Daphne and her quirks, including Daphne's small, sad family, and her spiky best friend, Thea.

Thea, who never gave Vic the slightest break or benefit of the doubt. Daphne had given him both, moved out of Thea's apartment several years ago and into Vic's house.

"Don't you want to follow the path?" he asked when Daphne led them toward the heart of the greenbelt. "How far are you going?"

"I should go as far as it takes," she muttered.

"What?" He was falling behind her now. Grazie wasn't keeping up either. Daphne yearned for glimpses of Eastpark Avenue. She pictured the waiting car, the man. The other woman saying something about embarrassment. The teenagers. The old lady looking back at her from the rear window.

Daphne shook her head and kept cutting through the park, toward the center. She was first to the fountain. Turning her back on the cascade made her look at the bench where she'd bent over and stretched her back that afternoon. Seeing Vic walk up with Grazie was like a superimposed movie as she tried to imagine herself there in brighter light. She turned, imagining the old lady who had scurried for the ferns and shrubs before the woman in black arrived.

"That's where I was sitting when I first saw her. She was ducking behind those bushes." Daphne gestured to the bench and brush before moving out.

She cut across the park toward Eastpark, walking fast.

Picturing the black-haired woman in the dark wool coat with her hand on the older lady's arm, Daphne made fists, pumped her arms, and started to jog. She burst from the park where the car had idled.

Behind her, Vic was calling encouragement to Grazie. Soon they were by Daphne's side. He took her arm with his free hand and murmured to his dog, told her she was a good girl. Daphne stared at the street and summoned a vision of the old lady being hustled into the running vehicle.

"Why did they take her in a car if she lived on Eastpark?"

Vic shook his head. "I don't know. It's what, twenty or thirty blocks long? This is about in the middle, maybe they live at either of the far ends. It could have been a couple of miles home."

Daphne pointed at the pavement. "Do you think the police should have come here with me?"

"What for?"

"To, you know, see it."

"I bet they've seen Eastpark Avenue before."

After a long pause, Daphne said, "I'll never see her again."

"The old lady, you're talking about," Vic said, his voice the careful tone of a man who'd been on this shaky ground with her a year ago, and every year before.

When Daphne didn't answer, he called her name again. She'd been running her hands through her hair and she let her palms cover her ears, huddling forward. She gasped when a man's hands closed over hers.

"Isn't this really all about Suzanne?" Vic asked as he pried her hands off her ears.

She yanked her wrists from his grasp.

"I know what day Sunday is," he said.

Her gaze searched the border of the park, the pavement, and the houses down Eastpark.

"And I know what other anniversary comes this week," he said, his voice full of soft sympathy. "Saturday."

Holding a hand up for silence, she flinched when he took her fingers in his, cupped her palm, traced her heart line, her life line.

"Daph, I think I even know why he did it."

She kept her face turned away. "This isn't about my dad."

"Your dad was about your sister. I know that. You know it, too."

"Vic . . ." Daphne's voice broke. "Leave it. Leave me alone."

"Aw, Daph." He rubbed the back of her neck, oozing sympathy if not empathy.

Vic's mother died thirty years back but from a long battle with cancer, not a sudden, criminal loss. When Daphne first told him how she lost her sister and her father, he'd explained his keen awareness of the inadequacy of sympathy, especially from one who has not experienced a similar theft of life.

Daphne had enjoyed his quiet interest as she told him, in pieces, about her family, their losses. He'd listened, truly listened, with a distressed expression, kind murmurs, and soft questions. She'd told him how her father was sure someone had seen something, how he held onto the hope that was never fulfilled with a new lead reported to the investigators.

She swallowed, as suspended in progress as was her sister's cold case. "I should have done something."

"Back then? For your dad? For Suzanne?" When she sniffed and shook her head, he tried again. "For the old lady? I think most people would have done exactly what you did or even less."

"I think most people should do something," she snapped.

"You didn't fail her, Daphne." He pointed to the street, to the park behind them. "You didn't fail here."

"I didn't do anything. When someone sees something, if they act, if they speak up . . ." Her voice broke. She knew where the thought would take her and where it came from. Her father's legacy—the belief that people must intervene for others—began a decade before he killed himself. Eleven-year-old Daphne heard it daily in those weeks before the worst Christmas holiday on record, those weeks when they still held desperate hope. *Someone saw something. Someone should have done something.*

Vic took both her hands in his. "People can't live their lives—no one can—dropping everything anytime there's a stray dog, a kitten in an alley, a late-night TV commercial with a starving child."

"Or an old lady asking for help?"

"And getting help, from her own daughter," he said, his voice insistent as a lawyer in closing argument.

"You don't know that," Daphne said.

"You said the woman called her 'mother' and—"

"And the old lady, the first lady, told me she wasn't the other woman's mother. She said 'I'm not her mother' in so many words."

"We both know what's likely and probable."

"What might you have done, Vic?"

"Daph . . ." He stroked her palm.

Choking off a strangled sob, she shook his hand away. "Come up with something, some kind of answer. What in the world would you have done? What do I do next time to know I did everything?"

He grimaced. "Maybe tell them to hang on a minute. Say you want to ensure the lady's okay. Explain your heart's in the right place, you understand if they feel you're butting in, but isn't that better than letting a stranger pass by into . . ."

"Terrible danger?"

He sighed. "Possible danger."

She nodded and jutted her chin forward. "M'kay. Great. Next time, that's exactly what I'll say." When her face crumpled, she sank into his embrace.

He kissed her bowed neck. "I wish I'd been here, been with you."

"You think it's different for you because you're a guy?" Her tone was more incredulous than challenging. Vic was not given to misogyny and theirs was not a relationship characterized by gender stereotypes.

"Hell, no," he said, massaging her large, hard bicep through her sweater. "But everything's easier when you're with someone."

"Minerva Watts!"

"What? Who?" Vic looked around in the dark, but no one else was there. Grazie flopped down on the wet grass, her legs stiff.

"The old lady's name. I just remembered." It rang clear as a dew drop now. "Minerva Watts. She told me her husband's name, too. John, I think."

"But her husband wasn't the guy in the car," Vic said, double-checking.

"No, no, of course not. He's dead."

"Dead? Who?" Lost again, Vic reached for Daphne's hand. "Slow down, will you?"

"Her husband. Minerva Watts's husband."

"What about him?" He tried to keep his hands on her shoulders, but she shrugged out of his embrace.

"He's dead," Daphne shouted. Then, seeing Vic fold his arms across his chest, she said in a calmer tone, "What?" And she searched the ground for clues.

"You're getting a little wound up. Did you notice?"

Smoothing her hair, Daphne sighed. "I just wish I'd see something here, like maybe she dropped something or, I don't know."

He checked his watch and clapped his hands, rousing the dog to her feet. "Come on, Graz. Can we go home now, Daph? Okay?"

As they recrossed the park, Daphne paused at the bench. "I'm going to call that police officer back and give him her name."

"Good idea." Under her stare, he hastened to add, "Really. It's great." "But?"

He shrugged and stayed silent.

"But you don't think it will change anything, do you?" She cringed at her tone, argumentative even though she too thought calling in Minerva Watts's name would make no difference.

"Daphne, what is it you would like changed? That people shouldn't grow old, shouldn't have troubles? Families shouldn't have difficulties that spill out onto other people's lives? Would you like no one's life to touch a stranger's, even for a minute?"

She reached for his hand and they finished the walk home in silence.

At their front door, Vic hugged her and told her everything would be all right.

Daphne twisted away. "I need to give Graz her nighttime aspirin."

"Cool beans." He grinned back when his phrase made Daphne smile, but she kept to herself how Thea had gone off on a tirade about his use of the expression just a week ago. "Love you. Can I go to work now?"

"Yes."

He grabbed his briefcase. Instead of watching him drive away, she checked Google but found no good match for Minerva Watts in Seattle. Drumming her fingertips against her phone as she thought about the old woman, she pulled the phone book from the back of the kitchen junk drawer, but it had no listing for Minerva Watts or M. Watts.

What had Mrs. Watts said? In her mind, Daphne stood in the park and Minerva Watts's feeble words came back. *I'm Mrs. John Watts . . .*

Daphne nodded with the whispery memory. She checked for J. Watts and John Watts in the phone book but got nothing. Sighing, she thumbed through the phone book's front pages and dialed again.

It was a one-minute conversation. The woman who answered with a quick, "Seattle Police Department," said she'd look up the officer who'd come to Daphne's house earlier and relay the message: the old woman said her name was Minerva Watts.

The lack of satisfaction clouded Daphne with uncertainty.

An old lady asked me for help, said she was being robbed. And I . . . did nothing.

How many people did nothing? How many times would it have mattered? How often might a life be saved if people made an effort and took action? If they got involved whenever there was a question, a hint of trouble.

Wouldn't Suzanne be alive? *Someone saw something.*

And then, wouldn't her father?

The dreadful impossibilities made her want to get the box from under the bed upstairs so she could read words that meant the world.

Lingering over those papers was an act she rarely permitted herself. The moping left her in a funk for days while her mind ran in endless spirals, but tonight she trod closer to the indulgence. Suzanne's old poems and essays—especially the *BETRAYAL* paper from her unfinished school year—left Daphne fraught with confusion and wistful love.

"You will have an even worse weekend than you're already going to have if you get that box out," Daphne warned herself out loud.

She picked up her phone and texted Thea, asking her to call or come over. *Now? tomrrw AM? next PM? Only wrkng half day*, Daphne added, with another round of thumb-flicking before she pocketed her phone and cajoled Grazie up the stairs.

Maybe Thea could find Minerva Watts and they could make sure the old lady was all right.

Thea could find anyone. Daphne wanted the courage to find someone, something.

Maybe Thea could find a particular retired homicide detective. Daphne didn't remember him, but remembered how her father kept checking with the man for months, for years. It was after the uniformed policemen had come to the door that Christmas break when she was eleven. Remembrance left her suspended in confusion and helplessness. The funeral memories could still make her shake, wrap her arms around herself like she hugged her cold body now.

Brushing her teeth while stripping with her free hand, she spat, rinsed, then pulled her phone from her pants. In bed, she willed Thea to call, to text, to save her. "Please?"

Grazie wagged in response to Daphne's plea. Sliding naked from the bed, Daphne pulled the comforter with her to cuddle the dog on the floor. Her fingers traced the edge of the cardboard box of her sister's things behind the bed's dust ruffle.

Picturing her sister meant a range of images. Suzanne's funky clothes, hair, and makeup filled Daphne's mind as the memories mobbed for attention. Feathers in her hair. Grating bits of orange peel into her tea, eating weird foods. Reading Eastern philosophy and Native American lore and Celtic myths. Her laughter made everyone in the room turn with an expectant smile. Her clothes stopped them dead.

She wore broomstick skirts and miniskirts and kimonos and jeans under tutus. Sometimes with men's jackets, trench coats. She'd been the first person in young Daphne's world to wear a camisole without a bra and call it good enough. Suzanne braided strips of tapestry into her hair. She shaved it, grew it, let it form dreadlocks.

Suzanne wrote poetry—sometimes naughty poetry about sex. She wrote plays and acted out the creations for her baby sister. She got As and Fs and laughed about grades.

Her leaving for college started three and a half tough years of Daphne aching for college breaks, aching for summer.

"I miss you," she'd say, meeting Suzanne at the curb when whatever boy she was with brought her home from the university for spring, summer, or Christmas break.

"I miss you, too, of course. I love you, Daffer."

Daphne would bask in the words. Even now, the memory of Suzanne's *I love you, Daffer* stopped time.

The safety of childhood shattered when her sister vanished. Not until Daphne had a youngster in her care did she relearn the sweetness of childhood.

When she met Vic four years ago, he had an adorable seven-year-old son and an easy eight-year-old daughter. The kids were charming at first, but Cassandra's behavior became uglier and increasingly catty with Daphne in Vic's life, and the woman's venom had infected two good children who had now grown into tough preteens.

Four years back, Vic had a healthy, happy, sweet-natured dog in Grazie.

He'd told Daphne his greatest secret, but for a long time, she didn't tell hers, how the secret shame of potential culpability changed her life's course.

CHAPTER 5

An odd sense of thwarting an attack smothered Daphne. She kicked hard and saw a helpless old woman in the backseat of a car, Suzanne's coffin at the altar, and a noose—all with herself no longer an observer but the assailant and the assailed. The world morphed, and voices—no, one familiar, safe voice—melted into her consciousness.

"Daph? Good morning." Vic's placid half rasp and hand on her shoulder made Daphne gasp herself awake like a diver breaking the water's surface. He laughed and shook his head. "Aw, you fell asleep on the floor with her."

Grazie thumped her tail from the folds of the comforter. Daphne pulled her hand from the box under the bed. "Morning."

She met his kiss halfway and bolted to her feet, checked the clock as she grabbed her phone, shook out her hair and secured a ponytail with three firm wraps of an elastic band. Under Vic's appraising half smile, she wiggled into her standard work clothes of a sports bra, T-shirt, and Carhartt jeans, feeling one long pocket along her thigh to ensure she had a carpenter's pencil. The canvas pants, originally brown and stiff as cardboard, had worn soft and light as Grazie's pale yellow fur.

"Hey, Grazie? Grazie!" The voice was Thea's, a quick, cusp-of-sarcasm tone, downstairs. The stairs carried sound like an intercom. Daphne had learned this not long after moving in with Vic, helping him in part-time parenthood.

Mom says people outgrow each other and she outgrew Dad. Mom says Dad's the reason we can't have decent cell phones and we have to go see G-Pop on Saturdays. Mom says Daphne's like a dyke.

Vic pressed his lips together. "Thea's here. Said you asked her to come over."

And I was hoping we'd have a morning together before I have to go to sleep, Daphne finished for him in her head. *And I wish Thea wasn't here at all.*

Grazie wagged her way out the bedroom door but stopped dead at the landing.

"I'll help her down," Vic said. "You can go see Thea."

—ᨈ—

They met in the dorm during Daphne's freshman year at Western Washington University. Thea's long red ringlets and skinny build made her stand out as much as her milky skin did. At the time, most girls wanted to be tan but not Thea. No indoor solar beds or bronzing oils for her. She was a year ahead and pushed Daphne, who had yet to declare a major, to consider journalism.

"All about investigative reporting, uncovering social injustice, getting the corporations, writing Pulitzer-worthy stuff," Thea promised. "We could be partners at it, get jobs together after graduation."

Daphne's parents had just wanted her to get any college degree and any good job. Suzanne would have wanted her to study everything, change majors eight times, join a lot of clubs and try every style. Daphne had ruined all those expectations, everyone's.

Standing in a house now with the two people she loved best, she knew neither of them understood her choices.

"Hey, you." Thea raised her coffee mug in an unspoken toast.

Pulling a fat handful of bread from the bag and eggs from the fridge, Daphne fed four whole-wheat slices into the toaster and three eggs into the microwave poacher. She plugged her phone into the quick-charger. Thea, who lived on coffee until the afternoon, looked aghast at the meal's size and offered one of the coffee mugs.

"Thanks for bringing this." Daphne let the bitter strength of double-shot Americano seep through her body.

"He told me about the lady in the park. You guys called the cops?"

Daphne exhaled, relieved beyond measure. They had overreacted making a police report, which meant she hadn't failed by not calling 911 earlier. She wasn't wrong for not throwing herself in front of the car, clawing out the other woman's eyes, wrestling the steering wheel away from the man.

"Sure," Vic said, patting his leg as he entered the kitchen, to call the old dog in with him. Daphne held her breath for more, but he added nothing.

Thea emitted a dismissive chuckle. "Well, if you're going to call at all, wasn't that a bit late?"

"Better late than never," Vic said.

"Not if some wackos already murdered the old lady," Thea sang, then snorted. "So you want me to see if I can find her for you?"

"Umm." Daphne let her gaze flit about the room. "I want to find, yeah, the lady's address would be a place to start. So, to check on a lady named Minerva Watts who lives on the other side of the park, what would you do?"

Vic picked up the fat Seattle telephone book, flipping to the Ws in the white pages. Daphne closed the book. "Not listed," she said. "What next?"

Thea wiggled her eyebrows. "I'd check records. Get all the house numbers for the street from a mapping program then run the addresses individually in the tax rolls until I got a hit on the name. Or I'd run the name through the Sewer Queen."

"The what?"

"My contact at city waterworks. And I've got telco—"

"Telco?" Daphne repeated the word without comprehension.

"Telephone company," Thea said. "I've got telco connections. And there are other databases I can access at work. But initial searching I can do online from any computer. My phone's charging in my car. You only know her name?"

Daphne stuffed more toast in her mouth. "Minerva Watts, probably on Eastpark Avenue, her husband was John. That's all. I don't know where to begin."

"So I guess you've begun by asking me." Thea moved for the laptop sitting in Vic's open briefcase at the end of the counter.

"Umm," Daphne hesitated as Thea fired up the computer.

"I'm going to bed," he said. But he stood there.

Thea's nails clattered on the keyboard as she typed one-handed, sipping coffee. She shook her head. "I might not get a match, given the demographic involved."

"What? Demographic? Why?" Daphne felt like a child who understood nothing.

"Because she's a thousand years old."

"Thea, stop it." Daphne slugged her coffee.

Vic stroked his chin in a way that acknowledged everything. "It was an older lady."

"Like this is an older computer?" Thea scraped her nails over the keyboard and an error message flagged on the screen as the computer beeped a protest.

"Hey," Vic said.

Thea clonked her ceramic cup on the counter and started using both hands to type.

"Just . . ." Daphne rubbed her scalp and took a deep breath. "If you could find an address, Thee, it'd be great."

Vic blinked at both women. Daphne waited, feeling somehow selfish for having slept while he worked last night.

Thea gave a quick shrug. "Little old ladies often do not have bills or property titles in their own names."

"Oh. But her husband's dead," Daphne said, catching her lower lip in her teeth. "I think quite a while back. She said something about that. Do you have to get property in your own name after awhile?"

Thea shrugged. "I'll see what I can find."

Daphne had been to Thea's desk at the newspaper's office, an expansive room of half cubicles and telephones with all sorts of computer and video screens lining the walls. She pictured Thea toiling through rolls of tractor-fed printouts, cross-checking special directories and dusty references. "How long will the basic searching you can do on the net take?"

"If I'm lazy? About an hour."

"An hour? Seriously?"

Thea sipped coffee then clanked her cup down hard enough to warn of breaking ceramic if she added more pressure. Daphne winced, pushed away a horrible memory, and imagined instead she could hear Vic's unspoken thought, the same admonishment he gave Jed and Josie. *Be careful. It can break.*

It's stupid, Josie had said, just the previous afternoon on their abbreviated Wednesday visit. *Mom has granite countertops. Granite doesn't break. Ceramic does,* Vic had told his daughter, soft-voiced. *Stupid,* the girl insisted.

Stupid is what Josie called the countertop when Vic labored to clean the old grout, too. Here, Daphne would have liked to agree with the girl but for the mean-spirited preteen angst Josie carried.

Vic shifted from one foot to the other and asked Daphne, "Would it be a huge inconvenience for you to take my car today so I can use your truck to pick up Jed's bike this afternoon?"

"Oh, no. I mean, sure, we can switch cars. It's a big commercial project I'm on today and I'm only working a half day anyway. I won't need much for tools."

"Thanks," he said, kissing her again. "I'm going to bed. I have to be at Jed's game this afternoon and it's all the way up in Snohomish. You won't forget Josie's volleyball game?"

"'Course not," Daphne said, kissing him as he drifted out the door.

Thea had layers of windows open on Vic's computer screen. "You're not sure about the street or anything, are you?"

"She said she lived on the other side of the park and I sort of assumed she meant Eastpark Avenue."

"You assumed that because you live on this side of the park and you live on Westpark. People do that, view the world from their own prism." Thea cleared her throat. "Well, if she lived on the block where you saw the car, there'd be maybe forty addresses to check in the block. Add ten blocks both ways to be safe. That'll take—"

"Forever," Daphne said.

"Maybe a few hours' work."

"A few hours?" Daphne felt a flood of relief. If Thea got the old woman's address today, she could go knock on the door this afternoon and see that everything was fine.

Thea nodded and grinned. "We used to have interns who lived for this kind of assignment. I loved bossing them around. Find me all the Joe Smiths who have a six-two-four phone prefix and own a food establishment in the downtown district. Get me a list of everyone who owns a racehorse that ran Emerald Downs last month and who drives a Jag XK. Run down everyone with a cosmetology license who lives in Ravenna."

"Why would you make someone do that? Because you're mean?"

"That, and because it's often the fastest way to locate someone I want to interview. News is a snappy event. When it's fun, anyway."

"Seriously?"

"Yes, news is more fun when it's fast-breaking. And yes, on all those examples. Like, a source mentioned this golden little tidbit he heard when riding with the friend of an acquaintance. He wouldn't name the person, but he slipped something about going to the track in the guy's Jaguar to see the guy's horse run. Hand that to a real research whiz with good Google-fu and you can pin someone down."

"Good Google-fu." Daphne murmured. "I don't have that."

"At work, we're way beyond Google," Thea said with a sniff. "But hey, I'm slumming here."

Daphne indicated the computer and spread her hands in invitation. "Slum away. You know specific websites to check offhand?"

"King County dot gov, for one." Thea's voice was less rapid-fire as she focused.

Daphne willed herself to not react when Thea again clonked her coffee cup on the ceramic countertop. To defeat the niggling memory, she asked, "You know those web addresses off the top of your head?"

"Well, yeah. Looking at address lists now and . . ." Thea muttered, clicking away, "Culling info from property tax records."

Thea punched more keys and Daphne heard the printer warming up at the built-in desk alcove where Vic liked to think his kids did their homework.

"It's amazing how much private information is out there, I guess," Daphne said. *How much should anyone ask about someone else's business?* "Why didn't the police do a computer search for the lady's address last night? They can access anything you can."

Thea snorted. "I think you overestimate how much they'll work on every single question from every single complainant."

"I'm a complainant?"

"Well, you were in this case." Thea nodded at the empty doorway where Vic had gone. "Or he was, since he's the one who called the police."

"Complainant. It sounds so whiny."

"So does complaining about it. Daphne, it's just the standard police term for a caller. The person who calls 911 or the nonemergency number and tells the dispatch center that there's been a traffic accident or a lost child or a burglary or—"

"Or a little old lady saying she's being robbed and kidnapped."

Thea lurched away to swipe a page from the printer. "You know, the whole thing actually makes no sense. Why would you kidnap someone in order to rob them? If I were going to rob someone, I would not kidnap said someone. And if I were going to kidnap someone, I think I'd be writing a ransom note to the person's family, not robbing them. You know?"

Daphne made shushing motions and groaned. "I don't know. I'd just like to know she's okay. I mean, what if . . . ?"

Thea rolled her eyes and made a dismissive puff of breath.

"No, no, listen." Daphne said. "Don't brush off the idea. Suppose there was some criminal enterprise that involved stealing from little old ladies, making them sign over all their property and—"

Thea cut both hands across the air. "Stop. If it was a great story, I'd be all over it. But it's not. I'd love it if it were, though. I could show up this new guy who thinks he's God's gift to journalism. Thinks he's the combined Woodward and Bernstein of our age. Doesn't seem to notice that one major paper in the city went online and our jobs are drying up. He's tall and gorgeous and flirty and always trying to buy everyone lunch and help with their articles and stuff. I don't like him."

"Because?"

"He called me a dumb bitch."

"That's terrible. And ridiculous. You're not dumb." Daphne patted Thea's arm. "You're the smartest person I know. I, I mean . . ."

Thea's sharp look muffled Daphne's stuttering attempt to recover. Nothing made a person gulp like Thea's curt *Leave It* glare. Then Thea crossed her arms and lowered her voice. "Okay, so tell me the real reason you called."

Daphne wondered if her face flushed as she nodded rather than fight

Thea's insight. "I saw something. And I don't want to leave things unfinished. I don't want things to end the way they are."

Thea beamed and reached for Daphne in a wide-armed hug. "That's the best thing I've heard in a while."

Daphne's return hug was uncertain. "Uh, yeah, well. I just, I need your help to find a guy, a detective who retired from the Seattle Police Department."

Thea's smile vanished. "What? Who?"

"The guy who was assigned to my sister's case. I want to talk to him."

Thea stared, openmouthed. "That's what this is about?"

"What did you think this was about?"

"Honey, I thought you were going back to school."

"What? School! Why would I do that?"

"To finish."

"God, no. I'm done with that. Forever ago."

Taking plenty of time pouring the last of the coffee from the paper cups into her ceramic mug, Thea asked, "Why did you quit school?"

Daphne sandwiched eggs in toast and ate in huge mouthfuls.

Thea sighed. "To get a retired guy's contact info, I'd have to go shmooze Henry—"

"He's one of your contacts at the police department?"

"Yeah, but even then, he's not going to want to tell me."

"But I want . . . I need to talk to him, Thee."

"Then you go blow Henry Fragher." Thea gave a wicked grin that melted to a kind expression when Daphne got near tears. "Listen to me. Your sister dying her senior year did not mean you shouldn't have graduated when your turn came. You only need a semester to get your degree. You could do it in a snap."

To keep herself from bawling, Daphne set about making her mid-morning sandwich, a peanut butter and jelly to go. "I don't want a degree. I want to go back in time. I don't want my sister's case to be suspended. And I want to fix yesterday. I want to know that lady is all right."

"Daphne."

With her eyes closed, Daphne raised both hands to stop Thea from pushing any further. "The retired detective? Can you put me in touch with him?"

"You're going to make me go smoke a guy I promised myself I'd never smoke again just to get you some police information?"

"Thee . . ." Daphne opened her eyes. Thea's smile grew strained.

"You know, you never used to call me that."

Daphne felt confusion drape over her. "What?"

"Not until you'd been with Vic a while and he started calling you *Daph*. Now you're doing it to other people. You're calling me *Thee* instead of Thea."

"Umm . . ." Daphne hesitated, rattled by a sudden crystallizing thought. Thea and Vic's half friendship slipped early on into the sort of adversarial mood sometimes found between friends of friends.

Thea's prior claim as Daphne's college friend and postcollege roommate competed with his now four-year live-in relationship with Daphne. Sometimes he asked Thea what groundbreaking interviews or investigations she was working on and she asked him if he and the other meteorologists had stopped any meteors of late. Their under-the-table animosity puzzled but had a comparison. Daphne remembered being eleven, feeling pangs over Suzanne going away for another semester. It would be the start of her big sister's senior year and who knew what would happen come graduation at the school year's end. And Suzanne had said something odd, that her best friend and her boyfriend didn't like each other.

The memory was a few seconds of life Daphne hadn't thought about before, only now making the link to her experience with Vic and Thea.

Suzanne's best friend and boyfriend didn't get along.

And Daphne couldn't think about the boyfriend without recalling the accusations that flew in the weeks Suzanne was missing, before they found her body.

After the murder, he was questioned.

At the funeral, as he was escorted from the church by uniformed police officers, awe-struck eleven-year-old Daphne had felt the seal of judgment fall on Ross Bouchard.

Thea tapped a few keys with her right hand. "If that old lady were actually in trouble, someone else probably—"

"Saw something." Daphne said, failing to keep the memories at bay. Her voice became a whisper. "I saw something."

"Aha!" Thea's victory shout was directed at the computer and she scribbled another note on the page she'd printed. "Address. Minerva Watts on Eastpark Avenue. Want to go run this thing down to the end?"

"Yes." The phone rang and Daphne checked the caller ID screen. "My mom."

"I can come with you if we go around ten."

"I can't, I've got work. Only a half day, though." Daphne shook her head as the phone stopped ringing with no message left.

Thea made a face. "You get all the fun."

"I ought to stop in on my mother. And I have to go to a volleyball game for Vic's daughter this afternoon. His ex might be there."

Snorting, Thea said, "You get all the dysfunction."

Fingering the slip of paper, Daphne read Thea's note: 11243 East-park Ave, original sale to John and Minerva Watts (taxes show under M. Watts now). She frowned as her mind circled. "The police could have done what you just did to get her address."

Thea licked her lips. "They could have, they just wouldn't for such a little thing. I mean, if someone has just been murdered in the street, they run it all down, but they don't pull out all the stops for every odd complaint that raises someone's eyebrows."

"Why not?" Daphne realized she sounded like a toddler, but she wanted to know.

"Don't be silly. They just can't."

"Am I silly to go there?"

"Yes. But going will put your mind at ease, so go."

Daphne looked at the phone, thinking of Vic picking it up the moment he had a notion. "Should I call the police and give them the address?"

"Did they fall over themselves when you called in the hot tip of her actual name last night?"

"Forget it. I am being silly on this."

Thea made each word a pronouncement. "Yes. You. Are."

"As soon as you can, please get me a way to contact that retired cop."

"Oh, Daphne, why?" Thea folded her arms and waited.

Daphne grabbed her Carhartt jacket. It was stiff and heavy, still the rich tan-brown of new canvas because she only wore it to and from work, never while working. When roofing, her shoulders needed to swing freely and the labor kept her warm, so she didn't need more than a sweatshirt. Vic bought the Carhartt jacket for her assuming she had a big liking of the brand.

How often did people assume something about another person? How often did they get it flat wrong?

Thea pulled out a lipstick from her capacious leather purse and asked, "Daphne, why do you want to talk to the retired cop?" She puckered and glossed.

Purseless, Daphne grabbed her wallet and truck keys from the kitchen counter, unplugged her phone from its power cord, and stowed her things in the jacket pockets. After buttoning the flaps shut, she remembered Vic's request and took keys to his car from the hook in the cabinet where they kept spares.

"Why, Daphne?"

Daphne looked back, mute. Of course the unanswerable couldn't be explained. That's why people didn't try.

CHAPTER 6

At the vast commercial building where Daphne's work schedule demanded today's half shift, the other roofers milled about, some at the bottom of the ladder, others waiting on the rooftop, but at the peak, not at the bottom left corner where shingling would begin.

"Have Mayfield start it," was the foreman's direction to Walt, one of the guys who stood in for Bob when he was at another construction project.

Daphne liked being referred to by her last name at the job site almost as much as she liked being the preferred roofer to start shingling. Some of the guys said the boss chose her to start shingles because Daphne was the smallest roofer. They thought her size made it easiest for her to crouch on an overhanging eave. But she knew what her foreman knew: she started shingles with perfection and only a roof well started could be finished to high standards.

Perfect starts were where she'd made herself whole. Daphne had never wanted to move up to supervising the roofing crew. Perfect roofing was enough. Bob, Walt, and Hal knew how many man-hours—a term Walt never failed to use—would be needed to complete a job and ordered different crew members to different job sites accordingly. Because of his ability to predict workloads, Bob had okayed her half shift today and Friday off.

She regretted the wasted day-and-a-half off now. She and Vic would have none of this afternoon or the next day together, which had been her hope when she requested the leave. Her seniority on the crew gave her good assignments and good time off, but nothing let her predict when Vic's life would be waylaid by his kids or work.

Just yesterday in the Peace Park, with her mind roiling about being the live-in girlfriend of a good man with kids—good kids—whose mother pushed their buttons, she'd wondered: *Do I need this?*

Frowning as she thought of her time in the park the last afternoon, of the old lady pleading for help, she pushed a hand into her right jacket pocket. The sheet of paper where Thea noted an address for Minerva Watts rested between her phone and wallet in the pocket.

"Hey, Mayfield," one of the guys teased from the ladder, "that all you got today?"

In her left hand and under her arm, Daphne carried a bare minimum of equipment, sure she'd get through to lunch on so little and not wanting to transfer more of her tools to Vic's car. She shucked her jacket at the water cooler, leaving it in the truck bed with the others.

"It's all I'll need," she said. Having no tools for the job was an error she'd not made since her first week in construction. When she switched cars with Vic this morning, she'd taken only her loaded tool belt and her favorite coil nailer, plus a hundred-foot silicon air hose. The silicon hoses were so much easier to handle than the old rubber ones. They didn't tangle, didn't drag heavily across unprotected tar paper, and flipped easily across the peak of a ridge.

At the mid-morning break, Walt tapped Daphne's shoulder as he headed for the ladder. "Boss wants to see you before you leave."

She paused in her sandwich, one booted foot on each side of the roof's peak. "Huh, m'kay." If he'd sent her to the boss as soon as she'd arrived, she would have been able to leave as soon as the lunch horn sounded.

Would the boss need her to work more than this half day? She had to get to Josie's volleyball tourney by three o'clock. Before the game, she wanted to check on Minerva Watts. And if they did need her to work this afternoon, suppose the job required tools she'd left in her truck? She reminded herself to call Vic and let him know she wouldn't make Josie's volleyball game if it turned out she had to work past noon.

When the lunch horn blared, Daphne was first down the ladder, heading for the Atco trailer and giving the customary rap on the door as she went inside.

"You wanted to see me, Mr. Wellsley?" She never addressed Dick by his first name. No one at the site did.

The owner and operator of Wellsley Construction, an outfit that had pioneered the Women-In-Construction program right when she'd needed her life changed, pointed to the chair opposite his desk in the trailer. "Sit down, kiddo. I'll get right to it. Did you do an off-hours job? Earlier this week?" He looked at a piece of paper in his hand, nodded, and added, "Tuesday?" Then he tossed the paper on his desk.

"I . . ." Daphne looked around the office and wondered if she seemed as unforthcoming as a kid, as Jed or Josie. She hadn't done anything wrong but was caught off guard with the inquiry.

Her boss waited with one eyebrow cocked, his manner pleasant enough but he didn't wait for her answer before adding, "I do not want union trouble."

She let her shoulders drop as she nodded. "Yes. It was a detached garage, a small one. Just a straight reroof. Tore off the old stuff, down to the wood."

"What else?"

"Nothing else."

"This shed, did it have rafters or trusses?"

"Rafters."

"How much work did you do on the old rafters?"

"None."

"'Bout how much repair on the subroof?"

Daphne cut her hands across her waist. "None."

"If it needed new shingles and paper, there must have been some water damage, kiddo."

"No, nothing else was needed, just new paper and new shingles. It was a cosmetic thing. They had a new house roof and wanted the detached garage to match. The roof was old, but it was solid. No damage to the sub, rafters all good. I didn't do carpentry there."

"So if Walt says you did . . ."

She looked up. Walt was the one who reported her as perhaps working beyond her scope? How did he even know she'd had a roofing job on the side? She loosened her elastic band one wrap, easing tension in her scalp. Fiddling with her hair when nervous wasn't her habit, but she wore her ponytail tight while working and always ached to loosen it as soon as she left the rooftop.

"It was truly a nonunion kind of job," Daphne said. "I didn't miss work for it. At the other site, on Tuesday, Bob let four of us go early because the sheet metal wasn't there yet. He offered afternoon work by seniority and I passed."

"Because you knew you had this other private job in the wings?" His phone rang and he grabbed it, telling the caller to hold on, then held the phone against his chest.

"Well, yes." Daphne cleared her throat, feeling like she should say more, but he brought the phone to his mouth and motioned her out the door.

She went. The boss was something of a father figure to her, a man who'd given her a chance the day after she lost her own father. She didn't want to think of father figures or fathers now. Her dad's final hideous choice left a residue of incomprehension and anger, left her mother alone. And Daphne, knowing she was the one person who could best balm her mother, despised herself for holding comfort back.

Sliding into Vic's car, she wished she were driving her truck. Not since her first days in construction had she been in a sedan—her father's car—at a job site.

"Oh, Dad . . ." She rubbed her forehead as his rants pounded in her head. *Nobody makes an effort.* Pushing a fist against her teeth, Daphne bit down and screwed her eyes tight to shut out his old mantra, but the memories ran and she had to stop the car.

The ten troubled years her father survived after his firstborn's murder would have seen his second daughter graduate college in one more half semester—if Daphne and he had both stuck with life plans. "Dad, I didn't know . . ."

She didn't talk to him often, save for the annual visit to the grave, but his words came back unbidden whenever she went home.

If she visited her mom, then slipped upstairs to talk in secrets to her missing sister, the memory of his voice—*someone saw something*—haunted her all the way up the stairs to her old bedroom.

Someone saw her, thought my girl needed help, saw him. Someone thought they should say something, do something. That's what happened. People don't make a goddamn effort.

At home, all the remaining questions and withheld explanations rang louder in a static world.

So she avoided her childhood home and her mother. But this choice left her scourged.

An image of her half-living mother summoned wild thoughts of shucking blame. Daphne wiped her eyes.

Had she blamed her mother, just a bit, for not knowing details of sorrow Daphne herself hadn't known?

She shook against the guilt and forced her mind to the task at hand, lurching Vic's car into traffic with one admission.

"Dad, I quit, too."

—–ᴍ–—

The Eastpark Avenue address Thea uncovered was easy to find and easy to believe as home for a little old lady.

Minerva Watts's house was tidy enough, but the eaves sagged and paint peeled in curls at the edges of sun-battered siding. Clumps of striving tulips pushed up near the windows. The bulbs had grown over-packed from years of not being dug up and divided. The home needed a new roof and the lawn was weedy. The lower windows and the front door had security bars that spoke of an elderly woman's fears. A thin crumbling walkway led to the front door.

The driveway lined the edge of the lawn, and a car—a navy blue Lincoln Town Car, Daphne noted—parked at the house had its trunk open.

Relax, it's a different car, Daphne coached herself. Just go say hello.

Because how could she go up to a stranger and say: Hey, you weren't in real trouble, were you?

I just wanted to stop in and see how you are. That could work but the words sounded odd and awkward as she rehearsed. Daphne rolled her eyes and tried again.

The other day, she began in her head as she parked Vic's car just past the house—wait, it wasn't the other day, some distant time. Less than twenty-four hours had passed since their encounter.

Okay, *yesterday afternoon in the park* . . . Daphne allowed her lips to move, though she did not speak aloud as she tried to summon what to say . . . *well, we saw each other and you were upset. You said some things and I just wanted to know if you're getting along all right. Do you need anything?*

Daphne pulled on her jacket, stepped out of the Honda, and pushed the car keys deep into one pocket of her pants just as Minerva Watts's front door opened. A man—the same man?—propped open the door's security gate, his back to Daphne. He wore a hip-length black leather jacket over jeans and running shoes and he grasped a cardboard box with both hands. Then he leaned into the open doorway and someone stacked another box on top of the one he held.

He made for the car with his double load. Daphne hesitated, deciding between following him to initiate a conversation and finishing her walk to the front door. Through the front window, Daphne could see a woman—the daughter, she reminded herself—standing in the living room, hands on her hips, her back to Daphne and the man outside.

I saw something and I . . . no, that would not be the way to start.

Knocking on the doorjamb as she stood in the open threshold, Daphne looked past the woman in jeans and a fleece sweater who held a small box on her hip. Beyond her in a powder-blue wingback chair, Minerva Watts sat wearing a quilted calico housedress over pink slacks, her bobby-socked feet tucked into blue loafers.

The old lady's face carried the unsure countenance of a scolded child about to break a rule.

"It was my grandmother Miller's brooch. Please don't take that." As she spoke, Minerva Watts leaned and peered around the woman in fleece and jeans. "Daphne!"

"Lady, I told you to shut it and—"

"Oh, Daphne!" Minerva Watts's smile showed sad joy.

The other woman whirled and looked Daphne up and down. "Yes?"

"Um," Daphne said, her mind reeling. *She remembers my name.* "I saw you in the park yesterday and the, um, Mrs. Watts here said—"

"I'm Mrs. Watts," Minerva Watts said, stating her name with purpose, sitting up straighter, smiling at Daphne.

"Mother, be quiet now." The woman pointed a finger at Minerva Watts, whose smile evaporated as she cast a worried gaze down at the cream high-low carpeting.

Daphne took one small step forward. The other woman raised a palm toward Daphne and the front door and cleared her throat, squinting at Daphne while she spoke to Mrs. Watts.

"Mother, it's time for your pill."

"Listen," Daphne said, a foot on each side of the threshold, "I know, I mean I don't know what's . . . Wait. I—"

Minerva Watts leaned forward, her bright and watery gaze fixed on Daphne. "Please help me."

"Guff!" The woman's shriek sparked the man outside to slam the car's trunk. Daphne turned on the threshold, her back against the doorjamb just as the man whipped his head around.

He glanced at the house and cut across the lawn in a jog, pointing a finger at Daphne, holding up his other hand like a traffic cop.

"You. Stand there. Hold up."

A few steps would put him on top of her.

"What?" Daphne said, blinking at the man. He was beside her now, six inches taller, eighty pounds heavier. She tried an encouraging, peaceable smile, looking from the man to the woman and back again. From the corner of her eye, she could see the woman bend to set her box on the floor.

The man put his hand on Daphne's shoulder. She stepped back but his palm changed to a gripping fist on her jacket. She froze. He looked into the house, nodded, then looked at Daphne again, his grip clenching deeper and harder.

She dropped her shoulder under his grasp, but felt his solid grip on her jacket.

In one breath, Daphne swirled, twisting out of her jacket and running across the yard, around the corner of the house into the side yard.

In those two seconds, she heard the woman shout, "Shit!" and something dropped, a door banged. Footsteps, fast and hard, pounded nearer. Daphne ran into the neighbor's side yard, across the next backyard, into the alley.

When she heard him running after her, she ran faster down the alley, panicked, and cut across someone else's property, desperate to escape the sound of the man chasing her. She ducked into the backyard of a house on the next street.

Somewhere behind her, a metal garbage can fell over and she heard the man swear.

Instinct made her want to run back toward the car, but the man was between her and Vic's Honda, blocking her escape, so she continued deep into the side yard of a stranger's house, crouched into some heavy rhododendrons, and pressed herself against a tall wooden fence. Perspiration trickled between her breasts.

A flash of motion caught her eye, too high to be the man, but she jerked at the sight of a person going by a second floor window in the next house, the one with the fenced backyard.

Don't tell him where I am, she willed the man in the house.

But then she thought, suppose the neighbor is a huge, decisive person who will tell any guy chasing a woman to back off?

But nothing happened. No one opened a window or called out or anything. Had the person upstairs not seen her come into the neighbor's yard and hide? She heard footsteps scuffing gravel in the alley, retracing, nearing her again. Should she make a break for it, run through the side yard and down the next street? If the man, Guff, saw her—and he was close now—he'd chase her again, grab her again. The sensation of physical desperation reminded her she lacked cardiovascular conditioning. For all her outrageous upper body strength, her endurance was poor and she decided she could not outrun the man. She was wearing boots, he wore sneakers. His reflexes were snakelike. Her hands shook in simple fear. She'd never been chased and she was sweating from more than exertion.

As she hid, an unbidden thought of her sister's final secret moments came to her. Had Suzanne run from her killer?

Call 911, Daphne mentally begged all the neighbors, wondering if any strangers were watching the spectacle of a woman being chased, hiding from a man. *Call and report him. Report me as a suspicious person. Just call the police. Someone? Anyone? Someone, see something. Help me.*

Again footsteps scuffed by in the alley. When she thought he was farther away, she edged deeper into the side yard, desperate to add a few more paces between herself and her pursuer. If she had to run for it again, she wanted a decent head start.

Or she could hide better. Up ahead were two overflowing plastic garbage bins, offering refuge. Daphne crawled from the rhododendrons on her hands and knees to secret herself between the stinking refuse and the wooden fence. *Bang. Boom. Bang. Boom.* Her heartbeat summoned all, but she could not hear the man's footsteps anymore.

A few houses away, possibly at Minerva Watts's home, a door slammed. Daphne felt the drumbeat of her heart, thumping to capacity within her chest, trilling in her ears. Then several car doors slammed in quick succession, their bangs sounding like gunshots.

Holding her breath, Daphne twisted, swiveling her head and neck. If she peeked out the other side of the garbage bins, she might be able to see across the alley, through the yard back to Eastpark Avenue. Creeping, she squeezed around the farther bin.

The unnerving sensation of giving up some of her cover made her heart pound faster. She pressed her lips tight, stifling a murmur and peered toward the street as an engine roared, gunned too hard in starting.

A big navy blue car sped by. Yes, the car from Mrs. Watts's driveway, the Town Car where the guy put the boxes. Two women were in the backseat, one small and cowering on the far side of the nearer woman— the fleece sweater woman who had called for Guff. Daphne pushed forward and saw he was the driver and that the woman sat with one arm over the old lady, the other hand holding a brown Carhartt jacket.

Daphne winced. The jacket held her phone. And her wallet.

They would know who she was, where she lived.

And they had taken the old lady. They had taken Minerva Watts. Again. Daphne abandoned hope of the best-case scenario or a happy answer—that strangers were having a bad day with a difficult older relative. She bolted for Vic's car, not thinking about what she'd do if they saw her and came after her again.

She gunned the engine, slam-shifted to spin the Honda around, and floored the accelerator, chasing the man who had chased her.

Fleeing straight down Eastpark, the navy Town Car was already more than a half mile ahead. Daphne rolled through two stop signs, checking left and right fast as she cleared the intersections. The other car was still pulling away, making her wonder if they'd blown the stop signs, too.

Get the license plate at least. Not having the license plate for the police officers last night was one of her failings.

She drove faster than she'd ever driven through a residential area, ever. She grimaced through it, held her breath. The neighborhood gave way to small businesses. More traffic would be coming with the University District.

Catch them, she willed herself, all attention on her forward pursuit.

They were approaching a green light at the top of a hill. She wouldn't be able to see which way they turned if they cleared the intersection without her. She pressed harder on the accelerator, city blocks whipping by as she gained on the escaping car.

The light turned yellow and the Lincoln vanished down the hill as the traffic signal loomed red.

Staring at the license plate in the bumper's center, Daphne stomped the accelerator. Less than a split second later, she gasped at the sight of a car coming at her left rear fender and another at her right front. Then the screaming of tires, the crunch of metal, people shouting, and glass breaking all jumbled in her head as the Honda spun a full circle in the intersection.

CHAPTER 7

Nausea welled up in Daphne's belly. An adrenaline spike shook her hands. Sweating and pimpled with goose bumps, she gulped in the breeze drafting through her shattered driver's window.

A man in a Seattle Sonics jacket came to her door as she turned her head like a swimmer needing a breath, her mind needing contact and help. "You fucking idiot," he said, his chest leaning into her window as he braced his hands on the Honda's roof. "How red they gotta be for you to stop?"

"I, I need a phone. I have to call the police."

"Jesus!"

Daphne closed her eyes. If the man's epithet had been any other, it might not have sent her mind crashing back to Suzanne's funeral. *Jesus. Jesus.* It was a name a Mayfield girl knew better than to say without respect. In her sheltered childhood, Daphne knew no one who spoke in such terms. Even her father never uttered any kind of curse until after Suzanne's body was found, then he cursed every unmoving stranger.

Daphne first considered the notion of propriety at eleven, when Ross Bouchard spoke out of turn at the altar and sang strange things about Jesus and Suzanne.

"Did you see that car? The navy blue Lincoln Town Car?" Daphne asked without looking at the man, her face turned to her lap, a swimmer no longer breathing, drowning. Her head swirled, remembering the Bouchard boy croaked something about how drowning men could see Him. She turned her head and gasped, "Did you get the license? Someone must have seen it."

"Jesus H. Christ," he said, and pushed himself away from her car with enough force to rock it.

She clutched her shaking hands in her lap, wanting to clap them over her ears to quell her father's voice. *Someone must have seen . . . someone saw something.*

Then she exploded, forcing the door open, wrenching a metal groan of protest from Vic's car. A horn bitched behind backed-up traffic. The Honda was still in the middle of the intersection, still pointing down Eastpark as if willing to make an effort, to pursue, though battered. On each side of the cross street, a crunched car waited at the curb. A blond woman in a green SUV with the driver's door gaping open pressed something white to her face. A small silver two-door, half its headlights punched out like a boxer with a black eye, sat on Daphne's right, the remaining hazard lights blinking in surrender.

"God, is anyone hurt? Seriously hurt?" Daphne called, swiveling in the road, facing the two-door, melting in relief when a young guy waved from the front bumper. His jeans were ripped at the knees and his T-shirt riddled with holes, but Daphne knew she hadn't shredded his clothing.

She jogged to the green SUV, calling to the woman. "Are you okay?"

The blond pulled a handkerchief from her face and looked at bloody smears. "I just dropped my kids off. I'm so glad they weren't with me."

"Oh. Oh, yes. Me, too," Daphne said, soaked in every kind of guilt, every feeling of human inadequacy.

The woman's focus shifted to something behind Daphne, someone. Daphne whirled, almost bumping into the Sonics man.

"I saw the whole thing," he said to the SUV driver, pointing an indicting finger at Daphne. "She blew the light. I'm a witness."

"Did you see the other car? The dark blue Lincoln?" Daphne asked him as she stepped away from the SUV for a futile peer down Eastpark Avenue. The Lincoln was gone, of course.

His face became a sneer. "There was no other car."

She felt her blood drain and rubbed her temples. "I need a phone. Now. I'm going—"

He shook his head. "You're not going anywhere." And he grabbed at her bare arm.

She yanked back hard. "Touch me and I will knock your head off," she told him.

He stared at her. Behind him, the woman gawked, her gaze covering Daphne as she eyed Daphne's hair, her dirty hands. Up and down, left and right. Daphne watched the woman ogle until she couldn't stand it and said, "I'm so sorry about the accident. It was an accident. Do you have a phone?"

"They said someone already called 911," she said. "We're just supposed to wait."

"Yes, yes," Daphne said, wanting to ask again if the woman had a phone. She swirled in the street, feeling drunk. At the far side of the intersection, the guy at the two-door was holding his phone, taking a picture of his bumper. Daphne saw now that his knuckles were cut. Dabs of blood on two joints dribbled down his fingers and he wiped his hand on his shirt before continuing to take pictures.

"Could I use your phone?" she hollered.

"What for?"

"To call the police."

"I already called them."

"It's about something else," Daphne said, waving her hands, shifting her tone between entreaty and urgency.

Beyond the SUV, just across the wide sidewalk, a convenience store's propped-open door advertised energy drinks, lottery tickets, and tobacco.

"I'm just going to use the phone in there," Daphne said to no one in particular as she pointed, then ran around the car feeling a bit like a kid playing fire drill games in traffic.

Inside the store, an older man with hair like aged steel stood behind the counter. He pointed to a basic black telephone by his cash register. "I make call already. Is good."

Daphne clutched both hands together to plea. "May I use the phone, please?"

He pointed to it again and she grabbed for the handset, dialing the three numbers. Outside, the man who swore at her stood by the green SUV, watching Daphne, his hands on his hips. She turned again toward the inside of the store. The man at the register was watching a girl at the beer cooler. Signs everywhere promoted lottery tickets. Be an instant winner.

"Nine-one-one, what is your emergency?" The dispatcher's voice sounded unstressed but clipped.

"Hi. I'm calling from an accident on Eastpark that just happened a few minutes ago and—"

"We have officers and an ambulance en route to an injury accident at Eastpark Avenue and Spencer Street, ma'am."

"Yes. Good. But I'm calling about something else. Just before. There was a man. A man and a woman and they took a little old lady. The lady's name is Minerva Watts and she lives on Eastpark and they took her in a navy blue Lincoln Town Car, but I didn't get the license.

It starts with a *Y* and then I think another letter. I was trying to get the plate and that's when the accident happened."

"Is this car involved in the accident on Eastpark, ma'am?"

"No, but—"

"Is it at the scene?"

"It's not part of the accident," Daphne said, waving her free hand in frustration. "The man who's driving it, see, he chased me. He and this woman took this lady, Minerva Watts. The woman called him 'Guff' and he grabbed me and I got away and he chased me—"

"What is your name, ma'am?"

"Daphne Mayfield."

"Where did the incident of a man and a woman taking an old lady occur?"

"At her house, 11243 Eastpark Avenue. Something's definitely wrong there. Yesterday, they took her from the Peace Park. I called that in, too. Didn't anyone call today? Someone must have seen something."

"Does Minerva Watts know the man and woman? Did she call the man Guff?"

"No. The other lady called him Guff."

"And Guff grabbed you?"

"And he took my jacket. My wallet and phone were in it. And he chased me and they were driving like crazy down Eastpark and I was trying to catch them so I could at least get the license plate, and then I had this accident and they got away, but I think you should—"

"Ma'am, slow down. An officer is on the way, okay? A police officer is on the way to you right now."

Sirens wailed outside and Daphne took a breath. "I hear them. I can hear them."

"Okay, talk to the officer. Good-bye."

"Bye," Daphne said to the dead line, going back outside to face more than she felt able to rectify.

Two blue police cars, sirens dying a block away, nosed up to the wreckage. The Sonics man pointed to Daphne then the Honda, SUV, and the two-door in turn. The first officer swung from his car, held a hand out to the man and talked into a shoulder microphone for several seconds before going to the SUV. A red and white ambulance bearing the words Medic One on the side pulled in behind the second police car.

"It's all her fault!" The Sonics man pointed Daphne out to the second police officer.

Had the dispatcher already sent another officer chasing across the city for the Town Car? Daphne pursed her lips, thinking how much time had passed, how big the city was, how impossible a minute's head start made pursuit of a fleeing car.

"She ran right through the red light. She was speeding, too."

The officer looked at the witness then Daphne. She resisted the urge to run to the officers and insert her non-accident needs. The fleeing Town Car was more important but the accident was the attention grabber. She rubbed her head and nodded at both men.

The first officer left the SUV and strode for the two-door, pointing to Vic's Honda as he went by Daphne. "Yours?"

She nodded again. When he told her to wait beside it, she walked to the car. How much longer? How far away would the couple with Minerva Watts get? How impossible would it be to find already? Where on earth would they be going?

Paramedics opened a large plastic tackle box beside the blond in the SUV. One pulled out a stethoscope and the other opened a dressing.

Feeling inappropriate on too many levels to gawk at the woman while the medics tended her cut head, Daphne turned, watched the first officer stop talking to the young man at the two-door long enough to nod and wave off the other cop. When the second policeman got in his car and drove away, Daphne tried to take a measure of calm. Maybe he would go after the Lincoln. The accident wasn't that bad. It wasn't.

Still, it seemed too long before the remaining cop headed back to her and the Honda.

"Saving the best for last," she muttered to herself and shook her head.

"So, you're the little woman who started this big accident," he said.

"Look, there's this whole other thing," Daphne began in earnest.

"Dig out your license, registration, and proof of insurance for me, all righty?"

Daphne turned to kneel on the car's seat, as she dug into the glove box for the registration, raising her voice to tell the cop about all that had happened right before the accident. When she popped up clutching the state's official registration, she saw the cop was not listening at her door, but walking around the Honda surveying damage. He wasn't even looking at her. Had he missed her whole speech?

"It was dark blue," she said, testing him. "The color of your shirt."

He bent at her rear bumper, touching swipes of green paint from the SUV. "No one else saw a blue Lincoln."

"He chased me. He has my jacket. My wallet. My ID and my phone."

"You were chasing another car and that's why you came through this traffic light like you did?"

"It didn't start that way, with me chasing him. It started with him chasing me. Around houses and down an alley and through yards."

"He was chasing you?"

"Yes." She gave one hard nod to affirm this fact.

"On foot, not in the cars?"

"Right. He ran after me." Daphne gave another nod, relieved he understood her.

"And why were you running from him in the first place?"

"I ran because . . . because he chased me. He grabbed me."

He hooked one thumb in his gun belt. "And then you chased him?"

"Yes," Daphne admitted, aware she sounded more than half crazy.

Shaking his head, he said, "Try again. Why did you chase him?"

Daphne took a breath. "Look. There's something wrong here, something going on. I think she's not that woman's mother. Minerva Watts is not her mother." She snapped her fingers. "*Lady*. She called her *lady*. And then when she saw me, she called the older lady *Mother*. Hey, did you hear about this car thing?"

He raised one eyebrow at her. "Yeah, suspicious incident on Eastpark. Navy Lincoln, northbound five or ten ago. Got it."

"You do know! Great! Then someone saw something. Someone else besides me, I mean. Someone called it in? Right?"

"You would be the Daphne Mayfield who called this in to our dispatch center from the JiffyMart?" He pointed over his shoulder to the convenience store without looking.

"Well, yes."

"Dispatch has radios. They use them to tell us out here in the cars what's going on."

"So you know what's going on?" Daphne wasn't sure she knew what was going on.

"Think so," he said.

"So, what are you going to do?" she asked.

He handed her some papers and pointed at her car. "Have a seat. Fill these out. Please be legible."

She sat behind the steering wheel like an obedient child. "Okay, for the accident," Daphne said, glancing at the forms which asked for information like her name and insurance provider. "But about the other thing?" She closed a fist over the papers and folded her arms.

He walked away.

She swung out of the car again. He could at least give her an answer. "Hey what's going to happen? Is someone doing something about it? What are you going to do?"

"I am going to handle this accident." He turned to the young man at the two-door and gave him similar pieces of paper.

"I mean, what are you going to do about that car? The one I was, you know, trying to catch up to?"

He gave a stony smile. "I am going to handle . . . this accident."

Two tow trucks arrived in a miniature convoy, their gumball emergency lights casting a weak glow in the afternoon sun. One hooked up to the green SUV.

She looked at her watch. Time was flitting away, wasting. She was going to miss the start of Josie's volleyball game if she didn't get clear of this accident soon. This was reality. No one was going to catch the Lincoln Town Car. It was just gone. A suspicious incident, just like the previous afternoon.

The shock of this realization was more defeating than it should have been. Daphne looked around the scene again. One tow truck driver pushed a broom across the asphalt, tinkling bits of shattered glass and plastic scraps of fenders and headlights into a pile. The scrape of his huge metal dustpan reminded her of the groans of the car door. The SUV made the same sound now as its front end was wrenched into the air by the tow truck.

"It doesn't run," the blond said, shaking her head. "It wouldn't start again."

"Well, you're coming with us anyway," a paramedic told her.

The pendulum swung to awful in Daphne's mental tabulation of the moment. She took a few hopeful steps toward the two-door, which the young man was cranking over. The engine almost caught, then died.

"Go. Sit. In your car." The officer put on sunglasses. "Ma'am." Then he said something fast and cryptic into his shoulder mic as he went to speak to the young man again.

The enormity of what she had done seeped within her. She would get a ticket. Her first. Would he look at her driving record and see that she'd never been ticketed before? Would he see that she was a good girl? She'd never even been stopped by a police officer before.

The ambulance door shut, shielding the paramedic and the blond.

Daphne turned away and saw the young man and policeman push the two-door to the curb.

"I bet a buddy of mine can get it started," the young man said.

"So long as it's not parked here more than twenty-four hours," the cop said.

My fault, Daphne nodded to herself as she watched the other driver leave on foot, rubbing his knuckles on his pants.

The guilty feeling was reinforced by the officer returning for a looming finale. She sat hunkered down in the Honda's driver's seat, wanting to try the ignition to see if it would start, pretty sure it would be drivable if she bashed the broken fender piece off the front tire.

Then the officer's body darkened her doorway. "Do you know how fast you were going?"

"No."

"What's your best guess?"

"Hundred and sixteen?" Daphne managed a weak smile.

He leaned over, closed his mouth and inhaled a deep, slow breath through his nose.

"Been drinking, lady?" His gaze flitted to the Honda's back seat and floor. Daphne was glad Vic kept his car clean and respectable looking.

"Oh, I wish," Daphne said, realizing now that the officer had been smelling her breath when he leaned over. "Sorry. Bad joke. It's just, I was trying to catch up and—"

"Heard that. Did you get the license plate of this suspicious car?"

Daphne shook her head but saw a distant flickering image in her mind, summoning a remembrance of speeding down the road staring at the eluding car's bumper. "Maybe part of it. A *Y* then I think another letter but I don't know. I don't know the rest. But I had to try. They took that old lady. They were at—"

"What's your address?"

She raised her voice just shy of real rudeness. "It's 11243 Eastpark Avenue. I wanted to make sure she was okay. I still do. You should, too."

He studied his notebook and muttered, "See, I think that if you were a law enforcement officer in reasonable pursuit of an actual criminal you would have gotten on the radio. And I still need to see your license." He waved the vehicle registration paper she'd given him.

"I don't have my ID because it was in my jacket and the guy stole my jacket. My wallet was in my jacket pocket."

"Uh-huh. Is this your car?" He eyed the Honda and its crumpled fenders again.

"It's my boyfriend's car."

"And his name is?"

"Vic. Vic Daily. Victor Daily."

"Do you know his full, legal name?"

"Victor David Daily."

He looked at her, pursed his lips. A feeling of inadequacy pinched at her. Thinking the officer wanted her to explain something she didn't understand, Daphne offered, "I guess his parents liked *V*s in names."

And his parents hadn't thought about a little boy being teased about venereal disease before he understood anything more than bullying. *VD, VD.* When he'd told her about being teased as a child, he'd laughed. But Vic's vulnerability, as a man missing his children—and as a little boy teased about his initials—tugged at her heart. Overwhelmed now by every failure, Daphne felt herself disconnect, a roaring in her ears. She felt faint, floaty.

"Miss, this car is not registered to a Victor David Daily."

Swirling out of the car to face the officer, Daphne's head bobbled as she jerked it back. Dizziness swayed her. Loopy as though she'd had two glasses of wine on a hot day, she still knew he was wrong. "Yes, it is."

He smiled, but in a way that made it clear he was sure he had the facts, the upper hand. "No. It isn't."

"But it is. It's Vic's car. It has been forever. Since before I knew him. I've known him for over four years."

"This car is not registered to a Victor Daily."

"What?" She held her head.

"I think you heard me."

Daphne shook her head and turned toward the car again. *Suzanne!* Staring into the rear seat's side window, she saw her sister's image. Daphne brought both hands to her face, then touched her hair, reassured that the reflection in the window copied her actions. Her ponytail had come undone and rhododendron leaves clung to her hair like feathers.

How long have I looked like her?

Suzanne would have been forty this Sunday. Forty. If she'd lived, would she be a mother by now? A grandmother? So, then her dad would be a living great-grandfather.

How much was missed when part of a generation disappeared?

"What's your date of birth?" the officer asked, but his voice seemed soft and Daphne stared at her Suzanne-like reflection in the window, imagining what life might have been like. Would Suzanne have moved far away or would she be here in the city? If she'd stayed, would she have done something with Daphne this Sunday? Would she want to spend her birthday with her little sister?

Suzanne's little sister was now more grown-up than Suzanne had ever been allowed to be.

Daphne squeezed her eyes shut. What would Suzanne have become? She'd have graduated college, maybe gone traveling like she used to talk about. She'd have done everything.

I didn't even graduate.

Suzanne would not have become a roofer, but she would have remained free and funky and more full of life than anyone else on earth.

"Birthday?" came a voice behind Daphne.

"Sunday . . ." Daphne murmured. On this birthday, Suzanne would have been forty years old.

"This Sunday?"

Daphne's answer mewled soft as a prayer without a thought to the voice asking questions. "Yes."

"And your full name?" The voice was male, not congenial. And then it snapped, "Miss?"

Daphne blinked and brought herself back from her memories. They weren't such nice memories, and too full of questions. She shouldn't wallow there.

The officer had one thumb hooked in his gun belt. It was the hand that held a little white notepad. The other hand clicked a pen on and off, on and off.

Well, Daphne decided, it's not like her present situation made for such wonderful wallowing either. Anyone would trade the present for the past if she'd had the sort of afternoon this was shaping into.

"What is your full name?" He sounded like he expected little from her and this was how his days went.

She shook her head. "I gave it to you."

"And then you gave me a different birthday than what the computer shows for Daphne Mayfield."

Daphne blinked. "My birthday's January six—"

"No, you said your birthday was Sunday. Sunday's a long ways from January."

Daphne shook her head. "I didn't mean that. That's my sister's birthday, Sunday. Mine is January sixteenth."

"Your sister."

"She's dead," Daphne blurted. And the real blurt of this weekend's two anniversaries was: her father found not the anniversary of the murder, but rather his dead daughter's uncelebrated birthdays hardest to take. Why? Daphne clamped her hands over her head to stem the headache. *Don't cry. Why am I about to cry?*

He clicked his pen faster. The hand holding the notebook lowered. "And where do you live?"

As soon as she started to give her address on Westpark, he waved her off. "Look, you just gave me an address on Eastpark Avenue. And even though you don't have your license with you, the computer tells me what your license has printed on it. And it does not show an address on Westpark either. It shows Mapleview."

Blanking, Daphne thought she might hyperventilate. "Okay. Okay. I know what it is, what's going on. Let's do one thing at a time, okay? I can explain everything."

"That'd be great. Thank goodness you're here. And you're ready to explain everything."

Don't cry, Daphne instructed herself. *Don't.* "My address, see, I, I just never changed it from home. From my parents' place. My mom's house, I mean. My dad's dead. It's my boyfriend's place, where I live. We live together. But it's his place. On Westpark."

Another blue police car appeared and a new officer approached, a woman with stripes on the upper arms of her uniform. Daphne brightened. A foreman, like the Wellsley Construction foreman, Bob. Roof here, roof there. Architectural shingles, three-tab. No roofing felt here, put felt on that one. Foremen made the job run, helped everyone be efficient.

"What's up?" the sergeant asked, making brief eye contact with Daphne before addressing the officer.

He pointed his notebook at Daphne. "Caused this mess. Clear reckless in blowing the light. No license in possession. Not the car's registered owner. Gave a false DOB at first. Doesn't give a consistent address. Gave a wrong first name on the car's Registered Owner. The license info on the computer gives a different address from where she says she lives, but the address she gives as a residence does jibe with the car's registration."

"Tried contacting the RO?"

"Yeah, but no luck."

"Medics seen her?"

The officer turned to Daphne. "You want the paramedics to check you out?"

Daphne shook her head.

"Take her in." The uniformed woman turned away, waving off further wasted time.

"You got it, sarge." He pocketed his notebook again and squared his chest to Daphne. "Ma'am, I need you to turn around."

Turning to face away from the cop was an idea Daphne embraced.

"Put your hands behind your back," he ordered.

She clasped her hands behind her. Enough patience would get this whole situation over with.

One of his hands gripped her fingers and he pushed the edge of something hard and cold against her left wrist bone. A quick burst of an odd metal ratcheting sounded and he pushed into her other wrist. Then the ratcheting sounded again.

He took her arm. "This way."

Handcuffs? I'm in handcuffs? Daphne's brain rejected the idea even as her shoulders asked her pinned arms to swing at her sides.

"Wait. What's happening?"

"You are under arrest for reckless driving. You will be in custody until your appearance before a magistrate or until you make bail."

She gasped but couldn't form words.

He could. "Have any weapons on you?"

"Of course not." *At least it was an easy question,* Daphne thought.

He patted her ribs and legs, pulling a carpenter's pencil from the long pocket on her right thigh. Then he led her not to her car, but to his, to the backseat, to the cage.

Everything in her body went into alarm mode. Daphne stiffened as he opened the rear door of his patrol car.

"No," she said, planting one boot against the door frame.

"Mm, yes. You are under arrest for reckless driving and you are going to have to prove your identity."

"I have to pee," she said, thighs clamped tight.

"Well, you're in custody now and you're going to have to wait until we get where we're going. Or you can go as you are."

Her eyes grew moist and she knew her chin was puckering. An involuntary bawl threatened to boil out. "Is this because of the car's registration? There's something wrong with Vic's car?"

"Oh, that didn't help. Car's registered to a Lloyd Daily but—"

"That's Vic's father!" Relief flooded Daphne's body, her brain. "Can I go now?"

He chuckled. "You can go to a holding cell. We're leaving in a minute." And he indicated the open rear door. "Hop in."

"Wait. The car is registered to my boyfriend's father. We live together, my boyfriend and me. Vic's father is—the registration must show the owner of the car as Vic's father, right?—Lloyd. He lives at the Green Springs Extended Care Facility in Woodinville." She shook her chained wrists. "Oh, God, please. Please? Please help me."

Then she winced at the painful memory of Minerva Watts's plea. *Please help me.*

"Get in the car."

"Please, please listen to me. Please don't do this to me."

"We are past done talking. Get in the car. Now."

Daphne looked around. The green SUV was gone. The two-door was abandoned. The ambulance had left with the blond.

I started and ended this mess, she thought.

Ducking awkwardly into the backseat of the patrol car, Daphne slid on the cheap vinyl upholstery, off balance because her arms were locked behind her back. Inside, the vehicle was surprisingly cramped. If she leaned forward, she could hit her head on a plastic screen. At the sides, she could hit her head on the vehicle's roll bar. Her knees pushed into the steel cage protecting the driver. Protecting the driver from her?

But I'm in handcuffs.

Dear God, I'm in handcuffs. In the backseat of a police car. On my way to . . . jail?

"Are we going to jail?" she asked as soon as the officer got in the driver's seat.

"Sort of," he said. "You'll go to the holding area first."

"What about my car?"

"Mr. Daily's car will be towed."

"Towed where? Can't it just stay here? Can't I just park it?"

"The tow truck driver's going to park it for you just fine. At the impound lot."

"No. Oh, no. I have expensive tools in there." When he made no response, she said, "I want to call somebody. I want to call Vic."

"My dispatcher called the listed number for him and got no answer—"

"Can't I try to call him?"

He nodded. "Sure. From the holding area."

"But I want to talk to him now." Her voice squeaked like a child's.

"That may be so, but it's not something I can help, is it?"

"Don't you have to give me a phone call?"

He smirked. "You watch too much TV."

"I do not. I hardly ever watch TV. God, what's the matter with you? You have to give me a phone call, don't you?"

He looked left, right, then at the car's headliner. "See any phones handy? No? Me neither. The way it works is, I give you a taxi ride and then other people have to deal with you. This is not a long-term relationship. You and I will soon be done with each other."

"Aren't you going to read me my rights?"

"Mm, I was kind of hoping you'd exercise your right to remain silent and we could be done with the chitchat." He followed this comment with something short and fast into a dashboard radio microphone. The radio blared a female voice making a short and difficult-to-comprehend response.

When he pulled out, pushing hard on the accelerator, Daphne was forced into the seat back, her body unstable in the awkward position, sliding on the vinyl seat.

The discomfort of leaning back in a car with her hands trapped in the small of her back was astounding. Her shoulders complained more than if she'd just spent the morning loading shingles the old-fashioned way. The outside of her wrists pulled on the hard-edged metal cuffs.

She knew her wrists would be red later, maybe bruised.

She knew Suzanne's corpse had borne similar marks and her life would never be the same.

CHAPTER 8

Two decades back, when the boy crooned about Suzanne's perfect body and cried, "*. . . you have no love to give her . . .*" and every adult at Suzanne's closed-casket funeral gasped, young Daphne's bewilderment at losing her sister muddied into a bleaker ache, a haunting.

That boy, Ross Bouchard, said things out loud, interrupted in church. In a funeral. He said strange, strange things and he used the shocking word *lover*. Even now, the old memories were confusing, but at the time, watching the scene unfold with a congregation stunned by a shrieking young man's impropriety, the words scandalized.

At eleven, sheltered Daphne hadn't quite understood the entire concept of sex, beyond knowing it had to be done in order to make children. It seemed like an embarrassing, faraway prospect to her childish eyes. Suzanne had told her not to worry about it, that a family with an early bloomer needed a late bloomer to compensate.

That's it, Daphne thought, *we never had the rivalry.*

Well, one doesn't compete with a hero. Someone a hundred times greater is not a rival. A rebel goddess, but not a rival.

Before Suzanne died, awe and confusion were what she provoked in her little sister. Then and now, Daphne felt puzzled by her big sister, baffled by all the wondrous, bewildering things Suzanne did.

Why run away to Lopez Island? Why braid feathers into your hair? Why go through a phase of wearing long, flowing robes and eating vegetarian? Why run away at all?

Suzanne always laughed and tossed her baby sister's uncertain questions aside with a spray of more puzzles: *Oh, Daffy, why did I sleep with my English professor? What was I thinking?*

What? Daphne had asked, bouncing on the bed in her preteen confusion. Partly wanting into Suzanne's world, she mostly wanted Suzanne to stay in hers. *I don't get it.*

Don't give it up early, Daffer.

What? Daphne's then-girlish confusion, doubt, and perpetual question of whether or not she fit in at all clouded her mind. Give it up early? She'd no idea what Suzanne meant.

Just don't worry about it, Daffy.

M'kay. She'd nodded to her big sister, happy to be relieved of the burden of worrying.

Because sometimes, Suzanne laded her baby sister with more than worry.

Sometimes, Suzanne left to young Daphne the duty of calling in the cavalry lest she had gone too far. Daphne hadn't quite grasped the whole concept of this either, but she'd known she was ready to do something important from the first time an alarm clock went off and Daphne awoke at five in the morning to find an empty bed across the room and a note from her big sister.

D- call this number and tell the woman who answers that we went out with Ross and the rest of the guys last night. We're going to drive up Mount Baker as far as we can. Maybe the snow was too much. She'll know what to do.

They hadn't happened too often, those notes Suzanne left to cover some secret contingency. Just enough for Daphne to be forever bound in their mystery.

D- if I'm not back by 5:30, tell M and D I snuck out last night and went to the party they said I couldn't go to at the U.

Besides, Suzanne always made it home in time.

Daffer- tell Mom I borrowed the car and she shouldn't worry but you'll all have to get to church another way this morning because if I'm not back by 5AM, I made a decision and I'm not coming back.

Suzanne's tiny travel alarm had chimed that morning at four fifty-five. At five, Daphne pulled on jeans under her nightshirt, staring at the bedroom door and then opposite, at the window where Suzanne snuck out onto the porch roof to climb down the trellis and vanish into the night.

Daphne had lowered her eyes and turned to the door again, prepared to go wake her parents and find out what happens when a girl handed over this kind of cloaked distress call. She thought she imagined the soft padding of footsteps on the roof beyond the window because she so wanted to hear them.

"Made it," Suzanne said, closing one hand over Daphne's, over the note. Her other hand kept the bedroom door shut, and her grin solidified, naughty and exhausted, as she flung herself into bed. "Hey, you're half-dressed. Do you want to wear some of my stuff for a change?"

Her sister had waved at the right-hand side of their closet, the Suzanne side.

The last time Suzanne snuck out was Christmas break. Her best friend and boyfriend had just driven her back from Bellingham, dropping Suzanne off first out of geographical convenience. That night, with her sister just settled back into Seattle for the holiday, Christmas died for Daphne, although she didn't know it right away.

Even the next morning when she awoke alone, even later in the day, after several calls from college kids asking for Suzanne, she didn't know.

Even throughout the evening and the next night, when it was clear

Suzanne was gone but they all hoped it was temporary, Daphne didn't know Christmas was over.

But after the body was found, after the funeral, after the dead Christmas, she knew.

For years and years afterward, Daphne found Christmas a joyless time. Not until she met Vic and he introduced her to Jed and Josie, whose childish enthusiasm at seven and eight for sharing Christmas together heralded everything good and happy, did the delight reawaken. Again she found the pleasure, the giving, the excitement, and general fun of decorations and treats and carols and too much cocoa.

The realization brought her to the not knowing.

Not every time Suzanne snuck out involved a note. She thought Suzanne had not left a note that final night.

But she didn't know. And now every time she visited her mom, every time she went upstairs to her old bedroom, every time she twisted the knob to her old closet door, Daphne stared, not at the empty left side she'd cleaned out back when she moved in with Thea, but the still-hanging side, Suzanne's.

She'd continued to share the bedroom closet with her dead sister. It would have felt wrong to take over Suzanne's side. There were few things Daphne felt comfortable wearing amongst her sister's eclectic collection, but by high school, Daphne did wear the occasional pullover or skirt that had been Suzanne's.

Being her mother's good girl meant dressing with more modesty than Suzanne ever considered. It meant not voicing the outrageous, the ill-considered tantrum. It meant remaining a late bloomer.

Not long after Suzanne's funeral, their mother had made an effort, boxed up Suzanne's school papers, diaries, and knickknacks, but she hadn't gotten to Suzanne's clothes or other belongings, and the sealed box had remained on the closet shelf until Daphne absconded with it.

She'd kept it under her bed when she roomed with Thea and she kept it under her side of Vic's bed now. Sometimes, she opened the box to read and wonder. On an earlier anniversary of this dreadful weekend—one of the two times a year she most thought of her sister—Vic had found her crying over Suzanne's papers on their bed and listened for hours as Daphne tried to make sense of loss.

The most eyebrow-raising thing she found in the box was the college essay Suzanne entitled *BETRAYAL*.

But she never found what she thought she'd find. With the span of years, with reflection borne of ache and maturity, Daphne wondered where it was, if it existed, what it said.

If she visited her mother this weekend—and she knew she should—she'd sneak upstairs to her old bedroom and cast about yet again for this one tangible thing, the thing no one but Vic knew about.

The note she never found.

—◊—

The patrol car cornered and Daphne leaned into the turn, splaying her legs to keep from falling over. The cop drove past a newsstand in the teeming downtown district and headlines from around the world teased her. Beseeching scents from open coffee shops and ethnic stores may have wafted on the street, but they failed to penetrate the car's closed back windows. Street sounds were muffled, too, but the police radio intermittently blared, making her flinch. Outside, people in suits appeared to talk to themselves and the air while they held half-private conversations via ear-mounted phones. The sense of deafness made panic flirt with Daphne's mind.

She stared hard at the street and all the freedom displayed, busy people doing important things or nothing at all, their choice. Shoppers passed the homeless who held handwritten begging signs. Kids in grunge clothes texted away at bus stops, ignoring each other.

The officer spoke into his radio again as he pulled into the garaged entrance of a gray concrete building. She took a breath and held it.

Another police car and a plain blue car of the same make and model she sat handcuffed in were parked in the bowels of the building, but she saw no people. A burst of electronic gibberish sounded back from the dashboard, but Daphne couldn't discern one intelligible word of the lingo. A buzzer sounded, and a fortresslike garage door sealed them inside. Her last view of normal life disappeared and they drove past a sign warning: *Secure Area – Authorized Personnel Only*.

Daphne thought about telling her officer—and he did now seem to be her appointed officer, though he wasn't one she'd have picked if given a choice—that she wasn't authorized personnel so maybe they should call it quits right now, but her spirit flagged and she couldn't make a joke.

He grabbed paperwork, swung out of the driver's seat, and stretched. Then he unlocked and opened her door.

"Hop out."

She stuck her left foot out, but with her hands manacled behind her back and no momentum, she lacked the balance to rise as she pushed off the floor with her other foot. The officer's hand on her elbow steadied her. She would have paused to regain her bearings, but he propelled her forward past a steel door that banged shut with a warning buzz as they entered a solid, off-white corridor. They were caged.

A few small keys hung from locks on little rectangular panels that looked like built-in safe deposit boxes. The officer unholstered his pistol and placed it in one locker, pocketing the key before he steered Daphne forward again. Now she saw the sign looming at the next steel door under a red light.

No Weapons Beyond This Point.

The light turned green, a buzzer blasted, and the next steel door opened. Daphne entered before the officer, directed by his left hand on her right elbow.

More forbidding signs faced her. She was not to smoke or spit. She was being monitored, although she didn't know what that meant. Video? Audio recorded?

A torrent of profane screaming shrieked through an open doorway just ahead on the left. In a room to the right, men's laughter roared, and dead ahead, behind plates of Plexiglas, the muted sound of a can of soda being popped open left her staring at a man's back. He wore a gray uniform. A janitor, Daphne thought before realization dawned.

Not a custodian, a correctional officer.

There were lots of gray-uniformed people here, men and women. The man in a sealed booth ahead slurped his soda, nodded at Daphne's officer, and pressed a button on a console before him. A buzzer sounded and more metal slammed.

Daphne found herself steered to the left and came face-to-face with an obese, sweating, tattooed young woman on a long plastic bench.

"What's your problem, bitch?" the young woman asked from the bench. A long metal bar ran just over the bench, behind the woman's shoulders. At the near end of the bench was an empty jail cell. In the back of the cell, Daphne saw a shoulder-high steel partition.

Daphne recoiled and peered through the open doorway opposite the cell, blinking at the computers and clipboards and papers within. With the scrape of a metal chair on linoleum, another man in a gray uniform appeared in the depths of the next room, leaning back in his chair, quick-sipping from a steaming Styrofoam cup. With a bare glance at Daphne and her officer, he let the chair's front legs fall back to the linoleum, whisking him from view. A man with a crew cut typed away on a computer in that room.

"Okay, contestant number whatever." A heavy-set man in a gray uniform appeared, accepted paperwork from Daphne's police officer, then gestured for Daphne to turn around.

He took Daphne's handcuffs off and gave them back to the police officer. She relaxed a tiny bit, rubbing her wrists in real pleasure.

"Fuck me, fuck me, fuuuck me." The woman on the bench sighed in a drunken drawl then kicked her feet out from the bench, splaying her legs wide.

Daphne studied her with furtive glances. The woman's tangled dark hair hung in her face. Tattoos snaked across her arms, bare shoulders, and neck. She leaned forward on the bench and heaved herself to her feet, letting loose another stream of verbal abuse, impugning the correctional officer's family, sexual appetite, and intelligence.

The man with a crew cut stopped typing and hollered, "Sit down, Josephina."

Josephina flung herself to the bench, flailing her huge legs in a fat, drunken tantrum.

"Put her in the tank," the portly man said, pulling on rubber gloves and waving Daphne toward the wall.

The tank? There's a worse place to go? Daphne prayed not to be put in the tank.

"Nah," called the other man. "She's just about to calm down." He pulled a piece of paper from a printer and entered the room smiling at the young drunk. "Aren't you?"

"Fuck you," she said.

"See?" He gestured for the woman to stand. "C'mon. Got a very nice room ready for you."

"Fuck you," she said, lying rigid on the bench. Another correctional officer called to the crew cut man, and he stepped away nodding, firing off names and numbers.

"Put your hands on those two squares."

Daphne flinched when the big man tapped her shoulder and ordered, "You. Put your hands on the squares."

Daphne looked at the wall where he pointed and saw two brown squares painted on the wall at shoulder height.

She gingerly placed her palms on the squares and closed her eyes while he patted her down.

"Great," he said. "Empty your pockets."

"They are empty."

"Inside out."

She reached into her front pockets, but unlike jeans, Carhartts pockets didn't pull inside out. She pulled her hands back out of her pockets and bit her lower lip.

"Have a seat," the man said, pointing to the end of the bench at the tattooed woman's feet.

"Seriously?" Daphne's stomach lurched at the thought of sitting here, of sharing space with that woman.

At the massive Plexiglas wall, the man behind the consoles pushed a plastic tray under a small access point. The police officer tossed Daphne's pencil onto the tray and waved several papers at her before adding them to the tray.

"Info on your traffic accident. Give the case number to your insurance company. They'll know what to do. And don't forget to send in this form or your driver's license could get suspended. That would make it a crime for you to drive."

Daphne closed her eyes, but tears formed and threatened to spill over unless she opened her eyes wide.

"About this jacket thing with this guy Guff . . ." The police officer had his notebook out again.

Tilting her face at the man, Daphne waited, then answered his spare questions. He copied down specifics about her jacket, wallet, and phone, then wrote a note on a business card.

"My card and the case number on this suspicious incident-slash-theft thing on Eastpark."

"What?"

He looked back at her.

She swallowed. "Never mind, I get it. Kind of."

He high-fived another correctional officer and walked into another room with the rest of his paperwork.

Don't leave me here, Daphne wanted to cry. But he did. From the bench, she could hear a man in a faraway cell and she wondered how big the cell was, how many men loitered farther back.

Competing scents of urine and disinfectant came to her as she sat on the grimy bench. The enormous tattooed woman squinted at Daphne's pencil in the tray.

Josephina wore a huge, tight black tank top several sizes too small for her double D breasts and rolls of rib fat. Still supine on the bench, she tilted her neck back and rolled her eyes up to fix a studying stare on Daphne.

Managing a weak smile, Daphne said, "I know a girl named Josefina. She goes by Josie. She's my, uh . . ."

Josephina worked her mouth as Daphne spoke, then swung her legs down, sat up, and let loose a tremendous wad of phlegm. The splat across the room silenced Daphne worse than the tattooed girl's grin.

"Do. Not. Spit." The order came from the crew cut man at the end of the room.

"I was aiming for the garbage can," Josephina said.

"I have to pee," Daphne said, not quite meeting the correctional officer's eyes, hoping the plea in her voice would be understood.

"We got a nervous pee-er here," Josephina announced, cackling. Her comment earned a laugh from the unseen man in a distant cell and a quick grin from the heavy correctional officer.

Closing her eyes, Daphne saw a replay of her pursuit of Minerva Watts, the car, the crash. She thought of her first encounter with Minerva Watts in the park. She had seen something, heard something. She made an effort.

Nothing good had come from her effort. Maybe those people wouldn't have taken Minerva anywhere if Daphne hadn't gone to the house on Eastpark Avenue in the first place. She opened her eyes when tears trickled from the outer corners.

"If I get a phone call, I'm using it to call 911 to report a crime." Daphne's remark sounded insolent even to her, but she was past caring. A battered phone with a long, stretched cord hung on the wall. She wondered if she could use it, if she had to dial one to get an outside line. Was she allowed to just walk over there and use the phone?

The tattooed woman leaned over to Daphne. "You know that's the kind of attitude that will keep you in here. Without a whole lot of phone calls." Then she burped, and Daphne's stomach flipped at the reek of alcohol vapors.

A woman in a gray uniform came and led Josephina past the phone to the nearest empty cell. Loud buzzing and clanging heralded the cell door's open and close. Daphne could not resist turning on her bench to watch the tattooed drunk.

Josephina waddled for the far end, pivoted and backed up, ducking behind a shoulder-high partition.

"So you're going to need bail and ID," the female officer said to Daphne, looking at sheets of paperwork as she led Daphne toward Josephina's cell. "Or are you just planning to be a guest of the Gray Bar Hotel until you see a judge?"

"What?" Daphne stared at her.

"I said, is there someone you can call to bring you positive identification and bail money?"

A cough choked Daphne, strangled her as she spoke. "Vic. I want to call Vic. He'll bring me identification and . . . and how much?"

"Are you paying attention at all?" The woman glanced at a form. "Your bail's five hundred."

"Can I call him now?"

"Number?" The correctional officer lifted a telephone from its cradle, one finger poised over the keypad.

Daphne gave Vic's cell phone number.

The woman dialed, listened, and passed the handset to Daphne. "Ringing."

Holding the filthy phone away from her mouth, Daphne threw a torrent of words into the phone, asking her boyfriend to bring her identification and money, ending with, "Um, thanks."

"Good?" The female correctional officer moved to hang up the phone.

Daphne entreated, "Can I try another number? Since it was just his voice mail?"

"'Course," she said, but another policeman arrived with another prisoner and the correctional officer led Daphne to Josephina's cell.

A buzzer sounded and the cell door opened. Daphne stepped inside like a sheep. She winced when the buzzer blared again and the cell door clanged shut.

CHAPTER 9

That boy should be in jail.

Pushing aside memories of her father's bitter mantra left Daphne thinking of the birth of his rants, that interim between Suzanne being missing and known to be murdered.

Daphne had climbed the stairs to her half-empty bedroom throughout that horrible Christmas break, hearing him pace and mutter below. *Someone saw something. Someone will say something. Someone will do something about what they saw.*

He'd caught this unfounded hope from the primary detective on Suzanne's case.

Someone saw something.

Her dad's chant in the week they first knew Suzanne was missing became his lifeline.

He would pray the three words as he paced in the basement, the yard. When sitting in his aluminum chaise lounge out back. While rubbing his chin as he brought the newspaper in every morning.

In the passing days of Suzanne being missing, he added to his assessment.

"She's a smart girl," he'd say. "Too smart maybe, but smart. She'll do the right thing. She'll get away; she'll get back to us."

And one afternoon, a uniformed policeman came to their front door with a detective. The other man was a plainclothes detective, but not the Missing Persons investigator her father had talked to daily during The Wait.

They'd had her body all day, confirming what they suspected as soon as some hikers' dogs pawed at the shallow grave where her naked corpse rotted as fodder for the earth.

And then, the funeral. Her father's prayer—someone saw something—continued. His goal shifted from getting his daughter back to getting vengeance.

The police brought the boy in for questioning. They interrogated him. They polygraphed him. And it was bad but not bad enough. They needed more.

Someone saw something. Daphne's father continued his mantra in a blind and desperate ache built on the foundation of the detective's certain assessment that they had not located the murder scene, that Suzanne's body had been moved. That wherever Suzanne met her killer, from the scene of the murder to the transportation and burial of her body, opportunities existed for passersby to notice something untoward. People, strangers, must have seen a girl meet a man. Maybe the girl was drunk, or where she shouldn't have been. At a party, a rave, a bar. Maybe she looked scared at some point. Maybe drivers on a narrow, rainy highway saw a man pull something bulky from his trunk or backseat. Maybe he carried a shovel or spade. But at some point, someone must have seen—

Someone saw something. That boy should be in jail.

—◆—

Beyond her cell door, behind a Plexiglas screen, a uniformed man clonked his coffee cup on the control counter and pushed a button. Somewhere, a buzzer blared and a door banged. Daphne thought of the policeman who'd brought her here in handcuffs, remembered the sergeant who'd come to the accident scene half an hour ago and told the officer to bring her in. She compared the mental image to the two police officers who'd stood on the threshold of her parents' house two decades past with news her sister's body had been found. And she thought of the police visit in between, ten years ago, when she and her mother were informed of her dad's suicide.

Turning from the jail cell door, Daphne brushed her hands against her pants. In a few strides, she stopped dead. Josephina stood behind the partition, her enormous breasts heaving in the tank top as she bent over, wiping her rear end. Daphne returned to the cell's door so Josephina's upper body was visible.

Swirling to face her jailers, Daphne pled, "I need another phone call. Please. Okay?"

Beyond the bars, the female correctional officer clicked one finger on the phone's hook then hovered over the number pad with her eyes raised toward Daphne. Daphne gave her another number and accepted the telephone handset through the bars.

Beginning a detailed message for Thea, Daphne looked at her cellmate and winced before asking Thea to get into the house using Grazie's dog door. "Then go upstairs, find my passport—I got one four years ago when Vic and I were going to—" She cut herself off. "And five hundred dollars in cash or cashier's check or a money ord—" Daphne shook with tears and wailed, "Just bring cash and my ID, Thee. Thea. Please. Right away."

And if this didn't work, she'd try Vic again, and then who? Her mother? Her mother would keel over if Daphne called her from jail. Still, she had to find someone who could get her out of here. And she wished she could call Suzanne, who would have been first and fastest to save her baby sister. She wished she could call her dad.

Instead, Josephina swaggered toward her, would be in Daphne's space in ten feet.

Clutching the metal bars, Daphne whispered to the female correctional officer, "Please, can I use the bathroom?"

"By all means," she said, gesturing to the partition at the far end of the cell. "Avail yourself of the facilities." Her last comment was made over her shoulder as she faced another police officer entering with a combative person in a hooded sweatshirt. The officer tripped the soundless, faceless kicking person to the floor and two gray uniformed staffers pounced.

"Tank," said the female correctional officer.

"No shit," said one of the men holding the fighter on the floor.

Josephina clutched the bars, swayed, and grinned at Daphne. Stepping to the partition, Daphne stared at the stainless steel, seatless toilet ensconced in the little area and took a breath. *Oh, God, oh, God. What have I done? What in the world have I done? How did things get to this point? How? How in the world?*

All she wanted was a chance to clear things up, right now, right away.

"Please, how do I get out of here?" Daphne asked, returning to the cell's closed door, desperate for the female correctional officer to not abandon her.

"The usual. Bail. Proof of identity."

"But my license was stolen."

"Then you'll have to get a replacement license at DMV."

"How can I do that when I'm in here?"

She nodded. "It's a stumper, isn't it?" She walked away. A thick door opened, the officer went through, and it slammed shut.

There was no one else in the cell but Daphne and Josephina. The wall had two old posters giving phone numbers she could call to report domestic violence or sexual assault. She read those posters over and over and over. She stared through the cell bars, stunned to be caged. She heard her father's bitter voice in that first year after Suzanne's funeral.

He should be in jail. My baby's dead. And he's out walking around. Her father's conviction that *that boy* had ended Suzanne's life—the horror of a brutal ending, too—competed forever with the horrible truth that no one was ever held responsible. Ever. A wrong unrighted.

Could a horrible wrong be righted? Daphne wiped her hands through her hair, pulled a bit of twig from a snarl and went quietly crazy.

The image of her reflection in the police car window returned, and Daphne saw herself as her sister, saw her sister alive with feathers in her hair. Heard a young man's voice come from an altar out of nowhere, to cry about children leaning out for love, forever.

—m—

After an indiscernible passage of time—whether minutes or hours, Daphne didn't know—with Josephina badgering her with all manner of questions and random blurts, a tall, clean-cut, gray-uniformed man approached the other side of their cell door and said, "Ms. Mayfield, you're up."

"What?" she asked.

He waved a clipboard at her, fluttering a paper that he smoothed down.

"You're going to sign, promising to appear in District Court, and you're going to be on your merry way. You made bail, or rather, someone made it for you." A buzz sounded and the cell opened. Daphne leapt like an obedient puppy, heeling at his side, ignoring the now quiet Josephina.

"Who? Is Vic here?"

He squinted at the form and raised his eyebrows. "A . . . Theadora . . . Roosevelt?"

Ready to bawl, Daphne edged away from the cell and started to go back the way she'd been led into the jail.

"No, ma'am, this way." He waved again, and she followed him through the unknown door and down a number of corridors. He stopped beside a heavy door marked *Lobby*. Ah, the lobby, Daphne thought. Where the good people are. This is why she hadn't been led out of the building the same way she'd come in.

The officer pulled the top form from his clipboard. "You must promise to appear for any and all court dates. Sign here."

Daphne held the paper against the wall and signed, noticing how her hands shook.

He tore one copy loose and handed it to her. She clutched the paper with both hands. *Freedom? Now?*

Opening his clipboard's catch, he pulled a carpenter's pencil and the police officer's forms from the maw. "Your personal effects. Please put these items in a pocket now."

She accepted her pencil, swinging a hand back to replace it in her thigh pocket, then winced. After folding the papers into another pocket and experimentally wiggling her shoulders, she winced again.

"Sore from getting in a car wreck, I bet," he said. "It happens." And he handed her another form.

"Do you know where my car is?"

He squinted at the last form he'd handed her. "Says there it was impounded."

"Right, yes. They had a tow truck come take it."

"So it's at the impound yard. Call the number on the bottom of that form." He pointed to the paper in her hand, then opened the door and gestured for her to step into the public lobby on her own.

When the door slammed shut, Daphne stood at the lobby's edge.

Loose lines of people crowded the front counter, their voices raised to staff behind solid Plexiglas. They held various forms and asked for pens and whether they had the right form and if they could write a check and whether they had to fill out paperwork. They were told they were standing in the wrong line and they were told they'd have to wait their turn. One woman's voice rose higher and higher about how her daughter was being treated.

The woman's enormous gray sweat suit stretched so hard across her paunch the fabric paled and she gasped for breath from the effort of standing, of stemming her stress as her turn at the counter arrived.

"I got the money. Why's my girl here?"

The answer came from a speaker in the Plexiglas, a woman with a computer and piles of paperwork. "Prostitution. Again."

"Everyone's probably being mean, right?" Bitterness coiled in her voice like a damaged snake.

The clerk didn't look up and her voice stayed measured, even bored. "I'm sure they're treating her just fine, ma'am."

"No. People aren't nice to her. They aren't nice to girls like my daughter. Big girls."

"Look, they're being nice, okay? Just like with everyone."

The woman's voice went higher. "But th-they won't s-s-see that mm-my daughter is b-b-beautiful."

Daphne stared across the room and somehow knew she was looking at her tattooed cellmate's mother.

Someone leaned around Josephina's mother and Daphne gasped a strangled whimper. "Thea."

Beautiful Thea stood looking over the top of her sunglasses like a movie star, a thousand questions in her eyes. Daphne sniffed in a huge breath but could not stop the tears from streaming down her face as she lunged to her best friend's side and clutched her in an unbreakable hug.

"You cannot believe the day I've had," Thea said.

CHAPTER 10

An old yellow Mercedes, blocky and curvy at the same time, sat cock-eyed in the end parking spot. Daphne ran for the passenger's side, calling for Thea to hurry, saying they had to get to a toilet right away.

"Didn't they have bathrooms in there?"

"No, they did not have *bathrooms* in there."

In a few blocks, Thea swerved to the curb in front of a Starbucks. Daphne bolted from the car.

"Excuse me, where's the bathroom?" she asked the barista.

The girl plucked a key with a giant wooden fob from a hook. "It's for customers only," she said, pointing to the back of the store.

"Thea, please buy a goddamn coffee," Daphne said over her shoulder. As she grabbed the key and ran for the back, she heard Thea request one goddamn coffee in her sweetest voice.

Back in the car, Thea paused, an opening in traffic wasted. She gestured a toast to Daphne then sipped the coffee, eyeing Daphne's shaking hands. "I don't think coffee's what you need," she said. "Are you going to tell me what's going on?"

Daphne waved at the road. Thea pulled her Mercedes out and Daphne took an enormous breath. "The short explanation is I was trying to catch up to a car, it had the same couple from last night. That couple took the little old la—Minerva Watts. They took her again. And I got in an accident and the car got away and I got arrested for reckless driving."

Thea rolled her lips in, looking dubious.

"Thea, that's it. That's what happened. And then nothing happened. The police didn't catch the car, or if they did, they didn't tell me about it. I mean, can't they do something?"

"What do you want them to do? Magically conjure up this car of yours and the people you saw in it? All they can do is broadcast a *locate* for the car, stop it if they find it, and send an officer for a welfare check at her house."

"Welfare? She's on welfare?"

"A welfare check is what they call it when they send an officer to knock on someone's door. Someone who doesn't show up for work, say, and a coworker's worried about—"

"If a coworker was worried, why wouldn't the coworker go check on the person who didn't show up for work? Why doesn't anybody make a goddamn effort?"

"Daphne, I'm just explaining to you the concept of a welfare check."

"Then isn't a welfare check what I did when I went to her house?"

"Yes, well, look how well that turned out."

"What am I going to do?" Daphne half-shrieked. "I mean, for God's sake, what happens next?"

"I think I take you home, you take a bath, we drink a bottle of wine, and we both go to work in the morning."

"I'm not working tomorrow," Daphne said. "I've got it off."

"Okay," Thea said, "reasonable enough. If I ever get my ass arrested, I'm taking the next day off, too."

"I already had Friday scheduled off."

"So take Monday."

"Could you just take me home now, please? God, how am I going to explain all this to Vic?"

Thea smiled and drove on in silence, but opened a bag on the seat between them. One by one, she offered Daphne treats. Fair trade chocolates, Bing cherries, French cookies.

"Is this your standard bail-someone-out care package?" Daphne asked.

Thea pulled more goodies from the sack and Daphne began her story with arriving at Minerva Watts's house, at the address Thea had written down in Vic's kitchen that morning.

With candied almonds, Daphne described the encounter at Minerva's threshold. With mozzarella balls wrapped in basil leaves, she told of shrugging out of her jacket, sprinting around houses and down the alley. Of hiding while she got dirty and her hair came loose and leaves stuck in her bangs. She was down to garlic-stuffed olives and the aftermath of the traffic accident by the time Thea pulled onto Westpark Avenue.

"He's still not home," Daphne said, her voice dull as she eyed the empty driveway.

"I brought something else," Thea said, lifting the almost-empty sack as she got out of her car.

"How long were you grocery shopping while I was sitting in jail?"

"All this stuff came from my house," Thea said. "I was home, working. Got your message and started grabbing stuff out of the fridge and my cupboards while it was playing. And I had to listen to the message twice. Thought about bringing wine but I know it's verboten at that facility—"

"Facility!"

"I stopped at a couple of ATMs to get enough cash. If you'd stuck with journalism and me, if you'd graduated and got on at my paper and suffered through doing the crime beat like I did, well then you'd know they don't take VISA at the jail."

Daphne nodded as they walked around the house, through the side gate and into the backyard together. "I'll pay you back," Daphne said as she crawled through the dog door.

Grazie stood, wagging and chortling. Enchanted, Daphne stayed on her knees and hugged the warm, golden fur while reaching with the other hand to let Thea inside.

"Hi, good girl." Thea pulled a soda can from her bag and popped it open. "You want a beef broth drinkie?"

In the kitchen, Thea poured the can of special canine soda into Grazie's bowl.

Daphne winced as she leaned in the doorway and watched the dog sample the offering. "That's your surprise?"

"The last treat," Thea confirmed.

"I hope people in Afghanistan and Somalia and wherever else don't know that you're buying flavored drinks for my dog."

"Why?" Thea thrust a hip sideways with attitude.

It needed an explanation? Daphne thought of jail and desperate people. She shook her head, realizing she'd been about to go down the road of offending a friend who'd done nothing wrong. How unreasonable was it for her to pick apart what Thea gave a beloved dog? Look at the choices she'd made today, the accident she'd caused. She'd butted into something she didn't understand and she'd gotten grabbed, chased.

"They have my ID, Thee. They have my mother's address."

"*They* could be just a misunderstanding. The whole thing. Other people have other things going on in their lives. And to us, in a glimpse, it looks bad or wrong, but if we knew the whole deal, we might know that there was no actual problem. And it's someone else's business. What you've done today, if you'll just stop and think—"

Daphne raised her palms. "She called her *lady* and then when she saw me, she called her *Mother*."

"You are making no sense at all."

Swallowing, Daphne tried again. "Two women. One is the older lady, Minerva Watts. She's the one I saw first in the Peace Park Wednesday afternoon—"

"Yesterday."

"Right. And the other one . . ." Daphne thought about her encounters with the police and her inadequacy at description. She could do better. "The other one was wearing a big black coat yesterday, jeans and a fleece sweater today, and she's younger. She's our age, maybe a few years older. That one called Minerva Watts *lady* but then, two seconds later, when she saw me looking at them, she called Minerva *Mother*."

"So maybe she just speaks that way, the other woman. Lady, mother, whatever. Haven't you ever done that?"

Daphne folded her arms across her chest. "I have never addressed my mother that way. *Lady*."

"I have never gotten arrested. I can't believe you did."

"Me neither, but believe it."

"Why didn't he cite and release you?"

Daphne rubbed her face, worn to the marrow. "I don't even know what you're saying, Thee."

"It's Thea. *Thhhee-uh.* And I'm saying the cop could have given you a criminal ticket. You have to screw up pretty bad to get physically arrested for reckless driving. You have to be racing in the streets or having sex while driving or hurt somebody, plus basically be an uncooperative crazy person."

"The last two." Daphne's grimace and shudder came with a flood of memories, the blond woman with the cut face, the young man and his bloody knuckles. The wreck could have been so much worse. "I've wrecked everything, haven't I?"

She pulled the paperwork from her pockets and threw it on the counter, then noticed the answering machine blinking in a consistent pattern of four blasts. Four messages.

Thea flipped through Daphne's paperwork, reading aloud. "Operating a motor vehicle with willful or wanton disregard of persons or property. A gross misdemeanor punishable by up to one year in jail and a fine of five thousand dollars." She looked up. "Wrecked things? That's a—"

"That's a yes," Daphne finished. Motion out the window caught her eye. Her truck was pulling in. "Vic!"

Jed and Vic stepped out of her Toyota pickup in the driveway. Vic turned to eye Thea's car as he came to the door. Daphne rushed from the kitchen, ignoring Thea on her heels and Grazie struggling to stay with both women. She threw the door open just as Vic's hand reached for the knob, wrenching it from his grasp. His glance wavered to Thea and back again.

"Hello, you're here. You missed Josie's game," he said. He sounded worn and disappointed. Jed adjusted his glasses and slouched past them toward the living room.

Daphne rolled her eyes, indicating the hallway where Jed had gone, mindful of hearing the TV turn on in the living room. She spoke through clenched teeth. "I got arrested. Why didn't you come bail me out?"

"I'm staying," Thea announced with gusto. "This is going to be good."

—m—

While Thea tried to interest Grazie in the remaining special canine soda, Daphne gave Vic the short version of her afternoon. He rubbed his jaw and pursed his lips.

"My," he said, reaching for Daphne while shooting quick looks in Thea's and Jed's directions. He wrapped his arms around her shoulders, kissed her hair, pulled a bit of leaf from a tangle, and said, "Do you perhaps want to get a shower and some clean clothes?"

Daphne nodded and twisted out of his embrace. Upstairs she startled at her reflection. Hair loose, a scrap of dried rhododendron bloom stuck on her scalp. Again the image of her sister entered her mind, even as she was able to deny that she looked like Suzanne. Suzanne was never dirty, just wild.

Daphne shed her clothes and stepped into the shower, soaping up and shaving to pare the sensation of grime from her body. She thought of being younger, at home, watching Suzanne shave her legs at the old house on Mapleview Drive.

"Mom," she said aloud, shutting off the water. Her mother might not be safe at home. Speed drying herself, she hurried back to the bedroom with the towel around her naked body.

Oh, no. Jed's here.

She was always uncomfortable being scantily clad when Vic's kids were in the house. She booted the bedroom door 'til it latched and phoned her mother.

Rising panic burbled in her chest as the telephone rang. The hum of adult voices downstairs, indecipherable through the closed bedroom door, made a background murmur of white noise she wanted to click off. In her ear, the ringing droned.

"Thursday night bridge." The answer came as she thought about the time and day and she nodded at her spoken thought. Her mother played with another widow and a sweet older couple once a week.

Her mother's answering machine came on.

Imagining that guy, Guff, would go to the Mapleview house was paranoid, worst-case-thinking, wasn't it?

Not trusting her voice and warning herself not to blurt about the mess she'd made of the day, Daphne mumbled a hello and was telling her mom's machine she'd call later when a voice picked up.

"Daphne? Is that you?" The croak of a dedicated smoker always sounded pleading.

"Yeah, it's me, Mom."

"Oh, Daphne, I'm late. Out the door this minute. I called you earlier. And yesterday, you know. I'm going to bridge now, but when I heard your voice on the machine, I came right back."

Daphne closed her eyes. Vic, too, couldn't ignore the phone when his kids weren't with him, thought no parent could. *What if it's them calling? What if they need me?*

"Well, when are you coming over?" her mother rasped. The request would soon turn into a wounded whine.

Frances Mayfield sounded like such a happy name, Daphne thought. She'd thought so as a child, back when she discovered her parents had first names, back when she was happy and believed everyone got along like her, a mid-pack girl, neither popular nor scorned.

Her mother baked cookies and had dinner on the table at six o'clock and cleaned the house and got frustrated with Suzanne, and that's how it was. There was no yelling, no swearing, and dad came home every night to hug his girls. They all kissed each other good night, every night, and they all said and meant good morning.

The kitchen stove and fridge were harvest gold. The telephone was the old-fashioned kind with a long, curly cord. Suzanne would have long phone conversations, swinging the cord for young Daphne—coming in for a glass of milk—to jump like a skip rope.

"I don't know, Mom."

Her mother's voice became begging. "But you're coming to see me, aren't you?"

As though they didn't live in the same city, less than ten miles apart. Daphne pressed the telephone's earpiece to her forehead and offered, "Maybe next week?"

"Well, you know what weekend this is. And Blanche says, she said to me—"

"Vic has the kids this weekend. Saturday and Sunday."

"Bring the kids."

"And you know he takes them to visit his dad on his Saturdays."

"I know. So come after you see him. Then after you all get here, we can all go lay flowers and then I'll make dinner for everyone. The kids can watch TV or play in the yard. What do they like to do?"

"Aw, Mom." Daphne closed her eyes. Above all, Jed and Josie wouldn't want to go to graves of people they'd never known.

"They'll be my grandchildren if you two ever get married instead of just playing house, you know. Are you ever going to get married?"

Choosing which question to answer made all the difference.

"They like to text their friends," Daphne said, knowing her mother wanted a different answer, knowing the woman wanted what she could not have—a family. The idea of her mother living as a family of one—a twosome only when Daphne came for a visit—wrenched her. *But there are things I want that I don't get to have either,* she thought, even as shame washed over her at the childishness of her reaction.

"I don't understand that whole texting business," her mother said and launched into a minor rant about kids these days and their cell phones.

Stifling a snort, Daphne thought about how Vic couldn't or wouldn't pay for smartphones for the kids or even for himself. She heard her mother's screen door creak and knew her mother was stepping outside onto the old porch. She knew why, too.

"There's stuff I don't understand, too," Daphne said, thinking that they would never talk about those big issues. They never had. She cleared her throat. "Like, why do you still smoke outside?"

"Don't get after me, Daphne girl. I do not need my daughter telling me whether or not I can smoke."

"I'm not telling you not to smoke. I'm asking why you still do it outside."

The screen door banged shut in the background and Daphne heard the flint scrape of her mom's cigarette lighter, knew why there was a pause before her mother spoke. The first big drag of poison from a Virginia Slim and the exhaling puff changed her mother's tone to something more hollow. Her mother's cat yowled.

"Nobody knows why anybody does anything, my girl. Don't you know that by now?"

Daphne sucked in a breath of her own, too many unutterable responses competing in her mind. She kept it all in and her mother filled the silence with a demand. "Come by tomorrow. I have a surprise. It's about this weekend."

"I have to work," Daphne lied, telling herself she was a lousy daughter.

"Off to be a carpenter again?"

Daphne kept her voice dull, expressionless. "I'm a roofer, Mom."

"He wouldn't have wanted you up on rooftops."

Daphne said nothing, concentrating on getting dressed one-handed while she held the phone to her ear.

"It's dangerous," her mother went on. "It's not for a girl either. When you started, I thought, well, our Savior was a carpenter, so maybe my girl is praying for—"

"Mom, I need to get off the phone. Thea's here visiting and Vic's got dinner going." The lies were close to true. After her mom had gone out for the evening, after she'd had a chance to think about that man having her ID, her old address, she could decide then whether to badger her mom into leaving the house for a few nights.

Frances said, "Well, I've got bridge so I'll let you go." And Daphne suppressed the urge to correct her, to point out the truth, that they would never let each other go.

CHAPTER 11

Leaving the bedroom with wet hair and fresh clothes, Daphne heard voices bickering in the kitchen below and sank to the floor in defeat. Vic and Thea were at it again. The hum of voices rose and fell. Daphne leaned against the doorjamb.

Thea's tone never diminished. "When her dad died—"

"Killed himself."

"Yes, I know. We all know what he did. This is America. Guns in vending machines, free when you buy a Happy Meal. Kids see a million acts of violence and death every morning with their cereal—"

"Oh, stop it." Vic's disgust brooked no lectures. "He didn't use a gun. I meant that he didn't just *die,* it was worse, but don't try to make it worse still. Stop it."

"You started it."

"I didn't start anything. I just pointed out that you didn't acknowledge how it was worse for the family because he . . . offed himself."

Daphne drew her knees to her chest and wrapped one arm around her shins, extending the other hand to pet Grazie without thinking. But the comforting touch of the dog's warm coat was absent. Grazie lay downstairs in the midst of Vic and Thea. She opened and closed her empty hand, pushed her body up the wall and swung the door open, telling herself to go downstairs.

The background noise of Jed watching TV became an added annoyance as he turned it up louder.

"Because it's such a lovely way you put it," Thea said.

"Offed himself?" Vic's voice rose to Thea's challenge now.

"Yes."

"Well . . ."

"I'm just saying her father's death still affects her," Thea told Vic.

"Her sister's death more." Vic's response was immediate, on top of Thea's.

"You think?" Thea's rebuttal showed cynicism. "But she was just a kid when that happened. Suzanne was twenty years ago."

"It was exactly twenty years ago the end of this year. December. Her dad was ten years ago this Saturday."

"Ever wonder why he did it when he did?" Thea asked, her tone different, making the inquiry of a journalist, an outsider. Someone who did not understand but wanted to, for all the wrong reasons.

Private pain wasn't to be explained to satisfy onlookers' curiosity, Daphne decided. Her mother had learned this, too, and whittled her exposure to friends down to a once-a-week bridge group. Not every prying question from a well-meaning friend or a stranger deserved an answer. Daphne rubbed her forehead. Frances Mayfield realized this truth and built walls after Suzanne's death, then again after her husband's.

"There aren't . . . answers for everything." Daphne's whispered words left her considering, wondering where they came from and if they were true. How had her mother known? How had she accepted unfinished facts?

Downstairs, Vic's voice became more modulated than usual. "It was the day before Suzanne's birthday."

The day before.

I think I even know why he did it.

Vic's comment yesterday hadn't seemed anything but plaintive, an attempt to say he understood what was not understandable. People did that, claimed to understand when there was no way they could begin to fathom. Daphne decided now she should have challenged him, not let him get away with thinking he understood.

"So," Thea went on to Vic as though this were an average conversation, "do you think that's what has her so worked up?"

So worked up? God, Thea painted an image of Daphne in a complete tizzy.

"Yes," Vic said. The whoosh of the gas stove shutting off and the flame extinguishing fit with Vic sighing his agreement, making him sound surrendering and sympathetic.

"What actually happened at her sister's funeral? Some guy wasn't supposed to be there, right? He got thrown out? What did he do?"

"I guess he was . . . out of sync."

"The boyfriend?" Thea's persistence in Daphne's absence raised goose bumps on Daphne's arms. And although she strained to hear a response from Vic, there was none. Perhaps he nodded, because Thea continued with, "Out of sync how?"

"Um, he acted suspiciously or out of turn or something. Got escorted out. Bad scene."

Unbidden memories of Ross Bouchard walking the church aisle—guitar clutched to his belly while he nodded at the cross and coffin—flashed in Daphne's mind. Gasps from her parents and other congregants created a chorus as her sister's boyfriend sang in a broken voice about Suzanne and knowing she was half-crazy.

"I know she thinks about it," Vic said. "I know he didn't pass his polygraph. After he came to her funeral and . . ."

"And . . . ?"

"And you should—"

"Don't tell me what *I should*," Thea told him.

Vic snapped. "Why don't you tell me what you know about what happened to Daph today?"

Thea snorted back. "Why don't you talk to *Daph* your own self?"

"I can hear you up here," Daphne hollered, much louder than she intended. Her voice pealed off the walls. She heaved herself up and stomped down the stairs, grabbing the end post to stagger for balance at the bottom. Vic and Thea leaned out of the kitchen, Vic shifting from foot to foot, Thea's fingers striking the doorjamb in a repeating drumbeat.

At the left of the landing, Jed stood openmouthed, looking from Daphne to his father.

"Sorry I was upstairs so long, everybody," Daphne said. "I had to call my mom."

Thea wiggled her eyebrows and made a face. They'd had many talks on how impossible mothers were. The gabfests had started in college and never stopped.

And when things had changed for Daphne and her mom, Daphne never made herself fix what was broken, she'd just moved in with Thea.

Vic turned and stepped into the kitchen. Daphne heard the clink of Grazie's leash from the refrigerator hook. A year ago, Grazie would have heard it, too, but her ears perked when Vic waved the leash at her, then his son.

"Jed, take Grazie for a walk." Vic held the leash out to his son.

"Why?" The boy's tone was a clear refusal.

Vic hooked the leash onto Grazie's collar. The dog's tail wagged; then she slumped to a lazy sit. He patted his leg, opened the door, and called her as he beckoned to Jed. "Thanks, buddy. We'll talk in a bit."

Jed rolled his eyes. So did Thea.

Daphne watched Vic avoid eye contact with everybody but his son. The boy didn't understand, but he didn't protest more. Thea didn't understand either, Daphne knew. And there was so much she didn't understand herself.

Vic still held the door open after his son and dog passed through, then moved down the walk and to the street. He gave Thea a stiff smile.

"Oh," she said. "I guess I'll be going."

He nodded. "It was good to see you again."

Daphne gave him a sharp look, grabbed her checkbook, and followed Thea outside. Using the hood of the car to write Thea a check, she saw a fat folder between the seats which had been covered with the bag of snacks. Papers splayed from the folder, printouts of newspaper stories. The headlines were familiar, but old.

Local Girl Missing. Body Found in Snohomish Woods. Body Identified as Missing Woman.

The headlines were twenty years old. When Thea plunked her purse and shopping bag on the car's roof, Daphne pulled the door open. "What are you doing with those articles?"

She looked where Daphne stared. "I was reading, that's all. I was thinking of you. I . . . wondered. I hadn't thought about Suzanne in a long time and . . ."

"And?" Daphne felt her teeth clench.

Thea's voice went to a whisper as she brought two fingers to touch Daphne's face. "And I'm a little worried about you, friend. So I was kind of trying to get inside your head. Maybe I could worry with you."

Something cracked inside Daphne and she shook her head, then palmed the fingers on her face. "Thanks then. Thanks for everything today, Thea."

Her best friend grinned and let her hand drop down to Daphne's hard shoulder. "Did you carry a billion pounds of roofing crap around again today?"

Daphne shook her head. "We usually load roofs with a lift or conveyor nowadays, especially on big projects."

"But haven't you ever thought all that physical work will make you grow a mustache?"

Daphne leveled a look at Thea. "No. I haven't. But thanks, I'll get started on that right away. Worrying about a mustache. Useful."

"I'm having a drink with Henry at eight." Thea winked and checked her watch.

"Who?" The last guy Thea mentioned dating had a long multi-syllabic name and the massive build of a Pacific Islander.

"Henry. Henry Fragher. He's a hotshot in the police union."

"Oh." Recollection flooded Daphne. "The guy you said you'd see—"

"Smoke," Thea corrected.

"Yes. That. I don't want you to—"

Thea smacked Daphne's shoulder. "Would you relax? I'm messing with you."

Daphne felt hope fade. "You're not seeing him? You won't be able to get me . . ." She glanced about for Vic, spied him at the open doorway watching them with his arms folded across his chest. ". . . An address or some kind of contact info for the retired detective?"

"Oh, no. I mean, yes, I'm seeing Henry. No, I won't blow him, and yes, I bet I can get a phone or addy for your guy."

"Mm, how?" Daphne imagined Thea going to jail for some wild indiscretion, too.

"Fact is, I'm going to look in his phone when he goes to get us drinks."

—⁂—

"She doesn't want to go," Jed said, padding up the walkway with Grazie.

Daphne opened her mouth, watching Thea back into the street, catching sight of a smudge in the asphalt between the Mercedes' tires. Then she blinked at the panting dog who wanted to go back inside and at the boy holding the leash who wanted the same.

"Thanks for trying," Vic called. As Jed and Grazie cleared the doorway, Daphne heard Vic project inside, "Be inside in a minute, buddy." And then the door shut and he was beside her, a hand on the small of her back.

"Where's my car?"

"It got impounded after the accident."

"You weren't hurt?"

She shook her head and noticed the headache it caused. She rolled her shoulders in exaggerated shrugs, testing. Movement hurt. "The side window shattered," she said, remembering the crumbled remains. "Maybe it rang my bell a little."

"You got in an accident and the result of the accident was . . . you were charged with reckless driving?"

She nodded, wordless.

"It would probably be a good thing if Cassandra didn't know about you getting arrested, if we can manage that."

"You think I want her to know? You think I want anyone to know? Jesus, Vic."

His jaw clenched in response, but he said nothing more. Daphne thought of how she'd playfully chastised him when they met and he'd semi-sworn, said *Jesus* when he spilled a glass in a restaurant on one of their first dates. She'd told him how she'd been instructed as a child not to speak that way. He'd never sworn Jesus again, but a few times when she'd let fly with choice words, he'd pointed out how she dabbled in profanity when stressed.

She gestured to the empty space where his car should have been parked. "I'm inconvenienced, too. My tool belt and my coil nailer were in your car. Vic, I needed you this afternoon and you weren't there for me."

He spread his hands in defense. "What was I supposed to do? I called your cell this afternoon when I got to Jed's game. I thought of you at Josie's game and I called you, just because I was thinking of you.

Then I got your voice mail. And you, you sounded insane, telling me to bring cash and identification and that you'd been in an accident and you were raving, but you didn't say *where* you were. I called your cell again and again, I called the house, I even called your work and—"

"You called my work?"

"Yes. They just told me you'd worked a half day and left at noon. It's what I'd expected you to do. I did not expect you to get arrested. If you'd been unable to reach me this afternoon, would your next guess have been to show up at the police station to bail me out?"

"I wasn't in a police station, I was in a jail. In a holding cell. But fine. No, I wouldn't have looked for you in jail. Not you."

"Not you either," he said, his voice soft and smile wry. "This was unusual—"

"A guy grabbed me today. I was trying to help, to make an effort for a little old lady and one thing led to another. I'm not perfect. Neither are you." She pointed to a smudged, bare clump of feathers ground into the street. "See that?"

"Who grabbed you exactly? What are you talking about?" Vic said, not looking where she pointed.

"It was a robin. You killed it Wednesday. You ran over it. Twice. Just yesterday." She headed for the door, ignoring him following her.

—⁂—

Inside, Vic pushed a button on the blinking answering machine. Its mechanical voice said, "Message one." Frances Mayfield had implored her daughter to call, to come visit. Daphne deleted the message.

"Message two." Then a woman's voice said, "Mr. Daily, this is Seattle Police Dispatch. I'm relaying a question for one of our officers at a scene regarding your vehicle. Are you there?"

After a pause, the line went dead and the message stopped. The machine clicked and said "Message three," in its stilted, careful English.

At the sound of his own voice asking Daphne to pick up if she was there, Vic hit delete.

"Message four." The machine's repetitive, electronic syllables made Daphne want to scream.

Then there was a man talking, his voice low and snarling. "You get it now? Something from ten years ago can come back and bite you in the ass."

CHAPTER 12

Daphne recoiled from the telephone, then rallied and punched the button to replay the last message.

Vic rubbed his scalp. In the living room, Jed turned the television up as the answering machine again voiced the electronic comment, "Message four." And then a man's snarl repeated. "You get it now? Something from ten years ago can come back and bite you in the ass."

"Who is that?" Vic asked.

She shook her head.

"You don't know?" His hands made fists on his hips.

She frowned and hit the message again, thinking of Guff rushing her at Minerva Watts's doorway. His words, his tone filtered back.

You. Stand there. Hold up.

One hand went to her right shoulder, remembering his grip on her jacket though she stood coatless in the kitchen now. Daphne hit the machine and played the message again. Low, the voice snarled its vague threatening words. A bit of menace. It sounded like someone disguising his voice, but it didn't sound like the man she'd seen carrying a box, Guff. No. Guff, the man who grabbed her and chased her, hadn't called the house and left this message.

Daphne shook her head. "Something from ten years ago? That doesn't make sense." Her father's suicide, a decade past, reamed her mind with new confusion. Nothing made sense.

"Then what would that guy be talking about, Daph?"

"I don't know. But do you believe me now? This guy Guff grabbed me. That woman called Minerva Watts *lady* at first but then called her *Mother*. Said it was time for her pill. Minerva asked her not to take—"

"Daphne!"

"What?"

"What does that have to do with something . . . ," he pointed at the phone, "from ten years ago biting you in the ass?"

"I don't know! How should I know? Maybe it's a message for you, not me. What did you do ten years ago? I didn't even know you then."

He shook his head. "Ten years ago, I had two little ones and a bad marriage and I'd just gotten my job at the Weather Service."

"So in ten more years you can retire and you're all set." As soon as she snapped off her retort, she regretted it.

He put a hand on her shoulder. "And you. Ten years ago, you lost your father."

"I didn't lose him. I know where he is. Just outside the church grounds. Just . . . not with his daughter."

"Daphne, what is going on?"

"You know what? The first thing you said to me was that I missed Josie's game. And you already knew I was in an accident. You should have asked first if I was okay."

"I could see that you were okay. Come on. We don't want to fight."

"Oh, I think I do."

He looked away, working his jaw muscles.

She folded her arms across her chest. "And that guy took my jacket, so he has my wallet. I have to get my mother . . . I don't know. Out of the house. She's playing bridge right now. But I have to go over there."

He grabbed her hand, then turned his wrist to check his watch. "But I need your truck so I can take Jed back to his mother's. We're late. I called Cassandra before we came home and asked for an extra hour, because I wanted to run home to check on you. I wanted to see if you were here. You weren't answering your phone."

"That guy got it when he took my jacket." Daphne replayed the quick conflict in her mind again, then remembered the wreck, the jail. The unfairness of it all brought tears to her eyes, but their appearance was infuriating. She wiped her face.

"But from the way you describe it, he was just sort of holding on to your jacket and you slipped out of it."

"And then he chased me, Vic. You know, I think Minerva Watts's grandmother's brooch was in that box Guff was carrying. He put it in the car."

"Do you hear yourself? Where in the world did that come from?"

"The box that guy Guff was carrying." Daphne snapped out of her numbness, "Look, whose side are you on?"

"Yours." He looked behind her and smiled. "I'm on your side."

Daphne turned. Seeing Jed behind her, she wondered how long he'd been there, how much he'd overheard.

"What's going on?" the boy asked.

"Oh, we just got an odd message on the machine, buddy. That's all," Vic said with a shrug. "You haven't used the phone, have you, bud?"

Jed shook his head. Vic nodded and said, "Go get in the truck and I'll run you back to your mom's house."

After the boy stepped outside, Vic turned to Daphne and snapped his fingers. "Have you been on the phone since you came home?"

She nodded. "When I was upstairs, I tried to call my mother to warn her."

"About this weird phone message?"

"No, about a guy having my wallet. Her address is on my ID."

"Okay, but we haven't received any calls, right? Nothing incoming? You haven't answered the phone?"

She shook her head, excited as she understood what he was thinking. They could uncover who left the message. There was a way.

Vic nodded. "Then we'll just dial star sixty-nine on the phone and get the phone number of the last incoming call. I don't think outgoing calls affect the ability to get the number of the last caller. And the last incoming call is from the man who left that message." He pointed to the answering machine.

She snatched the phone from him and he spread his fingers in a gesture of submission. Then she dialed three numbers and asked for a police officer, explaining that someone had her wallet and had grabbed her and chased her and now she had come home to a threatening phone call. And then she rolled her eyes at the dispatcher's vague answer of how long it might be before a police officer would come to her house and hear her complaint.

"What are you doing?" Vic asked when she hung up the phone.

"I get one chance to dial star sixty-nine and see who the last caller is, right? I want a police officer to witness it. I mean, suppose we get a phone call right now? Suppose Thea calls or anybody else. It'll show her as the last caller and we'll lose getting to know who phoned in this threat."

"You think it's a threat?"

"It's pretty weird, isn't it? So, I'm going to get a police officer here and he can hear with us who left that last message. And maybe he'll do something about it. I'll be a complainant," she told Vic, gesturing toward the telephone. Her head pounded. Nothing made sense, but she needed to articulate things. She would begin at the beginning with the next police officer and leave nothing out. He would see it. He would understand. He would find what was missing. Maybe it would be a female officer. Yes, that would be better. Daphne nodded. "It's just like yesterday when I called the police, I mean when you called, about those people taking Minerva Watts. I mean when they took her again today, it was like that."

"Her daily kidnapping?" Vic flipped one hand in a doubtful wave. "What?"

"Well, it doesn't make sense." He cupped her face with both hands. "Yesterday you see this couple with this older woman in the park and they go to a car. She says she's being robbed and kidnapped. Today you see the same thing. And you still believe there's really something wrong even though—"

"You weren't there. If you'd been there, you'd know."

"I'd know what?"

"That there is something wrong. Something's going on. She said it was her grandmother's brooch—"

He waved her off, his face perplexed. "What brooch?"

"I didn't see it but—"

"Exactly. You didn't see it. She wasn't making sense. She's a failing little old lady. She's Grazie without the fur." He stopped himself and rolled his lips in, then closed his eyes before continuing. "All I'm saying is, I want you to think about what you saw, what you've told us."

"Us?"

"Me. The police. Thea."

She nodded, her jaw set. "Because all of you understand there's nothing wrong and Minerva Watts is perfectly safe and I'm the one who's wrong here?"

"Daph, please. People do not get kidnapped one day and then again the next. By the same people? At about the same place? That is not kidnapping. That is a couple trying to handle an old lady in their lives."

"Then why'd he chase me?"

He spread his hands wide. "Why did you run from him? Isn't that why he chased you? Wouldn't you do the same, instinctively? If someone is at our front door"—he pointed to it—"and that person suddenly runs . . ." He gave a dismissive one-handed wave for explanation.

"No. No, Vic. And you know what? I am not feeling very safe with you, not with your attitude toward what happened to me today."

The front door opened and Jed stepped inside, accidentally bumping Grazie, who rested against the door like weather stripping. She struggled to her feet then collapsed, panting in pain.

"I think," Vic said, leaning over to calm the dog as Daphne knelt. "I think I have to put her down."

"No!" Daphne gritted her teeth, regretting her screech.

Jed patted the dog's head, then pushed his hands deep in his front pockets. "Don't put her down. Just don't. But Dad, are you coming? Mom's going to be mad if I'm even later getting back." He twisted his lower lip and looked at the dog. "Is she okay?"

A knock at the door made them all scramble, including Grazie.

"Who's here?" the boy asked, not calling through the door but looking at Vic and Daphne for an answer.

"I would seriously love to have just one thing going on instead of ten," Daphne said, sliding Grazie away from the door and rising to twist the knob. "Hello," she said, waving the short uniformed man with a red crew cut into the house. "You got here fast."

"In the area," he said. "What can I do for you? You've had a suspicious telephone call?"

"Dad, what's going on?"

"Jed, go grab the registration to Daphne's truck out of the glove box for me." Vic opened the door and shooed his son outside again. Then he turned to Daphne and stroked her shoulder. "Begin at the beginning?"

The cop eyed them in turn. "A threat on the phone? Is this related to the little pickup outside?"

"Threat on the phone, yes," Daphne said.

"Related to the truck, no," Vic said, sliding his arm all the way across her shoulders.

She felt herself relax into the warmth of his chest, told herself she'd had the third worst day of her life and that's why nothing clicked, but it felt good to have Vic's body against hers. She played the message for the officer several times, confirming for him she had no idea who the caller was or what the reference to ten years ago could be about. Then she told him about the woman in the park and the claims of kidnapping and robbery, about seeing the couple take Minerva Watts to a car, about reporting it to the police yesterday. Then she told him about going to the address Thea found today, and what the couple said, and all about the grabbing and chasing and hiding. About chasing them with Vic's car, the wreck, and the arrest for reckless driving. And coming home to this threat.

The crew cut officer never interrupted, never looked lost. Vic nodded all the way through her careful story.

"So, let's hit star sixty-nine and find out who called you last," the cop said.

"Great," Daphne agreed. And then he did and they all crowded around the speakerphone. A recorded operator's voice announced the last number that phoned the house. Daphne and Vic sagged together.

"It's Cassandra's number," Vic said, his voice dull.

"And Cassandra is?" the officer asked.

Daphne looked away. "His ex-wife."

"Ah, so this is an ex thing. Sounds like you know the drill? All about restraining orders to deal with harassing phone calls and such?"

"No," Daphne said. "I do not know the drill." She went to the front door, opening it just as Jed came inside with a paper in his hand.

"Your glove box is a mess. Is this the right thing? Your registration?" He handed it to his father and stalked off to the living room.

"Jed?" Daphne called after him, cutting off her annoyance with a deep breath when he ignored her. Then she threw the cop and Vic a glance and pursued the boy.

The living room was empty. She pushed open the kid's bedroom door.

"Jed?" Louder, going into the room calling him, Daphne made sure she produced enough volume for the cop and Vic to hear.

"What!" The boy's shot-back answer belied his pretense of not knowing Daphne had been calling for him. He sat on the floor leaning against his bed. Daphne felt a hand on her shoulder and wanted to shrug out from under it. Instead she shot Vic a look and he pushed his hands deep into his front pockets, exhaling.

Daphne rushed to speak first. "Jed, did your mom call since you've been home?"

"Nope."

"And you haven't answered the phone, right?" Making sure she missed nothing this time. "We didn't get a phone call that you know of? Not when your dad and I were outside after you walked Grazie?"

Jed shook his head but hesitated, openmouthed and silent.

"What?" Daphne demanded, trying to keep her voice measured.

He shrugged. "Josie called me."

"Jed! We've got the police here."

"But why? Why won't anyone tell me what's going on?"

"Someone threatened me or us or something," Daphne told him and shook her head, realizing how nutty and inadequate she sounded. She turned her back on the boy and stood puffing in the living room. "So after some guy left that message, Josie called. She's the last caller. She called while we were outside, Vic. Now we'll never know who that guy was. We'll never get to know why he threatened us, what he meant."

"Someone's threatening you?" Jed asked. "Who?"

The cop held up a hand. "Ma'am, generally when someone's being threatened, they know what they're being threatened about and they know who's making threats."

"Well, I don't."

"Any significance about ten years ago at all? For either of you?"

He eyed Daphne and Vic in turns. Daphne was sure he noticed the look Vic shot her, the blink of an acknowledgment of what happened ten years ago in her life.

When neither Vic nor Daphne said anything, the cop continued. "You know, it could just be a wrong number, too. Whoever the caller is, he could have just dialed the wrong number, left the wrong person this odd . . ."

"Threat," Daphne said.

"Message," the policeman said.

"I have to take Jed home," Vic said. "I'll be back soon. Come on, buddy." He walked away without kissing her good-bye.

Daphne wished the world weren't a place where a father drove his son away to his ex-wife's house and called that his son's home. She wished so very many things were different.

"Dad?" Jed called, hurrying after him. "Dad, what happened? Tell me what's going on."

—m—

"Let's go take a peek at the address on the other side of the park, shall we?" The officer stood on the threshold and beckoned her to come with him.

Daphne sucked in a great lungful and stepped one foot across the doorway, looked back at Grazie still on the floor. She addressed the cop while eyeing the dog. "Do you believe me?"

He reached for her arm. "I believe something may be a bit off. I'd like to take a look at the woman's residence on Eastpark. You can come and point out to me the route you ran. Maybe a neighbor or someone saw something."

Daphne shivered at the words and followed him outside, not wanting to lose this official person to talk to, this person who let her begin at the beginning. If she had more time, she decided, she'd even tell him about ten years ago and her dad, even about twenty years ago and her sister. Someone would know everything and could tell her what made sense and what didn't. "I don't have a car here," she explained. "My boy-friend had to take mine since I got his impounded."

"I'll take you with me. Let's zip around the park and check out the Minerva Watts place." They were within feet of his marked police car now.

Daphne took a breath, eyeing the back seat of the squad car as he jin-gled his keys. "Seriously, I . . . mm, don't have to go with you. I just . . ."

He opened his front passenger door and held it, looking back at her with a bland expression.

She smiled. "My parents told me never to get in a car with a man I didn't know."

"Your parents were right. Hop in."

Hop in, Daphne thought. The same words the other officer said after he'd arrested her.

Crackling police radio accompanied their drive. Her body trem-bled. "I got arrested because this guy stole my ID." Her tiny try for sym-pathy wasn't enough to make sense. She told him more details about the chase, the two chases.

"Sounds like you got arrested for driving reckless, blowing a light, and causing an accident, but hey, I wasn't there."

She looked at him sideways. "Okay, here's the one thing from ten years ago that stands out in my world." And she told him about her father.

"Who would call you and say that can come back and bite you in the butt?"

"No one!" Daphne's frustration bubbled out. "I mean, who? Why? It doesn't even make sense. But why would that message be directed at Vic? The only person in the world who doesn't like Vic is his ex-wife . . ." *And my best friend, Thea,* she amended in her head.

The officer nodded. "The caller didn't address either of you. The message may not have been intended for either of you. It may have been a misdial."

And then they were at Minerva Watts's vacant house at 11243 East-park Avenue, and Daphne imagined she could look right into and through the Peace Park and see herself in the middle of the greenbelt just yesterday, see Vic's dad's old house on Westpark Avenue bordering the far side of the park.

The officer told her to wait in his car. Her mind ran on and on while the officer knocked, waited, then walked around Minerva's house. When he knocked on neighbors' doors, she wished he'd left the patrol car's windows down farther, so she might overhear something. The woman who lived across the street was talking to the officer now, gesturing with the cop at the Watts house, the alley, down the road.

"She saw a dark blue car," the cop told Daphne when he returned to his patrol car. "Said the old lady's car's silver, that this wasn't the car that's normally there—"

"It wasn't?" Daphne chewed on this nugget, then shook her head in defeat. Every scrap was fallow, meaningless without illumination.

The cop shrugged. "Maybe family, a visitor."

"That couple. The dark blue Town Car must be theirs." Daphne stopped as the officer made a cryptic request into his shoulder microphone, asking for some kind of reverse check. The car's dashboard radio squelched the same voice from the officer's portable radio. Daphne looked from the cop to his dashboard and back again, not understanding the dispatcher's response. Something about a transfer pending. She trained her perplexed look on the officer.

He squinted at the house. "A check of all vehicles registered to a Minerva Watts at this address shows none. She had a 2012 Ford Crown Vic, silver in color, but just sold it to Fremont Ford."

"Just sold it?" Daphne looked at the house, too, wondering what, if anything, was in Minerva Watts's garage.

"Yeah," he said. "Records show a transfer pending as of yesterday."

"Yesterday? She sold her car, her Crown Vic, to a Ford dealership yesterday?" Daphne shook her head and looked back across the street.

"How long has the Town Car been hanging around Minerva Watts's house?"

He shook his head. "The neighbor didn't say."

"Ask her. Oh, please? Will you ask the neighbor how long the car's been around here?" Daphne's urgency came from her soul. "Can I go ask?"

The officer made a tight-lipped smile, then walked back to the neighbor's house. It was brown with a red door. No one answered his knock for some minutes; then he spoke to the neighbor lady again. Then he tried her neighbors, rapping on doors with his nightstick.

"Well, we don't know how long it had been there," he reported, "but the neighbor lady just noticed it a day or so ago."

At the house on the next block, Daphne pointed out the rhododendrons where she'd hidden, and the officer rapped on the door with a small flashlight, the metal making a ringing ping against a brass doorplate, but no one answered.

Moving across one yard to another, the cop lingered before he went next door to the house where she had seen someone in the upstairs window when she'd been hiding. The cop holstered the flashlight and drew his baton.

Daphne waited it out in the car, thinking and watching and reliving while the front door opened and the officer exchanged low words with occupants she could not see. And she wanted out, out of this car, this life. She wanted, craved, peace.

When he came back, she decided it was worth it, seeing things through. It would all be worth it if she got to understand. She didn't want to miss a thing, not anything, so she asked, "Why do you beat on people's doors like that?"

"Ever tried knocking on a lot of doors?"

"No." She made herself not ask if he'd ever tried roofing a six-plex, or a dozen of them.

He grinned and started the patrol car. "Hard on the knuckles." All the way around the park, he said no more.

"What happens now?" she asked as he pulled up at Vic's house. Her truck sat in the driveway.

"I write a little report and go to my next call." He tapped the radio on his dashboard then scribbled on a business card and handed it to her. "There's a bunch of calls holding in my area. I need to move on. Here's my card and the case number. Call if anything happens. And if nothing happens, you move on, too."

CHAPTER 13

Abandoned at the curb in front of her house—it wasn't hers, it was Vic's, no, Vic's *father's* house—Daphne blinked in disappointment as the police officer drove off. Then she saw Vic standing in the front doorway with a huge bouquet of roses and wasn't at all sure how she felt about him.

He waited for her to admire the red petals, looked undecided about something, then launched into, "So Thea was in the house, here by herself, looking for your ID."

"Vic, what was I supposed to do? I needed identification. I needed someone to get it for me from the house. What in the world was I supposed to do?"

"I don't know. Sorry. I'm just tired. I got up early this afternoon so I could get Jed's bike before I took him to soccer and . . ."

She sniffed when he didn't finish his thought. "Well, you'll sleep well tonight."

He reached for her. "With you. I can sleep with my arms around you all night. I love those nights."

She did, too, when life wasn't crazy and when his kids weren't around.

In the bedroom, both ready to call it a night though it was mid-evening, he stroked her left shoulder when she pulled her shirt off. "You're bruised. Is that from the guy grabbing you?"

Twisting to look at her shoulder in the mirror, Daphne prodded the purple blotch. "No, he grabbed my other arm—"

"God, I wish I'd been there!"

Pleased with Vic's sudden explosion, Daphne straightened as she rubbed her arm. "This bruise must be from the crash. The side-impact and steering wheel airbags went off. The car spun a full circle."

He shook his head. "The airbags went off? I think I was picturing closer to a fender bender, but something that still meant the car had to be towed. Quite a day. I'm just glad no one was . . . I mean, no one was hurt, were they? Anyone else?"

She told him then about the other two cars, the guy with the bloody knuckles and the woman taken away by ambulance.

"Yikes. I guess I had the impression you hit a power pole or something. I don't know why."

"I never said I hit a power pole. I got hit by a car from each side and it spun the Honda around in the middle of the intersection."

"The guy wasn't badly hurt though?" He waited for her head shake before continuing, "And you're comfortably sure the other woman is going to be all right?"

"Yeah. She said she was glad her kids—"

"She had kids with her?"

"Not with her. But she said she'd just dropped them off or something like that. She was glad they weren't with her."

Vic's shoulders sagged. "Picture what you did, Daph. You blew a light. You hit a woman."

She felt the stresses of the day and the last two decades break her open. When she opened her mouth to respond, she laughed, a great guffawing cackle. "Hey, I hit a guy, too." Daphne tugged at his sleeve.

"This isn't funny. Suppose her kids had been with her. Picture it. Picture them scared and crying." He shook his head. "I suppose it's because you're not a parent that you can make fun of potentially putting a kid in danger."

She clenched her teeth. "It's not because I'm not a parent, a mother. It's because it's over. There's nothing I can do about it. I wish it hadn't happened, but it did. In hindsight, yes, I should have slowed down, made sure it was clear before—"

"Before you ran a red light?"

"Remind me not to have you on my jury or defense team or whatever."

His eyebrows pitched up. "Does that mean you're going to contest your ticket?" He dropped his question when he saw her expression and raised his hands to stop the cycle of contention. "Can we just go to bed? Can I give you a rose massage?"

It had been his best move, she'd told him, the first time they'd slept together. A rose massage. He'd brought her a bouquet and startled her by tearing it up. Then he'd sprinkled the petals of twenty-three roses over her nude body, stroked and kneaded her skin, every muscle and curve. And he'd repeated every languid motion, stroking her with the last whole rose. It had taken hours. It had taken her to new heights of enjoyment, of seeing tenderness and affection in a man who professed pride in being with her.

Sinking onto the bed, Daphne asked him, "Do people seriously just go to bed like it's a normal night when something like this has happened?"

"Something like getting arrested?"

"No," she snapped, "something like seeing an old lady get kidnapped. Again."

"Daph, you really don't know what's going on with that lady, in her life, in those other people's lives. And I think you should face facts. Face the reality."

"Which is?"

"That you never will know, okay? You will never know. Some things, we just don't get to know. But those people, the lady, they're probably okay."

"You weren't there. I know what I saw. Something was going on." Daphne spread her fingers against his chest. "What gives with you? You wave off my concerns, but then when the cop shows up, you're Mr. Supportive, like you're playing a part."

He blew out a hard breath and took her hand in his. "You are tenacious and it's admirable, but once in a while, it would be good to let things go."

"How often has something like this happened?"

"Maybe once in a lifetime," Vic said, his voice beleaguered.

Once in a lifetime. The words echoed in her mind, lost from long ago. Once in a lifetime . . . what? Not helping someone?

Not helping because of not knowing was so much more excusable than not helping due to an apathetic lack of effort. A murder was once in a lifetime and most people didn't have murder in their families. A hanging? Once in a lifetime.

A girl like Suzanne, someone had said, she was once-in-a-lifetime special.

Who had said that? A boyfriend? That boyfriend, the last one? Ross? Yes, Ross Bouchard said Suzanne was a once-in-a-lifetime girl.

Oh, and her mother said the same when frustrated with Suzanne, having caught her about to take the car without permission.

Their mother had perhaps never known how Suzanne snuck out so many times. Her mother talked about Suzanne's sassing, funky clothes and hair, and that phrase on so many of the elder daughter's report cards: not living up to potential. Daphne swallowed at the literal reality of those teachers' comments. And her mother's counterpoint, when shaking her head and half-complaining about once-in-a-lifetime Suzanne, came in the same breath as she proclaimed how different Daphne was.

You're my good girl, Daphne.

"I have to call my mother again. I want her out of the house for now. Until I know if that guy having my wallet is going to be a major problem." She tried to think, to plan the conversation. Her mother might argue that she couldn't leave her cat for long. Daphne considered a counterargument, deciding she and Vic could keep the cat for a while. Maybe her mom would sleep at their house, too, but where?

"You have to cancel your credit cards," Vic said. "Should have already done it."

Daphne lurched from the bed, grabbed the phone off the nightstand, and pushed a useless button. "It's dead. Why's it dead?"

He took the phone from her and racked it back on the charger. "I'd guess you left it off the charger earlier. I'll go get the kitchen phone so we have one up here tonight."

Vic wanted a working phone beside the bed in case there was an emergency, in case his kids needed him, Daphne knew. She held out her hand. "Just give me your cell."

Vic slipped his phone off his belt clip, put it in her palm, then headed down the stairs for the house phone.

Her mother's voice held surprise with a one-word question. "Victor?" Although her mother still didn't have a cordless phone in the kitchen, Daphne had bought her a set of cordless units for the bedroom and living room.

"No, Mom, it's me. Just using Vic's phone. Um, how was bridge? Good?"

"I didn't have very good hands and I missed some things. Are you coming out tomorrow? I've been doing so much. Why don't you spend the weekend with me? Victor can come, too. And his kids. We can all go—"

"Oh, Mo-om." Daphne felt herself weighed down with these requests she didn't want to grant and realized her mother would not give up either.

Daphne wondered about the validity of her concern that the man who'd taken her jacket would go to her mother's house. She tried to weigh the best-case scenario against the worst, as Vic would measure it. People pursued victims in movies. With the salve of time, the whole afternoon at Minerva Watts's house turned surreal. Unexplainable and incomprehensible and somehow not real.

"Oh, Da-aphne," her mother said. "I have such a surprise for you. Just come out. It won't be a too-sad thing . . . like every year. We were saying at bridge, the other girls, they were saying you have to do things with kids. Kids don't want to just sit around in an old lady's house. You don't. And especially this weekend—"

"Mom, it's just—"

"No, listen to me, child. Blanche said there's this place we could go. We could all go. She takes her son and his wife and their kids up to a little resort in the apple country and they poke around at all those German-looking buildings and they pick apples and peaches in the orchards, although I don't think you can pick fruit right now. And they have Christmas stores, open all year. The hotel they stay at has a swimming pool and the grandkids love it. We could join them. We're invited. Victor's kids would like that, wouldn't they?"

"Um, Vic, Mom. Call him Vic."

"All right then. Vic. Vic's kids would like the hotel with a swimming pool. Blanche is going up with her son and his family this weekend and they've invited us, and there's no reason in the world you can't go, no reason to say no. You don't work weekends and neither does Victor. Vic. So we could all get away for the weekend and stay together. They're leaving tonight. You and I and Vic and his kids could catch up to them in the morning. Wouldn't that be good? It would. You know it would. Say yes."

"So, you could go away with them tonight? You'd be gone all weekend?"

"They've invited all of us. It's not peak season yet, so we'll get a good rate and there are vacancies on short notice."

"You should do it, Mom. You should go with Blanche this weekend. Tonight."

The pause killed. Her mother's voice returned, stiffer. "But you're not going to say yes and come along and spend the weekend, *this* weekend, with me?"

Daphne sighed. "No, Mom. I'm not. We'll have the kids and we'll visit Vic's dad Saturday morning and—"

"I told you the kids could come. They'd have fun. You just don't want to spend the weekend up in Leavenworth with me and Blanche and her lovely family. She's so lucky to have a son and daughter-in-law and grandkids who like to spend time with her. You just don't like—"

"Come on, Mom. That's not it." Well, it was, but it was a truth that left Daphne cringing. Spend a whole weekend trapped with her sad mother? Beautiful Bavarian Leavenworth, Washington, loomed like a prison—like Leavenworth, Kansas—when she thought of spending an entire weekend with her mother there. Aurgh.

"Mom? Make sure the doors and windows are locked if you don't go away tonight, okay?"

"Why?"

"Just do. I was thinking of you is all."

Her mother said nothing and the pause went on and on until Daphne sighed and said, "The truth is, my wallet and jacket and cell phone were stolen and my ID still has your address on it and I wondered if the guy who stole it might come to your house. You know? I just wondered."

"Why didn't you tell me that in the first place? Did you leave your jacket in your car at work?"

"It's a truck. I don't have a car—"

"Will you stop correcting me for every little thing? I'm your mother. You don't correct me."

"I'm sorry. I'm sorry, Mom. I am. I had a lousy day and—"

"Well, I'd imagine so, what with your jacket being stolen. Poor girl. Are you sure you didn't just lose it? Where did you see it last?"

Batting the conversation back to her mother, Daphne stepped over Grazie and thundered down the stairs, rolling her eyes at Vic while fending off her mother. She tried to pour a glass of wine with one hand, watched Vic chuckle, then relinquished the corked bottle to him. He was unable to stifle a grin while he poured two glasses, and he clinked them together before gesturing that he'd carry the wine up to their bedroom.

She heard the house phone ring as she ran up the stairs, screwing her eyes shut as she worked her mother's conversation to an end.

"I'll tell her," Vic said. Daphne peered over the landing and watched him finish writing a note, pick up the two wineglasses again, and climb the stairs with the note protruding from two fingers. She waited until she could stand his passivity no more, aggravated that he didn't tell her right away what he knew.

"Who were you talking to?"

He met her stare, set the wineglasses on their nightstand, and reached to kiss her while holding the note behind his back. "Thea."

"Hmm. You two still hate each other?"

"We don't hate each other," he protested. "We both love you."

"How long are you two going to not get along?"

"I don't know. How long were you eavesdropping on us this evening?" Vic brought his hand from the small of his back, glanced at a note in his palm, then folded the paper in quarters.

"What's that?"

"It's an address and phone number. And I have a quote to read to you from her, but I don't know what it means. Will you tell me what it means?"

Daphne looked at the tiny note between his thumb and forefinger, wondering hard about what Thea might have told Vic. "If I can."

"Okay, it says: Retired Detective Arnold Seton. Do not tell him where you got this address."

Daphne perked up. "And there's an address?" She snatched at the slip of paper.

Vic kept the note between two fingertips, extending his arm toward the ceiling. "You said you'd tell me what it means. What is going on, please?"

"I can go see him. I can talk to him. After all this time . . . what?" She raised her eyebrows as Vic scowled. She scowled back and hated being short.

He tossed the note on the bed and folded his arms. "And what am I supposed to do? You've wrecked my car. Am I supposed to take a cab?"

She bit her lip. "I'll pay for it."

"I don't want you to pay for it. I want my car." His voice was raised and he didn't raise it often.

"If I were yelling about something that just can't be, say if I were ranting about wanting my sister back, or my father, you'd tell me to be realistic. To not wish for things that just can't be."

He looked too chagrined to be defensive and said, "Well, I'd say it very nicely."

Her shoulders and ire dropped together. "You would," she agreed.

Vic sat on the bed and eyed the bouquet of roses on the nightstand. "There's something I want to say, to ask you, but it seems like there's so much distraction lately."

"Yes!" she exploded, wondering when he'd moved the roses up to the bedroom. "There's so much distraction these days. Why is that?"

He held a finger to his lips, to hers, then cradled her onto the bed and set the note by the double bouquet. After stripping out of his shirt and socks, he took his time undressing her. He pulled two roses from one bouquet and swirled one over her left nipple, then her right, while tracing the curve of her shoulders with the other.

She softened, succumbing to relaxation.

Vic placed one rose between her breasts and pulled back the green sepals of the other, making all the bloom show. He'd taught her the names of the parts of the rose, the pistil and stamen and sepal, with the first rose massage.

Back then, he'd crunched some of the magic for her when he'd admitted to learning the names from Cassandra, a master gardener.

"Tomorrow," Daphne breathed, closing her eyes. "I'll get things sorted out tomorrow. Get your car out of impound. See this detective Thea found."

"Then I want to go with you," Vic said, his voice hypnotic. "We can go see him together when I get off work."

She opened her eyes. "I don't want to wait until tomorrow evening. I have the whole day off work. I don't want to waste it."

"Daph, it's just one day."

"I don't want to wait. I'd go see him right now if I could." She looked at the clock and felt a niggling sensation that something was wrong, something else. What had she let lie? But the temptation to relax into Vic's seduction and be allowed to feel good pulled at her core.

Vic whispered, "I'll be off work at four. We can go together before I get the kids at six."

"I'll just go by myself. I'll take you to work, drop you off, and then I'll go. I've got the whole day off."

"Daph, you don't have to go at all."

"What?"

Vic stroked both hands across her hair, caressing as he murmured, "If I asked you to stop all this, would you?"

"All this . . . what?"

"All this tilting at windmills."

"I'm tilting at windmills?"

He nodded and nuzzled her neck. "And it could be dangerous." He held her face and smiled. "Didn't your parents ever tell you not to go talking to men you don't know?"

Her body went taut. "Every day since I was eleven."

His smile fell and he nodded. "Of course. Well. Well, they were right. It's someone you don't know. Some guy you don't know at some address you're unfamiliar with. At least wait so I can go with you."

"I'm going to talk to an ex-cop. They're not dangerous."

He tore several roses from the bouquet, and sprinkled a fistful of petals over her. Once she was littered from neck to thighs, he rearranged loose petals with two roses, tracing her breasts, her muscles, her belly button. Then he pulled a small silver ring from the change pocket of his jeans, and fed it onto one rose stem. Dangling the rose upside down toward her face, he twirled it back and forth. The cuts in the ring's metal flashed in the low light.

"I never gave this to Cassandra. I never even considered it. With her it was . . ." He stopped himself even before he saw her glare.

Daphne clapped her hands over her eyes, refusing to engage and see the metal band blurring above the rose bloom. "Why . . . are you talking about her now? Or at all?"

He pulled her hands from her eyes and shook his head. "I let my mouth run when it shouldn't have. She's not a thought I want in my head or yours right now. You mentioned some grandmother's brooch earlier, and it made me think of my grandmother's ring and the whole thing in my head about who I never gave it to and why, and who I want to give it to and why, and how I've been wanting to say something to you for quite a while . . . Wait. I'm fouling this up."

Clearing his throat, he rose from the bed and pirouetted three hundred and sixty degrees, then knelt at the bedside. "Starting over. This was my grandmother's ring. My mother set it aside and so did I. Will you marry me, Daphne?" He ended with both hands on his heart.

She stared as her mind whirled and then words boiled out of the mix of emotions and thoughts. "I can't believe you proposed. I mean, it's unexpected. Thanks. I mean, I love you, too. I just . . ."

The reserve in Vic's face ill-concealed his hurt and bewilderment. She turned away, knowing she'd caused so much distress today to so many, knowing she too was on the list of victims, of people who'd been put out by her actions. "Let me just manage one thing right now," she whispered as she reached for the light and clicked it off. "Let me tell you I love you and thank you, and let's go to bed. It can still be special. I'm . . . I feel so scattered right now."

In the dark, he said, "In the history of the world, no man ever picked a worse moment to propose."

"And no woman has ever been less . . . I don't know."

He fell asleep with her hands encased in his. Soon a disturbed slumber led him to pull a few inches away, half-rolling to his stomach, then pulling the covers above his shoulder. Daphne shoved the sheet and comforter down, ready to sweat, thinking about her reaction to his proposal. Part of her smiled, swooned a bit, and reveled in his desire. Part of her stayed stuck in questions past and present that had nothing to do with the man beside her. Vic's fitful sleeping, uneasy with the unnatural switch to his circadian rhythm, might have kept her awake, but she might have lain awake all those hours anyway, her mind rehashing and second-guessing in anticipation of the confrontation she'd earned for the morning.

A man she didn't remember, the man with the best chance of knowing, was going to explain to her what was missed.

CHAPTER 14

Daphne parked on a gravel driveway and checked the note again as she stepped out of her truck.

> *Retired Detective Arnold Seton. 216582 Amelanchier Street NE. Do not tell him where you got this address.*

The house was small, older. She saw a man deep in the carport and called to him. "Mr. Seton? Are you Arnold Seton? You were with the Seattle Police Department?"

He dropped his metal tackle box with a clunk and angled his body like a boxer's, his right leg stepping back, one hand darting under his jacket to his waistband. "Show me your hands."

"Shit," she said, dropping the note and throwing her spread palms into the air by her ears. "Don't shoot me."

"Who are you and what do you want?" The man didn't step out of the carport and Daphne stood rooted in the open, glancing down at the note, wondering if Vic's transcription of Thea's warning was face up.

"I'm Daphne Mayfield. I'm, I was . . . Suzanne Mayfield was my big sister. She was murdered twenty years ago. You were on her case. I was a kid then. I never got to talk to you or anyone who knew anything about it."

A half hour ago, she'd thought nothing could be more tense than driving one's new fiancé to work—driving him because she'd wrecked his car—while they were not speaking. He'd said she was being ridiculous to badger her mother into going away for the weekend with her bridge partner, said she'd managed to pick a fight with her mother on a terrible weekend. *Daph, you're creating friction with everybody.*

She tried to shake such distractions off as she peered at the man half-hidden in the carport. "Can I put my hands down?" With her arms overhead, her black T-shirt rode up. The low-rider jeans she'd worn in an effort to not stand out today the way Carhartts made her unique amongst all the jeans-clad people now left her belly exposed.

He stepped out of the carport, ignoring the tackle box he'd dropped. Crowned with thick gray hair, wearing loose blue jeans, a baggy flannel shirt, and a thin cotton coat, he looked about sixty, but the spring in his step made him appear younger. "Never told you to put 'em up. How'd you get my address?"

Daphne lowered her hands, put one toe on the note, and gave a weak smile. "A friend got it for me."

"Can you do better than that?"

"She works at a newspaper." *Nice fortitude,* she told herself. While not yet diming Thea out, she'd cave if the man questioned her harder.

He nodded, then shook his head and hooked his thumbs in his belt. "I know who you are. I remember the Suzanne Mayfield case. One of my few suspended cases. And she was my first."

"Suspended," Daphne said, mouthing the word, assessing its flavor as she bent to retrieve the note and pushed it deep into her right front pocket. Suspended described her family while they waited for news when Suzanne went missing, a state from which they'd never recovered, even with the discovery of the body.

Daphne recognized this permanent state of waiting as the demon that cloaked her and her parents throughout her remaining childhood and knew it had killed her father as much as the rope he'd brought to the hotel room.

She felt Seton's protracted consideration and wondered what he knew as he studied her. Struck by her category—the surviving sister of the murder victim in his first suspended case—Daphne fell silent.

Suzanne's life was suspended and so is mine.

"I hate that it was suspended," she said at last.

"So do I," came his immediate response.

"You guys thought maybe the guy she was seeing at the time did it." The thought made her father's voice play in her head. Remembering his bitter complaint—*that boy should be in jail*—put her mentally back in the jail cell, afraid to touch anything, wanting out of her cage. Yesterday. Just yesterday, she'd committed a crime, been jailed.

Tipping his head to one side, Arnold Seton looked at the high branches of hemlocks along his driveway, then over her head. "Do you have a boyfriend, a husband?"

She nodded. "Fiancé. Kind of." The word was newly personal and she was interested to try it out. Vic didn't know she'd gone into the park days ago to think about whether or not she could handle a future with him. He wanted to marry her.

Fiancé. It felt odd. Or did Vic not count as a fiancé since she hadn't yet responded to his proposal?

"If you were murdered, he's the first person detectives would look at."

"You're all that cynical?"

"That experienced."

"Seriously? It's like that?" When he nodded, she shook her head, but in defeat, not argument. "Was my sister's case the only one you never solved?"

"Please understand that numerous detectives, officers, and technicians are involved in an investigation as important as murder." He cleared his throat. "And we did our best, the very best we could."

"But . . ." Daphne chewed the inside of her lip, realizing questions would pour out of her mouth before she'd thought about them, before she identified what she wanted to know. She must not offend him or shut him down. She should know what she wanted. "But I mean . . . you said she was your first—"

"No, your sister's case was not the only one I failed to solve. Yes, it was my first . . . failure."

"Oh." Daphne grimaced, rolling her lips tight against her teeth. "In my sister's case, I mean, you probably don't remember it well enough to discuss it in detail. Even if you're willing to."

And please don't tell me you remember, but you won't discuss details because of some rule or confidentiality thing. She'd lost so much. A sister and a father. A decade and then another. Let no propriety block the balm of answers.

He rubbed his jaw and shifted his weight before saying, "I remember it pretty well. Murder scene never determined. Boyfriend acted hinky. Got himself thrown out of the funeral. Had a good alibi for the assumed night of the disappearance."

"Assumed?"

He shrugged. "We can't know, right? On the information we had, we didn't know exactly when your sister went missing."

Daphne nodded. "No, we didn't. Not the exact time."

He nodded. "Sometime in the afternoon, evening, night of, or next morning. It was a span of about twenty hours, if I recall." Then he added, "And I do."

"Do you remember talking to Ross Bouchard?"

"That the boyfriend's name?"

She nodded. "You interviewed him. He failed his polygraph."

Seton grunted and seemed lost in thought.

At last, Daphne said, "It wasn't him? You don't think he did it?"

"It could have been him, someone else she knew, or it could have been a stranger."

"The Green River killer was active back then," Daphne said, ready to show that while she hadn't been a part of the investigation as a child, she'd paid attention since adulthood. She'd looked up the old news articles and wondered. She'd prayed, like her father told her to.

"We thought about him, of course. But he was killing another woman that day."

"God," she said. Imagine the alibi: *I didn't murder her; I was busy murdering someone else.*

"Still there were a couple of other serial possibilities."

"Other serial killers?" The possibility seemed remote, and she shook her head.

"Yes." He nodded and studied her truck.

"Dear God," she said, feeling repulsed by his world. Under his silent, watchful look, she added, "Serial killers." The notoriety of it had occurred to her before, long ago. She'd been eleven and wondering who killed Suzanne. With the passing of decades, she came to realize it was a thing she might never know.

The not knowing, that was the killer.

"Don't you guys identify a serial killer's victims? Once you catch the bad guy?"

"No, not all, not always. There are other cases, like your sister's. Suspended cases, which means they're unsolved, in Seattle and outlying areas. Some of those killings are no doubt related. The Green River killer didn't corner the market on killing women."

Daphne shook her head again. "Well, there aren't that many serial killers, are there?"

"You'd be surprised."

"I've been surprised before," Daphne admitted, her voice worn. "But, serial killers? It's pretty rare, right?"

"Rare is a relative term. Most murders are not done by a serial killer. Many serial killers are never caught. At any point there are numerous active serial killers. Right now, there are several in process, I promise you."

"Seriously?"

"Welcome to the West."

"You mean . . ."

"We have more serial killers out here," he said.

Daphne shook her head. "But, I mean, but in my family, Suzanne . . . I never thought it was unsafe before she died. I've lived here all my life."

"Me, too."

"We have more killers than other areas?" Her voice sounded as small as she felt.

He nodded. "This coast is the capital for serial killers."

"Why?"

"Isolation's a factor."

"You mean, because there's more land out here? A lower population density?"

"I mean we have a bit higher divorce rate, a bit less religion, a bit less history in our communities. Less structure and other social support. People are more isolated from each other, from help."

"Loneliness," Daphne said.

"Yes, loneliness explains part of the problem. Our killers lack support growing up."

"Our killers," Daphne mumbled. Was this a stock resource every community had to some degree? Like, our industry? Our rivers? Our killers.

"And not just our killers. Our victims lack support, too. With fewer resources, being more on their own, they make better prey for our somewhat more common killer than is found in the Midwest, in the Northeast."

Prey. "I had no idea," Daphne said, shaking her head, shaking inside as his single word resonated. Prey. *Prey.*

Pray to God, her father said. Before he wanted vengeance, he sought prayers.

Arnold Seton shrugged and gave a wry smile, indicating something she couldn't decipher. That it wasn't her job to know? That she wasn't expected to understand, nor to do something about it?

He waved his arms, gesturing to include all points of the compass. "It's all linked. More death penalty sentences are handed out here than, say, in New England. Folks opposed to it say violence breeds violence but you are not talking to a guy who supports that theory. Violence often has to be responded to with violence, but chicken and egg arguments aren't too useful."

Uninterested in a death penalty debate, Daphne raised her hands in a gesture for peace and they stood in silence for a minute. Geese honked, out of place. The big birds shouldn't be here now. Water wasn't ready, the rivers icy with snowmelt.

"But I thought killers, I mean, a murderer . . . it's not usually a stranger, a random bad guy, right?"

"Well, most killings are done by someone known to the victim—"

"But when it's a stranger, like in my sister's case . . ." And she realized where she'd erred. "I mean, if it was a stranger who killed Suzanne, then why . . ."

He waved her speculation down. "It could make you crazy, trying to puzzle out the why. There are no good reasons. Movies would have you believe killers get into games with the police. Like we're playing chess with each other or something. Bad guy leaves little clues, maybe wants to get caught. Movies are full of nonsense. Bad guys don't want to get caught. And good guys, the regular citizens, they suffer Bystander Syndrome."

"Bystander Syndrome." She whispered the words with dread. "That's when someone doesn't help someone who needs help? A stranger?"

He hesitated. "It's . . . a collective response. When a group of bystanders see, say an accident, an altercation, something suspicious, but none of them move to help. They all think someone else will do something. Or should do something. Or someone else knows better what to do. And none of them moves a muscle."

"Bystander Syndrome." She sucked in a long breath, feeling gutted. He knew nothing more or new about Suzanne and her death. Of course he didn't. No one did. Conversation twenty years after the fact hollowed. Her mission failed. All she'd learned was there was a name for her inaction toward Minerva Watts in the Peace Park, and the West won the prize for the most serial killers.

Gravel crunched as Arnold Seton turned and retrieved his tackle box, then plucked a rod and reel from the carport wall, coming out with a smile as he waved it at her. "You fish?"

Daphne shook her head, not trusting her voice anymore.

"I'm a lunker," he said. "Spoons and bait. Don't get those fly fishermen. They say they're playing chess with the fish. That's giving a trout too much credit in my opinion."

She looked away from his tackle box. "That . . . syndrome . . ."

He raised his eyebrows, waited.

"Is there a name for it when there's one lone bystander?"

"You have"—he stopped, and raked his fingers through his hair in one slow motion—"you have something you want to tell me."

He wasn't asking, just stating the obvious, Daphne decided. But why not tell him about Minerva Watts? Arnold Seton wasn't Vic or Thea. He didn't know her and had no reason to push her into or away from getting involved.

And he'd been a cop for a long time.

"Do you have time to hear about this?" Daphne asked with a deep breath, checking for his nod. Then she launched into the whole deal, starting with seeing the old woman in the park Wednesday night and the couple hustling her away in a car. Vic's belated call to the police. The reassurances from the responding officer who said he'd put out a locate. And how, like Vic, the officer on Wednesday night thought the chance of there being a real problem was minuscule.

"And then that night, we walked back into the park and I remembered her name. Minerva Watts."

"Did you call that in to dispatch?"

"Yes," Daphne said, pleased when he nodded, like she'd just given the right answer on a pop quiz. "And the next day my friend who's with the newspaper, banged around on a bunch of websites or databases or something and found an address for Minerva Watts on Eastpark."

"And did you call that in to dispatch?"

She shook her head. "I went over there."

"To the lady's house? To this Minerva Watts's residence?"

Nodding, Daphne told him about those few minutes of her life. The hesitation. The odd, muted alarm that passed between the man and the woman. The sight of Minerva Watts inside, her face etched with barest fear. Her comment about the brooch. The other woman calling her *lady*, then *Mother*, then shouting for Guff.

"So he tells me to stand there and he grabs me. I kind of slipped out of my jacket—he was holding on to my sleeve—and I ran." She pointed a finger in the air, thinking it out. "When the policemen came the first time, I could hardly give them a thing, hardly describe the people I saw take the old lady—Mrs. Watts—or the car they drove. I couldn't even remember her name at the time, even though she'd told me her name a couple of hours before."

Seton shrugged. "That's normal. Quick description isn't something civilians get tasked with. I see you, I can spit into a radio 'white female adult, thirty-five, average size, brown hair pulled back, jeans and a black shirt.' But how often have you ever needed to immediately, succinctly, and accurately describe someone? Most people don't do description."

"I'll be thirty-two my next birthday."

"Close enough," he said with certainty. "My point is, civilians do not have to describe someone in a few words, in a manner that can let another cop hearing the description grab the target out of a crowd."

Daphne nodded. It made sense, everything this retired detective said made sense, but the words weren't a salve. Had she done everything for Minerva Watts? Had the police done everything for Suzanne? And how could anyone know? Maybe just one more question, one more option considered would have meant so much more, would have solved something. Maybe if she'd finagled an address earlier, then gone to Mrs. Watts's house Wednesday night instead of Thursday afternoon, things would be different. She wouldn't have ended up chasing after the Town Car.

What if the police had known Suzanne was missing a bit sooner? What if Daphne had reported how risky her sister ran, all the sneaking out and naughty things she did?

"Suzanne slept with one of her teachers once." Daphne's blurt surprised herself.

He rubbed his jaw again. "I don't recall if we had that detail. There's a cold case investigator at the department who should hear that from you."

"And something would happen? He'd investigate? Or he'd just write a little report with that little detail?" She heard the trace of bitterness in her voice and saw his lower jaw extend, set. She sniffed. "I've always wanted an explanation. I want to know who did it. And why."

"I get that. And I'm sorry." Seton set down his rod, balancing it with care against the carport. He faced Daphne with his thumbs hooked in his pockets. "Now, this deal over at the Watts residence—"

"He chased me," Daphne implored. She knew she sounded like a victim. She didn't want to be a victim. To not be chased, one just didn't run, right? But what if the feeling of menace told every fiber of her being to flee? "He chased me on foot."

"And then?"

"I got away." Now, she decided she sounded as nutty as Minerva Watts flailing in the Peace Park. *They're trying to kidnap me. They're trying to rob me.*

He pursed his lips, his glance flitting left and right, then checked his watch.

"I got arrested."

Seton cocked his head. "Not for running from that man you didn't."

"No. You see. I saw them leave . . ."

"While you were running?"

"While I was hiding. Then I followed their car and I caused an accident and got arrested for reckless driving."

There, she'd said it. She'd been wondering how to summarize the debacle for anyone else. Her mother? A lawyer, at some point?

"You were cited and released?"

"They took me away. I didn't have my driver's license with me by then because it was in my jacket and the guy who chased me got my jacket. My wallet and phone were in the pockets. The car was my boyfriend's, but it's in his dad's name and I forgot about that and I guess maybe I looked or sounded—"

"More than a little suspicious."

She nodded, glum. "I guess."

He folded his arms across his chest. "Tell me, why did you want to talk to me?"

"Because of my sister." Daphne heard the plaintive tone she used and squeezed her eyes shut. "It . . . just wasn't . . . enough. We never knew who or why or anything. I never understood. It never ended and it never got better."

"You mean because we never made an arrest."

"Yes. Sure. And, I mean, if you'd caught the guy—" Daphne opened her hands in front of him, looking for agreement. "It was probably a guy, right?"

He nodded, waiting with his lips pressed together.

"If you'd caught the guy, wouldn't you have gotten some information from him? Wouldn't we have gotten to know what happened? More or less? When and how? Where it happened. And why? Just, why?"

His shoulders softened as he exhaled and his tight grimace became sympathetic. "You know, when we go to the homicide unit, we get all kinds of training. From the best. And it's scary what we know about why twisted people perpetrate heinous crimes. Astounding what we can discern from analyzing the crime scene. One who's organized, one who's disorganized. Links. Quirks of the killer. A killer who knew the victim, one who didn't. One who feels bad about himself. It's scary. But it's also scary . . . what we don't know."

"I don't know why I had to lose my sister. She was so . . . great."

He gave the gentlest smile and a little commiserating nod. Probably he did that for every grieving family member he came across, Daphne thought. But he couldn't do more. He couldn't answer the unanswerable questions.

She swallowed. "I've taken up enough of your time. More than enough. Thanks very much for talking to me. I apologize for coming, even. I won't bother you again."

He heard all this without expression. If he'd been ready to admonish her, he'd changed his mind and instead walked the driveway to her car, holding her truck door when she opened it.

"There were," he said, "unanswered questions."

"Besides who killed her? And why?"

He studied Daphne. "*Why* is not a question with an answer that could satisfy you or any other reasonable person. There isn't and never will be a good answer to: For what reason was your sister murdered? Now, I hate that we didn't get a case built on anyone, but that is the way it goes sometimes. Otherwise, we'd be expecting that every single time we could point a finger at someone, say 'he did it,' we could know and be satisfied that we got that far. That would be perfection. Perfection doesn't exist. You had the misfortune to lose your sister through a senseless murder, then to be one of the families stuck with a suspended, cold case."

Daphne wiped her eyes. Railing about leads not discovered hadn't gotten her dad anywhere.

"I wish my father had come to see you years ago."

He twisted his mouth. "I talked to your father a lot. I remember your folks, remember dealing with them. See, when a case starts to go cold, we'll search the victim's bedroom. That's intrusive to the family. Lots of people get offended. They'll say we should be out catching the killer instead of sifting through the victim's personal things. They ask what we're looking for, but we can't say because we don't know. We're looking for anything. We want a name, a number, an address, anything, any clue when a case starts running dry. Anyway, I remember when we did that search." He smiled and nodded. "Spent a couple hours poking around and drinking your mother's coffee. She baked us cookies."

"You searched . . ." Daphne felt her face contort as she pictured her mother handling the situation twenty years ago. The best of intentions, complete misunderstanding. *Precleaning?* "You searched my bedroom."

One hand covered her mouth and Daphne turned away and refused, refused to cry as she pictured her mother stacking all of Suzanne's papers and notebooks, all the scraps with phone numbers or addresses. The fliers for raves. Everything paper in Suzanne's world. The poems and essays. *I've tidied your room, even the closet*, her mom had said when Daphne came home from school one day. And their closet, the closet she shared with a just-murdered sister, soon had a sealed cardboard box.

Oh, Mom. What did you do?

CHAPTER 15

Daphne felt herself wither under Arnold Seton's careful surveillance of her reaction.

He nodded. "That's right. Shared bedroom. But you weren't there that day. And your father was at work, but he knew we were going to be there. That search is pretty standard when a case isn't developing, see. Your folks got it, is what I'm saying. They didn't make the investigation—the search—harder, like some victims' families do. They let us search the girls'—your and your sister's—bedroom, flip the mattresses, everything."

She'd been eleven and not known. Her mother had been a housewife and not understood. Daphne pictured her mother in an apron, sanitizing the girls' room in advance of the police search of her daughters' bedroom, her good little girl and her murdered wild child. Frances Mayfield had boxed up Suzanne's naughty poetry and other papers.

"My mom didn't get it, I mean, Suzanne, see . . ." Daphne faltered as she concentrated on winning her battle to not cry in front of the detective.

Arnold Seton smiled. "Your folks, they're good people. I talked to your father more than your mother. He was the one wanting constant updates, asking about leads. He was real involved, kept checking in with me. He'd call me every six months or so, right up until I retired back in, let's see, I just started my eleventh year. Suspended cases go to the cold case guys when you retire."

"He . . . um, my father . . ."

The detective nodded. "Real involved."

"You retired ten years ago." Storm clouds threatened to rupture in her mind.

"I can't believe I've been retired that long. But yeah, ten years and a week now." He grinned and pushed his thick gray hair back, assuming a more somber expression. "I can't help you more. The cold case investigators are who you and your folks should talk to about your sister's case."

Tears formed as Daphne studied the soil. She stymied a wail. So. So, he didn't know about her father's suicide, didn't know how much hope her dad had lost when Detective Seton told him he was retiring and the suspended case would go join other dead cases. She opened her mouth, closed it. Did the man need to know another sad thing, another piece of loss stemming from his first unsolved homicide?

"What?" he asked.

No. Here was a gift she could give him. Daphne shook her head. "Thanks for talking to me."

He nodded. But after she sat in her truck's driver's seat and he backed up a few steps, he called out, "Your sister had a friend. I don't remember her name right off the top of my head, but she's the one who first noticed your sister was missing. Your sister wasn't reported missing for not showing up in class—"

"It was Christmas vacation," Daphne said. "The semester had just ended. Suzanne wasn't at the college, she was home."

"But not home that night, right?" he said, squinting as he recalled the details. "This friend had called your folks, wanting to talk to

Suzanne, was the one who first reported your sister missing. We always go back to the beginning, to the person who reports."

"Lindsay!" The name was out of Daphne's mouth before the thought coalesced. Lindsay . . . Lindsay Something. Daphne hadn't thought of Suzanne's best friend by name in years and years.

"Did you or your parents lose contact or did you stay in touch with her?"

"No. No, we . . ." Daphne's voice trailed. "We lost contact."

—∽∽—

An hour crept by in traffic as Daphne drove back from Arnold Seton's house. Almost two hours ached away while she stood in line at the Department of Licensing to get her driver's license replaced. Time slipped through her fingers like sand.

Downtown, she searched for a parking space near a building of smoked glass planked in brown stucco. She pushed through glass doors emblazoned with *The Seattle Times*. A woman at the front counter looked up and Daphne asked for Thea.

When the staffer said she'd check to see if Ms. Roosevelt was available, Daphne considered how Thea had befriended her at college. Other girls at the dorm had tried with too direct an approach, been pseudo-engaging. Daphne was the girl whose sister had attended the university and been killed during Christmas break.

Some of the old newspaper articles she'd read in grade school and high school detailed how the university offered grief counselors and held a memorial for Suzanne. Her English class had a poetry reading in her name. Another class planted a tree on campus with a plaque announcing Suzanne Mayfield would be remembered in their hearts forever. Daphne shrank from the curious who were drawn to the notoriety of murder, and she hated her minicelebrity status born of having a dead sister.

"Ms. Mayfield, Ms. Roosevelt will be out in a few minutes."

Nodding, Daphne snapped back from the reverie. There was plenty to worry about without dragging the past around with her. One unsettled and fresh issue niggling her thoughts was Vic's proposal and her own reaction.

Other moments deserved reflection, and Daphne had pushed them away. Back when Daphne got her union card and her first set of construction tools had early wear, she recalled Thea showing off her press credentials, saying she'd earned her wings. Thea had cut herself off from further boasting, as though it were unseemly or too professional, in light of the blue collar direction Daphne had taken. The moment had crystallized in time, a recollection Daphne could reexamine whenever she chose.

She'd always chosen not to study the moment.

Thea flung herself into the lobby, a wad of papers in one hand.

"Hey, you!" Her one-armed hug came without hesitation, and her voice was high enough to make the front counter woman gawk. "I'm doing a million things at once. What's up?"

"Hey," Daphne said. "I . . . wanted to see you."

"Let's go back," Thea said, nodding them through a doorway.

A few cubicle walls divided the vast open office beyond. Desks crammed with computers and files covered the floor. The walls were covered in newspapers, sections flopped over wall after wall. In every cranny, shredders, waste bins, and computer towers occupied floor space. A sign suspended over one set of tables read *News Desk*.

Breezing through the first open office, they passed a glassed-in conference room. The polished table within was huge, almost square, and held the majority of the sizable room. Thea strode on, past a corridor sign for the office's childcare area, past painted walls, vending machines, and people talking into headsets.

"I saw that detective," Daphne said in a low voice when Thea swooped around two corners and stopped at another desk piled with papers and folders.

"So, this is about Suzanne," Thea said.

"Everything's about Suzanne." Daphne shook her head, bringing a hand to her mouth. "I don't know why I said that."

Thea took a breath. "Even before, I mean . . . before she went away to college, you must have had questions about her."

"When she went away to college, I realized how much I missed her," Daphne snapped then winced. "I just mean, I never got answers. I was a kid and I didn't know who or what to ask. So I never did."

"And now you're asking. What are you actually asking?"

"Everything. I want an explanation. Explanations."

Thea pursed her lips. "And you don't want to let things go . . ."

Daphne spread her hands. "That's what Vic says. You sound just like him."

"I definitely don't sound like Vic."

"Last night, he was all after me to stop—what did he say? Tilting at windmills. And he proposed—"

"He can't stop you from checking on anything," Thea said, her voice severe. "How does he propose to do that anyway?"

Daphne opened her mouth, then shut down her automatic response, thinking hard. Looking down, she mumbled about the threatening phone message they'd discovered after Thea left the house the day before.

Thea raised her eyebrows and shrugged. "Weird. But maybe it was a wrong number."

"Right." Daphne told her about the police officer taking Daphne to the other side of the Peace Park, knocking on doors, discovering almost nothing.

"Look, Daphne—and I'm not trying to be mean here—picture your mother being older and forgetting things, not making sense, not understanding things. Fading out like you say Vic's dad does. And you have to pack up her stuff and move her. And she tells people you're not her daughter and you're kidnapping her. Can't you picture that happening?"

"Minerva Watts sold her car. And the car I followed isn't her car, isn't the one that's usually there." Daphne looked at Thea with hope, wishing the reporter's instincts would kick in and crucial questions would follow.

Thea shook her head. "I can't believe they actually did a neighborhood canvass for you."

"A what?"

"I can't believe they actually knocked on the neighbors' doors and asked questions just because some crazy lady spouted off nonsense."

"She's not crazy just because she's old. And dementia isn't the same thing anyway. It's not even the same thing as Alzheimer's." Daphne folded her arms across her chest.

Thea gave a withering roll of the eyes. "Hello? Crazy lady wasn't in reference to the old lady. You. *You* are the crazy lady."

"Ah. Helpful. Thanks." Daphne didn't try to hide her annoyance as she struggled to recall why she'd come to see Thea. The retired detective's parting words came back. Go back to the beginning. "What do you know about the cold case investigators at the Seattle Police Department?"

"I know," Thea's voice softened, "that they have a few cases they're working on out of a bunch they're not. On most cold cases, they have nothing to go on, but at some point every one of those cases was reviewed by their unit, step-by-step. And all their cases are reviewed at regular intervals."

There was more, Daphne could tell. "Right. M'kay, and . . . ?"

"And I know that your sister's case is not in their working pile. I checked. I'm sorry that's the way it is, but they have nothing."

Daphne felt her chin crumple and she rolled her lips in to keep herself together, until she managed to say, "That retired detective—"

"Who does not know how you found him?"

"N-n-no, not quite."

"Oh, Christ, Daphne. You are not cut out for this."

Daphne set her jaw. "No, I'm not. I never was. And that's fine with me."

Thea's gaze drifted down to her desk, flitting to files, Post-its, the computer screen with its open documents.

"Thee, find a woman named Lindsay for me. I don't know her last name but she went to school with Suzanne."

"No."

"What?"

"You heard me. No. As in, no, Daphne. *Daph*." Thea's last word blasted with sarcasm.

Feeling a flush rise, Daphne wondered what Thea based her decision on. Because Thea already talked to the cold case investigators? Because Daphne made Thea's name one syllable? "Thea," she said. "Seriously. Her name was Lindsay and she's the one who first reported Suzanne missing."

Thea stuck her fingers in her ears. "No. I won't do it."

"Come on. You could do it in a flash. It's just a little thing that retired cop mentioned. I want to ask this Lindsay . . . I just want to talk to her."

Thea cocked her head back, reeking offense. "Don't you think I have better things to do?"

"Look, Thea, what's the best-case scenario here?" Daphne asked, working it out one more time for herself: to have made the full effort or not. "And the worst?"

"Christ, Daphne. Fuck off, okay? Stop being self-important and melodramatic. Go ask for a deferred prosecution on your reckless charge and quit interfering and creating havoc. There's nothing here. Not with your sister's old case, not with the old lady thing. There's nothing—"

"Wait a minute. Yesterday, you were reading old articles on Suzanne's case. You had them in your car. What were you looking for?"

"Anything. But there isn't anything there. We have the old police reports. I looked at everything. I read all the old stories. This is a cul-de-sac. There's nothing."

"When I asked you to find a way to contact Minerva Watts, you did it in minutes. You're great at finding people."

"That was about your little old lady thing, not your sister from twenty years ago."

"No one on the planet has something better to do than to help a little old lady. She told me she was being robbed and kidnapped and—"

"And she wasn't."

CHAPTER 16

Huddled in her truck in the Weather Service parking lot, Daphne looked at Lake Washington through tears, her fingers hooked on the steering wheel. She sagged, dropping her face into the cradle of her elbows, and shook in silence. It was an amateur's bawling, a noncrier's cry. But her body convulsed on and on until the sobs wracking her became wet and noisy. She wanted to turn them off, turn off the world and its confusion.

Metal groaned and cool air rushed into the truck. A man had opened her door, put his hands on her body. She gasped in fleeting terror.

"Hey. Hey?" Vic stroked her hair. "What is it? Did you see that detective? Did he—"

He stopped as she waved him off. His quick compassion and peppered questions agitated her, but she recovered enough to say, "I had a fight with Thea."

He massaged her biceps. "Well, I'm assuming you won. Is she in the hospital? Is she alive?"

"Vic . . ."

His smile evaporated. "Call her. Apologize. Now, not later. Patch it up. You two have been friends for a long time. Keep it that way."

Daphne banged her forehead on the steering wheel, then looked up at him with a grim smile that fell as soon as she saw his considered expression.

His face torqued as he twisted his lips to one side and squinted. "It's not the only thing bothering you. I know this weekend marks a couple of lousy anniversaries. I know you're upset about that little old lady. And if I were in your shoes, I might have a good cry myself." He checked his watch. "We have time before I go get the kids. Let's get a bite to eat somewhere."

"But we have to get your car out of impound, figure out how much work it needs, where to take it. And I still have to get my wallet thing sorted out. I went to DMV and got a new license earlier. I canceled my credit cards, but that will make it harder to deal with the cell phone thing. I have to shut off the old one, get a new one. If we need to rent a car—"

"Can we handle one thing at a time, please?" he asked.

"Sure. Sure." Daphne sniffed. "I'm trying to decide where to start."

"Start with what's bothering you the most. What is it? Your family? Us? This fight you had with Thea? Do you want to tell me about it? What do you want to do? You're pretty agitated of late, Daph, and it's not like you."

Daphne couldn't make herself work through it, just one thing. And when she told Vic details about her fight with Thea, he shook his head and said, "I think I'm with Thea on this one."

"What? No! No, you're with me. You have to be. Hey, you asked me to marry you."

"You . . . didn't say yes."

She opened her mouth and shut it. Then she closed her eyes, opening them when tears would have leaked out if she didn't make way.

Vic massaged her shoulder while he waited for a response. Finally, he asked, "Did you see that retired detective?"

Daphne nodded and sniffed. "Now I want to find Suzanne's best friend. She was the one who first reported Suzanne missing."

He rubbed his jaw. "So, it went okay with the detective? It was fine?"

She sprung her fingers from the steering wheel in annoyance. "Yes, it was fine. It was great. My dad killed himself because he lost hope when the detective retired ten years ago. It was fantastic."

Bawling rocked her shoulders for a long time. Vic said nothing, one palm on her head, the other arm around her body, soft kisses into her hair. He knelt on the pavement, leaning into the truck while he caressed her.

His position couldn't be comfortable, she realized, working harder to quit crying.

When she could talk, Daphne made her voice slow and clear. "The retired detective mentioned her, this girl, Lindsay. So I want to find her."

"Do you recall her last name?"

"No."

"Do you remember where her family lived? Would your mother perhaps be in touch with her? You've said your mom saved Suzanne's old stuff. Do you think the girl's old contact information might be there? A childhood phone number or address might still be her parents' place. Or hers, even." He gave a self-deprecating grin. "Some people still live in the house where they grew up."

"If she's moved—and she probably has—then her old information won't put me in touch with her. She may have gotten married, changed her last name, but I don't even remember what her last name was back then. I don't know where to begin."

"Alumnus records," Vic said. "Did Lindsay graduate?"

"I don't know. Probably. I didn't."

He smiled and rubbed her neck. "Well, you can if you want to. Entirely up to you. Always was. But since you're not an alumna . . ."

"And Thea's the only graduate I know from Western Washington U."

"Oh, I see," Vic said, his gaze slung sideways as always when he was lost in thought. "Maybe the University office won't be obstinate. They might give you contact info on her right over the phone even though you aren't an alumna."

"Will you help me?"

He left her side and paced around the front of her truck, tapping the hood with a finger, and asking as he circled, "Is all this, in truth, about Suzanne?"

She glared at him through the windshield, then the passenger's window, glad for the excuse to raise her voice. "Neither, Vic. One's got nothing to do with the other."

He opened the truck's passenger's side and sank to the bench seat. "I don't believe that," he said, shutting the door too hard.

—◆◆◆—

The impound yard, within a vast, slatted, chain-link compound, appeared to be part compressed parking lot, part wrecking yard. Beyond the small booth at the entry driveway, flatbeds and standard-hooking tow trucks rumbled at the ready or jockeyed about, lowering impounded vehicles into position. Vic stared like a little boy fascinated with big trucks.

"I'd no idea what it was like here," he marveled, as they identified themselves to a man in a stained undershirt at the security booth. They shouted to be heard over the lot supervisor's crackling radio and an idling diesel tow truck behind him.

"And you have no idea what it was like being in Gitmo," she said, pulling her pickup over to park in the dust where the lot boss sent them.

Vic blinked. "No, I don't. Tell me, what was it like, your hour in jail?"

Instead of answering, she pointed down a row of impounded cars to a sad new version of Vic's old Honda. Crumpled fenders, missing bits of plastic in the grille and lights, with damage to the rear and right quarter panel as well. His vehicle looked forlorn amid the other impounds, some nice, some nasty. All pushed into tight rows as though they'd lost their eligibility to hold premium space in Normal Vehicle World, where cars are allotted an eight-foot-wide lane each.

Peering into the Honda's backseat, surprise and relief flushed through with the sight of her coil nailer and loaded tool belt on the seat. She grabbed her tools and stowed them under her truck canopy.

"It might be drivable once the parts hanging onto the front tire are pushed away." She tried not to look at Vic's face, warned herself not to, and then looked.

His jaw worked, the muscles in the side of his face bopping. Standing at the Honda's front bumper, Vic pulled off his glasses and rubbed the bridge of his nose, as though he found it a toss-up between eyeing the mess or squinting to examine the wreck with poor vision.

"Who's the only person you know who has gloves in her glove box?" Daphne said. But Vic wouldn't play, his usual easy countenance lost.

She went back to her truck and returned, pulling on leather work gloves, then yanking detritus off the Honda's left front wheel. Parts of the plastic broke but she couldn't manually clear away the stiff, wrenched fender. Fetching back to her truck, Daphne pulled her shingler's hammer from her tool belt.

While Vic stood in silence, Daphne hacked the remaining obstructive plastic off the Honda with her hammer's adze. "There." She opened her truck's topper and threw the broken bits of car body into the bed.

Vic stood, gloomy, staring at his car. It had been his father's. He wasn't sentimental about possessions, but he took care of things, made them last. And his budget had been tight ever since Cassandra threw him out of their marriage and he'd moved back home. Soon after, his father had to be placed in the care facility, straining Vic's finances to the near-breaking point.

Daphne felt guilty in her relative wealth. Flipping the heavy hammer in a lazy arc, she caught it when the blue cushioned handle spun opposite the forged head. It was a good hammer, a great one. She'd had it close to a decade. The toothed, gripping face was milled, forming one solid piece within the steel handle. A thumbscrew let her slide a thin cutting blade along the adze for fine work, and the adze could hatchet away serious material. The handle was coated in a special, shock-absorbing synthetic grip. The label advised users to always wear safety goggles when using a shingler's hammer but Daphne never heeded the warning.

"And the window's gone," Vic said.

"Yeah." Daphne looked away. On the next row, a tow truck driver angled a red convertible into an impound slot beside a navy Lincoln Town Car.

The navy Lincoln Town Car? She stared across the row of disparate vehicles.

Could that be the Lincoln Town Car she'd chased? Lowering her hammer, Daphne fit herself sideways past the Honda and the car behind it, then down the aisle, ignoring the tow truck driver's wave for her to not stand so close while he worked the convertible into a space.

"Hey, you need to move away." The shout came from behind her. The lot boss had left his security booth to flag Daphne down.

She took one giant step back, appreciating the improved view of the big navy blue sedan as the tow truck driver stepped out, glared at her, and worked handles on his truck bed to lower the convertible's front end.

The Lincoln Town Car had no license plate, but Daphne wondered if it had carried one starting with a *Y*. She pictured the man, Guff, driving the Lincoln. Driving too fast. She pictured the woman in the back, one hand holding Minerva Watts, the other gripping Daphne's Carhartt jacket.

The tow truck driver released his hook from the convertible's undercarriage and pushed a lever on his truck, winding his cable back up. Giving Daphne a snarling glance, he handed papers to the lot boss.

"Hot," said the driver, pointing to the convertible.

The man running the impound yard nodded, looking at the paperwork. "Yeah, dude, heard that. Just like the one it's next to."

Daphne looked from one man to the other. "That car's stolen?"

"You like that red rocket?" the tow truck driver asked. "It'd look good on you."

She shook her head. "The other one."

"The Town Car?" the lot boss asked. Surprise showed in his voice over which car attracted her interest.

"It doesn't have license plates," Daphne said.

The lot boss nodded. "It's stolen from out of state. The cop took the plates when he had it hooked yesterday. Plates were stolen, too."

"Wait," Daphne said, looking from one man to the other. The tow driver rolled his eyes and climbed into his tow truck. "That car's stolen and it had stolen license plates on it? I might know that car."

The lot boss raised an eyebrow and grinned. "You been in it? Been driving it? Bet that cop would like to talk to you."

"What cop?" she asked.

"The one who called to impound that Lincoln from The Ave yesterday."

The Ave, in the University District. Her dread of the traffic when she chased the Lincoln out of Minerva Watts's neighborhood toward the U District returned with a fresh tingle. When she beckoned for more, the man shrugged again, waving a hand as his explanation poured forth.

"The most interesting thing in the cop's day was a stolen car. He was all proud for checking it out right. Abandoned car, parked along the curb too long. Plate matched the make, model, and color, but he ran the VIN and bingo, hot car out of California wearing a stolen Washington plate from a similar car."

"I wasn't driving it, I followed it. If it's the same one anyway," Daphne said, feeling the lot boss's gaze on her. "Yesterday. The guy driving it stole my jacket. Was there a brown canvas jacket inside? It had my phone and wallet in the pockets."

The lot man shook his head.

"Can I look?" Daphne sidled over to the car to peek into the windows. A few paper napkins lay crumpled on the back seat. She walked all the way around the car. Was it the same one? She could picture the couple seated inside, Minerva Watts beside the woman in the back seat. But how could she know it was the same car? She turned to the lot boss. "Did you look in the trunk?"

He shook his head. "No keys. Guy's bringing 'em."

She brightened. "Now? The owner's coming here?"

"Nah," he said. "This poor dude in the Midwest somewhere. He gave me a sad story about his mother in California dying and he finds out she signed over all her savings, her pension fund, her house, everything, to some stupid charity right before she died. The car's the only thing he'll get out of her estate and only because he was already on the title as an *and*."

Daphne squinted at him. "What?"

"You know, Joe-*and*-Jane, instead of Joe-*or*-Jane. When a title shows a person *or* another person, then either one can sell it, but when it shows one person *and* another person, then both people have to sign to sell it."

"Oh." She looked across the cars toward Vic, on his phone.

"Yeah. Dude's calling here, telling me it wasn't the money—guess he'd figured he was going to get some inheritance, his mother had a nice place and funds stashed away—he was just so surprised. Dude's mother was something like ninety years old and never said anything about this charity before. And to top it off, the dude can't get in touch with these nonprofit folks, like it's already belly-up or something."

"Meaning, if his name wasn't on the title, the charity would have gotten the car, too?" she asked.

The lot man nodded. "Stinking charity cleaned out the guy's mother and she dies and then her car's stolen. What luck. I guess the Seattle Police contacted him about the car. He was calling here before it even made it to the yard. Told me the whole story."

Minerva Watts's voice pierced Daphne's memory.

They're trying to steal my house and all my money. And my car.

She pictured the lavender pantsuit and tan raincoat, heard the pleas for help in the Peace Park. And then Daphne thought of them putting the lady into a car—Mrs. Watts's own car, probably—and imagined the couple taking her to a Ford dealership, quick-selling the car below wholesale price. She stared across the row of cars at Vic. He was too far away for her to read his expression, but she watched him fold his arms across his chest.

When she waved him over, Vic looked over then back at his car.

"Sad story," the lot boss said. "I've heard this kind of thing—folks preying on old folks, wrangling what they can out of them, selling them some song and dance."

Daphne gulped and felt herself go cold. "Vic!" She turned toward the Honda again, but Vic was just a few strides away.

"I think the insurance company will require me to get several estimates," he said. "I hope they don't total it. It's an old car and they might not find it worth fixing. But it starts. The damage might be all cosmetic."

She stared into the Lincoln and pictured the car evading her, making it through the traffic light, Minerva Watts worried in the backseat, boxes of her things—including her grandmother Miller's brooch—in the trunk.

"What is it, Daph?"

Pointing to the Lincoln, she explained how it was identical to the car those people had used to take Minerva Watts and her things away from her house. It probably *was* the Lincoln she'd chased. She told him it was owned by a recently deceased old woman in California who signed over her bank accounts and house to a charity that then went defunct. And the car was stolen.

He raked a hand through his hair and twisted to look back at his Honda.

"Couldn't . . . I mean. Just suppose . . ." Daphne snapped her mouth shut. No. No way. Not possible, and not her business anyway. Had she been overreacting all this time, about everything regarding Mrs. Watts. But . . . what if?

"Couldn't . . . ," she tried again, but faltered as her thoughts ran wild.

"Couldn't?" Vic half-encouraged, half-teased.

"Couldn't there be a connection?"

"Between what and what?" he asked.

"Whatever's going on with Minerva Watts and whatever happened in California."

Vic pursed his lips. "It seems far-fetched. But . . . possible. Worst-case scenario."

Daphne nodded, insistent. "The wrong license plate was on it. The plate was stolen off a similar car. This car was stolen in California," she said, pointing to papers in the lot boss's hand.

"Where was it impounded from?" Vic asked.

The lot manager looked at his paperwork and gave them an intersection.

—∿—

Crunched outside, airbags blown, the Honda was ugly but still drivable. Daphne pressured Vic for all she was worth, pushing until he agreed to drop the car off at the best body shop he knew of, right away. When he protested about insurance and getting estimates, she brushed his arguments away.

"My accident, my fault. I'm paying for it."

When they pulled into the body shop parking lot, he hesitated again. "You shouldn't pay for it out of your pocket. This is what insurance is for. We should just go through the procedure, see what the insurance company wants to do."

"I'll get your car fixed. I want it fixed. I don't want this to drag out. Please. I don't want problems dragging on and on. I want to get clear."

The body shop attendant waited with paperwork on a clipboard. Vic nodded at the man, then pulled his phone from his belt clip and handed it to Daphne.

"What?"

"Don't you want to call Thea?"

"Oh." She flipped his phone on, wishing it were a smartphone so she could Google. Rolling her lips in, closing her eyes, she walked away from Vic as he signed papers. Back in her truck, Daphne dialed, trying to summon what to say when Thea answered.

"Hello?" Thea's voice held the reserve expected for a call from Vic's phone.

"It's Daphne. I—"

"Hey, you! I wanted to tell you I'm sorry for bitching you out earlier, I—"

"Oh, stop," Daphne said. "I'm sorry for being everything you said I was being. I felt pushed and pulled and I think of things being fine and things being catastrophic and I don't know what's what, so . . . wait, I think I'm not apologizing very well. But, Thea, I'm so sor—"

"Done," Thea said. "And I have a possible address on Lindsay Wallach for you."

"Wallach." Daphne sucked in her breath and closed her eyes. The last name sounded distantly familiar now that she heard it again. "Now I'm going to find Ross Bouchard. You could do it faster. I won't have computer access until I get home. Would you find him for me?"

"Oh, fuck it, Daphne."

"Well . . . I might as well finish, right?"

"I found this Lindsay woman. I found the Watts woman. You get one person a day out of me."

Daphne drummed her fingers on the phone and slumped in her pickup's seat. "But you could find him?"

"Now you're wanting me to show off," Thea said, her voice demure.

"You're always showing off." Daphne felt a weight drop, just a small one, but the load was lightened as she scribbled down an address for Lindsay Wallach, thanked Thea, and hung up.

Vic slid onto the passenger's seat, studying paperwork from the body shop.

"I'm going to find Ross Bouchard," she told him. "I'm going to talk to that boy myself."

"Ross Bouchard," he said. "The guy some people thought killed your sister."

She nodded.

"Then I'm going with you. No argument this time."

Daphne smiled and let him take her palm in his. "I don't have a way to contact him yet."

"Yet?"

"But I will." She offered her most satisfied smile.

Vic guessed. "Thea?"

She nodded. "And she gave me an address on Lindsay Wallach. There's enough time to go right now."

—ᴍ—

Baskets of bleeding hearts and other flowers lined the porch of the tiny trailer house. There was no answer to Vic's knock or to Daphne pushing the bell button. She tried to not feel pressured by his glancing at his watch, knowing she'd pressured him to make this quick trip to Lindsay Wallach's house right away. He had to collect his kids for the weekend.

Daphne looked at her truck and wondered about leaving a note. She knocked on the thin aluminum door again. Vic tapped his watch with one finger. A melodic voice rose with the rushing-air sound of wind in the evergreens.

"There's someone out back," Daphne said, stepping off the porch and striding for the corner before he could protest.

She didn't see the woman, not right away. She saw the weathered slab of plywood hanging on the trailer at the edge of the back deck. On the railing beneath the board, spent candlewicks jutted from puddles of cold, long-melted wax. Numerous faded items curled to the pins tacking them to the plywood—a rustic version of a bulletin board. In one corner dangled a faded purple and gold high school graduation tassel. Old photographs—of a beautiful young woman with feathers in her hair, wearing secondhand clothes—bubbled and delaminated the wood. Notes and cards, close to illegible with age, were tucked above spent candles.

"Can I help you?" the singsong voice called out from behind apple trees. The woman kinked a hose and the sound of water gushing stopped. "I didn't hear you come up."

"Lindsay Wallach?" Daphne's voice shook and she stared at the board instead of the woman she was addressing, too stricken to say anything more.

The plywood hung under the trailer's eave but showed years and years of weathering. The keepsakes had faded with their secret message, but the ghostly photographs of her sister's likeness in the few years after high school graduation were already etched in Daphne's memories. She didn't know why the board was here, but she knew what she was looking at.

The board was a shrine to her dead sister.

CHAPTER 17

Staring hard at the tattered notes to and about Suzanne, Daphne knew Vic stared hard at her, knew he could see her pure trepidation and shaking hands. When she stayed voiceless, he told Lindsay Wallach who they were and accepted two glasses of water, served on the back deck because they were not invited inside.

"What happened at the funeral?" Vic asked.

Lindsay Wallach shot him a shocked look. "What?"

Daphne looked toward the board. *The board, Vic.* But she understood him. He'd always raised his eyebrows over what he termed the bad scene of Ross Bouchard being hauled out of Suzanne's funeral after making a spectacle.

Vic shifted uncomfortably and said to Lindsay, "You were there, weren't you?"

"At . . . *Suzanne's* funeral? What, twenty years ago?"

Vic nodded and Daphne stayed mute, thinking about the retired homicide detective and his little nudge in this direction. *She's the one who first realized your sister was missing.*

"At the funeral," Vic asked again, "what really happened?"

When Lindsay threw Daphne a puzzled look, as though to point out that Daphne had, after all, been there for the entire service, Vic said, "She was just a kid at the time. I've heard a bit about it. What's the deal? Ross Bouchard was escorted out. What happened?"

Lindsay winced at the Bouchard name. Daphne gazed at Lindsay's face, watched her eyes close to avoid the stare.

"Ross sang," Lindsay said, her gaze shifting from Vic to Daphne and back again.

Vic eyed Daphne. She'd told him many times about the singing, about the congregation's gasps over the weird words the boy had wailed at the altar.

"It was just a tribute to Suzanne. An old Cohen song that just fit her. And him. And it was, the whole thing, a boy with a guitar, him singing about loving her . . . well, it was too hippie for that stuffed-shirt church. And Ross was broken up, half-crying so he was kind of talking the lyrics, and he came off pretty weird." Lindsay looked at the shrine and back again. "Why? Why are you asking now? What in the world brings you out here today? After all these years?"

Mute, Daphne looked again at the board and its faded mementos of Suzanne. She felt Lindsay's gaze follow hers, heard Vic clear his throat.

"Saturday," he said, "tomorrow, is the anniversary of Daphne's father's suicide."

"Oh, I-I didn't know," Lindsay said, her voice a soft, pained gasp. "You, your dad, your poor family. Some people get more than their share. That's terrible. When did he . . . ?"

Daphne still couldn't speak. Vic looked at her, nodded, and told Lindsay, "It's been a while."

"Well," she said. "I'm sorry he died. Sorry he did that. Old news, apparently, but I didn't know. The poor guy. You poor girl, Daphne."

Daphne remembered sparing the retired detective this detail, wondering about her own character that she'd liked it a second ago when Vic dropped it on Lindsay, foisted bad news on Suzanne's old friend.

"Tomorrow, huh?" Lindsay asked.

"Yes, tomorrow." Daphne's voice was measured, careful. But she couldn't last, her voice breaking as she asked, "Do you know what day Sunday is?"

Lindsay glanced at Vic who watched Daphne then folded his arms across his chest and told Lindsay, "It's Suzanne's birthday."

"Oh . . ." Lindsay exhaled. "I always think of the anniversary of, I mean, I remember Suzanne more in December . . ."

"When she died," Daphne sniffed.

"Yes." Lindsay faltered, seeming lost in thought.

"Why do you have that board over there?" Daphne asked at last, pointing to it now without looking at it. Satisfying Vic's curiosity was not the same as satisfying her own. What he had wanted to know all along, and what she wanted to know since they'd arrived, were in different directions, past and present.

Lindsay opened her mouth, hesitated, then said, "I don't. I mean, I just didn't ever take it down. It's been there a long, long time."

Daphne felt herself soften and she wished the sun would stay on them, but the sky clouded. She wanted, needed, warmth.

Twenty years ago, she was my sister's best friend.

"Can I use your bathroom?" Daphne asked, her voice hoarse.

Lindsay waved toward the door. "On your right as you go inside." Daphne stepped inside but heard Lindsay say to Vic, "So . . . her father's death still affects her."

His soft response was immediate, clear to Daphne because she'd heard him say the same words only yesterday. "Her sister's death more."

She found the bathroom, a tiny thing with a triangular shower crammed next to a toilet and a small corner sink. Washing her hands in the minimal flow of cold water, Daphne looked at herself, at her palms, and turned her wrists over. The unsettling specter of Lindsay, out here in the woods in an ancient, crummy trailer, tending a little orchard, felt somehow morally suspect.

Because she survived? Because this is her version of survival? Daphne shook her head. *Don't go there,* she warned herself. *You might not stack up so well yourself.*

Uncomfortable answers arose to other uncomfortable questions.

When she and Vic began as a couple, he told her about his divorce and talked of how he strove to improve his children's lives by not engaging Cassandra's bile. Passivity helped, he told her. Things had been worse before he figured out how to avoid Cassandra's wrath. Vic had shrugged when Daphne suggested taking the fight to Cassandra and told Daphne he was a work in progress.

And now she decided, she was a work not-in-progress. Recognizing this made her wonder how long she'd been suspended, and whether it was an inherited condition.

Had Lindsay inherited this trailer house? Daphne tried to picture her perhaps coming here as a college girl, coming with Suzanne, with Ross. She thought of best-case and worst-case possibilities, tried to delineate the givens.

A man like Vic, a person like him, Daphne decided, would take a heavy breath and find it all an opportunity to be more thoughtful. He'd said this sort of thing before, to his son and daughter, and to Daphne. Never quite a lecture, just a considered nod and a hug and the comment that whatever upsetting thing had just transpired could be an opportunity for him and whoever else to work harder, to practice more patience, more kindness. Daphne wasn't sure she wanted to work harder.

Cold. It was cold in the trailer, stagnant. Daphne thought of what it might have been like twenty years ago. What Suzanne might have seen. It was December then. It would have been even colder.

And that December Suzanne was attacked by someone. Just someone. Not knowing more was still as random and strange as it had always been.

Longing for the air on the deck, Daphne allowed herself a tour of the little house. The narrow hallway led to one small bedroom with veneer buckling on the walls.

It was just a thin home. There were no other secret shrines. Nothing untoward raised her hackles. Daphne wanted back outside, to escape from the cool, dark interior of Lindsay Wallach's home.

"What did her dad do for a living?" Lindsay was asking Vic.

"He sold insurance." Vic's tone was cool enough to demonstrate this was not going to be an engaging conversation, but he was willing to tell what he knew. He was part of the Mayfield family, in the way that people close to one family member adopt. Lindsay Wallach had long ago filtered out and away from the Mayfields.

Daphne stepped back onto the deck and slid the door shut, reassured that Vic and Lindsay had not relaxed into friendship, but awaited her return.

"It's a special kind of grief to lose someone unexpectedly," Lindsay said, her acknowledgment spoken with the care of somber pronouncement one might make to the close relative of a dead friend. "With someone still young, with such promise, it's even worse."

Pointing again to the board beyond the deck railing, Daphne asked, "Did you make that?"

Lindsay cleared her throat. "Do you know about the, um, the gift of bones? The idea that a person might need a place to go . . . to grieve?"

Daphne felt her jaw tighten. Her mother had talked about the gift of bones after Suzanne's body was found. Her mom was a grave visitor. The habit of mourning was a large part of Daphne's dread for this weekend and its anniversaries. Daphne found no solace at the cemetery. "I know about it," Daphne said. "We had the gift of bones two weeks after Suzanne disappeared. And then we had the funeral."

"She had . . ." Lindsay began and stumbled, "a horrible death. I'm so sorry about that. Sorry for you."

Am I supposed to say thank you? Daphne wondered.

"But," Lindsay continued, "a great life. Suzanne had a great life. Don't you think? Do you remember her well?"

Vic eyed Lindsay. "When her sister was murdered, I think Daph's memories got all the stronger. She wasn't going to get any more of them."

"Are you looking for something else here?" Lindsay asked. "Are you searching? Ross said all of us are searchers until we're freed."

"You stayed in touch with him," Daphne said.

Lindsay hesitated before nodding. Daphne took a deep breath, saw Vic do the same, and gestured for him to say nothing. It was time. After all these years, she'd find Ross Bouchard and confront the man so many thought was the killer who got away with her sister's murder.

Daphne stared at the plywood board of old photos, the fluttered, faded colors of the high school graduation tassel above the old candles. "He made that board, didn't he?"

"Before she was found," Lindsay said, nodding as her voice caught and she was unable to speak.

Daphne set her jaw. Someone else crying, even threatening to cry over Suzanne, would make her crash. Don't do it, she willed Lindsay. *Don't you dare do it.* "He made it right after she went missing?"

"The second week. Then he added to it afterward, for a long time. Years. He used to live here, but often he went off to his father's place down in Oregon." Lindsay squeezed her eyes shut. "Ross said a girl like Suzanne comes along once. Like once in a generation or in a lifetime."

"He was right about that," Daphne said.

Lindsay cocked her head as if struck by some personal thought. "I know how much Ross cared about Suzanne."

Talking right on top of her, Vic said, "I know he failed every lie detector test he ever took about her."

Lindsay's eyebrows perked up an inch.

"You didn't know that?" he asked her, his voice harsh now, even cruel.

Hallelujah, Daphne thought.

"He failed the polygraphs when he was questioned about Suzanne's death," Vic said, a judgment sealed.

A long exhale escaped Lindsay's pursed lips. "Well, he must have felt guilty."

"Why?" Vic and Daphne said as one. Daphne continued, "Why did he feel guilty?"

Lindsay's voice grew small and strained. "He was with me. That night. The night before, you know. The night when Suzanne took off, went off wherever she went, did whatever she did. Something reckless, I'm sure. She'd found us here, together, said she was going to find some action—"

"But you . . ." Daphne felt tears sting her eyes on her sister's behalf. She thought again about Lindsay filtering out of the Mayfields' lives. Suzanne had known this would happen before anyone else. She'd known it fresh and painful in the last hours of her life. "You were her best friend."

"Yes. And I was twenty-one. So was he. I'm sorry I went after my best friend's boyfriend."

"She told me you guys didn't even like each other! Her best friend and her boyfriend don't like each other. I mean, they didn't like each other."

Lindsay and Vic gaped at her.

"And Ross Bouchard—" Daphne began.

"Was sorry, too. Sorrier. I mean . . ." Lindsay hesitated, her gaze casting about and hands fluttering. "We liked each other, Daphne. We tried not to. I was, and am, as sorry as I can be, but I forgave myself. And Ross, well Ross never got over it."

Feeling Vic's gaze shift to her, Daphne met his glance but couldn't hold it. There was too much in his face. Sympathy and questions, his and hers.

And then Lindsay told them, "He's dead, you know."

Vic closed the distance and put an arm around Daphne, who managed no words from her open mouth.

Lindsay cleared her throat, and when she spoke again, her voice held the raspy catch of grief. "It was a couple years ago, March. He'd been a drinker, tried to dry up and relapsed lots of times. A few months before, he'd been back in central Oregon, out on the rimrocks. A favorite spot of his. I'd been there with him. The ground just falls away. His body was found below. At the top of the ledge were a lot of empty beers. At the bottom . . ."

There didn't seem to be anything else to say. Daphne's mind created an image of Ross Bouchard—not a man approaching forty but a boy dating her sister—in a suspended free fall from one of Oregon's high desert mesas. She shook her head and inclined her chin at Vic, glancing away to indicate readiness to leave.

She needed air, wanted to drive too fast, to leave this place. They said stiff good-byes and slipped around the trailer to her truck.

Before Vic entered the passenger side, Daphne said, "When I went away to college, I felt out of place. After the first summer, I had a hard time going back. After the second summer, it was worse. My mother promised the angels would come, but the next year my father killed himself."

"I know, honey." Vic pressed his lips to her hair as soon as they got in the truck's cab.

She fired up the engine and shoved the transmission stick. "The angels never came."

He held her hand, kissed her hair again. "There are different kinds of angels."

Lindsay ran at them, waving. Daphne braked and lowered her window.

"When he sang at her funeral," Lindsay said, breathing hard, "you have to understand this, he sang with a whole heart."

Using the black mood plied by the encounter with Lindsay, Daphne pressured Vic and his tight schedule until he agreed they had just enough time to drive by the intersection where the Lincoln had been discovered and towed.

"What's the big deal?" he said again. She'd already explained how she wanted to see it, and he'd explained how he thought he might be late getting his kids.

"What's the big deal with you?" she fired back. When he kept quiet instead of letting it become an argument, she made a point of staring out her window. Let him look at the back of her head, if he was looking at her at all, she thought. *I dare you to tell me to watch the road while I'm driving.*

"Left here," Vic said. "The guy at the impound lot said it was the northwest corner, on the northbound side, right after the fire hydrant in the first curbside spot."

She blinked at him and pretended not to notice his stretch, which ended with a twist of his arm in a disguised gesture to check his watch again.

Following the directions, she mused, "I wonder why they towed it in the first place."

"It was a stolen car, Daph." He stretched his legs as best he could in the little truck cab. "If that Lincoln at the impound lot *was* the same car you followed yesterday, it makes sense that they felt nervous about you. I mean, if they were driving a stolen car that had stolen license plates on it, they would be a little nervous about any contact. They wouldn't want anyone to connect the dots."

Daphne wanted to be pleased that he was interpreting the facts, that he considered the possibilities about whatever was going on with

Minerva Watts, but her tone became challenging. "So that's why they drove like crazy down Eastpark?"

"I don't know. I was just talking about the Lincoln being impounded from this street. Some cop noticed it was a stolen car."

"But you don't know that by looking at it, right? What attracted some cop's attention to it in the first place?"

He pointed to the sidewalk. "Well, it's metered parking. Maybe with the meter unpaid, they just ran a check. Maybe the license plates were already reported stolen, too."

She nodded, distracted, and stopped her little truck in a parking space the Lincoln may have occupied mere hours before. When had it been parked here? "The impound yard guy seemed to think it was kind of noteworthy that the VIN was checked. That's how the cop realized the Lincoln was stolen out of California . . ."

He checked his watch. "Can we go now?"

She let her Toyota idle out of the parking space. There was no traffic behind them on the road. It was a general business district, with a few oncoming cars. "And you'll drop me off at home and go pick Jed and Josie up?"

"Daph, there's not really enough time now. We have to go together."

"I can just see Cassandra making a big deal about four of us in the truck. I don't want us to both go get the kids and then all of us to squash in here."

He checked his watch and frowned.

"You could just drop me off at a coffee house or something and come back for me . . . ," she offered, looking left and right on the street to see if there was some suitable Internet café where she could pass an hour or so.

"Just dump my kids at the house and come for you?"

"The kids can stay at the house alone. They have keys. You'd . . . we'd be home soon."

He slouched. "I should have just taken the Honda as it was. It ran. It might not be worth fixing, it's so old."

"Hey, there's a car rental place," she said, perking up as she saw the business at the end of the block. "Let's rent a car there."

His face stayed impassive. "We can make do with just your truck until the Honda's fixed. The guy said it might only be a week or two."

"Come on," she said. "With four of us in the house for the weekend? How can we all go see your dad in the morning?" She pointed to the small space between them on the bench seat. Her little Toyota pickup had seatbelts for three. Stretching to four was claustrophobia-inducing. Given her loose tools, work gloves, and other equipment in the cab, it was cozy for the two of them when they were getting along.

He looked away. "I guess one of us could stay home in the morning, miss seeing my pop. You or one of the kids. Or maybe we could all cram in here."

She parked at the car rental agency. "I want to rent a car. It will make the time while we're waiting for yours to get fixed easier. It will make this weekend easier. I'll pay for it. Look." She pointed in the window of the business. "There's no other customers in there so it will be a fast transaction. Come on."

She was out of her truck before he could argue more. He caught her at the rental agency's door and opened it for her.

Inside the business, the lone young woman behind the counter whispered into the phone that she had to go. Then she hung up and asked how she could help them.

"We'd like to rent a car," Daphne said. "I'd like to."

The young woman had red-streaked black hair and a nose piercing. She pulled a multipage form from underneath her countertop and clicked it onto a clipboard. "Okay, you just fill out this form, initial here, here, here, and here"—the woman checked various boxes on the form as she spoke—"then sign at the bottom. And I'll need to see your ID and a major credit card. What kind of car did you want?" She pulled out several sets of car keys from a drawer and played through them, her long fingernails clicking like claws.

Daphne blinked at the clerk, then placed her shiny new driver's license on the counter. "If you don't take checks, I'll pay cash. I don't have credit cards with me."

The clerk hesitated, her fingers still playing through sets of rental car keys. "I still need to see your credit card, even if you're paying cash. We need the number for your deposit. A major credit card. Like Visa or MasterCard or American Express."

Turning her back to the clerk, Daphne faced Vic, glanced at his front pocket, where he kept his wallet, and gave him a meaningful look. "I don't have a credit card right now. My wallet was stolen."

Behind her, the clerk repeated, "We don't rent cars to someone without a major credit card."

"Vic, the bank's closed already but I can draw three hundred out on my ATM. I can do it tomorrow and Sunday, too. I can give you nine hundred over the weekend, see? I will take care of the Honda, of my accident. Just use your credit card and rent us a car, please."

"Let's go, Daph. I'm going to be late getting my kids. We don't need another car. We can get by, make do."

She stared beyond him to the front of the office. Tourist posters adorned the walls and a large display of fliers offered various diversions for the visitor. Daphne kept her gaze trained in the middle ground between Vic and outside, on the display case. "I want this. I can't do it. You can. So, do this for me and I'll pay you back. Please?"

There, if he didn't comply, he'd be using his possession of credit cards against her loss, winning through attrition.

He hooked his thumbs into his front pockets.

They never argued like this. One always gave in soon enough. And they never did it in public. Daphne stiffened. "Vic, what's the problem?"

"You. You're just fixing problems with money," he said. A blush seeped across his neck and face even as he voiced his protest.

"What you just said doesn't even make sense." She white-knuckled her own belt loops.

He gave a tiny nod and stepped up to the counter, where the clerk eyed them as an interested spectator of their spat. Vic shrugged, as much to the clerk as to Daphne, and said, "I'm not the only one not making a lot of sense, am I?"

His long-suffering attitude was more than Daphne could bear. She walked away and out the door.

CHAPTER 18

Outside the car rental agency, Daphne looked across the sidewalk at her truck and took five deep breaths. They were about a mile away from where she'd had the accident the day before. Inside, Vic was renting a car because she demanded he do so. She pushed back through the door, but avoided the service counter. Instead, she loitered at a display stand of traveler information. Wooden racks held dozens of tourist fliers. A smaller display occupied another wall, promoting local offerings. A bed and breakfast inn, an alpaca farm, blackberry preserves, a weekly community street fair. Another B&B. Daphne thought of a little bed and breakfast where she and Vic stayed on Lopez Island years ago, their first getaway together. It was before she'd met Jed and Josie, although of course she knew about them. Her fingers trailed over the cards.

Fliers for island getaways and driving trips, including trips to Mount Baker, beckoned. Snowboarding! Skiing! Inland attractions beyond the Cascades called, too. See Apple Country! See a Bavarian village right here in Washington!

She thought of her mother, taking a minibreak with Blanche. She wondered if her mother's bridge partner and family were glad to have her mother along for the weekend, and she scrunched her shoulders, stifling regret and relief at having not succumbed to her mother's pressure to go along.

This guilt drove her back to looking at the fliers for a distraction. Pike Place Market. The Space Needle. Winery tours. More hotels, motels, and other places to stay. Local guest houses and vacation rentals, a place called the Rainier Court Vacation House.

If she and Vic could get away together again—next weekend he wouldn't have the kids—maybe they could figure things out. She watched him accept his credit card back from the clerk. Did he think they needed to figure things out? Probably not. He'd talked several times over the last winter about them going to the next level, whatever that meant. He'd been the one to suggest she move in years ago. He made do, he was happy. She knew it was her life alone that brought murk to mind, no matter the distraction she might want to blame on Jed and Josie and their hideous mother.

I need to figure things out for myself.

Should she go away? Alone? She pulled out a flier for a local spot, the Rainier Court Vacation House.

"I happen to know that place is rented out," the clerk called out to Daphne, while pointing to places on the contract for Vic to initial. "Someone rented it when they got their car here yesterday."

"Oh, I'm just . . ." Daphne waved the clerk off, mindlessly folding the flier in half, in quarters. Then she shrugged and pushed the card deep into her jeans pocket.

If she wanted to escape Vic's house to think, she could go to her mother's house. She could go home.

But then she'd have to look at Suzanne's empty bed as she went to sleep.

—m—

"See you at home?" Vic asked as he got into the white four-door rental. Daphne nodded and mused again on the nature of home. As soon as he said the word, she pictured his blue saltbox, Grazie, and noisy or silent kids on alternate weekends. She pictured herself and Vic making dinner together, sharing one plate, trading foot rubs on the couch.

Daphne drove and thought about that home and how it had come to be hers.

Jed and Josie were beautiful and interesting and scary. Sometimes they were so special and touching. And sometimes—conflicted, pulled children that they were—Daphne ached for their anger.

When she first met the kids four years ago, the school year was starting for them. They hadn't seen their father for weeks and weeks. They were huggy and smiley and exuded desire to please him. And so had come their ready acceptance of Daphne, who'd been equally ready to please Vic, reciprocating the kind and loving attention he showed her.

Before Vic, she'd never dated a guy with kids. Now that she'd been with him in her late twenties and early thirties, seen friends have to figure out the stepparent thing, she realized the odds of such encumbrances increased with age. And she felt guilty for thinking of a boy and a girl as encumbrances. Not that she didn't like them and love them, but they were victims of a nasty divorce, and Daphne had come to see that their past made all the difference in their present.

She loved Vic, knew she was happier with him, more comfortable, than she'd ever been with any other man—not that there had been very many. There was the plumber, a guy who'd become a jerk and then got jerkier, showing his true colors, and she'd ended up deciding she would never date a guy associated with work again. There were a couple of men Thea had set her up with, educated men with plans. Men who smoked and talked and talked and found her lacking when she didn't know or care about international politics. There was the guy she'd met on her own, flirted with at a restaurant. He'd been rough and she dumped him hard within a week. There hadn't been another man with children, though.

Thea had told her many horror stories of dating divorced men, dealing with the kid thing. Daphne's first months with Vic were kid-free because Jed and Josie were away at their maternal grandparents' for the summer, but they were in Vic's thoughts, his spoken memories, his wishes. His obvious concern and love for his children intrigued Daphne, no matter how Thea warned that a man with kids was not worth the extra effort.

And when she'd gotten her first chance with them, when they were seven and eight years old, they were still awed by their father living in what had been their G-Pop's house, instead of with them and their mother. They were quiet and friendly and responsive, and they thought Daphne was pretty cool. Daphne thought they were pretty cool kids, too.

And Vic's ex had hated it. Cassandra reached into the kids' minds with tentacles of hate. In response, Vic had put his arm around Daphne and told her again and again how he loved her, how special she was. Daphne wanted to believe him when he said they could figure it out, work it out.

He was the first man who listened to her and asked the right questions, made the right murmurs when she talked about her family. She still felt shame that it took her so long to tell him all she knew and feared about the past. She still felt honored that he told her so early in their relationship about realizing—after a blood bank donation—that he was not his son's father. That he'd set aside concerns about paternity because fatherhood was what he felt. He loved and cared for his children like a father, and this defined him.

Cassandra had cheated on Vic just like Ross Bouchard—and Lindsay Wallach—had cheated on Suzanne. Daphne grimaced at the thought, comforted by reassuring recent memories of how Vic had handled their encounter with Lindsay.

Sometimes Vic could drive her nuts or say the wrong thing, but what balanced that was knowing she wholly returned the favor. By now, she knew they could be a couple for the rest of their lives. But for Cassandra's manipulations, she'd seen no reason for them to ever stop.

And by now, she'd driven toward downtown instead of going straight home, ruminating all the while.

Pike Street ended in the quintessential Seattle indoor-outdoor market, and she pulled into a rare parking space just as someone in a Hummer pulled out. The fish throwers were hollering to each other, tossing whole salmon. Teeming crowds circulated, parting to pass around street musicians and buskers.

At the farmers' market section, where bins of every produce imaginable offered color and shape, Daphne bought a phallic-looking butternut squash, with a long, thick stalk and bulbous end. Vic had never outgrown his childhood lech for baked squash, and Daphne, never much of a cook, had found it a challenge to try to get there with him. He said hers was the best he'd had, better than his long-dead mother's.

She bought some chocolates for herself and Jed, some jicama for Josie, who was of late on a calorie-conscious kick, and she dawdled over a display of herbal remedies intended to cure arthritis and joint pain. What in the world would they do with Grazie?

What would she do with herself?

"Home, I guess," she said aloud, and smiled when she didn't draw strange looks from passersby for talking to herself.

—⚏—

Two strange cars hogged the driveway at Vic's house, forcing Daphne to park on the street. After a moment, she remembered the white four-door was Vic's rental car, but the other was different, at once sporty and luxurious. A woman with frizzy hair sat in the front passenger seat, looking at the house's open front door. Daphne paused at the car. The woman stared ahead, refusing eye contact, so Daphne continued on, a shopping bag in each hand.

On the brick steps, a sleeping bag and loose pile of books blocked the entrance. A voice that didn't belong there bounced inside, a woman's voice.

Daphne felt herself wilt. Cassandra was inside the entryway, bursting out of a white camisole and black Capri pants. She shouted to the kids about the white car outside and whether their father had bought a new one, like she suspected, or if it was a rental, like he claimed.

"We don't know," Jed said, his voice plaintive.

"Don't keep secrets from me. No matter what he tells you." The woman's scorn was for everybody.

"Mom! We're not keeping secrets. Not from you." Josie's frustration gleamed from every pore of her red face.

"Don't take that tone with me, missy. Just because you get away with murder over here where there are no rules. I'm your mother and you will respect me."

"I do, I do, Mommy." The girl's voice sounded teary with stress.

Hamstrung, Daphne thought, as Josie pled. Those poor, good kids were hamstrung by their mother.

It would always be this way.

She stopped Vic as he stepped outside to retrieve the books and sleeping bag. "Ahem."

"Daph, hi." His face brightened from the impassive mask he wore in front of his ex.

"I don't like Cassandra inside." They could tell she was in their kitchen now.

"Me neither," he whispered into her mouth as he kissed her. "If she stays more than a minute, I'll push the fridge over on her."

"Fair enough."

She followed him inside, but he went down the hallway with Josie's things. Daphne turned into the kitchen and came face-to-face with a woman who had four inches, thirty pounds, and piles of temperament on her.

"Oh, look," Cassandra said. "It's my husband's fiancée." After a smirk and a beat, she added, "My ex-husband's."

Daphne felt gates in her mind clang shut, decisions rendered about how the evening would go with Vic and whether or not she'd even stay tonight. Had Vic announced that they were engaged? If he had, could she legally kill him for the offense?

She set her shopping bags down on the counter and stepped back to the front door, holding it open for Cassandra with a set smile.

And Cassandra did return to the front door. She nodded to her friend in the car and raised her voice while pointing at Daphne.

"Vic's girlfriend."

Daphne knew Cassandra was making an announcement to neighbors and traffic passing by. She tried to think how best to deal, what to say and do, and she knew Vic's mind churned the same muddy waters. Back when they first met and she'd asked about his ex, he'd told her the woman was unfailingly awful to him and he was determined not to treat his children's mother the same way. He didn't want the kids to see behavior so unworthy. Daphne loved his determination to take the high road and followed suit from the beginning.

He came to her side and took her hand.

And then Cassandra said, "Our divorce wasn't even final when he shacked up." She turned on the front threshold to face them. "And yesterday you blew off your daughter's volleyball game."

"Daphne was going to go to Josie's game," Vic said, "but she was delayed. It almost never happens. It's never happened with Daph. Again, I'm sorry I was late to get them this afternoon."

"Cassandra," Daphne said, "we had a threatening phone call yesterday."

"I don't make threats." She turned on Vic. "I told you. It was a promise. If you're late again, if you don't meet your commitments, you can expect things to change."

Vic made eye contact with Daphne, closed his eyes, and gave an almost imperceptible shake of his head. Daphne nodded then roused herself because Cassandra stepped past them to the kitchen. Now Daphne remembered the fat white purse she'd seen on the counter when she set down her grocery bags. In the kitchen, she decided Vic had one minute to get his ex out of the house. Emptying her grocery bags, Daphne smiled at him when she saw his hopeful appreciation of the produce.

Cassandra eyed the vegetables too and gave Vic a wistful look. "I used to make you squash and eggplant. I made it right here for your dad, too." She looked around the kitchen. "How's Lloyd? Does he ask about me?"

"You can go visit him," Vic said. "You can take the kids to him, too."

Daphne smiled. They'd worked on this, on not getting baited into whatever Cassandra wanted to hash over.

Four years ago, when Daphne met Jed, Josie, and the wicked ex for the first time, she thought she was ready. Vic had prepped her, warned her, given examples of the outrageous, skin-prickling comments Cassandra made.

She'll outright lie to the kids and start screaming if I contradict her. Tells them I don't pay child support. She tells them wrong times to give me for pick-ups or teacher conferences. I've learned to barely talk in front of her and confirm everything. Believe me, Daph, it's best not to engage her at all.

Daphne had agreed with Vic, even advised him. Answer what you want, not whatever she demands. Be oblique. Without knowing from where she got her ideas, Daphne felt certain they'd work better than milk with a cat like Cassandra.

The woman amazed Daphne, like watching a human train wreck that never finished, never released a final clang and let dust settle. The mental games became more sly, inventive, and unpredictable. And more, Daphne had seen how the woman's venom seeped into her kids. The problem had increased, instead of becoming manageable. Hers was a poison with a cumulative effect.

Cassandra slid a knife from the butcher's block holder. Her other hand stroked the length of the squash before slicing the shaft just above the bulbous end. Daphne saw Vic's hips twitch, one thigh lifting in unconscious protection of his crotch as the butternut squash shaft fell to the counter.

"So, Cassandra," Daphne said, thinking of how Vic, for all his waffling about Minerva Watts, had been in her corner in front of the cop, in front of Lindsay Wallach. "I'm sure you're busy and you need to go. Thanks for dropping the kids off."

Cassandra lifted her purse, swung it from her shoulder, and at the door looked toward the living room where the TV covered the kids' voices. Daphne thought she could read the woman's mind, thought she saw Cassandra's mental cogs turning on how to incite the kids.

"Just stop it," Daphne begged.

Cassandra froze, then whirled to the entryway. "Cheer up, Jose," Cassandra hollered before she stepped outside.

Vic came to the door and stood beside Daphne.

Cassandra made her parting shot as she got into her driver's seat. "I shouldn't have to do everything. They're your kids, too."

Vic's jaw set, and Daphne gave Cassandra an unappreciated—much as she tried to will the woman to look at her—glare. She watched Cassandra go. And right then, she loved Vic through and through for not calling Cassandra on the lie.

The kitchen and living room and entryway all held pictures Daphne and Vic had put on the walls. He'd encouraged her over the years to make the place her own. He'd asked if she thought they should paint the walls, and what color. When she'd said she thought the plates and tableware would be more convenient in the cabinet closer to the dishwasher, he'd nodded and pulled canned goods out of the shelf where they'd always been stored, swapping the cupboards' holds to the way things were kept in her childhood home. They'd smiled at the little ways different families made houses into homes, the different clicks and wavelengths people employed.

—⟪⟫—

Daphne used Vic's computer to find the phone number of the Ford car dealership the police officer had mentioned when they were in front of Minerva Watts's house the day before. The clerk answering the phone sounded cheery for the end of the day.

"I'm calling about an, a, um, a transfer pending? I think you bought a car, a silver Crown Victoria, from a lady named Minerva Watts. Just this Wednesday. Two days ago." The awkwardness of asking on a whim left her stammering.

"We don't often purchase vehicles from individuals, ma'am," the clerk told her in a hesitant tone. "Are you saying the vehicle was traded in?"

Daphne shook her head, feeling the wash of uncertainty born of conversing and probing out of her element. Then she reminded herself the woman couldn't see her. She cleared her throat and said, "No. I think it was sold to you, to Fremont Ford. I think you bought it. Not a trade-in. Can you check on that, please?"

"Please hold," the clerk said.

With the click, Daphne's mind wandered to Minerva Watts's car, then to the home on Eastpark Avenue. What was in the garage? In movies, she'd just go over there and break into the house, see for herself what was in Mrs. Watts's garage.

A long wait with soft rock music passed before the car dealership clerk came back on. "Yes. It was purchased as a wholesale, um, this Wednesday."

"A wholesale," Daphne said, mouthing the word, furrowing her brow. "Do you know who came in to sell it? An older lady? A couple? All three of them?"

"Ma'am," the clerk's tone became more closed, "is there a problem?"

"No," Daphne reassured the woman, in an automatic, unthinking response. "I don't know. Maybe."

"Ma'am, we have sales staff here until ten p.m., but the manager who handled this purchase is not in right now. It's Friday night. Would you like to call back Monday?"

"Uh, sure." Daphne hung up, despondent over the prospect. She could lose momentum by Monday. And if something dire were going on, Monday could be far too late.

CHAPTER 19

When I was sixteen, I dumped on my little sister like I was Hitler.

Daphne wasn't hiding, sitting on the bed with the door closed, the old box of Suzanne's papers and keepsakes strewn over the comforter. But downstairs, the kids had been noisy and hungry and half-arguing. After the four of them ate dinner, Jed and Josie taunted each other to the point of shrieking. Vic was bleary-eyed from the disturbance to his sleep schedule.

Ten minutes earlier, she'd kept herself from saying anything when Jed removed his glasses while petting Grazie. He left them on the floor for those few minutes. Of course, Josie came along and stepped on them. The damage might not be total but he'd smacked her leg and she'd kicked him in response.

"You . . . asshole." Josie's voice rose to end in a screech.

"Josie!" Vic said, lowering his newspaper and blinking. "Language."

Daphne bit the insides of her cheeks, stemming a snort. He'd been napping in the easy chair and his dismay at his daughter's comment struck her at once as out of touch and charming in its hope for a gentler world.

The TV was on. Vic retreated behind the newspaper. Grazie slept through it all like a dream and Daphne had to rouse the old dog to get her to come up to the bedroom refuge.

She slid off the bed now, limp papers in her hands, to avoid glances at the nightstand and its harbinger. This morning, when she'd left to see Arnold Seton and Vic was getting ready for his day, he'd picked up his grandmother's ring, flipped it like a coin, and placed it back on the nightstand without a word. While he handled it, she'd stayed silent, dreading discussion, relieved beyond measure when he didn't use words.

Sinking to the floor to keep the nightstand's top out of view, Daphne burrowed her toes in Grazie's fur and read, reread.

BETRAYAL, by Suzanne Mayfield, was a fine essay, a heartfelt, well-organized recounting of a teen having refused to take an excited baby sister out as soon as Frances and Reginald Mayfield would allow their just-licensed daughter to drive without a chaperone.

. . . And she so wanted to go with me that day and I so didn't want her along. But for absolutely no good reason. For no reason at all. I dumped her. I broke her heart and . . . Suzanne's confession spared nothing.

The composition received an A+, even with red-penned notes here and there about run-on sentences and adverbs and starting sentences with conjunctions. The English teacher had written comments about her sentence structure and use of the passive tense, then added a final scrawl: *You are such a sensitive girl, Suzanne!*

Daphne shook her head. *BETRAYAL.* She'd read the essay so many times. How much worse a betrayal was it for society to fail a member, for a member as vibrant as Suzanne to be a murderer's victim? How much of a betrayal was it for a man to be unable to face his dead daughter's coming birthday and to quietly take his own life in a hotel room to avoid facing that black day?

How much was she to blame for having never told her parents about Suzanne's sneaking out at night?

She dreaded facing this idea, believing it was something to be mired in. Wallowing served no good purpose. But after today, she wallowed anew, finding some personal culpability in so many tragedies. And she marveled at the fortitude Lindsay Wallach had shown to call right away, as soon as she suspected Suzanne was in trouble.

Daphne stacked the essay papers with Suzanne's other old notes and cards and closed the box, slipping it under the bed, thinking about the grade, the great grade, and the professor's other written comment: *Did you talk to your little sister about this?*

She imagined the professor rising from his bed in the middle of the night, unable to sleep, wanting his beautiful, essay-writing, wild student to have made nice.

She pictured Ross Bouchard, years later, drunk and slipping to his death from a high rock ledge.

Or perhaps, he threw himself to the canyon depths, thinking about Suzanne as he fell.

"Suzanne," Daphne whispered. "Su . . . zanne." Her voice broke and she stemmed a cry by pressing her lips together, bringing a hand to her mouth as she balanced rights and wrongs.

But betrayal? No. Daphne didn't remember Suzanne dumping her. She had no recollection of the first day Suzanne was licensed, of begging to go for a ride with her big sister. Yet, Suzanne had ached over betraying Daphne.

Daphne wondered why it gave her an odd comfort to know her sister ached for her when she didn't even recall an injury.

—ᴍ—

Downstairs, Daphne poured a glass of wine and pulled the newspaper from Vic's sleepy grasp. "Need some fruit?" she asked.

He smiled and accepted, sipping before he told her, "A glass of wine is not a fruit serving." He gave the glass back. They both knew he never took more than a few sips when his kids were home. "What's on your mind, Daph?"

"The person in California who owned that blue Lincoln is dead. And that person was an older person who, at the last second, willed everything over to a charity that went belly-up right away."

"What in the world are you talking about?" Vic asked, eyes wide as he looked around the room, then behind Daphne.

"Minerva Watts told me that first afternoon that they were stealing her car. And now she's suddenly sold her car wholesale to a local dealer. Maybe that couple forced her to sell it." Daphne turned and saw Josie standing at the living room's edge. The girl's glance flitted from her father to Daphne and back.

"I want to know she's safe," Daphne said.

"That," Vic said, "is a very reasonable thing to want. I'm just not sure how it's achievable."

Daphne picked up the phone on the end table.

"Who are you calling?"

"My mom. I want to ask if she remembers Lindsay." She snapped her fingers with a sudden recollection. "Oh, she's gone for the weekend." Hoping her mother's bridge partner and family were enjoying the extra company, Daphne stashed the guilt of not going away with her mother and instead took in Vic's little family. Jed had sequestered himself in his room now, but the door was ajar, and she could see his foot dangling off his bed. He's reading, Daphne guessed.

Josie took Daphne's usual spot on the couch beside Vic, who had dozed off. Daphne restrained herself from leaning down to kiss him before she turned away.

Besides, if she didn't go back upstairs, poor Grazie might awaken alone up there and make an unnecessary trip down the steps. Daphne understood that Vic was pacing himself, trying not to cling to Josie, who had a sleepover planned for the next night. Vic would lose one precious night of his daughter being under his roof.

She felt a surge of sympathy for them both as she headed back for the stairs with her glass of wine.

Fingers tapped her arm and Daphne turned on the bottom step to see Jed's hopeful face.

"Can you talk to Dad about me staying home tomorrow?"

Daphne sank to sit on the step. Vic could be awake again or be tuned out, dozing or reading, but she couldn't tell from the stairs. "You don't want to go see your grandfather?"

"G-Pop."

"Right," Daphne said, remembering how the kids had flared a few weeks ago when Daphne dared use the family's pet name for Vic's father. *You don't call him that! You don't know him like us!*

"It's just, sometimes, well, it's such a drag going there. It's kind of creepy, too. Don't you think? I mean, some of those old people are kind of creepy. They stare and say weird things and the whole place smells weird."

Daphne nodded, her thoughts swinging to Grazie upstairs. "You know, one of the things I like and admire about your dad is the way he cares for his father."

"Because you don't have a father?"

"Because the way your father cares for his father is admirable. Your G-Pop is in a tough situation."

"Forget it," the boy said, turning for his room.

She heard his door shut and knew Vic had lost any glimpse of his son from the couch. She was startled to see her wineglass empty and Josie standing in front of her, scrutinizing.

"I'm going to get myself something to drink," the girl announced.

Daphne rose and followed the girl into the kitchen. "Goodness, I was just thinking of myself when I came downstairs, wasn't I? I'm sorry, Josie. What would you like?"

"I'd like to get it myself." She pulled milk and juice and discount soda from the fridge. "Isn't there any Diet Coke?"

Daphne nodded and pulled out the special stash of cans she'd bought to share, recalling Vic's purchase of the on-sale, store-brand, non-diet soda and how she hadn't contradicted his choice out loud, but bought what she and Josie preferred on her way home from work. Opening a cupboard with quiet care, Daphne got the glass with roses on it, the one Josie liked best.

Josie's shoulders started shaking.

"What's going on, Jose?" Daphne swallowed and corrected herself from using the girl's parents' little nickname. "Josie? What is it?"

"L-l-lainey said she didn't want to hang out with me anymore."

The most recent best friend, Daphne remembered, not allowing herself to get caught smiling about how Josie and her girlfriends were always declaring one or the other a BFF, with a very short understanding of what *forever* means.

Josie's chin crumpled and her body shook with muffled sobs. Daphne let her arms encircle the girl's small, unhappy body. Her lips brushed against the auburn hair, her voice addressed the pain right into Josie's double-pierced ear. "Oh, Jose. Oh. She said that? Ow. God. Oh, Josie, Josie. That must have—"

"It hurts." Josie's arms folded as she hugged her own body and her jaw went forward. She sniffed, a ragged, wet sound that ended in a hiccup. "She's such a—it was such a—"

Daphne nodded, screwing her face in anger, matching Josie's expression. "Such a bitchy thing for Lainey to say."

"Yeah." The girl's detachment vanished as she condemned the girl who'd hurt her and she let herself lean into Daphne's sympathy, crying in earnest.

Daphne stroked Josie's hair while the girl added details of the trauma—other kids who heard and laughed, the snickers and stares. Murmuring in sympathy to the doubled-over girl, she spied Vic in the kitchen doorway. She shook her head and mouthed, *Go away*. Vic's mouth opened and one arm extended for his daughter and girlfriend.

No, Daphne mouthed.

Jed walked up behind his father, headed for the kitchen. The boy looked at the females in the kitchen, then at his father. His tongue poked the inside of his cheek, distorting his face.

Vic hesitated, then let his extended arm go around Jed's shoulders. He steered his son away, glancing back at his daughter crying in the kitchen just once.

Josie took a final sniff, wiped her face, and smoothed her hair back. Daphne sat up a bit, leaning into the counter instead of the girl.

"I don't care anyway," Josie said. "I mean, I shouldn't. No one should want to sit with someone who's so bitchy. She can be a real bitch."

Daphne reached the table near the stairs in the entryway in two long steps and grabbed the Kleenex box, pulling out tissues for herself and Josie.

—※—

Back in the bedroom after the kids had gone to sleep, Daphne pulled her keepsakes box from under the bed and stowed it on the closet shelf—just like at home, at her mother's house.

Reopening the box top, she filled her hands with Suzanne's papers. She frowned, thinking about how her mother had compiled the box not long after the funeral, stacking all Suzanne's papers and photos and scraps and notes, then taped the cardboard carton shut. That the box had appeared on the girls' closet shelf—on Suzanne's unused side—and stayed there until Daphne moved out and took the box with her had never seemed significant before she talked to Arnold Seton.

While she understood why her parents hadn't told her, at eleven, about the police search of her and Suzanne's bedroom, she alone knew her mother had unwittingly sabotaged the police's sifting for clues.

Back in high school, when she was big enough to wear some of Suzanne's clothes, she'd cut the box open and discovered her big sister's personal papers, the beautiful, tantalizing bits of Suzanne. Once, when their mother caught her on the closet floor, the *BETRAYAL* essay in one hand and Suzanne's old, girly, flowered address book in the other, Daphne had felt like a trespasser. But her mother had stroked her hair and told her it was all right for her to look. *Just you. You're my good girl.*

Daphne again averted her gaze from the nightstand and felt Vic watch her. When he stepped into the bathroom, she sank to the bed and ogled the item that didn't belong on the nightstand.

One rose wilted there, with Vic's grandmother's silver ring slid all the way up the stem. The bloom's unwatered petals curled, the ruby color fading.

He came out of the bathroom bare-chested, holding his glasses, using his shirt to polish the lenses. "My vision's blurry. I've got to see the eye doctor, get a new prescription."

Daphne felt a memory prod. "Jed broke his glasses."

"Maybe I have a brain tumor. Maybe that's why things are blurry."

"Actually, Josie broke them. Jed left them on the floor and she stepped on them."

Vic stared through the window. "Do you think that's it? Cancer? I can't even make out the leaves on the trees out there."

Daphne gave an uninterested sweep of the front yard. "I can't see the leaves either. You don't have cancer. We just don't have clean windows."

He kissed her good night and sighed a few words about what a day, what a week. And she thought so, too, but wondered if they thought of the same events when they reflected on traumas, small and large.

"My sister used to leave me notes," she said.

"Yes. You've told me."

Suzanne's last note, the one she never found—the one that might not even exist—wasn't a secret that rocked him when she confessed it more than a year into their relationship. But his own secret—Cassandra cheated so early in their marriage that Jed was a stranger's biological son, so who knows if he was Josie's birth father either—rolled him and remained a private detail he kept from everyone but Daphne.

She knew it threw him yet he compartmentalized, put it away. That's what he told her, showed her. He lived it down, moved past it somehow.

Vic looked at the box on the bed and studied her. "Did you find something new at your mom's house recently? I mean, something you hadn't seen before?"

"No. And I never will." She waved Suzanne's papers at him, at this man who loved her. "Right?"

"Right." He used both hands to massage her hand, fingers kneading.

"I've combed through that room, every inch. When I was twelve. Thirteen, fourteen, fifteen. I remember doing it again when I was sixteen, the same day I first got my driver's license." Daphne pictured her new licenses—the one she got on her sixteenth birthday and the one she got today. She still needed a new wallet and replacement credit cards. "Do you think my mom should do something with our bedroom?"

"With our bedroom?" Vic's baffled expression as he stopped rubbing her hand made Daphne want to smack him.

"Mine and Suzanne's. Our old one."

He let go of her hand. "Hmm." Rubbing his chin, he took a breath and paused before answering. "I think it is up to your mother what she does with her house. Sometimes I think it would be better for people to move on with more . . . demarcation . . . when they've lost someone, the way you've lost your sister and father. But I think loss of that kind is very traumatic and personal and no one ought to tell anyone else how to grieve in the first place or how to handle such loss in the second place."

Tears topped Daphne's smile. "That was quite a speech."

"I'm glad you liked it."

Vic's kind outlook toward her mother sometimes chafed Daphne, who'd grown used to Thea's snarky support about how difficult mothers could be.

Sleep wouldn't come soon, but she knew it would come. Yesterday, a man called Guff had grabbed her and she'd ended up in handcuffs within the hour. They had taken her jacket, they had taken Minerva Watts. And here she was going to bed, as though nothing bad had happened. She knew better. She remembered being eleven, Suzanne missing more than a week. They thought—hoped—that Suzanne might have run away again, been on a lark, but Lindsay insisted Suzanne must be in trouble, said she was missing. And at night, with hours eking past, they went to sleep. They said they couldn't and then they did, all of the Mayfields, even her father. Eventually, the exhausted slept. Just as she and her mother had somehow slept after her dad hanged himself in a hotel room.

This is how life is done, she knew. One minute at a time.

CHAPTER 20

Jed was already up when Daphne slipped down the stairs Saturday morning. Wearing his spare eyeglasses, with his cheap electric guitar slung at his hips, he opened the fridge and pulled out the orange juice. She was about to tell him to use a glass instead of drinking from the container, when he poured juice into a coffee cup and raised the carton to her.

"Want some?"

She melted. "No, thanks." And she thought, *No, thanks, buddy.* That's what Vic would say, would get to say. Daphne cleared her throat. "It's nice of you to ask."

"Want to hear me?" Jed thrust his electric guitar forward.

Daphne turned from her coffee making. Jed pulled the guitar up to his stomach, fingers clutching at the strings. She nodded.

The thin squeaks were hesitant, then went on. And on and on.

"It sounds better with the amp," Jed said after a lengthy effort.

"It sounds fine this way."

"You don't want to hear it anyways."

"I do," Daphne insisted.

He pulled the guitar strap free of his body. "I wish Dad worked normal hours."

Daphne went back to her coffee making. "Why?"

"He's always tired. He's no fun."

Josie came out of her tiny bedroom—she hated that Jed's was bigger than hers, had once made a show of measuring and calculating the two areas to prove her case—and looked pointedly away from Jed.

Daphne clipped in a sigh. So the kids weren't getting along this morning. She thought of so many days early on when they'd been out of sorts and fussy. At first it got better as the divorce became more distant in time. And then it got worse, because the kids grew older, smarter, more perceptive. And their mother's poison matured, too, worked through the kids. They became more hurt, the family more riven.

Cassandra had dragged out the divorce proceedings for almost two extra years although she was the one who threw Vic out, who filed in the first place. Oh, how she filed, postponing court dates, asking the Superior Court for a litany of discovery on his finances, even on Daphne's. Oh, how she demanded witness statements and threatened to make the kids testify.

Jed shrugged and slumped off to put his guitar away. They could all hear Vic helping Grazie down the stairs.

Josie leaned toward Daphne and spoke in a soft, crying rush. "You have to understand. It just would have been better if our mom and dad hadn't gotten divorced."

Considering the out-of-the-blue comment, Daphne swept the girl with a level gaze. Josie's hair, like every other girl in her grade, hung straight and simple but brushed with care. Her clothes, too, were standard, the low-cut jeans, camisole not covering her belly, and thin hoodie that couldn't have kept her warm.

"Yes," Daphne said. "It would have been."

Josie's eyes widened. "Oh, my God. You think you and my dad shouldn't even be together? And here you are! You are so twisted."

What should I have said? Daphne wondered as she walked away, stepping out the front door for air while she pretended to want the newspaper.

—⁓—

Green Springs Extended Care Facility necessitated a forty-five minute drive, one-way. Every other weekend, Daphne dreaded the drive as much as she knew Jed and Josie did. Perhaps the novelty of the rental car would make the trip smooth for the kids.

Daphne pursed her lips, considering the vehicles outside. This morning, she'd slid into the same jeans she'd worn the day before. Pushing her hand into the pockets to find her truck key, she felt stiff paper and pulled out a police officer's card and a folded flier for the Rainier Court Vacation House. The larger card made her think of nothing so much as escape. Her brow furrowed as she recalled the car rental clerk's comment—that she happened to know the vacation house had been rented out the day before yesterday. But there were plenty of inns and B&Bs.

After peanut butter on toast for everybody, Vic smiled all around and said, "Everybody ready?"

"I'll take my truck and meet you guys there," Daphne said, and was first out the door. Outside, she counted from one-one-thousand to ten-one-thousand before the front door opened and Vic stepped out alone. The kids must still be getting themselves together inside.

"Daph . . ." Vic began his protest on the steps, putting both hands over hers.

"What!" She yanked her arms free from his grasp.

"Josie said she was mean to you this morning."

"She wasn't," Daphne said, moving down the steps without looking at him. When he reached for her arm again, she faced him with her hands shoved into her hip pockets. "Let me talk to her."

"Let me talk to you," Vic said. "I've never loved someone more. I know I'm not perfect. But we're good together, Daph. You know we are. You know I love you. All these years. I remember what kind of ice cream I bought you the second time I ever saw you—"

"We had ice cream the *first* time we met."

"Yes, but it wasn't the first time I saw you. I came back with Grazie, the Wonder Dog. Back when she used to walk faster than two miles an hour."

"You saw me and came back? Fetched your dog and came back to meet me?"

He nodded.

"Huh," she said. "I'm trying to decide whether or not to be creeped out by that, Stalker Boy."

"No! Not creeped out. Definitely vote for not. Swooned, maybe. Daph, come on. I wanted to meet you. And I'm so glad I did. Where am I going to find another girl who's so interesting and gorgeous and good for me and understanding and crazy and kind to my son and daughter and father and dog? What other woman could even listen to Jed murder *String Cheese* songs?"

"That was *String Cheese* he played for me this morning?"

"Please don't tell him you didn't recognize it."

"No, no," she assured him. "I wouldn't do that."

He kissed her left ring finger, stroked its empty length. "I know you wouldn't. Daph, listen. When guys propose, women tend to say yes. And they say it right away."

"I'm not them."

"No. You're not. That is all about why I want you. You're not like other women, Daph. You're special. You are a once-in-a-lifetime find."

The words gutted her and she frowned. She didn't reply, having no answer to give. The kids came out and piled into the rental with Vic.

Throughout the near-hour drive in Seattle traffic, Daphne glanced at her truck's rear view, watching Vic and his kids in the rental car.

—∿∿—

It had been a toss-up, Vic had told her the first time he took her to meet his father. He'd talked so much about when he had to put the old man in care, how hard it all was, right down to choosing his father's final home. When his father signed the house over, Vic took an equity loan and chose between two decent facilities, Green Springs and Memory Lane, going with the former because the name of the latter made him want to scream.

Outside Seattle, in the town of Woodinville, as leafy as the name suggested, a walking path curved around the large lawn bordering the moss-colored nursing home. Its single story stretched in four wings that joined at a courtyard nestling Green Springs's central dining and recreation rooms.

"What's he like today?" Daphne asked an aide at the desk as they walked by.

"Like always," the heavyset woman in white said, her smile huge.

Vic nodded and turned to wave his kids forward. "He's okay."

Daphne ground her molars. If this visit was like the last one, Vic would be upbeat, his father would ask about Cassandra, and the kids would be uncomfortable. And maybe Josie would have an outburst that reminded Daphne of Cassandra.

Lloyd's roommate was a man named Charles Pafford, whom he called Bud. As they approached, Daphne pushed the scent of urine away and heard Bud's hoarse, craggy voice from the end of the hallway. "When they come, I'm going to be introduced to the man who's going to be my grandchildren's new father."

Daphne winced, thankful that only she and Vic knew he had proposed to her. Lloyd Daily nodded to Bud as Vic, Jed, and Josie stepped into the room behind Daphne.

"I don't much care for the word boyfriend," Bud said, his gaze coming to the door, seeing the four visitors. "Makes a man sound like a boy."

Lloyd nodded again, then turned in bed to see his family. His face brightened and he held his arms wide. Josie went first, slipping in for a hug, patting her grandfather on the back. Jed waved, hovering at the foot of the bed.

"Is he getting too big for hugging?" Lloyd asked Vic.

Vic's laugh was instant, if forced. "Maybe he thinks so, Pop. How are you today?"

Bud pressed his buzzer, making a yellow light shine outside their door and a soft chime ring. An aide came in and conversation stalled until Bud had been helped out of bed and down the hall on his walker.

Lloyd shook his head. "They won't come, his family. They never do. But Bud keeps hoping."

Josie sat on the edge of Bud's plastic visitor chair. Jed slumped into Lloyd's chair by the window.

"Is Cassie here?" Lloyd asked.

Jed snorted.

"No, Pop," Vic said with his usual calm, his face wooden as his hand dropped to his father's shoulder. "Cassandra and I are divorced. You know tha—"

The old man waved a hand. "That's right. That's right. I know that. You don't have to tell me. I know. Sorry. Sorry. I don't know why I said that." He pointed a finger at Daphne at the foot of the bed. "I know who you are."

She smiled at him, her heart breaking.

"You're the roofer!"

"That's me," she said, "I'm Daphne, the roofer."

The kids drummed their heels on the chair legs.

Three and four years ago, Daphne used to come and pick Lloyd up, drive him to the kids' T-ball games. Lloyd had loved it then but had become less and less able or brave enough to leave his home.

Put your name on it, Josie. That's what Lloyd used to say when he watched his granddaughter at the games, roaring when she swung, incredulous that the little girls and boys didn't always know which way to run, that the fielders sat down in their boredom and dawdled in the grass. Astounded that boys and girls played together, he'd marveled at the coed play, shaken his head, and asked Daphne again and again about her work.

"I want to see them next week," Lloyd said at last, when Vic had covered every conversation topic he could, an hour had passed, and Lloyd's attention flagged.

"Two weeks, Pop," Vic said. "I get them again in two weeks. Every other weekend." He reached for his son's shoulder.

Jed rolled his eyes and was first out of the room. Daphne kissed Lloyd and followed Jed but didn't catch him until the courtyard. Exiting through the rec room meant a longer walk to the car, but less walking inside the Green Springs building. Daphne pushed through the closest exit door, too.

Outside, the boy's mouth pinched and he rubbed his scalp, looking just like Vic.

Was he crying? Daphne squinted. "Jed?"

The boy squinted back and kicked the ground. "Did you know that G-Pop wears a diaper?"

Daphne nodded.

Jed toed his shoe in the lawn and whispered, "Sometimes I hate coming here. I wish I didn't, but I do."

She slipped one arm onto his shoulder, then her breath caught when he slipped his around her waist. He turned the gesture into a motion more akin to pushing Daphne away, and she let her arm drop.

"I wish I didn't hate it," he said. His miserable tone became wistful.

"Hey, buddy, would you have liked to . . . I mean, maybe sometime, would you like to get away for the weekend? You and your sister and me and your dad? Like to Leavenworth?"

"Leavenworth?"

"I had a chance to go this weekend. We were all invited. Maybe we should all go away sometime. I'll talk to your dad if you need a break from coming here every Saturday."

"But then G-Pop would feel . . ." Jed shook his head and spread his hands in a hopeless gesture. "It's like you can't fix it, you know?"

"I know. I do."

He rolled his eyes, let loose a disgusted snort, and stalked off, trailing his father and sister, who had cleared the courtyard and would beat them to the parking lot.

"What should I have said?" Daphne asked no one, her voice soft. "That I'm sorry I wanted to be nice?" She tried to convince herself that the boy wasn't rejecting her. It wasn't personal.

At her truck, watching the three of them go to the rental car, Daphne remembered the way the kids' hands felt in her palm four years ago, when they were hand-holders and huggy. Recalling the softness, she nodded. She imagined those hands—little kid hands no longer in her palm—and remembered managing to give them slipping-away, finger-light squeezes today. She remembered stroking Josie's hair the night before.

Daphne glanced down at her empty palm, her fingers brushing nothing at all.

In the distance, Josie raised her chin at her dad, making an imp's grin. "This is the best thing you could rent?"

Jed laughed at his sister. She flashed him a return smile and got into the backseat. Josie had been up front on the drive over. Fairness was crucial to Vic in how he treated his children. If they were driving several places, the kids took turns in the front seat, and on one-way rides, Vic seated them both in the back.

"It's just a car," Vic said, sounding tired. Then he smirked at his kids and said, "Yes, it's the very best I could do."

Daphne's soft hand turned into a fist.

CHAPTER 21

Pulling in behind Vic's rental car at home, Daphne paused, her hand on the ignition, letting the truck's engine run. She watched the kids go up the steps, saw Vic watch her through the windshield. She moved her hand from the key to the shift lever and backed her truck out again.

Vic hurried to the street. "Where are you going?" he asked, leaning in her window.

"I'm just going," Daphne said.

He looked ready to press her, to cajole her into hanging out with him and Jed and Josie for the rest of the afternoon.

If he told her not to be distant or asked her what was wrong, she'd scream.

The truth was, so much felt wrong amid so much right.

Then Vic smiled and kissed her. "See you soon?"

"Right," Daphne said, faking a smile. "Yeah, of course."

She drove down Westpark Avenue to the end of the Peace Park, where she hesitated at the cross street until the car behind her honked and she was startled into turning along the edge of the park just to get out of the irate driver's path.

At Eastpark Avenue, she drove until she reached Minerva Watts's house, where she slowed her truck, then parked on the street. She sat there for a long time, thinking and not thinking.

Suppose she'd never stepped into the Peace Park Wednesday, had never seen Mrs. Watts, never heard her haunting cries about being kidnapped and robbed?

Dementia? Or was the old lady making a real complaint about a terrible offense? Could it be both?

She drove on, picturing the scene two days earlier with the Lincoln escaping down Eastpark, the black-haired woman holding Minerva Watts, holding Daphne's jacket. But today, she was in her truck, not Vic's Honda, and she was not chasing the Lincoln. And something . . . something else. Her mind niggled, processing, trying to find what she missed. Of Minerva Watts's and her own troubles? Of Suzanne?

Daphne shook her head. "Of myself."

Is that what I'm missing? Part of me?

But with a mile and then another, she cleared the intersection where she'd caused the wreck, and drove down the hill where the Lincoln had fled.

Sticking to the main roads, flowing with traffic, she reached the intersection where the stolen Lincoln had been abandoned. The dots connected.

"That impounded car had to be the same Lincoln I followed," she said. She let her truck idle down the street to the far corner, just as she had done with Vic the day before.

Suppose, just suppose, Daphne thought, working it out aloud.

"They were getting away from me, afraid they were caught. They had to get rid of the car. And there's this rental agency at the end of the block. One of them went inside and rented a car." Sitting outside the rental agency's office, she wished she'd described the people—Guff and

Lisa Preston

that woman—to the clerk when Vic signed for a rental car the previous afternoon.

I could have asked what kind of cars were rented yesterday afternoon, asked if the clerk remembered a little old lady.

But maybe one of them kept Minerva Watts in the Lincoln at the other end of the block until the rental car was procured.

After shutting her truck off, she trotted to the agency's door, tugged on it even though it was locked, and stared at the placard showing the hours. "Closed," she said as she gave the handle a final shove.

She could return to the agency when it reopened and ask all her good questions. If the same clerk who had rented to Vic the day before was working—the clerk who remembered details well enough to say that the Rainier Court Vacation House had just been rented—then Daphne could ask questions. She could ask for descriptions and . . . And that clerk knew the vacation house was rented because someone had reserved it from the car rental office.

As soon as the thought congealed, Daphne gasped.

Reaching into her jeans pocket, she pulled out the cards, repocketing the police officer's card as she studied the vacation house flier. She shook her head, got back in her car, and started the engine again. "It's a lot of ifs."

But she drove on and felt prickles on her skin when, fifteen minutes later, she was on the east side of the city, at the mouth of Rainier Court. Again, she snaked the cards from her pocket. Within the folds of the vacation house flier was the police officer's card. She turned it over and read the words next to the case number: *Officer Taminsky Threats/Suspicious Incident.*

She studied the flier. One side showed a little map to the vacation house and photos of the inside and exterior of the property. A shot of the living room and fireplace. Shots of the front and back views—the Sound and thick woods—and one of the green exterior, with its prow front. Below the photos, a sales pitch shouted to those considering choosing a vacation house over a hotel or bed and breakfast. Adjoins a natural greenbelt! Commanding views of Puget Sound and Mount Rainier! Centrally located! Available weekly or monthly!

Rainier Court—like the little streets adjacent—was a long cul-de-sac. Daphne drove down the lane, claustrophobic with the street's narrowness. Heavy, dark trees from an untamed woodland loomed over the houses deepest in the cul-de-sac.

Daphne stopped and peered at the house numbers on each side of the road. Counting, she realized the house farthest into the cul-de-sac, the one with the imposing front prow, was the rental house. It didn't stand out, this place rented out on short term called the Rainier Court Vacation House.

A vacation house? Daphne studied it from her safe distance. It was just a green two-story house pushed into a green hill.

The car rental clerk's words echoed. *Someone rented it yesterday.*

It was someone who had just rented a car from the car agency.

A late model white sedan sat parked in front of the house and she wondered what kind of car the agency might have rented to someone in the minutes after the Lincoln had been abandoned. Studying the clean sedan in the distance, she said, "That is *so* a rental car."

But she couldn't find the courage to drive up, knock on the door, and see what happened. She could just try out silly words, fitting a worst-case scenario.

"Hello," she said, leaning under her rearview mirror to better see the house at the end of the cul-de-sac. "Are you the creepy couple holding Minerva Watts? And are you robbing and kidnapping her? Did you take her grandmother's brooch? Did you sell her car? Are you making her sign over her house? Or is she your mom and going loopy so you're having to deal with her finances?"

She stared down the block at the house and decided there were different kinds of courage. She couldn't go down there—those last ten lots to the end—and knock on the door. She would sound like an ass to someone on vacation or she would end up in another confrontation with a couple who may be victimizing a little old lady. Or dealing with a failing mother's dementia.

As doubts amassed and her fortitude failed, sweat clustered at her temples. "I am making myself crazy."

She backed her truck into the nearest driveway to turn around. At the mouth of Rainier Court, she peeked into her rearview mirror at the vacation house far behind her now. "Did you ditch a stolen car? Did you rent a fresh car? Is that where you saw the flier for this rental house?"

She turned the corner, passed another cul-de-sac, and hesitated as the road abutted a vast tract of undeveloped land, the same land that curved around to envelop the cul-de-sacs. "Are you holding little old Minerva Watts in that house? Are you stealing all her stuff?" She kicked the floorboard. "Where's the brooch? Where's my jacket and my wallet and phone?"

Crazy. She knew how crazy she'd sound if she called the police right now.

Besides, she didn't have a cell phone anymore.

The land the flier called a greenbelt wasn't an area of manicured trails like the Peace Park, but rather one of the many pockets of random wilderness all over Washington State. And the forest afforded a much better way to take a closer peek at the vacation house. Daphne parked, stepped out of the truck, and slipped into the woods.

Under the assorted evergreens, the ground teemed with ferns and blackberries. Vines twirled in the canopy above her head. She hiked, aiming to penetrate the woods as deep as the cul-de-sacs, paralleling them before cutting across to pass the first street then guess her way to the back of Rainier Court. Looking back, she lost sight of her truck, the street, anything other than occasional glimpses of streetlights and power lines.

Avoiding oozy black mud that smelled of rotting vegetation made her trek longer. Early season mosquitoes lifted from the wetness as she trudged up and down a hilly section. The sun vanished from view within minutes of hiking into the deep woods. She slipped in the peaty ground climbing another hill and reminded herself that Rainier Court had indeed been an uphill street to the vacation rental. She pushed closer to where she guessed the houses should be, although all was wilderness.

The trek took longer than she'd thought it would. With no trail to follow and rough ground, perhaps fifteen minutes passed before she edged closer to where houses should be. The prickling on her skin made her rub her arms. She saw brown siding, heard a distant voice and a door slam. She faded back.

Wondering if she'd gone too far and was now skirting houses on the street after Rainier Court, she saw a bare flash of a white car at the front of the house's green prow.

Daphne clung to the trees, sinking deeper into the hemlocks and cedars and firs as she moved to spy on the back of the house.

Tucked into the green hillside, the back of the Rainier Court Vacation House appeared single story, but it was the upper story relative to the front of the house. A deck, moldy and crusted with lichen, faced the woods. A sliding glass door with the curtain drawn veiled the inside, but two shadows hunched over a table. To the right, nearer the front of the house was a window that might have been over a kitchen sink, to the left, a small window and more drawn curtains over another window. A silhouette showed there too, rocking, someone slight in build. A child? A small person?

Slipping from the woods, Daphne stepped onto the deck. The wood was slick, the top fibers soft and blackened from the constant wet of the north-side woods, never feeling sunshine. In the cold, she crept across the surface and moved to the door to listen.

She heard nothing but wondered, *What if it's her? What if Minerva Watts is here?*

And still, doubts. *What if I'm just interfering? Suppose there's nothing sinister going on at all? Suppose it's just a couple tasked with caring for a little old lady?*

She stepped off the deck. Little old ladies can be difficult to tend.

She thought of Lloyd and his unwillingness to leave the sanctuary of his rest home in the last year.

I'm not her mother. Just this morning, Lloyd had temporarily forgotten who Daphne was, had forgotten Vic was no longer with Cassandra.

"How do I know for sure?" Daphne whispered under the window where someone rocked. Loud as she dared, she called, "Mrs. Watts?"

And then she gasped as she heard a door open at the front of the house and voices rose. A man said something sharp but unintelligible, then a woman snapped, "Just do it!"

They were out front, by the car. Daphne crept back onto the deck and made a tentative push on the sliding glass door. It gave, unlocked. She moved it open just far enough to slip in sideways, and swept the curtain from her face. A big reclining chair sat to her left, in the room's corner. The vacation house offered a great room, half living room of carpets under padded furniture, and half dining area with a dark table and four matching chairs on a stone floor. Rows of papers lined the table, making her think of the dining table at home every April when Vic did his taxes.

The front door slammed and quick footsteps approached. Daphne flung herself behind the corner recliner, deciding in a split-second that pushing back through the curtain was too much of a giveaway. The fabric would flap, be sucked out the open door in her wake if she fled onto the deck.

Could whoever entered the room hear the banging of her heart? Daphne made herself very small behind the recliner, memorizing its tweedy brown pattern. It was clean, as was the carpet under her knees. No dust bunnies. She willed the curtain to remain still to disguise the open sliding door. She prayed for no draft to alert whoever had come in, and wondered if she'd be hidden from someone coming to close the door.

But they'll wonder why the door's open. Then what do I do?

The scoot of a wooden chair on stone made her breath catch. Someone banged on the table, then hurried away, back toward the front door.

"Guff," a woman hissed, "you forgot the other credit card."

Daphne chanced a peek at the woman hurrying away. It was her, the one Daphne had seen bully Minerva Watts away in the Peace Park, the black-haired woman who had shouted for Guff at the Watts residence.

Daphne noticed something else on the table, beyond the papers: a fresh bouquet of roses. And then a pack of cigarettes and a lighter. Daphne let her mouth twist as she eyed the rich, red blossoms from her refuge. These rose petals would not be rubbed on the other woman's body, she decided, hearing echoes of the woman's short tone. They were makeup roses. *She's mad at him. He knows it, doesn't want her pissed off.*

That is a woman not getting along with her man, Daphne decided, smirking at the bouquet on the table.

The man and woman's voices carried, but not enough for Daphne to make out words in their conversation by the car outside. She heaved herself from behind the recliner, hesitating with one hand on the sliding glass door, the heavy feel of the curtain on her wrist. Staring at the table, she moved, cringing as she brought herself closer to the voices outside in order to peek at the notes and papers.

A yellow notepad held careful rows of numbers and brief notes. A Diners Club card and a Sears charge card beside the pad were in the name of Minerva Watts.

The black-haired woman's muffled voice encouraged, demanded. "Just go . . . get it done . . ." Then her voice grew nearer, dismissing the man, returning to her lair.

"This one isn't as Alzheimer's-y as the others." The man's parting comment pierced Daphne into retreat. As she whirled, she saw her first glimpse down the hallway before throwing herself behind the corner recliner again.

How long would that curtain cover the open glass door? *No wind, no wind,* Daphne prayed. She allowed herself the thinnest of glances toward the table where footsteps sounded on stone.

The woman wore black again, tailored slacks and a sweater. She reached for the cigarettes, leaning across the table and then, with the table creaking under her weight as she leaned farther still, she low-ered her face to the bouquet and bit into the nearest blossom. Daphne could just make out a hint of the woman wiping her mouth after the odd morsel, then the woman stalked back out the front door with her cigarettes and lighter.

Daphne pushed herself up and sprang down the hall, past the bath-room on the left. The next door was closed, latched with an odd metal add-on lock that encircled the doorknob and ratcheted onto the decora-tive molding that trimmed the doorway. A travel lock. Daphne flipped it off, slipped into the bedroom, and startled Minerva Watts.

The lady sat on the bed, arms clutched around her own thin shoul-ders. She still wore pink slacks under a quilted calico housedress. A pair of blue loafers rested on the floor at the bedside.

"Mrs. Watts, do you want to go with me?" Daphne asked, her voice soft but urgent.

"I want to go home."

"Yes, yes," Daphne whispered, diving to the floor. She worked to put the shoes on the cool, stiff feet, neatening the bobby socks as nec-essary to get the shoes on, given the time crunch.

"Who are you?" Minerva Watts asked.

"I'm Daphne. I'll take you home. M'kay? Follow me." Daphne kept her hand over Minerva Watts's, leading her away to safety.

"Yes, Daphne."

"We have to be quiet. No talking right now," Daphne whispered.

"Yes, Daphne."

She'd not heard the front door open again. The woman, Daphne hoped, was out front, busy smoking. Maybe the man had driven away.

Where would he go? Back to Minerva Watts's house? Pawning something? Running up Minerva Watts's credit cards?

She guided Minerva behind the curtain, gripping the old lady's elbow as they crossed the deck, steadied her on the stairs, fearing every moment the lady would slip and fall. The old woman remained

cooperative, giving every indication of understanding the situation—
they were making an escape and they had to be quiet. They had to
hide. Daphne wanted to rush long and deep into the trees, but instead
dodged from one large tree trunk to another for cover. Minerva Watts's
gait was too slow for better progress.

"Hurry, hurry," Daphne whispered, throwing a look over her shoulder. She could still see the house. If the black-haired woman came
inside, opened the curtain, and looked out the back deck door, she
might see Daphne and Minerva Watts.

As rambling as Daphne's solo, unsure hike to the house had been,
it was much faster than she would be able to trace her way back to the
truck with Mrs. Watts.

"We have to hurry," she hissed.

Twice, Minerva let out little cries of "Whoops" or "Goodness" and
flashed apologetic looks when Daphne shushed her.

I'm pushing her too hard.

The ground dipped behind three tree trunks growing together,
offering a shield. Daphne crouched in the perfect minicrater, gesturing
for Minerva Watts to duck down with her.

The old lady slipped on the uneven ground and ended up on her
rear. Daphne squatted down, feeling safer than she had in the last ten
minutes of her life.

"My," Minerva Watts said, dusting her hands together before leaning close to Daphne's face and whispering, "Is it Saturday today?"

"Yes," Daphne said, pleased. Everything would be easier if Mrs.
Watts was mentally together, not an Alzheimer's victim. "Yes, it is."

"Two nights I've been in that bedroom. There is no bathroom in
there."

"I'm sorry—"

"Sometimes, oh, this is awful, but sometimes, I have to get up in
the night. Well, that woman wouldn't let me out to the bathroom at
night. And the first night, I didn't make it. The second night, last night,

I knew. I knew, so I didn't drink anything all afternoon and evening so I wouldn't have to go." The old face looked pained, embarrassed, then too distressed to contain the tears and little sobs that shook her thin shoulders. "I messed myself. Yesterday, she told me to just let my clothes dry. But look."

Minerva pulled her housedress up and half-turned on the forest floor, pointing to the yellow stain on her pants. "I'm so embarrassed. And I don't have any underwear on. I, I couldn't bear to put them back on again. I'm not properly dressed, Daphne. I'm only half-dressed and I'm in dirty clothes. I so want to freshen up. Can you stand to be with me?"

"Yes, I can," Daphne breathed, thinking of her mother, who wanted nothing so much as her daughter's company.

"Three days and two nights, I've been there in that bedroom." The old lady's indignation rose. "They wouldn't let me leave."

"I'm sorry," Daphne whispered, her hands clutching Minerva's fingers as though in prayer. "I am so sorry. I guessed, but I wasn't sure. I should have come for you yesterday. A day is so long. Too long." And it had taken her a day to get the Eastpark address from Thea. Daphne swallowed. "Three days is . . . forever. I'm so sorry I didn't figure it out sooner. I wish I had. Please understand, I am so very sorry."

Minerva patted her hand, looking overwhelmed by the apology more than her predicament. "Well, you're here now, dear. Dear Daphne." She beamed, then frowned as shouts came from the house and Daphne raised a warning finger.

Staring wide-eyed back at the house, unable to make out the words yelled from the deck, Daphne watched with one eye and saw the woman at the rear of the rental house.

As quietly as she could speak with clarity and without looking at Minerva, Daphne said, "Don't move. Don't speak. That woman is looking for us. She knows you're out of the house. Do not move."

CHAPTER 22

Daphne held her breath and tried to imagine the worst-case scenario as she hoped for the best. They had about two hours of daylight left, but the tree canopy refused most of the overcast sky's light, making the forest dark. If they were still, if that woman didn't come into the woods, if she'd done the right thing, then things would be okay.

She looked at Minerva Watts sitting on the forest floor. The lady looked as though she might like to hum. Her finger stroked the fir-needled ground, a pleasant expression on her face.

She smiled at me when I came to her house. She remembered my name, called me Daphne.

She didn't remember my name today. She asked me who I was today.

The worst-case, Daphne decided, *is I just spirited away a little old lady who was supposed to be in that bedroom.* And once she acknowledged her doubt, it built, flooded. *I don't know her. In truth, I don't know anything about this situation. What if Vic's right, they're just some people having a hard time with an older*—no, *the credit cards. I saw them.*

But people taking care of older relatives have to deal with financial arrangements. They handle the elderly person's credit cards and deeds and titles. She remembered Vic going over his father's finances at home, intercepting a charged purchase originating in another state for a fancy stereo, an obvious fraud perpetrated on an old man. Vic never established how the unknown criminal had collected Lloyd's credit card number, nor could he ever be sure whether the old man had been convinced by a predator to hand it over or if the card number had been outright stolen somehow. He'd gotten the charge reversed, ordered a new credit card number, and offered to store his dad's cards for safekeeping.

Feeling the uncertainty, Daphne clung to Guff's comment to the black-haired woman: *Not as Alzheimer's-y as the others.*

They were bad people. They were, right? She wasn't, was she?

And Mrs. Watts said they wouldn't let her use the bathroom. If that were true, it settled things. If it were true.

She whispered, "Do you know them, Mrs. Watts?" and swallowed hard. Was she doing the right thing? Her words became a whispered torrent. "Do you remember me? In the park?"

"Of course, Daphne, I—"

"And a few days ago?" Daphne's words came in a rush. "And then, at your house? Do you remember seeing me before today?"

"Pardon, dear?"

"I . . ." Daphne turned and studied the vacation house.

Suppose she hadn't run from Minerva Watts's house when Guff had grabbed her shoulder? Would everything have been sorted out then? Couldn't she just confront the woman, explain her concerns, and demand the police be called?

Doubt. When boiled down to the essence, wasn't doubt what kept people from intervening? A lack of certainty? Because if people knew someone was in trouble, they helped, didn't they? That was the deal, the bargain of being part of the human family.

Holding her breath, Daphne tried to decipher her gut feeling. She hadn't always suspected Minerva Watts was in trouble. On their first encounter—Wednesday in the Peace Park—Daphne had been absorbed in her thoughts, startled and disturbed by an old lady claiming kidnap and robbery. Frowning, Daphne found no gut feeling to fall back to from that day. She wasn't a gut-feeling kind of girl.

And then a decade-old memory sifted up. At twenty-one, the evening her father left the house for the last time, she'd gone to bed early, tired of college and feeling like she didn't belong. The empty spring break stretched ahead before she'd have to go back for her final half semester. She'd kissed her mother good night, then her father.

He'd held her extra-long, told her she'd always be his good girl, had been steamy-eyed. As she'd gone upstairs to sleep across from Suzanne's empty bed, an unnerving feeling had prickled her. A doubt. Her father had been behaving strangely.

But by morning, after hearing he'd taken his own life, she'd reacted like a child, wondering only what her mother had or hadn't done or said.

When her mother later talked about his death—in halting, teary words of confusion and loss, repeating endlessly that she didn't know—Daphne had stood mute. They hadn't known he was so sad, so bleak, he couldn't face Suzanne's birthday.

Just yesterday she'd realized her dad couldn't live down the detective's last talk about handing the suspended homicide over to the cold case unit, but she didn't blame Arnold Seton.

She shouldn't have blamed her mother.

Minerva had said from their first contact that she didn't know the black-haired woman.

As she chose what to do, Daphne squinted at the back of the vacation house. The woman in black cupped her hands to her eyes, making a visor as she peered at the woods from the deck, swiveling as she searched left and right. She stepped off the deck and looked around the house's side yards.

Minerva Watts cocked her head and smiled, misty-eyed, at Daphne.

She's safe now, Daphne decided. Whatever else, she's safe now. Shoulders shaking, she thought of things she'd imagined as a teen when she learned bits and pieces of what happened to her sister. They never knew where the murder occurred, just where the body was dumped. She was tied up. She was raped. She was strangled. And, as the investigator hoped, as her father prayed, *someone must have seen something*. When Suzanne met a man, when the man got violent, when he moved her body, all were chances for another stranger, a good person, to see, to act, to aid.

But whoever saw something didn't intervene in a stranger's life.

I've come this far, Daphne encouraged herself. *I will make Minerva Watts safe before I go asking questions.*

Motion would make them more visible, easier to spot. Daphne kept her breathing shallow and watched with one eye between tree trunks, glad she was brown-haired, hoping Mrs. Watts's calico housedress was low enough in their little divot in the earth.

If that woman didn't just plunge headlong into the woods, they might be okay. If the man didn't return to the house and didn't come into the woods after them, they were safe. Daphne looked for a stout branch on the ground, moving her head as little as possible in the search.

Motion caught her eye back at the house, and she aborted her search for a weapon to watch the woman go back inside.

Twisting on her knees, Daphne leaned into the old lady's face. "Who are they, Mrs. Watts? Who are those people? They were with you in the Peace Park, the first day I saw you, and then the next day at your house, and here. Who are they?"

"I don't know. I don't know them, dear. They're stealing everything from me."

Daphne's mouth opened and closed as she hesitated, trying to believe.

Don't hesitate, she told herself. *Do something.*

"Okay, we're going through the woods to my truck now, Mrs. Watts. When we get there, we'll drive to the nearest phone and call the police." Daphne tugged at the frail old arm, making her stand. "It took me ten or fifteen minutes to walk in here. Okay?"

"I'm not dressed for going out, dear." Minerva's protest was demure.

"Oh, that's all right." With continued physical insistence, Daphne forced Mrs. Watts along, feeling she must seem just like the black-haired woman in the Peace Park, bullying an old lady.

They made forty yards of progress before Minerva lost her footing and tumbled to the ground. Daphne clung to her, trying to cushion the fall.

"Are you okay?" Daphne hovered, using her fingertips to touch Minerva's side, knee, and wrist.

Minerva Watts stayed prone on the musty soil.

Daphne fell to her knees into the humus and whispered, "Can you get up?"

"Fairy Slippers," Minerva cried. "I've found Fairy Slippers. It's been so long since I've seen Fairy Slippers. Imagine finding such a treasure now."

"You're not making sense," Daphne said through her teeth, desperation making every muscle knot. *Please don't be a crazy old lady.*

Minerva Watts stayed face down and talked to the ground. "Oh, the Calypso. I haven't seen one since I was a girl. Younger than you, much younger. Imagine, us finding Fairy Slippers."

Dear God, suppose Minerva Watts has dementia? Suppose I extrapolated, imagined things, and drew connections that did not exist? If Vic and Thea and the police were right and there was nothing wrong, what have I done?

She had kidnapped an old lady.

"Do you know, dear . . . Daphne," Minerva said, her smile growing wistful, "there are flowers you see once a generation?" She reached out a trembling hand, extended a finger, and touched a tiny bearded flower growing between two small rocks.

"Mrs. Watts," Daphne began, "Minerva? I think I've made a big mis—"

"These are Fairy Slippers," Minerva said, pointing to the flower while she twisted her prone body to beam at Daphne. "Fairy Slippers are what you call Calypso Orchids, but I don't recall their proper Latin name. They're rare, you see. So rare. And they don't live very long, not long at all."

"Mrs. Watts . . ." Daphne looked deep into the woods, wished for her truck, and cast a wary eye in the direction of the vacation house. Were they halfway to the truck? No, less than a quarter of the distance, she decided, remembering the steeper hills and the mud she'd traversed.

Mrs. Watts caressed the two-inch-tall flower's miniature purple-spotted beard. A doleful look replaced her excitement at her discovery of rare wild miniature orchids in the woods.

"They haven't any nectar, you see."

"Mrs. Watts . . ." Daphne pulled at the woman's shoulders and cast a look down the pink-clothed legs. Minerva Watts didn't seem to be hurt from her fall. Suppose she just picked the lady up and carried her?

"You don't have to call me Mrs. Watts, dear."

"Minerva. Minerva, we have to—"

"When I was a girl, they called me Minnie," Minerva Watts said. "I always liked that. I liked it when they called me Minnie. And then when they had the Mickey Mouse Club, it was a good joke. Minnie Mouse. Do you know about the Mickey Mouse Club? Yes, I was Minnie, when I was young. Even younger than you, dear."

"I'll call you Minnie, if you like," Daphne said, flushing at the thought of addressing a lady of Minerva Watts's years by such a casual nickname.

Should she grab her and run for it? She could carry someone of Minnie Watts's weight. She could. But on this ground, chances were high she'd slip and fall if she ran while carrying Minnie. She might hurt the fragile old lady.

We'll just have to go slowly, but make it back to the truck. What else can we do?

And then Minnie's eyes watered, one tear slipping down the cheek closer to the ground.

"What is it, Minnie? Minnie? We need to go now, Minnie. Minnie?"

"I'll never see them again." Minnie hovered one index finger above the rare orchid. "Never again. Never. They're so beautiful. And rare. You have to find them in the wild because . . . because they can't be cultivated. Fairy Slippers. I expect I'll never see them again."

I want to see them next week, too. Lloyd's words, the hope behind them, flooded into Daphne.

Of course Vic would make his children go visit their grandfather every weekend he had them. Daphne's mind reeled. How much was missed when a generation—or a part of a generation—disappeared?

She lifted Minnie to her feet, relieved the lady could stand, could walk a few halting paces.

In ten yards, the ground got brushier, and Daphne let go of Minnie to reach forward and part a path in the brush.

"Oh!" Minnie cried as she slipped. Daphne grabbed her but one of Minnie's loafers fell off.

Don't be hurt, Daphne prayed. Please, please, don't have a twisted ankle.

"Minnie, are you all right?" She knelt and tried to let go of Minerva Watts's hands, but the lady clutched at her. Daphne looked up then away from Minerva's watery eyes. The paper-thin skin of her liver-spotted wrists deserved care, not the hard grasp Daphne had thrust on them when she grabbed to prevent another fall.

She caressed the old hands. The clutches loosened and Daphne pulled free to smooth the old woman's stockinged foot.

"I'm tired," Minnie said. "I need to take a nap."

And you're probably dehydrated from withholding water from yourself, Daphne thought. "But Minnie, I have to get you out of here. We have to go." She wriggled the cast shoe back onto Minerva Watts's foot.

"Dear, I can't. I cannot take another step. I don't go hiking and trekking."

"Oh, Minnie." Daphne swung her arm wide in despair, brushing into nearby leaves. At once, she recoiled, her hand burning as though bitten by dozens of ants. "Ow!"

"That's stinging nettle," Minerva said, pointing to the greenery draping toward them from the mud. "It hurts you the most when it's in full flower."

"Aw, Minnie." Daphne felt air and much more deflate from her body. She couldn't ask a frail old woman to make an escape by hiking through undergrowth and hilly, muddy, rutted ground. What had taken her ten minutes on the way to the vacation house demanded a half hour's bushwhacking over bad footing at an old woman's pace. Minerva Watts was an old lady wearing loafers. Daphne was asking too much. "Maybe we could just cut across the woods to the next street. I could get my truck and move it closer."

Daphne weighed the plan of cutting through to the next street instead of taking the woods all the way to her truck. She stood on a stump, nodding as she looked in the direction where the street between the woods and Rainier Court should be. "We're close to the end of the next cul-de-sac. If you wait here, I could run ahead and move my truck to that street. Would you wait for me right here, Minnie?"

Minerva turned a kindly smile as though she were being told dinner wasn't being served right away, but if she'd be a good guest, it would be hot and on the table in fifteen more minutes. "Of course, I'll wait for you, Daphne."

"Promise me, Minnie. Promise you'll wait right here, okay?"

"I promise."

Daphne cast one fearful look in the direction of the vacation house. They weren't far from it, but they were in dense cover. With one parting squeeze to Minerva Watts's arm, Daphne bolted in the general direction of her truck, running like life depended on speed. She leapt over rocks and roots and stumps. When vines twirled around her ankles, she kicked her feet free. When she crashed to her hands and knees in muddy grime, she shoved herself to her feet and ran on.

On the main street, she fired up her truck and spun a one-eighty. Her tools flew and clanged in the truck bed. She floored the accelerator, braked hard at the intersection, and zipped down the nearest cul-de-sac, squealing to a stop by the last two houses. Flying from her truck, she ignored a man who gawked at her while checking his mail, and darted through the side yards between the houses.

Barging straight into the woods, Daphne felt winded. She was no runner and it was tough footing with undergrowth that trapped her legs. She wove between trees, searching for the spot with the stinging nettle, searching for pink and calico.

"Ow!" Daphne yanked her hands up when the thigh-high nettles slipped their acid onto her palms. "Fuckety-fuck."

It hurts you the most when it's in full flower.

Where was Minnie? Was this the spot? Daphne swirled, searching the trampled ground, then turned again, casting about in the woods. She found the stump, the exact footprint in the woods where she'd left the little old lady. Daphne saw the path she'd forced into the brush when she'd run for her truck and saw brush she and Minnie had trampled when they'd progressed from the vacation house.

Had Minnie tried to follow her? Daphne climbed onto the stump, craning her head. The flash of pink was brief and low, a flit through trees, back toward the Rainier Court Vacation House. Launching herself, Daphne dodged trees, trying to retrace the route that had brought her and Minnie to this spot. By the time she got close enough to glimpse the deck, she could see Minnie, cloaked in a long black wool coat, held close by the black-haired woman. They were walking around the vacation house, heading for the front.

Daphne charged, gasping, feeling her heart bang against her chest wall. Before she neared the back deck, Minnie and the other woman were out of sight. An engine roared to life and car doors slammed. Daphne pelted around the house, screaming as the threesome pulled away in the white car.

Minnie Watts sat crammed between the man and woman in the front seat of the white sedan. Daphne's pulse increased in a crescendo that teased of what she wouldn't achieve as she chased the car down Rainier Court, falling farther behind with every stride.

When the car reached the main street and she didn't, Daphne screamed again. "Stop! No, stop! Wait!" She raced after the car with all her power.

With the car's violent lurch as the man took the corner onto the main street, Daphne found new speed, but she couldn't scream in top flight. She passed the next street, but it was hopeless. Pulling blocks farther away in seconds, the car fled, outstripping her human strength. She thought it turned right on another main street up ahead but couldn't say which one because it was so far away. Daphne's lungs demanded several sucking gasps before she had enough breath to cry out to the entire neighborhood.

"Call the police! Help! Call 911!" Then she ran again making another block before the rank futility of her effort seeped through her core. Too winded to cry, she slumped, elbows and knees on the pavement as she struggled for breath.

CHAPTER 23

The threat of screeching brakes forced Daphne to her feet. She rose from the asphalt still gasping for air, and wiped her face.

A car door opened and a man's voice asked, "Ma'am, are you all right?"

She turned. It was a uniformed police officer, with a patrol car behind him. She lurched toward him, then twisted and pointed down the road in the opposite direction.

"There's a car, a white car. You've got to stop it."

He indicated the passenger's side of his car. "Get in." As he got back behind the wheel, he leaned across the seat to open the door for her.

Daphne threw herself around the front bumper and into the police car, drawing her knees up, wanting to put her feet against the dashboard to brace herself.

"Seatbelt," he said.

She buckled herself in, ready for hot pursuit, but he drove not much faster than the determined side of normal, no screaming tires, no lights and siren.

He spoke rapid-fire and cryptically into his dashboard radio, a number of other voices and squelch returned, and then he said, "Ten-four."

"It went up and turned off to the right down here somewhere," Daphne said as they arrived within a few blocks of where the car had turned off.

"Describe the car. Make? Model? And start talking about why we want this car."

"It's white," she said. "Just white." Shit! The car color, that's all she had. Daphne took a breath. "It's a four-door. A sedan. And it's a late-model, like, new. Clean. I bet it's a rental."

"Foreign? American?"

"I don't know."

"And which road did it turn down?"

"I don't know. One of these. I was way back there. One block from Rainier Court. I was on foot."

"Okay," he said, braking his patrol car to the curb. "What's going on between you and the occupants of the white sedan?"

"They took a lady. An older lady named Minerva Watts. They're holding her and I think they're stealing from her."

"Who are they?" He spoke into his radio again, but Daphne couldn't make out the quick code.

"A man and a woman. I don't know their names. Guff. The woman called the man Guff. I don't know if it's a nickname or what." She looked around as he turned his car around with a smooth one-eighty in an intersection. He was driving them back toward Rainier Court. She sat up stiff and straight, rising with her voice. "Wait, what are you doing? Go after that car."

"What's your name?" he asked. And as soon as she told him, he said, "Miss Mayfield, other officers are closer than I am to that car. If they see it, this white late-model four-door with three occupants, two women, older one named Minerva Watts, and a man named Guff, they'll stop it for me and I can work from there. Right now, you and I will begin at the beginning."

As he passed Rainier Court, Daphne pointed. "There. That's where it started. I mean, today it did. This goes back to Wednesday. It's kind of complicated."

He pulled up to the end of the last cul-de-sac, to her ill-parked truck, and they both got out, walking the few feet to her truck.

Giving her a pointed glance of appraisal, he said, "So, neighbors call about a young white woman in jeans and a black T-shirt. They say she drove up at a high rate of speed in a Toyota pickup with a camper shell on it, and she went running between these houses into the woods. And the neighbor calls back, says the woman is now running and screaming on the next road—"

"Rainier Court," she supplied.

He nodded, gave a quick smile, and said, "Right before I arrive, this woman is screaming, running down the main road, down Everson, and she's shouting for people to call 911."

"That was me."

"So I gathered. We got another call from a Rainier Court resident." He walked around her truck, peered in the windows. "Why do you have all these tools in the back?"

"I'm a roofer."

He raised his eyebrows.

"You said begin at the beginning," she told him. "I'll try to make it brief."

She described driving to Rainier Court, feeling intimidated about going straight to the front door, then parking on the main road and hiking through the woods until she arrived at the back of the vacation house. She skipped how she got into the house, concentrating instead on Minerva Watts's credit cards arranged on the dining table, the man and the woman, their comments, the add-on lock that kept Minnie confined to the bedroom, and the few details Minnie had related.

The officer turned in place, shifting his weight from one foot to the other, and answered a squawk on his radio with a mumble as he listened to her story. He asked how far into the woods she'd gone after moving her truck to this cul-de-sac, and everything she could tell about the couple leaving with "the Watts woman."

"Oh, God. I never should have left her. I never should have left Minnie in the woods alone. I left her! I left her by herself." Sobs made Daphne tremble even as she told herself to pull it together.

He spoke into his radio some more and this time Daphne caught a bit of a woman's voice. ". . . registered to a Daphne Mayfield on Mapleview Drive."

My truck, she decided. *He ran some kind of check on my truck.*

"Let's go take a peek at the end of Rainier," he said.

"Yes, good. Rainier Court. Can I drive myself instead of going in your car?"

"Sure."

Another patrol car was there, parked right across the driveway of the Rainier Court Vacation House. A blond man in uniform stepped away from the neighboring house as a woman in sweatpants hurried back inside.

The blond officer shrugged at the officer following Daphne. The two men conferred by one patrol car, with the blond officer shooting skeptical glances at Daphne.

"There's more," she called out. Closing the distance between them, Daphne told them in a rush, "They're holding her, stealing her money, kidnapping her. You have to believe me. You have to do something." She could not lose ground with the police. This new guy and the blond man had to believe her.

The first officer continued to regard her with a set, grim face. And the blond guy said, "Calm down, ma'am."

She wiped tears from her face. "I don't want to calm down," she said. "Please, please, believe me. No one believes me. Look, I have this card, this officer's card." She pulled it from her pocket. "Officer Taminsky. He knows what's going on, I mean until today. He doesn't know about today. He knows about before."

"Before," the first officer said, taking the card and then stepping away to spurt words and numbers into his radio. When he gave her his attention, she told him the rest, the before. Wednesday in the park, Thursday at Minnie Watts's house.

"And she asked them not to take her brooch. And the woman called her *lady* but when she saw me, she called Minnie *Mother*, and poor Minnie, she was so glad to see me, just like today." Daphne took a breath and told them about Guff grabbing her, about the car accident and getting arrested for reckless driving, then again how one thing led to another today.

"And the guy said 'this one isn't as Alzheimer's-y as the others,'" Daphne reminded them, wondering how many others there were.

"How 'bout a security sweep around back," the blond officer said to the first. "Make sure the place is secure."

The first officer nodded and told Daphne, "Wait right here."

Waiting in front of the vacation house, Daphne thought about how she'd told Minnie Watts to wait.

Bits of motion in neighboring windows caught her attention. She was being watched by people who hadn't so much as stepped outside when she'd screamed for help.

Turning her back on those unhelpful neighbors, she squinted up at the officers' silhouettes moving upstairs in the vacation house.

As soon as they came outside, she asked, "Did you find anything?"

"We weren't searching the house, per se," the first officer said.

"No," said the blond, "just making sure it's secure. And there's nothing remarkable in there."

Daphne clenched her jaw. The couple would have taken their papers and Minnie's credit cards. She pictured the details, the roses on the table. What happened to the little add-on lock she'd pulled off the bedroom doorknob? She had a vague memory of dropping it when she knelt on the floor to help Minnie don shoes. She swallowed and faced the first cop.

"That woman put her coat over Minnie and—"

The blond cop looked at Daphne for one second, then told the first officer, "Sounds like she was taking care of her. After all, you say she addressed the Watts woman as her mother and—"

"Suppose she put the coat on her to disguise Minnie?" Daphne fired back. "To make her harder to see, harder for me to find her?"

The blond made little calming motions with his hands. "Suppose they ran because you chased them?"

"No, listen to me. That woman, Minerva Watts, she's in trouble. These people are holding her, keeping her against her will. And I think they're stealing from her." Daphne snapped her fingers, remembering another piece. "She just sold her car wholesale to Fremont Ford. You can check that out." As soon as she said this, she remembered the dealership telling her they couldn't check on the sale until Monday.

The first officer squinted, as though he were trying to believe or trying to pretend while he listened to her talk again about the first car, the impound lot men's comments, and what Officer Taminsky had learned when he checked out Minnie's house on Eastpark and talked to the neighbors.

"Quite the circle-jerk," the second officer said to the first.

Daphne looked at him. "What?"

"Maybe they're running from you because you're chasing them and you're chasing them because they're running from you."

Circular reasoning wasn't going to get her out of this mess, wasn't going to help Minnie Watts. Daphne felt her tension grow, credibility slipping as the blond cop headed for his patrol car. Desperate to be believed, she repeated, "The guy said 'this one isn't as Alzheimer's-y as the others' and he was kind of in a tiff with the woman—"

The first cop pointed a finger at the house. "With Minerva Watts?"

"No, with the other woman." Daphne eyed him. When he'd told her to get in his police car right away and pursued the white car, he'd given up because they were too late to catch them. He'd chased without needing more of a reason from her, right from the start. She studied him for hope.

"Miss Mayfield," he said, "people just say 'this one' sometimes. It does not mean there were others. It's just an expression."

"Not this time." Her jaw thrust forward. "Not in this instance. Look, I think there were others. Saying she wasn't as Alzheimer's-y as the others means there are other victims. See, this stolen car from California ended up here in Seattle." She explained more about the impound, the abandoned car on the same block as the car rental agency and how the clerk had mentioned this house had just been rented. She talked about what the impound lot boss had said regarding the survivor coming to collect the car and the car being all that could be collected out of an estate because the owner—an old person—had recently signed things away to a charity that went defunct. And maybe the same thing was happening now, here.

"A lot of ifs," said the first cop.

"But he said 'this one' like there were others." Daphne felt angry tears on her lower eyelids.

"This one," said the blond. "The others. Could be just an expression."

Daphne shook her head. "Those people are holding that old woman. She was locked in a bedroom!"

"Sometimes people have to do that with their older relatives," the blond cop said as he turned to go.

She watched him drive away but couldn't stand the sight and closed her eyes. When she opened them to the sound of another vehicle, Officer Taminsky was pulling up. The first officer stepped to Taminsky's driver's door and they conferred for some minutes.

Daphne walked over. After all, they hadn't told her to stand where she was.

"Yeah, I checked that on the way over," Taminsky was saying. "A day-shifter impounded the car. Dispatch says they got calls associated with that impound from an out-of-state owner. Sounds kind of complicated."

"Quite a few ifs," the first cop said again.

Daphne nodded, then shook her head. "Not too many ifs. I wish they'd stopped and you could have talked to them. I tried to stop them. Why didn't they stop? Why didn't someone come out and help me stop them? Why didn't someone else call for help sooner?"

"Why didn't you call us instead of going into that house?"

"I don't have a phone, remember? Guff got it when he grabbed my jacket Thursday. He grabbed me." Then she pointed to the neighboring houses. "Lots of people must have seen. Someone should have called 911."

"Someone did. We had two calls on you."

"They should have called sooner."

The first cop eyed the houses around them. A few faces were visible at windows, watching the spectacle. "People don't always call the police when they see something suspicious. They're reluctant to intervene, can't decide what to do. They relieve themselves of the job. Officer Taminsky is going to finish up here, Miss Mayfield. Bye now."

Because he was willing to see, Daphne showed Taminsky where she'd parked her truck on the main road, where she'd run into the woods. They went behind the house, too, and she showed him where she and Minnie had hidden.

"You made an unlawful entry into the house."

Daphne closed her eyes. "What is the worst-case scenario?" she asked. She imagined being arrested again.

"I think we're both imagining the same worst-case," he said. "That there's a couple victimizing this Minerva Watts. That impounded Lincoln, well, it's odd, the history there, what we're hearing from the man claiming the California Lincoln, the other person on the registration and title."

She nodded and let the tears fall. *He believes me. This will get fixed.*

He raised an appraising eyebrow. "That Lincoln was abandoned not long after you followed it from Minerva Watts's home, not far from where you got in a traffic accident while pursuing it."

They dumped it because I pursued them, she realized. And that's why it ended up in an impound yard with Vic's car. "So what will you do? What happens now?"

He tapped his radio. "I've had another drive-by done at the place on Eastpark Avenue. There's no answer, doesn't seem like anyone's been there."

"No," she said. "It looked vacant when I drove by today, before I came to Rainier Court. I bet they haven't been back since Thursday, when he grabbed me and I ran." She cleared her throat. "They have her. They have Minnie Watts. I had her and I let her go." Daphne's voice dropped hollow and softer with each word.

"Ma'am," Taminsky said, "we'll find her. This will not go on and on. It will end. We will figure it out."

"But wait. Right now, what happens? You've got to *do* something."

He explained that they'd done what they could. He promised to let her know of any new developments, promised he'd verify everything he could, not let it go. He said again he'd do what he could to figure it out.

"You guys don't always figure things out," she said, desperate and sure.

"Ma'am?"

"There are things that never get figured out. Things that never get solved. Ever." And she knew it was true, knew she was right. "This is the third time since Wednesday that some cop has taken information from me and done what you guys call issuing a locate. And nothing's happened. You don't find her. You don't stop whatever's going on. There's lots of times you guys don't figure it out."

He nodded.

She stopped there, not wanting the fact that police had never figured out who killed Suzanne to derail the search for Minerva Watts. She knew Minnie Watts wasn't safe, even with the niggling doubts the police presented, making it sound so reasonable that it could all be a misunderstanding. She knew in her bones that Minnie wasn't safe, wherever she was in the city, with those strangers.

But Minnie had been safe, for a few moments, when she was in the woods with Daphne, kneeling amongst the Fairy Slippers in the rocks.

———⟋⟍———

"Where's your dad?" Daphne asked Jed, two seconds after she came through the front door and followed the sound of the TV into the living room. The boy—tonight looking like a boy-man in one of Vic's old shirts—was on the couch, his glasses shoved to the end of his nose as he tried to read without them.

He pushed his glasses back and studied her. She wiped sweat from her face and flapped her shirt, feeling a trickle of perspiration course down her ribs. She'd never stopped sweating from her sprint through the woods, down Rainier Court after the car, dealing with the police in her fury and desperate hope. Pushing stray hair back from her face, Daphne's fingers found moisture. She knew she must look greasy, like she'd been on a roof all day, shingling. Dirt smudged her jeans, clung to her shoes.

"He took Josie to a sleepover." He stretched his legs and crossed his ankles. "How 'bout you make me a nice five-course dinner?"

"What?" Daphne's chin dropped as she stared at him.

He grinned. "He said I should try not to bug you when you came home, so I thought I'd start with that."

A strangled snort erupted from Daphne's nose. Then she coughed and a fit of giggles burst forth.

"I'm not that funny," Jed told her.

"Stress," she explained. "Do you need some dinner?"

He inclined his head toward the table. Daphne swung around and saw the milk jug, and a paper towel smeared with mustard and bread crumbs. "Dad told me to make myself some sandwiches."

He'll clean it up, she thought. *He doesn't need to be told.* "I'll be upstairs."

Jed nodded and returned to his book.

Grazie wouldn't get up and come with her, even with plenty of pleading and encouragement. The dog flumped to lie on her side.

—m—

Cross-legged and alone on the bed, Daphne waited. For an idea, for hope, for Vic.

The phone did not ring.

She decided the police had forgotten to call, they'd been too busy, but they'd found Minnie. They had to find her, make her safe.

Then she called the police department and went through two dispatchers, explaining at length who she was and the numerous contacts she'd had with the Department and how she was hoping for an update.

"We have Officer Taminsky on the street on another call, Ma'am. We've relayed your request and he's telling the dispatcher on that radio channel that he has no new information for a Daphne Mayfield at this time."

Daphne fell back on the bed, phone on her chest, and wept.

When she heard Vic drive up, park, come in, and speak to Jed, make a small fuss over Grazie, then climb the stairs while ushering the dog along, Daphne pressed her lips together. When he opened the door, she felt a valve release as her mouth opened, but he spoke first.

"I think I'm going to put her down," Vic said, looking down at the dog. Doubt and resignation marked his face. "She's so delicate. And we don't know how old she really is. Nine? Younger? Twelve? Older?"

Daphne knew she could make this a short conversation. Determination surged through her mind. "She deserves another chance."

Vic's lips twisted. "It would be hard, the recovery. Demanding on all of us." They talked about doing the hip surgery in oblique terms these days, as it had all been hashed through before and the decision was waiting to be made.

She made her decision. "I get that." Her voice was harsher than she meant it to be and her hands shook. Then she started to cry and said, "I found her."

CHAPTER 24

Vic turned his attention from the dog, straightened up and let Grazie steady herself the last few feet to her bed. "You found who? Minerva Watts?"

Daphne felt her shoulders drop, felt gratitude ooze through her core over his guessing right, remembering Minnie's name and using it. "Yes. I found her and I was helping her escape and they got her back, and they got away."

He gaped while she related her tale, pulling the flier for the Rainier Court Vacation House out of her pocket, flailing her hands while she described everything. When she finished, he opened his mouth to reply but blew out a long exhalation instead.

"If I ever see that couple again," Daphne said, her voice resolute, "I'm going to kill them."

A sad, wry expression played on Vic's lips and he jostled her shoulder. "Really? Are you a good killer?"

She pushed his hand off her shoulder and gave him a sour look. "Do I need to be particularly good at it?"

He shoved his fists in his pockets and studied the floor. "One possibility is that couple is victimizing a little old lady—"

"Minnie Watts."

"And another possibility is that they are taking care of this . . . Minnie, or Minerva Watts, and some stranger broke into the house and talked a confused old woman into sneaking off into the woods. They found her, alone in the woods, and a strange woman ran at them, screaming and—"

"No. Don't. I am not listening to doubts. I'm through with that. I am done." She made her warning as close to a threat as she'd ever made.

"Can we talk about something else? Please?" Vic rolled his eyes and drew his fingers through his hair. "Josie's all pinchy and you're upset—understandably so—but I'd love some peace."

Daphne listened harder to the hum of noise downstairs now and realized there were two voices, a girl's with the boy's. "Why is Josie even here?"

"Because she is my daughter and this is also her home," Vic said, his voice level, trying for evenness.

She glared at him for the little lecture. Although the kids lived at their mother's home far more than his, Vic's adamant position that his home was also theirs echoed from her first days of couplehood with Vic. She'd long backed his position and knew he was aware of her support. "I mean, why isn't she at her sleepover?"

He threw his hands up in dogged exasperation. "Some kind of mix-up. No one there, no answer on the home phone. Now Josie's cranky and—"

"Does this sleepover mix-up have to do with that little bitch Lainey?"

"Who?" Vic stared at her. "Lainey? The lady we saw yesterday who knew your sister? You're calling her a little bitch?"

"That was Lindsay, Suzanne's friend. Supposed friend. No, I'm talking about the girl who hurt Josie's feelings, but you know what? You act like I don't connect with your kids and yet here you are way behind the power curve, because I know. I know and you don't, do you? About what happened to Josie at school on Friday?"

Vic's gaze flicked away. "I know all about it. Cassandra told me. Some girl, Leslie or something—"

"Lainey." Daphne allowed herself a satisfied smile.

"Gave Jose the brush-off at school yesterday."

"It was in the cafeteria. She didn't want to let Josie sit with her."

"It was just a little thing between little girls. A little rivalry. It was inconsequential, Daph, it doesn't matter," Vic said.

"It matters to them," Daphne said. And when he said nothing, because he was an expert at letting a stupid argument die, at not engaging wrath or other hard emotions, she said, "Well, at least you won't lose a precious night with her due to a sleepover."

"If you weren't being sarcastic, you'd realize you're right," he said.

"I'm not being sarcastic. I'm serious. I'm extremely serious."

But Vic didn't look convinced.

—m—

Downstairs on her way to the kitchen, Daphne tried a smile at the kids. Josie looked the other way. Daphne pretended not to notice. The milk was still on the table.

"Jed, don't leave the milk out." Daphne made her tone light. She turned just enough to make sure the boy shifted off the couch and slouched toward the table.

Josie shot her a look.

The answering machine showed no calls. Daphne swallowed and stepped through the kitchen to the laundry, opening a can of dog food, mixing it with kibble and water and aspirin. She took pains to stay hidden when she heard Vic come downstairs. The kids mumbled to him, then the front door opened and shut.

She was alone. "Grazie? Dinner." Remembering that Vic had brought the dog upstairs, Daphne guessed she was asleep in their bedroom.

The phone rang and she snatched the receiver, praying for good news. "Yes, hello?"

"It's me," Thea said.

"Hey." Daphne walked through the kitchen, checking the table. It was tidied. She heard a noise behind her and voices outside, then spied Jed on the couch. Vic and Josie must have gone out front.

"You sound down," Thea said. "And I don't think I'm going to be cheering you up."

"What is it?" Daphne asked.

"That guy, Ross Bouchard. His last address was the same one I gave you for Lindsay Wallach, but a few years ago outside of Madras, Oregon, he was found—"

"I know," Daphne groaned. "He's dead."

"You know? How'd you find out?" Thea's surprise was at the edge of offended.

Daphne made a dull-voiced explanation of seeing Lindsay Wallach and remembered to thank Thea again for having come up with an address on Lindsay in the first place. In fits and starts, Daphne described going to Rainier Court, then backed up and reviewed going to the impound lot, the car rental agency, everything that led her to the tangled woods behind the vacation house, and how that had turned out. An unlawful entry, a chase, a police response, and yet another failure.

Waiting in Thea's silent pause, Daphne stood at the kitchen sink. Water pooled onto a dinner plate in the sink, turning a bread crust to goo. She scraped the crust off the plate, trying to tune out Jed cranking up the TV volume in the living room. Through the window over the sink, she could see Vic and Josie with a volleyball.

Vic had strung a white rope between two trees and worked either side of the line, opposite his daughter to receive her serves, or on the same side, setting up the ball for her to spike.

Sighing, Daphne asked Thea what she thought about the Rainier Court debacle. There was no response. "Thea?"

"Still here." The sound of typing rattled in the background.

Daphne wondered if Thea was working on an article or surfing the net or what. Thea wasn't interested in her drama. And there was too much going on at home anyway. "You ought to have kids. They're great for having someone to clean up after," Daphne said.

"Yeah, sounds like fun. Someone to clean up after." Thea snorted.

Daphne wondered aloud about the odd phone message and then listened to Thea marvel about the strangeness of the threat, something from ten years ago.

"I mean," Thea said, "ten years ago . . ."

"Right," Daphne said, casting about for focus.

The milk sweated on the kitchen counter next to the refrigerator. She'd been so intent on checking the table for the jug, she'd missed it right on the counter. Bread crumbs littered the counter next to the milk, and the mayonnaise jar sat behind the milk. Gritting her teeth, she yanked the fridge door open and returned the warm milk and mayo to the fridge.

"So what're you doing?" Thea asked in the tone of someone making a weak conversational effort while she was otherwise engaged.

Daphne frowned, listening to Thea's occasional keyboard punches in the background. "I'm cleaning up after the kids. They've left a little mess for me. Isn't that sweet of them?"

"Yeah, sweet. Makes you want to drown them in frosting or maple syrup or something."

"Jell-O," Daphne insisted.

Thea cleared her throat in considered assent. "Okay, pink Jell-O. Listen, Daphne, I've got to check some stuff . . ." More typing clattered in the background.

"M'kay, bye." Daphne tried to keep the disappointment and abandonment out of her voice.

Two-handed now that she was free of the phone, she took the plate, holding it just under the counter's edge, sweeping the ceramic clear of crumbs with her other hand. Her palm felt hot and sticky. The mundane tedium of doing housework while wondering about Minnie Watts's safety made her want to cry, made her hands tremble. She took a breath and considered her situation, the reality of living one moment then another. The past. The present, with all its worry about Minnie. The kids, the dog. Vic.

The summer she met Vic, Daphne heard about Jed and Josie but didn't meet them for two months because of the kids' trip to Cassandra's parents' home. Daphne saw their pictures, saw Vic miss them, and felt a natural empathy to a good person wanting a good thing: to be a good father.

Once the kids returned from visiting Cassandra's parents, Jed and Josie were home every Wednesday night and every other weekend, Friday through Sunday, sometimes Sunday night, too, with Vic taking them to school Monday morning. He called them every night. He e-mailed them. He helped them with their homework and listened to them. And Daphne felt her admiration grow for Vic, even as a remoteness seeped into her while she learned the kids' wants. Awareness of this emotional stepping back came with a realization that she didn't want to examine her own offhandedness.

She didn't want to look at how reluctant she was to spend time with her own mother, how she avoided the combination of clinging and coolness served up on Mapleview Drive. Shaking her head, Daphne made for the stairs with the dog's bowl, but hesitated and found Jed in his bedroom. She knocked on the half-open door and waited for him to look up.

"Jed, the milk was on the counter. I put it away for you."

"Talk to Josie. I put it away." He pulled his glasses off and looked at her bleary-eyed. "Will you talk to my dad about getting my eyes fixed?"

Daphne swallowed, counting to three, then four. Jed hated wearing glasses, had wanted his eyes lasered ever since he'd learned about such surgeries.

He closed his book. "Will you? Mom says Dad could afford it, but she can't."

"It's not a matter of affording, I don't think," Daphne said. "Your dad—"

"If one person says one thing and another says something else, how can you know what to believe?" Jed leaned back on his bed and stared at the ceiling.

"Listen to me, Jed. Your dad does not have stacks of extra money, no matter what you may be told by anyone else. But your dad wants you to be happy. I think you and your sister are the most important thing to him. And that's how it should be. He wants you to be happy and have what you need. And he knows you want to have your eyes fixed and he'll pay for it for you as soon as you're old enough."

"How do you know?"

"He told me."

"When?"

She waved her hands. "A long time ago, when I first heard about this. About you wanting to get eye surgery. But you're still too young for it. Your eyes aren't done growing so they just can't do it now. When you're old enough, it will happen."

"I wish I could have it now."

"I know you do . . ." *Buddy.* Daphne stopped the endearment from rolling off her tongue, knowing she'd just picked it up from Vic, and Jed might blow up at her for using it.

The front door opened and slammed, Vic's voice booming, "Where is everybody?"

Jed grinned and threw himself out the door, waving for Daphne to clear his bedroom, shutting the door as he went to whisper to his father.

In the living room, still holding Grazie's bowl, Daphne edged to the stairs. Josie had a smile or two and was red-faced from her volleyball exertions. Vic looked happy and Jed was giggling some secret in his ear.

Then Vic gawked and said, "You told her what? Listen to me . . ." And then Vic's voice sunk too low for Daphne to hear what he said to his son, but it was done with intensity and an arm around the boy's shoulder.

The image was too intimate to behold. She was an outsider and stepped in silence to the landing, looking back once, seeing Vic lean down. He snugged one arm around his daughter's shoulder, holding her close, murmuring into her ear. Josie shot Daphne a look, then cocked her head as her father whispered. Daphne went up the stairs, thinking of waking Grazie, feeding her, telling the old girl how the aspirin would make her hips feel better.

"Daphne?"

She turned in the upstairs hallway. Josie was almost to the top landing but didn't climb the last three steps. Daphne kept her arms wrapped around Grazie's bowl and went back to the top of the stairs.

Josie gingerly touched Daphne's wrist. "It's really sad. I mean, about your sister." Daphne took a breath to speak but stopped as Josie continued, "And your dad."

"Yes," Daphne said. "It's really sad."

—⟋⟍—

Vic stood in the bathroom waiting to brush his teeth. "I don't know what we're fighting about, Daph."

"We aren't fighting," she said.

"I know this weekend has difficult and painful anniversaries for you but—"

"She didn't accidentally leave the milk out. Jed put it away. Then I had to put it away because she got it out and left it out just to annoy me."

"Seems to have worked."

"Jesus, Vic." Daphne smacked her hands on the bathroom counter. A container of bath crystals he'd bought for her several years ago—she'd never used them—fell over.

Vic swept the little flood of pink crystals into his palm, then let the dust settle into the garbage can. "Daph, I think you ask the wrong question sometimes."

"What?"

"What? Just think about it, will you? Wondering whether a child will sometimes try to annoy you, get under your skin—"

"Oh, I'm not wondering. I'm announcing it as a fact and getting no support from you."

He raised a palm. "I support you. I do. I get that she's getting under your skin. But she's eleven."

"Eleven is old enough to put the milk away, isn't it?"

"You ask the wrong question. Isn't eleven young enough to get a little bit of a break from you?"

"You know what? You're in a bad mood because you're tired because your sleep schedule's screwed up because you went to day-shift hours yesterday. Well, I didn't screw up your work schedule. That was you. And wasn't your shift-change-training thing optional? You said that, last month when we talked about getting a long weekend off together."

"How often do I change my schedule and go to training? Once a year?"

"Yeah? Well, my union has a meeting every first Wednesday of the month. But how often do I go? Never."

He snorted. "It's a roofers' union. They just go to drink."

"We're roofers and waterproofers and allied workers."

Vic raised his hands. "Excuse me, madam."

Daphne left him in the bathroom, swinging the door shut between them. On the far side of the bed, she knelt and raised the dust ruffle. Their luggage was there but no box nestled next to it. Panic rose, then she remembered moving Suzanne's papers to the closet shelf. There, she caressed the box with a fingertip. Back at the bedside, she pulled out her suitcase.

Grazie scrambled and stood quivering, panting. Suitcases meant travel and her natural want was to go along, to be included. But now she panted, hind legs propped wide, and collapsed. The bathroom door opened as Daphne winced at Grazie's pain.

Vic said, "I have to put her down."

"You give up on her, you give up on me." Daphne's shoulders rose in defense.

"What?"

She sneered and made a mocking echo. "What?"

He stepped around the bed, drawing closer to her and stopped dead when he saw the suitcase.

"You're . . . leaving," Vic said, his voice full of air and defeat and wonder.

"I'm just . . ." Her voice trailed. What would she put in the suitcase? What did she need? Nothing. "I'm going to go crash at my mom's. Just go think. Or not think." Should she put the suitcase back and take Suzanne's box? *Don't cry.*

She couldn't speak, but there was nothing else to say. He followed her down the stairs, dumbly carrying her empty suitcase.

Josie stood in the kitchen doorway. Her eyes widened. "Daddy?"

Vic set the suitcase down. With a fixed gaze, Daphne walked past the girl, opened the door, and took a breath on the front porch. When she tried to shut the door, someone grabbed it from the inside. Daphne let go without looking back and moved down the brick steps.

"Daphne, don't leave," Josie called. "I . . . I'll be . . ."

Vic's voice was soft. "Jose, come inside."

Starting her truck, Daphne saw Vic, his face dim in the dark, a mask. He held his daughter and kissed her hair.

CHAPTER 25

A shin-high gray shadow boiled out of the house on Mapleview Drive. Daphne gasped but, hampered by an armload of tools, her reflexes amounted to flinching.

"Cinderfella, you scared me," she told the rumbling cat. "Inside, now. I've come to keep you company."

Stepping across the threshold at home pelted Daphne with memories. Here was the tile floor where her mother dropped her father's coffee mug the day police came to tell them about his suicide. Straight across was the living room with the same furniture she'd grown up with, the carpet where Suzanne had taught her to play checkers. This home had seen Suzanne fight with their mother about what Suzanne wore, about whether she could extend her curfew, go to a party, see that boy. Daphne closed her eyes.

If she turned to the right, there would be the kitchen and the dining area toward the back of that long room, also full of memories. To her left were two sets of stairs, one down to the basement—where her father had paced and ranted when Suzanne went missing—the other up to the two bedrooms.

Daphne pinched tears from the inner corners of her eyes thinking about those two bedrooms, the one she had shared with her sister, the one her mother had shared with her father.

Last month, when her mother started talking about this weekend, Daphne had snapped. Snapped at her mother and hung up. She'd scheduled time off from work for these last two days.

But she hadn't followed through, hadn't acted on the impulse to break away from her family's old patterns. No matter how fleeting thoughts of escape might tantalize her, she couldn't finish the deed. She'd known it the second she heard the hurt in her mother's response. They couldn't change.

Daphne dumped her loaded tool belt and coil nailer by the kitchen doorway. With the neighborhood not as good as it used to be, she didn't want to leave her tools in the truck overnight.

In her mother's living room, Daphne flopped on the couch. The heavy cat jumped on her stomach, making her grunt, then hopped onto the couch arm, his tail rattling pictures on the end table. Suzanne's high school graduation graced one frame, Daphne's the other. The sight of the telephone behind the framed photos made her think of calling Vic. She wanted to. She didn't want the night to end this way.

She didn't want them to end at all. She didn't. But sometimes, it was just too hard. If it hadn't been for this weekend with the anniversaries of her father's death and her dead sister's birthday, she could have kept herself together.

Or if it hadn't been for Minnie Watts.

Minnie, are you safe?

No. Daphne shook her head. Minnie is not safe. She looked at the phone again, wondering if she should give her mother's phone number to Officer Taminsky in case he had an update.

No. No need. Vic would call her if he received news. Vic was like that. He'd never let a spat stand in the way of doing the decent thing.

She pulled Cinderfella to her chest, pressing her face to warm fur as she rose. From the living room, she could see a great deal of clutter in the dining area and she half-wondered what unnecessary cleaning her mother had been up to. The cat nuzzled her as she carried him up the stairs.

When she'd moved out of this house and in with Thea, Daphne had once referred to the cat her mother adopted as her replacement. Her mother had snapped that no one could replace a daughter, and Daphne didn't try to get lighthearted with her again.

Cinderfella loved to be carried. Her mom said he was too heavy to carry and he had to walk himself around. His rumbling purr filled Daphne's body as she held him. Loose hair tickled her nose as they rubbed faces.

The pleasure of petting a friendly animal brought to mind first meeting Vic, with Grazie making introductions. Before he'd gotten to the point of buying them ice cream, he'd been trying hard with chitchat.

"I'm a meteorologist," he'd said.

"Are those necessary anymore? I mean, isn't the weather monitored with computers? Or can't we look out the window or stand on a rooftop?"

"Well, there's even more to me, you see. I'm dual-educated. An oceanographer and a meteorologist."

"Oh." Daphne had no snappy comeback material for oceanography majors.

"What do you do?"

"I'm a roofer." Having loaded drywall that day didn't change her love of being on building summits.

He'd gaped, stunned as people always were when faced with a young woman who chose her trade. "Don't buildings pretty much already have roofs on them?"

They'd both laughed at his weak effort, and she rewarded him by indicating the empty spot on the bench. After a great chat, he'd bought three vanilla cones while she held Grazie's leash. Daphne wanted to feed Grazie the extra cone, so Vic held two cones while she and the dog made a great mess. After, they'd walked and talked and turned the encounter into lunch. They chose a place with sidewalk seating, so they could keep the snuffling, chuffing mass of yellow fur at their feet. Daphne could not stop petting the dog, telling her what a fine girl she was. Something clicked, felt comfortable, in whatever she or Vic said right from the beginning. They talked about everything. The city, themselves. The present, the past, people and work and coffee and how good those sandwiches were.

When he asked about her family, she told him. She told him the whole deal about her sister and her father, stopping just shy of Suzanne's contingency notes and the guilty question blanketing Daphne ever since. Before, she'd always gotten the signal from men that they couldn't take it all in, but Vic was different. He didn't get distant or bored with her, didn't become standoffish or fidgety at her family's tragedies. He listened, his face contorted in beautiful sympathy. It was a first, all of this great kindness in a new man.

Just into couplehood, he told her his great secret—that Jed was not his child. That when Cassandra admitted this, he'd wondered whether Josie was his and then he'd put the thought away, but not because he necessarily thought Cassandra hadn't let another man father their daughter, too. He'd thought instead of changing the kids' diapers, of holding them when they were sick, of reading to them and playing with them, of taking them places. He took them to school, extracurricular activities, and their friends' houses. And he knew in his bones that he did what a father does, so he was their father.

He was a good father.

When he'd told Daphne about managing to reconcile the truth about his son's paternity, and how he chose to be Jed's father forever because he'd served as Jed's father, and because he loved Jed and wanted the best for the boy, Daphne had been impressed by Vic's handling of his great secret and cowed by her own—*what if my sister left me a note that last night and I never found it, never told a soul?* She didn't reveal her secret, her secret fear.

But as the anniversary of her father's death and her sister's birthday approached on her and Vic's first year together, Daphne succumbed to circling the drain. The doubly hideous anniversary always brought her down. While Vic stroked her shoulders and nuzzled her hair and told her how sorry he was for her pain, she told him about the note she never found, about how she wondered so many things, like why her father quit life, and why Suzanne was killed and by whom, and whether a final note existed at all.

He'd wrinkled his brow and asked a lot more questions about Suzanne, general things that brought Daphne to gush about an adventurous, beautiful, young iconoclast who'd awed her kid sister. Then she told him more about the sneaking out and the notes.

Vic had talked about the unlikelihood of there having been a final note. He'd told Daphne she'd done enough, done all she could. She could safely step aside. There probably wasn't another note, not that final night, since she never found it.

But, Vic, I can't ever know for sure. As soon as the words were out, her mouth hung open; then she'd snapped it shut it, closed her eyes. Leaning against his chest, she told herself to stop it, just stop it. She wouldn't say that again—complain about not knowing—not to a man living as a father of a boy who was not his child. Not to a man who held himself as the father of a girl whose paternity he doubted.

Instead she told Vic she agreed that all the worry and wonder in the world wouldn't bring back her sister or her father and this was the way it was.

But sometimes, especially this one weekend every year, it was a hard reality to live.

——⟋⟍——

"So, I, uh, ran away, Cinder-kitty," she told the kneading, purring cat.

Suzanne ran away, and was gone for a weekend the first time. She'd told Daphne when she came back that it had just been a lark, and Daphne, then seven, had pictured songbirds in trees, morning larks.

"Where did you go?"

"Lopez."

"What's that? Is that a man you went to see?"

"It's one of the San Juans, Daffy. Don't you ever look at a map?" Suzanne had braided Daphne's hair as she talked.

When she and Vic were a firm couple, several months after meeting, he'd asked if she'd like to get away for a weekend.

"Maybe to Lopez?" Daphne had said, heeding the ancient, lurking call of the island. She longed for the possibility of understanding her sister and the places on the planet that spoke to a wild child.

He'd nodded and checked the ferry schedule, booking them for a night at a bed and breakfast on a rocky beach. They'd left his car in Anacortes and walked onto the ferry. She'd been disappointed that it was just an hour's ride on the water.

She didn't find answers to her sister there, but Vic was beside her and attentive. He was a man in his own rut who made room for her because he wanted her in his life. And she wanted him right back.

——⟋⟍——

Upstairs, Daphne released Cinderfella when he asked to go into her mother's bedroom. It had been years after her father's death, Daphne recalled, before she stopped thinking of the last room on the right as her *parents'* bedroom.

And she still thought of her old room as the one she shared with Suzanne.

"Hang on, Cinder-cat," she said, and turned the knob to her old bedroom. The dent in her old bed—from the last time she'd sat there to talk to Suzanne's ghost—was gone. Her mother had straightened out the girls' old room. Daphne smiled, thinking of her mother, the perpetual housewife, tidying and minding her household, even though the deep cleaning—releasing the hoarded past—was more than Frances Mayfield had ever done.

Suzanne's bed had a new dent, a full-length imprint.

Daphne's fond feelings turned wistful as she pictured her mother there, aching again over her murdered child.

She should leave her mother a note, she decided. She could put it in her mom's bedroom.

Something concrete, a bit of learning about the past, occurred to her. She could leave a note of real substance. *Remember Lindsay? I found her, Mom, and . . .*

Opening her old closet to find a bit of surplus notebook paper and a pencil, Daphne was stunned. Bags and boxes of clothes and kids' things were compiled in the previously untouched girls' closet.

Some of the bags were labeled *girls clothes* and another pile was marked *garbage*. A box of old novels and textbooks had a big black question mark on the side. School supplies were gathered in a carton marked *Boys and Girls Club* and another box was labeled *Salvation Army*.

I have a surprise. A little sound of understanding, of sorrow, escaped Daphne as she looked at her mother's hard work, recalled her mother's promise.

"Good for you, Mom." She swallowed down a cry. "Good for me. For us. Thanks."

Taking a piece of paper and a pen from the box of school supplies, Daphne began her note: *Mom, remember—*

The cat yowled from her bed.

Daphne nodded. "Come on, Cinderfella."

Crumpling the note paper, just as her face crumpled, Daphne tried with moderate success to resist a good bawl. Of course her mother remembered Lindsay Wallach. Why wouldn't she? Her mother needed no help in recalling misery and pain and unanswered questions.

Swallowing, Daphne decided that she would never mention seeing Lindsay.

But she thought of the part the ex–best friend had played in Suzanne's death. Lindsay Wallach and Ross Bouchard cheated on Suzanne. They broke her heart.

They broke my sister's heart on the last night of her life.

How strong had Lindsay Wallach been to sound the alarm on Suzanne's behalf?

Suppose I'd told our parents? Just tattled on Suzanne once for all the sneaking out? Suppose Suzanne had stopped because I told Mom and Dad?

Identifying this old guilt with new clarity offered bare answers.

Then Suzanne might have made safer choices. And then her father would never have been so bleak he decided to stop living.

And there was other tattling she could have done, things she'd kept quiet. Suzanne had said things. Suzanne had written things.

So, Daphne would make an official visit.

And Daphne would talk to Lindsay one more time. She would thank Lindsay for raising the alarm the moment her gut told her Suzanne was missing.

It was too late to call tonight, but she promised herself she'd thank Lindsay before the weekend was out.

Cinderfella pawed at her mother's bedroom door, his purr erupting into little meows as he begged.

"She's not in there," Daphne told the cat, but cracked the door open for him.

A spare suitcase gaped on the bed, a note and photos beside it. Daphne pushed the door all the way open.

The largest suitcase of her mother's luggage set lay open and empty on the bed beside a few folded sweaters and slacks. Her mother had had a hard time deciding what to take on her weekend away and had come to opt for the smaller of her two suitcases.

And Frances Mayfield had been looking at two photos of gravestones. Daphne picked up the note.

> *Frances-*
> *Don't hold off, don't hold back. You can see them anytime,*
> *talk to them anytime. Come away with us and have a*
> *nice weekend.*
>
> *-Blanche*

Daphne fingered the note and swallowed, looking at the first photo. *Suzanne Emily Mayfield Beloved Daughter and Sister*

The headstone represented all that remained of her beautiful, wild sister. Daphne shook her head and knew why she still talked to Suzanne in their old bedroom, never in the cemetery. She leafed this top photo over the other and thought about how she did talk to her dad at his lonely grave.

Reginald Mayfield

A girl buried in consecrated ground, and her father, whose body lay outside the church's plot. His headstone represented how one man had been cruelly shortchanged in life. She remembered how shortchanged she'd felt ten years ago when, in the living room below, police told her and her mother that he'd taken his own life, alone in a hotel room.

Of course I was confused, Daphne thought, remembering how she'd wondered what her mother had or hadn't said or done. *I was twenty-one.*

How does a girl just accept losing her father? Then she gasped at the thought poking her mind.

Did I hold you back, Mom?

She booted the cat from her mother's bedroom. "We're sleeping on the couch, Cinder."

Back downstairs, Daphne stepped into the dark kitchen and inspected the clutter in the dining area at the back of the room.

Dim illumination from the streetlights added to the sepia-like feel of nostalgia. Her mother had pulled countless socket sets, screwdrivers, a few paintbrushes, an ancient chainsaw, and other old tools of her dad's from the garage. Different coffee cans of bolts and screws and nails and nuts each had a masking tape price tag of fifty cents. Garage sale signs, more masking tape, a pencil, and a spiral notebook listing items ended the stacks of goods on and around the table.

"Oh, Mom," Daphne breathed. Pleased and heartened for her mother's big steps, she fingered her father's things. There were extra picture frames, spare fixtures, an unused basketball hoop, and a lamp her dad had kept on his desk at the insurance office. There were many pieces of the past whose meanings were long gone.

Daphne wondered if the garage sale was scheduled for the next weekend. Vic wouldn't have Jed and Josie. She could help. Vic would come, too. He would offer to come without her having to ask, he was that kind of man. He'd always been willing to spend time with her at her mother's house. And he'd be ready for a distraction, missing his kids.

And she would miss them, too. She wanted Jed and Josie to be all right.

She wanted to tell the kids good night right now. As hard as quasi-stepparenting was, not doing it was harder because she loved Vic, loved Jed, loved Josie.

Cinderfella jumped on the table and stepped amongst the clutter, knocking one picture over. Daphne grabbed the glass frame and stowed it behind the chainsaw.

"You are a big, naughty, klutzy cat who almost deprived my mother of a"—Daphne peered to check the masking tape price tag in the low light—"twenty-five-cent sale item. And you shouldn't be on the table."

With a deep breath, Daphne beamed at her mother's cleanup efforts. She pulled her abandoned note from her pocket, ripped it in half to get some clean paper, and tried anew.

Mom, Can I have Dad's old chainsaw and some of these other tools? -D

A sharp jangle from the old-fashioned wall phone in the kitchen made Daphne gasp. She could remember standing on this faded linoleum, waiting for cookies to come out of the oven, watching Suzanne pass hours on that phone, sometimes flipping the long cord back and forth, teasing Daphne into playing jump rope games. It used to drive their mother up the wall, Suzanne letting Daphne skip over the kitchen phone cord. In all those long-passed years, the phone, like all else, had not been upgraded.

So Daphne felt a bittersweet smile tug on her mouth as she lifted the receiver without clicking on a kitchen light. "Hello?"

"It's Thea."

"It's after eleven," Daphne said.

"I know. Wake you?" Thea waited for Daphne's negative murmur before asking, "What are you doing over there?"

"How'd you know I was here?" Daphne countered. She could tell this would be a long one with Thea, and she got a glass out of the cabinet, half-filling it at the sink and wondering if there was something better in the fridge.

"I called your house and Vic said you were at your mom's. What's up?"

"Nothing, I just . . ." A noise outside the house, something that could pass for boots on the back porch, made Daphne flinch.

"Marry him."

"What?!"

Thea said, "He told me."

Daphne inhaled, long enough to stem the sniffle that wanted to escape. "Just because a nice guy loves me and treats me pretty well and understands me pretty well and is a nice guy—"

"He is a nice guy." Thea cut in.

"Nice to children," Daphne said, "and animals. We've talked about Grazie, you know, putting her down or getting her hips done, and he just about breaks up over it."

"So, he's nice to kids and animals."

"And to old people," Daphne said. "You should see how he is with his dad. And he's great with my mom."

"You're not."

"No. I'm kind of crappy with her."

"So he's nice to old people," Thea went on. "And to you."

"Yes," Daphne agreed now that the list was complete. "And to me. Anyway, just because of that nice stuff and 'cause I love him, it's no reason to go around marrying him."

"Oh, hell, no," Thea said. "You know that tiff you and I had a couple of days ago? Did you know he called me and asked me to use my alumna status to get that Wallach chick's contact info for you? He said it would be the quickest way and this is the shittiest weekend of the year for you, so would I please help you out. And he was right."

Daphne felt the familiar clench in her stomach thinking of her best friend's usually snide attitude toward Vic. "Why don't you like him, Thea?"

The reply was a verdict. "Well, shit. He says things that no one should say."

"Like?" Daphne felt her eyebrows rise.

"Like *cool beans*."

Daphne's protest was immediate, adamant. "He does not."

"He does, too. And I mean, come on. No one says *cool beans* anymore. No one."

"Vic does, sometimes," Daphne admitted. "Listen, where are you?"

"Driving."

Daphne snorted. "Where are you, Thee?"

"Um, out."

"Out?" Daphne drained water from the plastic tumbler.

"Just driving. I was in your neighborhood—I mean, near Vic's house—and I called, and Vic told me you were at your mom's and you'd left him and he'd proposed a couple of days ago. You never told me he'd proposed—"

"I started to. We got distracted, I think."

"Well, I think you should marry him."

"Why? Seriously, why do you think I should marry him?" Daphne turned as she asked this. A prickly feeling of someone watching made her glance around the kitchen, stepping over the cord as she circled. Was she feeling examined just because Thea was being nosy? Daphne nodded, calming herself down. No one was watching her. No one except her best friend was paying attention to her. It was just darker in the old neighborhood, with taller trees blocking city light and glow.

"As they say in court, Daphne, asked and answered." Thea's tone changed and the reception became clearer. "The lights aren't on and nobody's home."

"What?"

"I'm at that address I gave you a couple of days ago, on Eastpark. Listen, I was doing quite a bit of research earlier, Nexus searches and more. The thing about this Minerva Watts lady . . . and the stolen car from California? It's possible the old woman who owned that California car, that Lincoln that you chased—"

"I know what car you're talking about," Daphne said, yanking the fridge open.

"It's possible she was murdered. It all fits. Too many pieces fit. So it is more than possible there really is a couple victimizing old people in a systematic way and maybe your Minerva Watts is their next victim, their Seattle one."

"What!" A shadow moved outside and Daphne swung the fridge door shut, mindful that she'd just been backlit, visible to anyone outside.

She told herself to calm down. A tiny clink of broken glass rattled. Daphne looked for Cinderfella amongst the goods on the dining table, telling herself she should switch phones and take him to the living room, get the cat away from the tools and picture frames and old lamp.

Then a cool draft whispered through the house, coupons clipped to the fridge fluttered, and Daphne knew the back door was open. The living room floor creaked as someone crossed the room. One wall separated her from someone coming toward the kitchen.

Daphne looked with horror down the long phone cord connecting her to the far wall at the kitchen's opening. A small revolver—unbelievable, but there—entered the room in a man's hand. And then another hand, this one in a black leather glove, reached for the telephone hook.

"Thea, call the cops. Now."

CHAPTER 26

Flinging the telephone's handset, trying to ignore the sound of its plastic body skittering across the floor as the coiled cord beckoned it home to the receiver, Daphne stepped deep to the wall, beside the fridge. But that man—it was Guff—already knew where she was and would be on her in seconds.

Daphne pressed herself against the cold metal of the refrigerator, aware of how its hum changed when she leaned into the monstrous old appliance. The wham of her frightened heart threatened to make her shake. Guff was coming. He was a few yards away.

She had to do it fast, very fast, with all her power. If it didn't slam over, but only rocked, he'd be warned. And there was no time for anything more than full, immediate success.

It's the legs. It's the legs. Hunching her shoulders and abs as her hands gripped the upper back corner of the fridge, Daphne curled her body, stepping her feet up the wall toward her hands. She braced in a fetal position, body in the air, clinging to the refrigerator's upper corner, toes high on the wall as she eyed the little cupboard above the fridge. A cheap cabinet. And she could see in her mind's eye what her mother stored up there. A big milk glass platter for serving the Thanksgiving turkey. A punch bowl. They'd been part of the family forever and would be ruined if she flipped the fridge. The cabinet would rupture when the back end of the fridge rocked forward.

Pushing her feet against the wall with every leg, arm, and core muscle, she forced the refrigerator to crash, doors to the floor. She rolled toward her father's old things as she fell. Guff's startled cry and the sound of breaking glass, splintering wood, and cabinet items scattering was punctuated by a heavy, whomping thud as hundreds of pounds of metal met the man and smashed him to the floor.

Daphne jumped to her feet, hoping her heart would stop thudding aggression and fear. It didn't.

The man grunted. Motion in the dim light sent terror through her legs like electric sparks.

A sick, wet sound came as Guff lifted his head and then gave up, smacking it back into a little pool of blood.

She'd pinned him. One unmoving boot toe protruded toward Daphne from under the fridge. His left arm flailed above his head as his right shoulder made damped motion, the right arm trapped beneath the fridge. She guessed his trapped arm was on his torso. She wondered where the gun was.

"Ah! My leg. Knee . . ." He wheezed.

Stepping away from the wall, she skidded on a piece of broken cabinetry. Her father's things, her mother's pending garage sale setup, were behind her. In order to get to the light switch and the telephone, she'd have to climb over the fridge.

Well, why not?

Daphne planted her palms in the middle, noting the fridge didn't rest flat. When she vaulted the facedown appliance, Guff eked out pained breaths. She scampered farther from him, flicking on the lights and pausing in the kitchen doorway as she scanned the floor for his gun.

The odd black shape—there had never been a pistol in her parents' house, she was pretty sure—was on the floor near the kitchen sink. The phone was at her feet in the doorway, its plastic cracked. Shards of milk glass and extra baking pans littered the floor and countertops.

Guff eyed her, struggling for breath as another word formed. "Bitch."

Daphne looked down at him, fear and fury melding together. "Where's Minerva Watts?"

He grabbed the edge of the refrigerator with his left hand and pushed, but the harvest gold block of metal kept him pinned. His breathing got raspy and he didn't bring himself to try again.

Picking up the phone, Daphne glanced at the hook where he'd disconnected her from Thea, but hesitated. Had Thea heard her and called the police already?

The police would listen to her now. They could put it all together. But how long would it take? Suppose the other woman was waiting for Guff to come right back? She could be around the corner, holding a gun on Minnie. Suppose they planned to make their escape, leave town right after he had come and dealt with Daphne. Had they already killed Minnie? How long would it take to find out where they held Minnie if police asked, then waited for his cooperation?

How long would it take to make Minnie safe?

How long did she have?

Daphne walked to the sink and toed the pistol toward the doorway.

A gun was not one of her tools. She drew her tongue across her front teeth in wicked pleasure.

"Wait here," Daphne told Guff as she kicked the pistol into the living room, feeling like she'd scored a goal. Out of his sight, she pushed his pistol under the edge of the couch with her foot.

A decision burst. She grabbed the roofing hammer she'd wielded on the Honda the day before. A distant siren wailed. The police might be coming here already. She might not have much time.

Crouching just out of Guff's reach, Daphne raised the special tool, showed him its sharp adze.

"Shingler's hammer," she explained. "Tell me where she is. Now."

He looked at her, opened his mouth, and turned his head in a half shake of refusal.

Cutting off the gulp her throat wanted, Daphne drew her arm back to swing like she was at T-ball practice with Josie, years ago.

The man's shoulder on the floor made a different sort of target than a white plastic ball on a post, asked for a vertical blow instead of a horizontal swing. Asked a very different mentality of the swinger. Daphne swallowed hard and raised the hammer. "I think you're going to tell me where Minerva Watts is."

His breath came in pained gasps between words. "You . . . are a crazy bitch."

"Not even the point," she said, locking in on Guff's exposed shoulder. "I want to know where Minnie Watts is and I want to know right now."

He pressed his lips together, puffing through his nose.

"Put your name on it, Daphne," she shouted as she closed her eyes and brought the hammer down.

The sick thwack, blood, and Guff's following scream didn't surprise her—she'd signed up for it—but when the fridge shifted as he struggled, she raised her hammer and eyebrows.

The distant but definite wail of sirens called and she knew it had to be now. He had to tell her. No asking nicely, no taking time and bargaining or giving his girlfriend a chance to escape again. Now. Not later, not after waiting until he felt like offering a little information in exchange for some legal benefit. Not after he had taken the time to weigh the pluses and minuses of being cooperative, balanced his crimes against what the police knew, what his fallout would be. Not after he got an attorney and exercised rights and took time to choose whether or not to let Minnie be safe.

Now.

Daphne stood, looking across the fridge to the dining table. "How about I see if I can get the old chainsaw running?"

He wheezed.

She vaulted the fridge again, causing him to gurgle in protest at the added weight. He grabbed at her with his free arm, but it was futile. A few feet away, she was safe. She hefted the chainsaw.

"Wow, feels like there's some gas and oil in it," she lied. It felt too light, unfueled, the scent of petroleum products much fainter than it should have been. She flipped the choke and power switches, then yanked the starter cord. The little engine gave a quick accompanying roar but didn't catch. She pretended to adjust the choke, pretended a confidence she didn't feel.

"This will be a faster way to cut your arm off. A lot easier than hacking it off with my hammer's adze. And I don't know how else to make you tell me what I want to know." She yanked the starter cord again, holding the chainsaw as close to him as she dared.

His eyes went wide and rolled back in his head.

"Hey, don't pass out," she said. Slight red light played through the room. The police were on the street, down the block.

They were here too soon. She raised the chainsaw.

"I will cut your fucking head off," she told him. "You will tell me right now where she is or I will kill you. This is your last chance." She yanked the starter cord again and knew she was assaulting this man who, at the moment, was vulnerable and at her mercy.

His lips formed soundless words, a bubble of spittle popping from his teeth. He rasped as his chest heaved as he strained to breathe.

"What? Say it," she demanded.

He opened his mouth but no sound escaped. Then he managed, "Q-Q-Quality Inn. Exit one-fifty-four. Two-seventeen." His free hand made a feeble gesture.

"I-5?" she asked. "Exit one-fifty-four off of Interstate Five? Room two hundred seventeen at the Quality Inn?"

He nodded assent and his head lolled back.

"Seattle Police!" The shout came from the front door. She hadn't locked it earlier.

Guff blinked and looked away from Daphne, toward the kitchen's doorway to the rest of the house.

She set the chainsaw aside and swallowed. "Help! Help me, please."

Footsteps crossed the other room and then a uniformed man and woman appeared near the kitchen phone. Daphne waved from beyond the overturned refrigerator. The officers took in the trashed kitchen, her, and the man struggling for breath under the fridge in a glance.

Both cops moved to the edge of the fridge and grabbed, readying to lift.

"He's got a gun," Daphne said. "He's an intruder. I was over here on the phone to my friend and the first thing I saw was his gun. He was going to kill me. I asked Thea to call the police. He's working with some woman and they're holding a lady named Minerva Watts. Holding her against her will. They're robbing her. I think they've done it before, to others."

Leaving Guff pinned, the officers released the fridge. He moaned and tried to speak.

The female cop leaned her face quite close to Guff. "What's in your hand under the fridge?" she demanded, cocking her head to listen to his faint mumbles.

Daphne couldn't hear Guff's response, but the cop keyed her microphone, asking her dispatcher for "paramedics and a rescue assist."

Then she turned to her partner. "He says his leg's hurt. Says he doesn't have a gun."

"It went across the floor when I pushed the fridge over," Daphne said, pointing to their side of the fridge. "Then out the kitchen door. I kicked it under the couch in there." She pointed to the wall separating them from the living room.

"You pushed the fridge over?" The woman eyed the room again.

The male officer stepped back into the living room. The woman studied Daphne. "Whose house is this?"

"Mine. My mother's. I'm staying here tonight."

"Is anyone else here?"

Daphne shook her head, then hesitated. "Not that I know of. But then, he's an intruder and I don't know if he's alone."

The male officer leaned into the kitchen, the revolver dangling from his pen. "I'm going to clear the residence, then grab my camera," he told the woman. "Medics are almost here."

She nodded and looked at Guff. "Hang on, sir. The fire department's going to help you out."

"Hey," Daphne hollered from the darker dining area, waving from behind the fridge. "You have to listen to me. There's an emergency still. There's this whole thing . . ." Pointing to Guff, Daphne told the woman cop about Minnie Watts and previous police encounters and Guff breaking into the house with a gun. She talked fast, without stopping.

She said that after the fridge fell, Guff grabbed at her and she swung wildly in self-defense with her hammer, said she'd asked him where Minnie was and he told her the hotel and room number once he realized he was stuck.

"Please, you have to get people over there right away. The Quality Inn on I-5 at exit one-fifty-four. Room two hundred seventeen. You have to make Minerva Watts safe," Daphne finished.

After listening these long minutes, eyeing Guff and Daphne at turns, the cop keyed her mic and said several things on several different channels. Daphne heard lots of "ten-fours" and other codes.

Best of all, she heard the hotel location repeated and the words, "Immediate welfare check on a Minerva Watts."

The male cop used his radio, too, calling for Officer Taminsky and a sergeant, but Daphne could hear none of the other end of his conversation because he wore an ear bud jacked into his radio.

As paramedics entered, Daphne longed to vault the fridge—or clamber up and bounce on Guff. The cop told her to jump over Guff's head. When Daphne hesitated, the officer pinned Guff's free arm and again told Daphne to jump.

She jumped.

They asked if they could look around, accepted Daphne's nod, and told Daphne to wait outside by the police cars.

From the front yard, Daphne watched paramedics and more fire department personnel crowd into her mother's kitchen with their gear, tackle boxes, and a stretcher. On the street, a collection of police cars clogged the lane. Daphne could see an officer with stripes on her shoulder talking to the first woman officer in the living room. A fire engine and an ambulance hogged the neighborhood street.

She recalled being twenty-one, still living at home, when a neighbor a few houses away had a chimney fire. The flames spread to the roof and the street had filled with emergency vehicles and neighbors watching the spectacle.

The fire erupted the same week a fledgling feeling of competence as a roofer began to soak into her hands and mind, just before she'd moved in with Thea. Watching the firefighters stand on that smoking roof, chainsawing into the very heart of a burning home, creating smoke ejection ports to force the fire where they wanted it—making safe passage for the crew inside—she'd wanted to join in. Destruction appeared as satisfying as building, as roofing. To break something down and then rebuild it seemed maybe even better than starting something anew. So, the little odd jobs that commenced with removing an old, rotting roof drew her. That was why last Tuesday she'd stripped and reshingled an old shed's roof, done it solo.

But she'd come to realize she'd rather a structure be built so well it would last a lifetime. She could do the necessary deconstruction, but to live, she loved building.

Turning now from the street and its emergency vehicles to gawk through her mother's windows, Daphne gasped when a hand touched her shoulder just as the firefighters inside righted the refrigerator.

Thea's eyes were wide. "Are you okay? What happened?"

"Um, well, look," Daphne said, pointing through the kitchen window at her handiwork inside. In the wrecked room, paramedics and firefighters lifted Guff's bloody form to the gurney.

"Did you kill that guy?"

Daphne's smile twisted. "Nah. He's still alive. Besides, he came here to kill me, Thea."

"That Lincoln owner in California," Thea began, but stopped as the fire department crew maneuvered the gurney through the front door, the male police officer escorting them. Guff's face was gray and the back of his head had stained the pillow crimson. One paramedic tried to put an oxygen mask on him.

Guff swiped it away and rasped to the police officer. "That bitch hit me and she was going to cut my head off with a chainsaw!"

"My, what an imagination he has," Daphne said. "I guess it takes a lot of imagination to conceive the kind of crimes he does. Taking old people's money, killing them . . ."

The cop looked at her.

"Or is his girlfriend the brains of their enterprise?" Daphne asked.

The cop was about to say something but stopped and cocked his head as though listening to his ear bud. Then he pressed a button and spoke into his shoulder mic. "Ten-four." He listened some more. "Copy that. And what's your ETA?"

She stiffened. "Whose ETA? Who's coming?"

"Officer Taminsky. He's in another precinct. He responded to a complaint you made earlier? We have two detectives en route as well and officers on scene at the hotel. Now, Ms. Mayfield, you can go inside.

Officer Howe needs to talk to you about what happened after the refrigerator fell." He looked at Thea, who stood now with a notebook and digital recorder out. "Press?"

"*Seattle Times,*" she nodded.

"You cannot go inside without the owner's permission."

"Yeah, yeah." Thea grinned.

He headed for his police car, following the ambulance.

What happened after the refrigerator fell.

Daphne thought of the mess in her mom's kitchen that began when she dropped the telephone. *The phone.* She figured she'd violated the law by striking and threatening a man who posed no immediate threat to her and felt caught. Thea might have heard what she did. Thea sometimes recorded phone calls, too.

They would know. Everybody would know how she'd tortured Guff, made him tell her where they held Minnie hostage.

She'd used force when it was legally wrong to do so. She'd assaulted Guff.

She would go to jail.

From the front door, the first female officer—Howe?—waved her in.

Daphne's voice fell low and urgent. "Thea, did you hang up? How long were you on the phone after I asked you to call the police?"

Thea's gaze narrowed as she studied Daphne. "I called the cops and called Vic, all as I was driving over here."

"Ms. Mayfield? Come inside, please. I need to clear up a few things," Officer Howe called from the door.

Daphne did her best to maintain a poker face as she felt Thea studying her. She imagined Thea's pending question, *What did you do, Daphne?*

She thought of Vic's often restrained, impassive expression and did her best to mimic the look. And then she saw him, coming on foot through emergency vehicles, his face full of worry. He closed the distance between them at a run.

"Daph? Are you all right? What's going on?" He grabbed her as he spoke, hands climbing her arms, taking her shoulders, hugging her, then holding her away again to search her face.

"Yes."

"Yes, you're okay?"

"Yes." She would keep saying yes to him. They would be okay. "What time is it, Vic?"

He looked at his watch. The diesel roar of a departing fire engine drowned out any chance of talking. Vic cocked his wrist to show her the watch face. After midnight. Daphne felt satisfaction, maybe the beginnings of peace, trickle into her core.

She gave Thea the hotel location and Thea bolted for her car. She brought Vic inside and told him in front of the police a version of what happened. She began at the beginning as the two female cops, Howe and a sergeant, worked to deconstruct the events, but Daphne kept things as simple as she could, pretending confusion or fear or whatever it took when the questions edged too close to self-incrimination. She wanted to build, to go forward, not get swamped in what happened earlier in the kitchen. Or elsewhere.

A detective arrived and she gave him her consistent statement, too. Vic stayed close until his cell phone rang as Daphne finished up with the detective.

When Vic waved from a few feet away, holding his phone to his chest, Daphne slipped over to him. "Thea's on the phone. She's with Minerva Watts," he reported. "Everything's going to be all right."

It was Sunday, by minutes, but it was a pretty good start of a Sunday. It was Suzanne's birthday.

It was the day after the ten-year anniversary of her dad's death, and she had something to tell him. And she didn't have to go to his grave. Like Blanche wrote to her mom, she could talk to him anywhere, anytime.

"Dad, I didn't quit."

CHAPTER 27

In the town of Leavenworth, Washington, Daphne searched for her vacationing mother. She used her best game face, dragging and tired instead of refreshed by the restless nap she'd snagged with Vic after the police left. The early drive she had to make in order to arrive in central Washington before her mother came home left her yawning.

The resort her mother's bridge partner had chosen was nestled in the forest, behind the Bavarian-style main streets, abutting ragged, snowy mountains. The apple trees were in flower, not offering fruit until fall. The weather was warm enough to relax by the pool, but not to swim. Frances Mayfield sat on a deck chair with her feet propped up, smiling across the water at a posing family.

Blanche beamed, a baby in her arms, bookended by a young couple. The man held a wiggling toddler. A hotel employee snapped a picture of the five and handed the camera back.

Daphne greeted her mother with calming words, said she didn't want her mother to worry when arriving home to a bit of a mess.

"You're here! Oh, Daphne, I'm so glad. Don't worry about some mess. Nothing else matters now that you're here."

"Well, hear me out. I need to explain," Daphne said, thinking of so much she ought to say that had nothing to do with a man breaking into the house and Daphne wrecking the kitchen. She and Vic had patched the broken windowpane in the back door before they left. She would install a new door as soon as her mother picked one out, but for now, she began at the beginning.

Frances listened to her daughter explain, amazed. "A man broke into the house? Did he steal anything? Imagine getting robbed while you're on a weekend vacation."

"There's more, Mom."

Her mother looked across the pool to the little family again, cupped her hands, and called, "Look, Daphne came after all. She came to be with me."

Daphne waved at Blanche and her family. Frances leaned in to hug Daphne, who swallowed like mad. "I'm sorry I didn't come with you in the first place. This, of all weekends."

Frances smoothed her slacks. "Well, you're here now."

Blinking, Daphne remembered Minnie forgiving her in the woods for not coming sooner. "Mom, there's a lot I need to—"

"Yes, this break-in, now. Blanche told me to have emergency phone numbers right on the refrigerator. That's why the police knew to call you, isn't it?"

Taking a breath, Daphne said, "You need a new fridge. I'm going to buy one for you. See, I was already there, Mom. I went over last night to stay."

She hesitated under her mother's next question about why she was at the house. Not that she wasn't always welcome, Frances told her.

"I kind of had a fight with Vic. I was upset and out of sorts and wanted to get away."

"Oh. Well, that will be all right, won't it?" Frances waited for Daphne's head to dip in agreement before saying, "Imagine someone breaking in on the one night I'm not there, but you happen to be home. Goodness, for your sake, I wish you hadn't been there that one night."

Daphne opened her mouth and shut it, looking at the mountains beyond the quaint facades of Leavenworth's main street. Here, she could believe they sat poolside in Germany. In a faraway land, everything could be different. In make-believe, she hadn't held her mother back and she hadn't placed childish blame on her mother over her father's death. The family hadn't built walls in their minds—suspended themselves—when Suzanne's case was suspended. They could handle things.

In that imaginary place, her father had handled his grief, his dead daughter's birthday, the fact that they might never know who committed Suzanne's murder, never see justice.

Daphne pressed her fingers to her mouth and shook her head, eyes closed for a flicker before she made herself open them, not wanting to upset her mother.

Frances Mayfield shook her head, her gaze narrow. "Why do you shut me out?"

"I'm not, I, I just . . ." And then Daphne felt the wall crumble. She softened her shoulders and spent a long time telling her mother the whole story, all about Minnie, everything that happened since Wednesday afternoon.

Her mother praised her for intervening, for trying hard when it seemed like such a small chance, so crazy, that Minnie Watts could be experiencing a genuine catastrophe. She marveled over her daughter's resolve and asked more questions, and Daphne told her no, it hadn't seemed like something they should talk about at the time, but she wished it had. It did now.

"Goodness," Frances said at last.

"Right." After a time, Daphne said, "Mom, did you know Suzanne used to sneak out at night? She did it quite a bit."

Frances tilted her head. "She wasn't a bad girl, Daphne, but she wasn't a good girl like you. I knew. Mothers know their daughters."

Daphne slipped her palms into her mother's hands. "You're cleaning out all the old stuff, all the . . ."

The squeeze of her mother's hands relieved her of having to say more when her voice cracked.

"It was just so hard," Frances said, her voice super soft. "I never got started with it before because it was just so hard . . . to start."

"I'll help you finish," Daphne promised.

—⁓—

Daphne spent a week at the family house, helping sort old belongings, her father's, her sister's. Monday morning she had a new refrigerator delivered. Monday night, she took her mother to meet Minnie Watts on Eastpark Avenue. Minnie said she used to play bridge and would love to start again. On Tuesday afternoon, Frances took Minnie to a beauty parlor, then shopping.

The next weekend, ready to move back in with Vic, Daphne brought the Sunday paper in as her mother introduced Minnie to her bridge partners, Blanche, and the others.

"And everyone here knows my daughter, Daphne," Frances said.

"Oh," Blanche said, studying the new partner playing at the Mayfield house. "You know Frances's girl?"

Minnie smiled and squeezed Daphne's arm as Daphne hugged her.

—⁓—

Thea's breaking scoop made the front page and flew to other major papers. Her editor sent her to California. She uncovered a case in Arizona perpetrated before the Lincoln owner's death, too. She interviewed former neighbors and employers. Guff—Edward Gufler—and his girl-friend, Andrea Osborn, had worked for a financial firm. They'd located and planned their victims from the company's records. Minnie was to be their next murder. The Arizona man and California woman were dead and had signed over everything right before they passed. Thea thought there was a victim in Oregon, too, and was still searching obituaries for more matches.

And Thea withdrew her earlier advice to Daphne to ask for a deferred prosecution on the reckless driving charge. "Turns out you can only get that if your wrongful conduct, as they say, is the result of or caused by alcoholic or drug-addicted actions. Or if you're just plain mental."

Daphne snorted.

"Just plead no contest," Thea said with a grin. "I'll be surprised if they don't dismiss charges before you even have to plead. I bet they just dump the reckless charge. I bet they read the papers. You're a fucking hero. But that Gufler guy sure said some interesting stuff about you while he was in the hospital."

"I bet he did." Daphne tightened her grin.

—m—

Vic's patience was there as he helped her haul another load of her father's things home, and she recognized the manifestation of love.

When they took a breather, slow-walking Grazie in the Peace Park, he said, "I want to do the surgery. I want to go all the way. I'll take some leave and you can and the kids will give up some fun time. We'll all take turns nursing her."

Daphne considered this, not wanting to be placated, wanting him to want it. "This is very different from what you said you wanted last week."

"Last week I . . . I didn't know."

"Know what?"

"That I cannot take an ounce less of tenderness in the world. I know people come first, I do understand that. But Grazie has helped me, and you. She's helped us raise the kids, and she'll always be a part of us."

Daphne braced herself for him to balance this comment against the other side of the equation, for talk about money and bleeding hearts and there had to be limits, best-case and worst-case scenarios, the suspension.

But there was nothing more. No slight roll of his eyes, sigh, or diminishing words, however kindly spoken.

She reviewed the change. "You're sure?"

"I'm sure. I do not want to be less than I can be. I want to be as kind as I can be, as compassionate as I can be. I want to engage all the way. Like you, Daph." Vic took her hand, squeezed. She squeezed back. "Well, that's solved then except for the doing it part. It will be hard. A bit of a battle. But I'll get it scheduled this week. We should do it in summer, as soon as we can."

She drifted, lost in thought about how some things stay unsolved. What a battle it was, and would remain, some parts of their lives. Cassandra. The dawning teen years with Jed and Josie. And she felt the need for many deep breaths.

He pressed his body to hers.

"It'll be fine," Daphne said, determined although every bit as daunted as the prospect deserved. She thought of his kids, at least one of whom was not biologically his, and again admired Vic for doing right by them with such marvelous patience. "But you're right, it'll be a battle."

He looked at her and she knew he realized they were talking about more than Grazie's hip surgery.

"It never ends," he said.

"Battles, duties. They should go to the end, not be cut short just because it's hard or uncomfortable," Daphne said. "But the main thing is we're supposed to care for one another. Including family and strangers and old, hurting dogs. Until the end."

Vic cleared his throat. "So we'll buy our old dog some new hips."

"Yes," she said.

"Solved." With another squeeze of her hand, lingering on her left ring finger. "When my first marriage soured, you know, as Cassandra showed this other side of herself and just wouldn't stay faithful, wouldn't make amends when she'd muck things up, wouldn't even try—"

"She didn't deserve you. She doesn't deserve Jed and Josie either."

"But they're hers."

"Oh, I know. I get that. Just saying, m'kay?" She swallowed, noticed his appraising look, and asked, "What?"

"You try so hard with my kids and I know it's hard, but I . . . was satisfied with what you and I had."

"Satisfied?" Daphne shook her head. "I want to do better than that."

"I get that. Maybe I always did, but it's a little scary to shoot for better than satisfied. It was good enough for me. You seemed content. I thought we were content, but you've changed. I've seen it in the last few days."

"I only changed in the last few days."

"But, what? What did you change?" He appeared to have pondered the question and been unable to find the answer.

"I don't want to be . . . suspended. I saw that I was. I want more, better."

"I have better, having you. I'll do better." Vic nodded his promise. "I'll engage. We'll not be walked on by Cassandra, not tolerate her damaging the kids."

Daphne felt the flood of possibility, of reasonable hope and real love. And she loved the realization that she loved her life. "I used to think the best thing about your house was being so close to the Peace Park."

"What do you like best now? The failing furnace? The ceramic counter with its hard-to-clean grout?" He rubbed his wry grin. "Hard to compete with this park. Do tell, Daph, what do you think's the best thing about the house?"

She took her time before replying, making sure he would understand. "The man inside."

Daphne knew when she came back to Vic's house, she would wear his grandmother's silver ring. A lot of people at work—the guys—never wore rings. She'd never worn one, never had one to wear, so didn't join in the anti-ring conversations.

But she recalled their talk. The electricians didn't wear rings, most of the plumbers wouldn't either. Quite a few of the hammer-swingers—framers, roofers, and drywallers—gave excuses about hands swelling while working, about a fear of the metal band catching while loading rock or plywood, about concern of a hammer strike gone awry crushing a ring-encased finger. They said it could be a hazard. You could lose a finger over it.

She'd find out for herself.

—◆—

The regular foreman, Bob, stopped in on the building project long enough to give his stand-in some instruction. Daphne saw Walt talking to Bob, making some point about more roofers.

"Morning," Bob said, giving Daphne a nod.

Walt turned and reddened, said nothing, and went back to trying to convince Bob they needed more crew. Hal and some of the other guys were strapping on their tool belts. Daphne grabbed her coil nailer and headed for the ladder, sensing enough tension between the bosses already filtering to the worker bees. They would put in extra hard today, she knew. The guys were climbing the ladder a bit earlier than usual, all had caught the vibe.

They weren't behind on the roof, she decided. This was a power struggle between a foreman and a wannabe foreman.

"Wants his cousin hired," Hal said on the roof. "I bet Walt promised him work. No way will Bob take the guy once he sees the name."

"Why?" the guy on Hal's other side asked.

"The cousin got himself fired here his second week, way back. Long, long time ago. I remember it, though. He mouthed off more than he worked, running other folks down. Bob sent him packing right away."

Daphne stood up. "Was that back when Mr. Wellsley started the Women-In-Construction thing? Like, ten years ago?"

Hal rubbed his head. "Yeah, I guess."

"There was a guy who was a bit of a jerk to me, nothing I couldn't ignore, but I kind of remember him."

"Could have been a lot more of a jerk behind your back. I mean, he was. A lot more. He was out of line." Hal stood as the small air compressor on the roof fired up.

She wanted to think more about a guy years back being out of line and wondered how much worse he'd been out of her earshot. Looking across the slope, she saw Walt crest the ladder, stride onto the roof, and switch on the air compressor.

"Let's get the lid on this thing," he hollered.

"Hey, Walt," Daphne yelled back.

He turned back for the ladder as though he didn't hear her.

She flipped the switch to kill the air compressor and be heard. "Did your idiot cousin call my house last Thursday? Leave a snotty message?"

Walt turned two shades redder as he looked around, not meeting her stare. Hal and several other roofers watched.

She shook her head. "You've been mad at me for ten years over your cousin getting fired? That's ridiculous. You're ridiculous. It wasn't my fault. I didn't do anything wrong. Whatever stupid thing he did or said to get his ass fired, it's his doing."

Walt's jaw set as he looked away. "You're holding up the work," he said at last.

She flipped the air compressor back on. She would go to the eave and start the shingles' exposure and reveal with perfection.

Come the morning break, she'd call the Seattle Police Department's Homicide division and speak to a cold case investigator about Suzanne sleeping with her English teacher.

Something from twenty years ago could come back and bite a professor in the ass. Surely he wasn't supposed to be bedding his students. Maybe he had done more.

She'd turn Suzanne's boxed papers over to the investigators, too.

At the water cooler later, she paused by Walt, but he wouldn't look at her. Back on the ladder, Walt still beneath her, she waited until he chanced a glance up.

"Be nice," she called down, "or I'll push you off my roof if you ever come up again."

Applause sounded from the roof above. She climbed up, peering. Hal nodded around, enjoying the audience of grinning roofers. "Kiddo, I said it years ago and I'll say it again. You've got stones."

Daphne grinned, pulling herself to the rooftop. "I don't need stones."

ACKNOWLEDGMENTS

Countless thanks to my husband, Barry.

To my editors, Alison Dasho and Bryon Quertermous; and to my über agent, Mark Gottlieb.

AUTHOR Q&A:
LISA PRESTON, AUTHOR OF
Orchids and Stone

1. You've written several nonfiction books on animals, specifically on the care and training of horses and dogs. Why did you turn to novels?

I've always been a bookworm and loved good fiction. As a child, when I finished a wonderful novel, I would hold it and not move, just absorb for long minutes afterward. I felt gratitude and wonder and knew I wanted to someday return the favor of transporting readers to another person's interesting world. I loved finding meaning and truths in stories, and I liked learning what the characters did, what happened next.

2. Where do you write?

Mostly at home, with my feet on an old, scarred rolltop desk. I'm someone who never learned to type properly, but I can hunt and peck as fast as many people who did take the right class in high school. Everything I've written has been on one little laptop or another—I've never owned a desktop computer. When I'm rewriting, working on a hard copy, I can be anywhere. I might go into town with a manuscript and have coffee or a glass of wine or a slice of pizza while I slash and scribble.

3. What is your writing process like?

My approach is pretty organic. Different ideas will capture my imagination and ask if they can be in a story. Sometimes they fit together and sometimes they don't. One notion leads to another and I might write pages that will have to go away later, but I'm sketching, getting to know a character, how she or he speaks or lives, so I just let it flow.

Things start to click. I don't outline before starting, nor do I write one chapter at a time or even in chronological order. If I'm thinking about a scene, conversation, or event that will come later, I page down and write away.

4. What inspired the idea for *Orchids and Stone*?

One day when I was in high school, the entire student body was sent to a church to attend the funeral of a recent graduate. I didn't know her or even know *of* her. I was standing in the back of a huge, packed church when a young woman was called to speak. She managed two words—*my sister*—before she crumpled up crying. Seeing this survivor so bereft rocked me, and the tragedy cut deeper when I learned that her sister had been murdered. I still tear up at the memory of her raw pain in front of that altar.

Life took me to interesting places and interesting careers. I worked as a fire department paramedic and later became a police officer, routinely encountering situations like domestic violence, going undercover to buy crack cocaine, and chatting with children about their sex lives with their dads. People tried to kill me and I was prepared to use force. I made arrests, served search warrants, cooled down countless squabbles, and handled a lot of traffic accidents. Every day presented scenarios of people not at their best. But sometimes people were at their best. Sometimes, someone stepped up and gave aid or information that was life changing for a stranger. People and the choices they make captivate me.

The novel is from my imagination, although different ideas sparked various parts of the story. A friend called one day because she found Calypso Orchids in her woods, and I thought about what this rare, wild orchid could represent. I saw a woman roofer one day, slinging shingles along with the guys. My husband and I pulled the car over one day because a little girl was bawling horribly at the edge of a vehicle turnout. I asked the man and woman some distance away if everything was okay, and they said they weren't with her and they had no idea what her problem was. Getting that child home to her parents was the only choice for me.

5. The novel's scenario of a little old lady claiming people are kidnapping and robbing her provokes urgency but could be explained away as the raving of a person with dementia. Do you think people have an obligation to help strangers?

On some level, we certainly ought to help others, but the reasonable extent of our intervention can fluctuate with the scenario and personal factors. There are regular news reports of bystander syndrome and some of these are shocking, but it can feel a bit too pointed if we Monday-morning quarterback an event and remark on what others could have done differently. If the story had begun with chapter two and readers put themselves in the park, many would not have intervened. Obviously, I wanted to write about someone who was driven to take one step and then another to render assistance, going as far as it took to solve the problem.

6. Why did you choose such an unusual and physical job for the central female character?

Not surprisingly, I can identify with a woman making it in a physical and male-dominated career while keeping her femininity. I like out-of-the-box thinking and choices. But Daphne needed a reason to intervene in the coming scenario, so her career choice wasn't random. It was rooted in her reaction to personal tragedies. No spoilers here, but readers often comment on chapter one and its end.

7. What are you working on now?

My next novel. Really, I write, run, ride, rinse, and repeat.

BOOK CLUB QUESTIONS FOR
Orchids and Stone

1. Imagine that you are Daphne when Minerva Watts asks for help in the park. Would you dismiss the plea as crazy talk? When the other woman claimed to be Minerva's daughter, was Daphne relieved of any civic duty to help Minerva even though Minerva kept asking for help and said she was not the other woman's mother?

2. The loss of innocence had a profound effect on Daphne. How has her past affected her reaction to Minerva Watts? Is it natural for a person's resolve to fluctuate?

3. Vic said that lightning has struck twice for Daphne. How do the Mayfield tragedies ten and twenty years past continue to impact the central and peripheral characters?

4. Family stability is a recurring motif in *Orchids and Stone*. How do Lisa Preston's characters, particularly Daphne, attempt to compensate for the loss of a traditional family? Do the obstacles Vic and his children face differ in nature because of the reasons the two families are fractured? What about Daphne's parents?

5. Minerva Watts shows Daphne rare wild orchids. What does the orchid represent? Does anything else replace this symbol? What symbols and themes recur in *Orchids and Stone*?

6. Daphne's father felt his job was to keep his daughters safe. To what extent do traditional roles dictate life choices for many people? Do you know someone working in a field that is not traditionally occupied by people of that age, gender, or other stereotype? Can stepping beyond tradition be both empowering and limiting?

7. The suspension of Suzanne's murder case is echoed in other characters' lives and choices. In what ways do Daphne and her mother compensate, and are their methods successful? In what ways have other characters made, or not managed to make, healthy progress in their lives?

8. Daphne sometimes experiences tension because her best friend and her boyfriend do not get along well. How do relationships between friends impact other friends? What does the difference between Daphne and Suzanne's experience in this area reveal about the characters involved?

9. Daphne wants to know more about her sister's death. Vic tells her that there are some things we never get to know, and the retired homicide detective tells her that why is not a good question because there is no good reason for Suzanne's murder. Can an unanswerable question be a motivating force? Have you been influenced by a desire that could not be satisfied?

10. What do you think happened to Suzanne? Do you agree with Daphne's decision about the cold case investigators in the final chapter? How does the balance between letting things go and not letting things go impact our lives?

11. At the heart of *Orchids and Stone* is the question of how far one should go to help others. Discuss how different people in the story display varying levels of tenderness and aggression toward others, especially vulnerable characters. How often might we help or hinder strangers? Have you ever witnessed bystander syndrome?

12. How does the physical resolution scene at Daphne's mother's house in the second-to-last chapter comment on violence? Is it ever justifiable to threaten or assault someone? What if the person is helpless at the moment? What do responses to this idea reveal about disparate views on our humanity? What questions remain at the conclusion of *Orchids and Stone*?

ABOUT THE AUTHOR

 Lisa Preston was born the day of the great Alaskan earthquake and lived in the frozen North for twenty years. She has worked as a college teacher, fire department paramedic, and a police sergeant, using her downtime to earn odd degrees such as a minor in Canadian Studies. She lives in western Washington where she writes and rides the wilderness on Akhal Tekes.